Also by David Moody

Hater

Dog Blood

Them or Us

Autumn

Autumn: The City

Autumn: Purification

Autumn: Disintegration

Autumn: Aftermath

David Moody

THOMAS DUNNE BOOKS ⚏ NEW YORK

ST. MARTIN'S GRIFFIN

THOMAS DUNNE BOOKS.
An imprint of St. Martin's Press.

AUTUMN: AFTERMATH. Copyright © 2012 by David Moody. All rights reserved. Printed in the United States of America. For information, address St. Martin's Press, 175 Fifth Avenue, New York, N.Y. 10010.

www.thomasdunnebooks.com
www.stmartins.com

Library of Congress Cataloging-in-Publication Data

Moody, David, 1970–
    Autumn : aftermath / David Moody.
        p. cm.
    ISBN 978-0-312-57002-6 (pbk.)
    ISBN 978-1-4299-2685-0 (e-book)
    1. Zombies—Fiction.   2. Survival—Fiction.   3. Regression
(Civilization)—Fiction.   I. Title.
    PR6113.O5447A9523 2012
    823'.92—dc23

                                                                2011040981

First Edition: March 2012

10   9   8   7   6   5   4   3   2   1

Dedicated to The Survivors

Acknowledgments

In the previous Autumn books I've already thanked a lot of people: the editors and teams at the various publishers involved with the series around the world; the artists I've worked with on cover designs, Web sites, and marketing; and my friends, family, and fellow authors who've all been tirelessly supportive.

But there are plenty more people I've yet to acknowledge. There are far too many of you to list here individually, and I'm sure to miss someone out and cause offence if I try. So this impersonal, blanket "thank you" will have to do.

As I write it's almost ten years to the week since the first *Autumn* novel appeared online, and this book marks the very end of the series. My sincere and heartfelt thanks to everyone who has helped me in any way, shape, or form over the last decade. From those who've read the books and provided feedback, to the thousands who downloaded the first book back in the day, to those who've helped promote each new novel along the way, I appreciate your support more than you can imagine. Thank you.

And as I first said back in 2001, please keep spreading the infection!

PART I

Twenty-Six Days Since Infection

1

Jessica Lindt died three days short of her thirty-second birthday. That was almost a month ago. Since then she'd spent every second of every day wandering aimlessly, often drifting in herds with other corpses, occasionally gravitating toward the few remaining signs of life in this otherwise dead void of a world. Jessica had no idea who or what she was any longer: she simply existed. She responded to the infrequent movement and noise around her, but didn't know why or how. And yet, somehow, she occasionally *remembered*. In her dull, decaying brain, she sometimes saw things. They were just fleeting recollections, clung on to for the briefest of moments at a time, gone before she'd even realized they were there. Split-second memories of who she used to be.

Her body, of course, had changed beyond all recognition, bulging in places where gravity had dragged her putrefying innards down, becoming brittle and dry elsewhere. Still dressed in what was left of the Lycra running gear she'd died wearing, her feet were badly swollen and her lumpy, bruised ankles were now almost elephantine in appearance. Her distended gut sagged, inflated by the gases produced by decay and a substantial insect infestation. Her mottled skin had split several inches below her drooping right breast, allowing all manner of semi-coagulated yellow and brown gunk to escape.

Jessica's unblinking eyes were dry and unfocused, but they saw enough. The movement of the lone survivor standing in the house up ahead of her was sufficient to attract her limited attention. Suddenly moving with more speed and something almost beginning to resemble a purpose, she lumbered toward the small, terrace cottage, then smacked into the window with force and collapsed backward, ending up on her backside in the gutter. She'd been down less than a couple of seconds before others attacked her, attracted by the noise and assuming she was somehow different to them. They tore what remained of Jessica Lindt apart, and soon all that was left of her was an imprint on the glass, a few lumps of greasy flesh and a wide puddle of gore which the others clumsily staggered through.

The survivor stood on the other side of the window and waited for the brief burst of chaos outside to die down again. His name was Alan Jackson, and his faith in human nature was all but exhausted—not that there were any more than a handful of other humans left alive. He'd been standing in the shadow-filled living room of this otherwise empty house for what felt like hours, staring out at the sprawling crowd of several thousand corpses which stretched out in front of him forever, wondering how the hell he was going to get through them and out the other side. He could see his intended destination in the far distance, his view of the ancient castle distorted by the tens of thousands of swarming flies which buzzed through the air above innumerable rotting heads like a heat haze. He hoped to God—not that he'd believed in God for as long as he could remember, certainly not since the beginning of September—that this was going to be worth the risk.

In the three and a half weeks since the population of the country—most likely the entire planet—had been slashed to less than one percent of its original level, Jackson had thought he'd seen it all. From the moment the rest of the world had simply dropped dead all around him, right up to now, his life had been a ceaseless tumult of death and decay. It was everywhere. It surrounded him constantly, whatever he did and whichever way he turned. It was inescapable. And he was fucking sick of it.

Another one of the bodies staggered past the window, a twitching, dried-up stump where its right arm used to be. Christ, how he hated these damn things. He'd watched them change virtually day by day; gradually regaining a degree of self-control and transforming from lethargic hulks of impossibly animated flesh and bone to the vicious creatures they had become. He didn't dare think about the future, because he knew that if the pattern continued—and he'd no reason to think it wouldn't—they'd be even more dangerous tomorrow. He tried to remain focused on the fact that if they continued to deteriorate as they had been, in another few months they'd have probably rotted down to nothing. Jackson was no fool. He knew things would undoubtedly get much worse before they got any better.

Standing alone in this little house, a fragile oasis of normality buried deep in the midst of the madness, it occurred to Jackson that even though he'd outlasted just about everyone else, his life was still little more than a fleeting moment in the overall scheme of things. Mankind had crashed and burned in a day, and he probably wouldn't last that much longer, and yet it would take decades, maybe even hundreds of years before all trace of the human race would be gone forever. His skin and bones would be dust blown on the wind long before the streets he'd walked along to get here today were fully reclaimed by nature.

It made him feel so fucking insignificant.

All the effort he'd put into his life before the apocalypse had counted for nothing. And the worst part? It wouldn't have mattered a damn if he'd tried ten times as hard or if he'd not bothered at all. Everything that had happened was completely out of his control. *A man makes his own chances*, Jackson's old dad used to say when things weren't going well.

Yeah, right. Thanks a lot, Dad. No amount of handed-down wisdom and bullshit is going to help me get past those bodies out there today.

Jackson was dawdling, and it wasn't like him. His reluctance to move only served to increase his unease. It was because the way ahead was no longer clear. Up until recently he'd had a definite plan: to keep walking north until he reached those parts of the country where there had been fewer people originally, and where the effects of the disaster might not have been so severe. When it became apparent that things were far worse than he'd thought and the true scale of the chaos had been revealed, he'd been forced to reassess his priorities. His original aim had been too ambitious, and he decided instead just to head for the nearest stretch of coastline. Having the ocean on one side would make his position easier to defend, he thought, and also, when he looked out to sea it would be easier to believe that the rest of the world wasn't such a ruin.

Three days ago, Jackson had had another change of heart.

It began after a chance encounter with another survivor. The kid had been the first person he'd found alive in several days. He was an archetypal angry teen, all long hair, leather and denim, piercings and a patchwork of bad tattoos he'd inevitably end up regretting if he lived long enough. Adrenaline, fear and untold levels of pent-up sexual frustration surged through the kid's veins, and a cocktail of drink and drugs had clearly added to his volatility. Jackson had found him in the gymnasium of what he presumed was the school the kid had previously attended, rounding up corpses in an improvised

8

corral. The sick fucker clearly had some deep-rooted issues, and had been trying to settle a vendetta or ten with some old and very dead friends. He'd been flagellating the bodies he'd captured, mutilating them beyond recognition as if he had a serious point to make. Sick bastard.

After a halfhearted attempt to try and deal with him, Jackson had left the kid to fester, deciding there was nothing to be gained from trying to reason with the clearly unreasonable, and knowing that neither of them would gain anything from being with the other. To him, the unpredictable kid presented an unnecessary risk, and to the kid, Jackson was just another authority figure to despise and kick back against. As he'd walked away from the school, Jackson had wondered if useless, broken people like the kid were all that was left. That night, the enormity of what had happened to the rest of the world weighed heavier on his shoulders than ever before, heavier even than the backpack full of survival equipment he'd been lugging around since the first day.

The encounter with the kid had made him stop and think, and after that he'd begun to realize the futility of walking endlessly. With the dead becoming increasingly animated, just being out in the open felt like it was becoming more dangerous by the hour, and Jackson knew it was time now to stop and think again. It wasn't as if he had anyone else to worry about but himself. There had been someone who'd mattered once, but she was long gone and best forgotten. He didn't want anyone else now, didn't need them in the same way they needed him. He'd come across several groups of survivors before the kid in the gym, and they'd all, without exception, asked *him* to stay with *them*. *We should stick together*, they'd inevitably say to him, *we could do with having someone like you around*. And that was the problem: they needed him, never the other way around. He'd realized he didn't actually need anyone. More to the

9

point, having other people around seemed to actually make things *more* dangerous. All it needed was for one person to panic and make a mistake, and untold numbers of dead bodies would be swarming around them in seconds.

Another surge of movement outside the unimposing little house made Jackson focus again. Up ahead on the other side of the road, one corpse had attempted to fight its way deeper into the vast crowd. All around it, others reacted to the unexpected movement. They tore into each other, vicious fingers stripping decaying flesh from bone, creating a sudden firestorm of sickening violence. And as the first few reacted and began to fight, so did more and more of them until huge numbers of the damn things were scrapping vehemently over nothing. As the bizarre swell of activity gradually petered out, Jackson wondered whether he'd actually been running away from the rest of the world, or at the very least trying to hide from it.

Yesterday morning he'd stopped at a prison. His first instinct had been to avoid it, but common sense said he should stop and investigate. *You have to think about things differently these days*, he told himself as he cut his way in through a no-longer-electrified chain-link fence. *After all, places like this were designed to keep people away from each other, and that's what I want.*

The prison proved to be a damn good place to shelter for a while. The kitchens were well stocked to cope with feeding hundreds of hungry inmates, and the vast majority of the dead prison population remained conveniently incarcerated in their cells. Jackson spent a couple of hours walking along numerous empty landings which all looked the same, swigging from a bottle of wine as lifeless prisoners threw themselves against the bars on either side of him, straining their arms to try and reach him. It had been like visiting a zoo and intentionally goading the animals.

He broke out onto a section of flat roof where he sat cross-legged and watched the sun sink as another day ended. Unperturbed by the cold, he lay back and looked up into a dark sky filled with more stars than he could ever remember seeing before, their individual brightness intensified by the lack of any ambient light down at ground level. And yet again, his personal insignificance became painfully apparent. He felt like a piece of gum that had been spat out on a pavement, like the last chunk of meat and dribble of jelly in a discarded tin of dog food. He might have mattered once, but not anymore.

Half drunk and completely depressed, Jackson had slept intermittently. It was when the sun had finally started to rise on yet another day, that he looked up and saw the castle.

It had seemed like a good idea at the time, but Cheetham Castle (as it had been signposted for miles around) was surrounded by vast numbers of the dead, many more than he'd expected to find. He could see the gray stone tower of the castle gatehouse through the living room window, towering proudly above the heads of the writhing crowd, still visible in spite of the smog-like swarms of insects. He'd checked out the full scale of the crowd from an upstairs window earlier, and the size of the humongous gathering both terrified and intrigued him. Whenever the dead amassed anywhere in these kinds of numbers, he'd long since discovered, there was *always* a reason. He hadn't wasted much time trying to work out what that reason was, primarily because it was impossible to do anything but guess from this distance, and also because the castle looked like an ideal place to spend the next few days while he worked out what the hell it was he was going to do with what was left of his life.

From upstairs he'd seen that the castle was between half a mile and a mile away from this row of houses. Between here and there was a road, a gravel car park—and several acres of grassland which contained several thousand corpses. Interestingly, they had all stopped short of the building's walls, prevented from getting any closer, he presumed, by the steady slope of the large hill upon which the castle had been built. It was simply too steep for their weak legs to climb.

The castle walls themselves appeared relatively strong from a distance. It was difficult to gauge their height from the house, but they looked to be reassuringly unscalable. For a while, though, Jackson had given serious consideration to trying to improvise a grappling hook and rope so he could drag himself up and over like some bizarre Robin Hood pastiche. As it was, his best option would clearly be the gatehouse, over to the far right of the castle from where he was currently standing. Judging from the numerous signposts he'd seen on his way here, this place had probably been a reasonably popular tourist attraction up until a month ago. The castle owners would surely have done everything in their power to make it easy for the public to get inside and part with their hard-earned cash. At the very least, getting to the castle would afford him a little much-needed breathing space before moving on again. The steep climb gave him an obvious advantage over the dead, and the view from the top of the rise would no doubt be spectacular.

Jackson packed up his few belongings, finished eating the last of a packet of cereal bars he'd found in the kitchen, and readied himself to fight.

He stepped out into the open and pressed himself back against the wall of the cottage. The cool air outside stank, and he was acutely aware that every move he made seemed disproportionately loud. Every footstep thundered, and his every breath seemed to echo endlessly. He remained frozen to the spot as he assessed his limited options, moving only his eyes as he scanned the wall of dead flesh up ahead of him, virtually all of the corpses now standing with their backs to him. It made sense (as much as any of this made sense) to try and work his way around closer to the gatehouse and look for a place where the crowds were thinner. Whether he'd find such a place or not was academic; whatever he did and wherever he did it, his success today boiled down to being able to charge his way through the decay and come out the other side.

He began to shuffle slowly along the lane, mimicking the slothful movements of the dead and trying to blend in with those which, even now, were still dragging themselves closer to the castle and joining the back of the pack. One of them sprung out at him from a hitherto unseen gap between two buildings. Whether it was an intentional attack or an unfortunate coincidence, it didn't matter. It took him by surprise and he swung it around and slammed it against the wall he'd been following, then clubbed its brains out with a short length of heavy metal tubing he'd taken to carrying with him as a bludgeon. He dropped what was left of the bloody corpse in the gutter, then looked up as another one began moving toward him, alerted by the noise of his violent attack. This creature had a badly damaged right leg, and its unsteady gait made its approach appear more aggressive than it actually was. Jackson angrily shoved it away—reacting before he'd fully thought things through—and it clattered back against a wheelie bin which thudded into several others. The noise echoed through the air.

Shit.

He knew before he looked around again that he was in trouble. Many of them had noticed him now, and their reactions had, by turn, attracted even more. He might as well have fired a starting pistol into the air because, up ahead and behind and all around him, huge numbers of the dead were reacting to his presence. They began to peel away from the edge of the immense crowd like a layer of dead skin, and he knew he had to move fast. Fortunately, several of the pitiful monsters lost their footing in the confusion and were trampled by their desperate brethren. He glanced up at the castle in the distance, visible intermittently through the crisscrossing chaos. Could he still make it? It had been a while since he'd taken a chance like this. Christ, he hoped so.

Jackson swung his heavy rucksack off his shoulders, using it to smack the closest few corpses out of the way as he did so. He ran, kicking out as a foul, bald-headed creature with a hole eaten through its face where its nose used to be lifted its arm and lashed at him. He jumped up onto the bonnet of a Vauxhall Astra—his sudden change of direction causing temporary mass confusion—then climbed up onto its roof. He stashed his metal pipe, then opened one of the backpack's side pockets and dug deep inside, finding what he needed almost immediately. As more of the dead tried to grab at him with hands drawn into spiteful claws by decay, he took out a packet of fireworks wrapped in a clear plastic bag. Ignoring the creatures as best he could, and occasionally stamping on fingers which got too close, he unwrapped a rocket and fumbled in his trouser pocket for his lighter. Distracted trying to light the blue touch paper, he didn't notice when one of the bodies managed somehow to grab ahold of the bottom of his right trouser leg. The crowd around the car surged unexpectedly as more of the dead arrived, and the body holding onto Jackson was pushed back. When it appeared to tug at him, he tried to pull away and over-compensated. The heel of his boot slipped down onto the curved surface of the windscreen and he lost his balance, crashing down onto his backside and leaving a deep dent in the hood. He screamed out in pain—the noise attracting yet another sudden surge of dead flesh—and almost dropped the rocket he was trying to light. He spat in the face of another wretched carcase (because he didn't have hands free to do anything else) then scrambled up onto the roof, straightening his legs and sliding his backside up the glass. The touch paper caught suddenly. Jackson ignored the intense heat and the shower of sparks spitting out over his hand, and aimed the rocket down into the center of a pocket of seething corpses a safe distance away. The firework whooshed away before coming to a sudden stop, embedded in the chest of a dead car mechanic who reeled back on its heels and looked down at the jet of flames sticking out of its belly—just before the rocket exploded.

The noise and flames had exactly the effect Jackson had hoped. Almost immediately the focus of attention shifted away from him and toward the mechanic, who was still staggering around despite the fact he was burning up. Jackson lit a second rocket and aimed it up into the air. The piercing scream it let out as it raced up toward the gray clouds was enough to distract an enormous number of corpses, and as they lifted their tired heads skyward he jumped down from the car and ran for all he was worth. He crossed the road and the gravel car park, then tripped over what was left of a barbed-wire fence which lay flat on the ground, already trampled down by the crowds. He lit a third rocket as he picked himself up, and shoved it into the gut of something which looked like the kind of kid he'd have done his level best to avoid. It looked down at itself, bewildered, jets of blue and green flame suddenly spitting out through various holes in its chest. Stupid thing still had a baseball cap on, glued to its head by a month's worth of dry decay. And it was the wrong way around, peak at the back. Jackson bloody hated it when they wore their caps back-to-front like that.

As the corpse exploded behind him, he dropped his shoulder and charged deeper into the heaving throng. Many of them were now trying to move away from the castle, heading back in his direction to get closer to the flames. He felt like a derailed bullet train, smashing bodies away on either side, not entirely sure where the

15

hell he was going or where he was going to stop. He just kept moving, knowing that every step took him closer to the castle in the distance.

Deeper into the dead hordes now, and here they had no idea he was close until he made contact. Some were still trying to fight their way toward the fireworks, but most were looking the other way, facing the castle. He simply pushed them aside and clambered over them when they fell. And then, unexpectedly, the ground dropped away in front of him. Within a few steps he found himself suddenly having to wade through a mass of tangled, fallen bodies rather than running between and around those still standing. A few steps more and he was knee deep in churned remains. He looked back and saw that he'd stumbled into a wide ditch—the overgrown remnants of an ancient moat, perhaps. It was filled with bodies, trodden down and compacted into a repugnant gloop beneath his boots. Despite being trapped, some of them tried to keep moving, and Jackson ducked as a dripping, virtually fleshless hand swung past his face, sharp, bony fingertips just missing the end of his nose by millimetres. He was struggling to keep moving, the decay sucking him down, and then the reason for its depth became clear. The deep furrow here had acted like a valve: the dead had been able to get in easy enough, but none of them could get out again.

Jackson kept moving and eventually found himself on level ground again. The corpses on this side of the ditch were fewer in number. Despite being soaked through with gore and desperately needing to stop and catch his breath, he kept on running, sidestepping one cadaver which came at him, then handing off the next as if he was a rugby player weaving around the opposition to score a try under the posts. And then he realized he was finally beginning to climb, and he looked ahead and saw the castle looming, the imposing wall of old stone stretching up toward the rapidly darkening sky. His thighs burned with the effort but he kept on pushing until he passed the last of the bodies, then slowed as the ground became steeper and exhaustion got the better of him. He moved at walking pace now, struggling to keep climbing. He looked back over his shoulder at the crowds gathered at the bottom of the incline and on the other side of the trench, waiting impatiently to pounce should he slip and fall.

Once he'd reached the castle walls, Jackson followed a roughly meter-wide pathway around the edge of the decrepit fortress toward the front entrance, but it was obvious there was no chance of him getting inside that way. As well as the fact that the huge wooden gate was shut, there were more bodies here, all crammed onto a narrow wooden bridge. He pressed himself back against the stonework and looked down toward the house he'd been sheltering in, trying to assess the situation. A gently curving track wound its way up here from the car park below, and its relatively smooth surface and steady incline had enabled a stream of bodies to make the climb. Over time the main gate had become blocked by an impassable, clogged mass of rotting flesh. Jackson shuffled back the other way, only moderately concerned. Despite the inconvenience of still not having found a way into the castle, he realized it was also a good thing. *If I'm having trouble getting in*, he thought, *then the dead have no chance.*

He'd worked his way back around half the perimeter of the immense ruin, looking for another entrance or a place where the wall was lower, when he stopped to look down at an engraved brass tourist map set into stone. Obviously a popular viewpoint, as well as affording him a clear view for miles around, it also gave him a clear appreciation of the true size of the vast crowd waiting for him at the foot of the hill. Thousands of blank faces looked in his direction, an almost incalculable number of them stretching away to the right and left, wrapping around the base of the hill and sealing the castle off.

The brass map had accumulated a light layer of filth which Jackson wiped away with his sleeve. He tried to make out some of the local features it had been designed to highlight: the port of Chadwick some thirty miles east (he was closer to the coast than he'd realized), the smaller town of Halecroft to the south. A reservoir, the ruins of an abbey, a wealth of other beauty spots and landmarks—none were of any obvious use to him. He was on the verge of giving up for the day, wondering if he should just finish walking around the castle then find enough level ground up here to pitch his tent for the night before moving on in the morning, when something caught his eye. Another entrance. A *secret* entrance? This was the stuff of bullshit and legend, but it appeared to be real: a smaller, far less obvious way into the castle through a passage carved into the hillside. There was a brief explanation of sorts on the map—something about smugglers getting in and tyrants getting out in times past—but none of it mattered. He orientated himself, worked out roughly where the hidden entrance was, then headed straight for it.

A padlocked gate, a cage of green-painted iron railings set into the hillside, and an unexpected gaggle of more than a hundred corpses were all that stood between Jackson and the entrance to the tunnel. He stood several meters above the dead and composed himself, watching as several of them tried unsuccessfully to scramble up the wet grass to reach him. Hands shaking with nerves, he lit his last firework and aimed it at the back of the ragged gathering. It shot away from him, and before it had even hit the bodies, he was sprinting directly at them. The rocket exploded and they turned and moved toward the light and noise *en masse,* giving him a few seconds of space to fight his way through to the gate, metal cutters held ready. With the dead already turning back and beginning to grab at him, he struggled to get through. The padlock clasp was too thick and too strong, but he managed to cut through a link in the chain it secured. Knowing that the firework had burned out and he had again become the sole focus of attention, he wrapped one end of the chain around his hand several times, then began swinging it around wildly like a whip. Its effects were remarkable, slicing through rotting flesh whenever it made contact. With the arc of the chain providing him with an unexpectedly large bubble of empty space, Jackson threw the gate open and disappeared down into the tunnel. The dead followed, but they were no match for his speed. He started back to shut the gate, but there were already too many of them pouring through after him.

The pitch-black and close confines of the damp tunnel walls combined to make him feel uncomfortably claustrophobic, but he had no option other than to keep moving. He ran with arms outstretched, climbing upward and bracing himself, knowing that at any second he might reach a dead end. *Christ*, he realized, far too late to be able to do anything about it, *this bloody tunnel might not even go anywhere*. The passage was several hundred years old at least—it could have collapsed, been shut for safety reasons, been rerouted back outside to the bottom of the hill . . . And all the time he could hear the dead behind him, chasing him down with an almost arrogant lack of speed and absolutely no fear whatsoever.

The lighter. He dug his hand into his pocket and felt for the reassuring metal outline of his lighter. He was running low on fluid, but what the hell. He flicked it on and the unsteady yellow light illuminated the rough carved sides of the passageway immediately around him. Moving with increased speed now that he could see something, he burst into a large, low-ceilinged chamber with

19

various displays mounted on the uneven walls. Something about smugglers, gruesome pictures of starving prisoners . . . it looked like this had been some kind of dungeon. That'd be about right, he thought as the lighter began to burn his fingers. He swapped hands—not that that made much difference—and desperately searched for another way out. Another short sloping passageway now, leading away at about ten o'clock from where he'd entered the dungeon, then another large open space beyond. He let the flame go out again, conserving lighter fluid as he ran across the width of this second space. He slowed down to walking pace again and felt for the wall with outstretched hands, increasingly aware of the sounds of the clumsy dead following close behind, their shuffling, scrambling noises amplified by their confines. His fingertips made contact with cold stone and he worked his way around to the left until he reached another doorway cut into the rock. He carried on along yet another tunnel, feeling his way forward with his left hand, trying to flick the lighter into life again with the right, the dead sounding closer than ever now. The lighter flame caught, and Jackson saw there was a wooden door directly ahead. It looked relatively modern, and reassuringly solid, and yet he felt the hairs on the back of his neck begin to prick up and stand on end. *If I can't get through*, he realized, the sounds of the dead continuing to increase in volume, *then I'm fucked.*

He hit the door at speed, slamming his hand down on the latch, and it opened immediately. He fell into another space as it swung shut behind him. Up ahead was a body hanging from the wall, its arms shackled, and he screamed out in fright before realizing it was a plastic dummy, dressed in rags and strung up for effect. He stumbled back with surprise and tripped over his own feet, hitting the deck hard and dropping his lighter, which he heard skittle across the floor. The sudden pitch black was suffocating, all consuming.

He crawled slowly forward, running his hands along the ground from side to side, desperate to feel the warm metal of the lighter. He found boxes and packaging and what felt like the plastic feet of another executed dummy, but no lighter. He kept crawling until his head hit wall. He yelped with pain and rocked back. In the distance he thought he could hear the dead advancing with renewed speed now, almost as if they were feeding off his pain.

Head throbbing, Jackson felt along the wall until he found the edge of a door. Was it the same one he'd come through or a different one? Had he somehow turned a full circle in the darkness, and if he went through this door, would he be running headfirst toward the dead? He stood up and tried the handle but it wouldn't open. He shook it, pulled at it, then shoulder-charged it. It gave way and he flew through, landing on his hands and knees in the middle of a small shop. There were shutters down over most of the windows, but he could see enough. *Exit through the gift shop*, he thought as he picked himself up, then shut the door and blocked it. He jogged down to the other end of the cluttered room, weaving around displays of key rings, mugs, stuffed toys and other equally useless things, then shoved another door open and burst out into daylight.

He was standing on the farthest edge of a large courtyard inside the castle walls, looking down the business end of a rifle barrel.

"Nice fireworks," the man aiming at him said. "Now who the fuck are you?"

"I'm Alan Jackson," he answered, breathless, "and I've had a hell of a day. Mind if I come in?"

2

The castle's walls were virtually impenetrable, and its proud, elevated position at the top of the natural rise was ideal. The dead were unable to get anywhere close, save for an unsteady stream—a bizarre slow-motion parade—which dragged themselves tirelessly along the road from the car park, up to the bridge and the impassable wooden gate where they formed an unmoving clot of increasingly decayed flesh. The inconvenience of having a few hundred of them nearby like this was nothing compared to the constant nightmare of thousands which Jackson had become used to.

Inside, the once-magnificent ancient fortress was far less impressive. The outer wall and the gatehouse were the oldest parts of the site still standing. Some inner walls had been reduced to little more than crumbled piles of stone, battle-worn and weather-beaten into submission over the centuries. Along the full length of the eastern side of the outer wall, several hundred years newer but in no better state, were the remains of a series of inner buildings. What had once been stables, a bakery, a great hall, living quarters and various other rooms were now all open, roofless spaces alike. Some had been repurposed by the most recent owners of the estate; a few areas either strengthened or replaced completely with out-of-character prefabrications to make a series of interconnecting rooms: an L-shaped display area and museum with a small onsite classroom in one corner, a café with a small but reasonably well-equipped kitchen leading off it, and at the end stood the gift shop through which Jackson had made his dramatic, unannounced entrance.

Jackson spent a lot of time up on the roof of the gatehouse tower, looking out over the battlements like a medieval lord of the manor. He felt as if he was under siege. The dead continued to amass all around them, waiting on the horizon like a germ-choked army of old, poised to charge. Except he knew they couldn't. For now.

Kieran Cope, the man who'd shoved a rifle in Jackson's face when he'd first arrived, became his man-at-arms. Kieran was tall and slim, and his manner of dress was very different to Jackson's. Rather than the practical, hardwearing clothing which Jackson almost always wore, Kieran favored jeans, T-shirts, hoodies and jackets. He'd been here since the beginning, and had so far been spared the rigors Jackson had endured out in the field. Kieran looked less like one of the few remaining survivors of a global apocalypse, and more like a student who'd just wandered in from a night at the pub.

Jackson's arrival had revitalized the flagging fortunes of the handful of people who'd already made Cheetham Castle their home. Apart from Kieran there were two others, though there had originally been three. Before the apocalypse, Melanie Hopper had juggled three jobs—one cleaning, the other two in local bars, mostly undeclared and paid in cash to keep her below the benefits threshold so she didn't lose her council flat but could still go out drinking most nights. She'd been vacuuming in the museum when everyone else had died, and had barely noticed anything until half an hour after the event when she switched off her music, took out

23

her headphones, and found Shirley Brinksford sitting in the middle of the courtyard, sobbing.

Shirley, by contrast, had been a reluctant sightseer. She had just pulled up in the car park with her unbearably dull husband Raymond for another excruciating day touring local relics. She'd been looking for a way out of the relationship for a while, but not like this. Dropping dead at the wheel and driving the car into a ditch had been the most exciting thing Raymond had done in almost thirty years of marriage.

No one spoke much about Jerry—originally the fourth person at the castle. Stricken with some kind of god-awful muscle-wasting disease, Jerry had been spotted trundling along the road outside the castle very early on, steering his electric wheelchair with his right hand, which proved to be just about the only part of his body he still had any control over. No one dared say as much to any of the others, but they all wished they'd never found Jerry, because it had been abundantly clear that there was nothing they could do for him. He needed round-the-clock help, and constant physical and medicinal treatment, and Kieran and the others hadn't been in a position to provide for any of their own requirements, let alone Jerry's. They did what they could—tried to feed him, tried to communicate, tried to keep him clean and safe and warm—but it was hopeless. It was a relief to all of them when he died in his sleep.

The decision of whether or not to stay at the castle had been a simple one for Jackson. To his surprise, he found himself thriving on the sudden responsibility of trying to coordinate the small group of people and make their castle hideout as strong, secure, and comfortable as possible.

Getting out and gathering supplies had been a priority. When Jackson had first found them, they'd been desperately ill-equipped for survival. All they'd had was a little food, the flatbed truck in which Kieran had arrived, Raymond Brinksford's car, and Melanie's (presumably) dead boyfriend's souped-up and clapped-out Ford Fiesta. Kieran's rifle (which he'd found in a house nearby) and half a box of ammo were the extent of their defenses.

Leaving the safety of the castle was a necessity, and they did all they could to reduce the risks. Kieran, Jackson, and Mel headed out for the nearest village, bulldozing their way out through the castle gate and over the bridge in Kieran's truck, and returning several hours later with a full load and two more vehicles. Although being down among the dead was always fraught with danger, the strength of their castle hideout was such that they could afford to make as much noise coming and going as they damn well pleased, safe in the knowledge that only a fraction of the dead could reach them.

"We get out," Jackson said, "we get what we need, then we get back. It's as simple as that."

And for a time it was.

In spite of the differences in their relative ages and backgrounds, Kieran and Jackson worked well together and their joint expeditions into the dead world became more audacious, bound by their shared desire to survive. They took diggers from never-to-be-completed roadworks and building sites nearby, and used them to keep the gate and the wooden bridge relatively clear. From a holiday camp by the side of a river which they spied from the gatehouse, they towed up six large caravans. Warmer and considerably more comfortable than any part of the castle including the prefabs, the caravans were used to provide additional accommodation. And that accommodation was soon needed, because as well as attracting the attention of almost every corpse for miles around, the activity in and around the castle also attracted the attention of several other pockets of survivors who'd been hiding nearby. Although not in any great numbers, people began to creep through the shadows

25

to get to Cheetham Castle. Some broke through the lines of the dead like Jackson had on his arrival here; others waited and threw themselves at Jackson's feet (or, more accurately, in front of his vehicle) when he and Kieran were out gathering supplies.

The number of bodies beyond the castle walls seemed not to matter so much as long as the number within the walls continued to grow too. Five people became ten, then more still. Jackson spent hours watching from the gatehouse battlements, scanning the dead world for signs of life and hoping even more people would arrive. But after a while, no more came, and the population of Cheetham Castle settled at seventeen.

3

It had been almost a month since Jackson first arrived at the castle, and weeks since anyone else had made it through the hordes of bodies still gathered outside. Jackson and a handful of others sat on deckchairs around a large bonfire burning in the middle of the courtyard. Behind them, other people busied themselves in their caravans, doing all they could to keep themselves occupied, still struggling to find any semblance of normality within the bizarre surroundings of the castle walls.

"Well, I'm with you, Steve," said Bob Wilkins, swigging from a bottle of lager. The drink made the cold night feel even colder still, but he was past caring.

"Me too," Sue Preston, sitting next to him, said. A short woman, the amount of extra clothing she had on tonight made her appear round, almost double her normal size.

Steve Morecombe—a tax inspector until his job had been added to the apparently endless list of now completely redundant vocations last September—looked at each of the others in turn. He zipped up his anorak as high as it would go, then turned back to face Jackson. "You're the boss. It's your call."

27

"This is bullshit," Kieran protested. Jackson silenced him with a glance, then knocked back another slug of whiskey-tinged coffee and winced at the bitter aftertaste.

"Not bullshit, Kieran," he said. "Common sense."

"It's got nothing to do with common sense," Kieran argued. "It's because this lot are too damn scared to—"

Jackson glared at him again, and he immediately became quiet.

"First things first," Jackson said, returning his attention to everyone else, sniffing back the cold and wiping his nose on the back of one of his fingerless gloves. "I'm not the boss. I don't want any of you turning around and pointing fingers at me if this all goes belly-up. We're all in this together, okay?" A few quiet mumbles. No dissention, not even from Kieran. "I think Steve and Bob are right."

"It makes sense," Bob said. "The way I see it, we've done all the hard work we need to for now. We've stockpiled enough to get us through the winter, and no one new has turned up here for weeks. We need to start focusing more on those that are already here, and forget about everything that's going on on the other side of the wall until it's safe. If we think we can batten down the hatches and survive the winter with what we've already got here, then I think that's what we should do."

"Agreed," said Steve, rubbing his hands in front of the fire.

"I think you're wrong," Kieran said. "You're making a mistake. Things are going to start getting easier out there, not harder."

"Maybe in another couple of months," Bob argued, "but not yet. I think there's worse to come before things get any better, and if we don't have to take any risks, then we shouldn't be taking any."

Jackson looked at Bob, then over at Kieran on the other side of the fire, trying to gauge his reaction. The arguments continued, and he stared into the flames, concentrating on the glowing embers and hoping to shut out the noise by focusing on the crackle and pop of burning wood.

"The risks are minimal, the potential gains are huge," Kieran said.

"A risk's a risk," Bob replied, "no two ways about it."

"We should put it to a vote."

"You know you'd lose. Face it, Kieran, you're the only one who wants to keep going out there."

"Bull. Mel said she'd go if—"

"Way I see it is this," Jackson said, cutting across all of them, tired of the bickering. "What Bob and Steve are saying makes sense, and Kieran, I think you're wrong. But the thing is, if we do this, then *everyone* has to buy in and we *all* have to follow the same rules. Food and drink will need to be carefully controlled so we don't run short. Folks have to be free to leave here if they're not happy, but they need to know that if they willingly walk away, we'll not be chasing after them. Agreed?"

He looked around at the people sitting with him.

"Fair enough," said Sue, sinking deeper into her seat, her face disappearing into her padded jacket.

"Kieran? You know you can't go out on your own."

At first Kieran didn't react. Jackson stared at him until he grudgingly mumbled, "Okay."

"I'm in," Steve said. "I'd rather bloody starve myself for a couple of months than go out there again unnecessarily."

"Probably do you good, you fat bastard!" Bob joked, relieved that the conversation had gone his way.

"So let's do it," Jackson announced, "and we'll see how things go. I say we should keep the gate locked until those fuckers out there have rotted down to nothing. You reckon that's going to be six months maximum, Sue?"

"Give or take," she replied. "But don't forget, I was a sister on a children's ward, not a mortuary nurse. It was my job to try and keep people alive, not watch them after they'd died."

"The only exception," Jackson continued, ignoring her negativity, "the *only* exception, mind, is if we get wind of there being other people like us nearby. I don't much fancy sticking my arse out there and risking getting bit, but by the same token, we can't just turn our backs on people we might be able to help. The more of us there are here, the better. That sound fair?"

A few more mumbles and nods. No one answered properly, but no one argued either, not even Kieran. Apart from Aiden Parker, who was just a kid of twelve, most of the people at Cheetham Castle were older than Kieran, and none of them shared his energy or his apparent (and untested) fearlessness. His confidence had been steadily increasing, theirs reducing.

"Just one more thing," Jackson said, stopping those people who were already halfway out of their seats and heading for their caravans and bed. "This is important. Just remember that we're safer here than anywhere else any of us has come across, but nowhere is completely safe anymore. If anyone does anything that puts the rest of us at any risk, I'll personally drag them to the top of the gatehouse and throw them over the battlements. If we're patient and sensible then we'll all get through this mess and come out the other side in one piece."

Fifty-Eight Days Since Infection

4

He'd seen this coming long before the rest of them. Driver had suspected this place was too good to be true the first moment he'd driven his beaten-up old bus along the twisting road which led up to the front of the hotel. *Way I see it*, he thought at the time (though he didn't waste his energy trying to explain to any of the others), *there's plenty of different ways to survive, you just have to make sure you're all pulling in the same direction.* And that was the problem they'd had here—too many chiefs—and that was why he'd planned to take evasive action long before the shit had actually hit the fan. He'd already seen the cracks starting to appear.

Ask any of the others, and they'd all have said Driver was incapable of showing any emotion. What would they have thought if they could see him now, perched on the end of his bed, head in his hands, sobbing like a frightened child. They thought he left his beard to grow wild because he was lazy; the truth was, he grew it to hide behind. But they were silly, foolish people, more concerned with one-upmanship and scoring points over each other than anything else. They'd all been so preoccupied with their bickering that they hadn't questioned him when he'd feigned sickness and hidden

33

himself away in this room, as far from everyone else as he could get. In fact, they'd positively encouraged him to do it, figuring it would be best for all concerned to put maximum distance between him and themselves. And so, armed with little more than a stash of food he'd been steadily siphoning off for himself on the quiet and very little else, he sat alone in his room on the top floor of the east wing of the hotel and watched as the rest of the idiots threw away everything that they'd worked for.

He'd expected the end to come soon, but never with such speed. Within a couple of days they'd lost everything. It had begun with the usual fights over food, then some chaotic stupidity as some of them had tried to attract the attention of a helicopter they all knew full well was never going to see them, then someone—he wasn't sure who—had cracked under the pressure and the floodgates had well and truly been opened.

It was time for him to move.

His gear packed, he crept back downstairs and waited outside at the farthest edge of the hotel grounds until he was sure that this really was it and there was no turning back. Carrying the remainder of his food and water, a few items of clothing, his well-read newspaper and little else, he watched from a distance as those cracks he'd seen widened to chasms with incredible speed. He'd heard several explosions out on the golf course, and some idiot had then taken his precious bus and managed to crash it, blocking the full width of their only escape route. He cursed the fools he'd wound up with. They'd written him off long ago, but he didn't care. He was used to it. *Just because I don't talk all the time or get involved in their pointless bloody arguments, it doesn't mean I don't care.* They'd grossly underestimated him, assuming that he wasn't interested in their ongoing fight for survival when, in fact, nothing could have been further from the truth. They presumed he was a selfish, uncaring bastard. Bloody hypocrites!

Driver stood by the boundary fence and watched the unstoppable descent into chaos begin. *When it comes to the crunch*, he said to himself, *I'll be the one who gets them out of this mess.* He felt like he knew all of them intimately—their strengths and weaknesses, likes and dislikes—and yet none of them knew a single damn thing about him other than the fact he used to drive buses for a living. They assumed that was all he was good for, but the reality was it was what he'd *wanted* to do. He'd had his fair share of different vocations—ten years in the Royal Navy, a spell working as a tour guide across Europe, a first-class honors degree in Greek history and art . . . they knew *nothing* about him.

Up ahead, a considerable distance away from him but still far too close for comfort, he saw the bodies beginning to surge through the gap in the fence he'd seen Martin Priest use previously. Contrary to what Martin had said, however, that gap wasn't the only way through. Taking care not to be seen—there'd only be another bloody argument if they saw him trying to leave, then no one would get out of here alive—he ran across the wet grass over to a section of fence where he'd found a couple of loose railings two days previous. He was able to lift the railings, squeeze through the gap, then replace them without anyone noticing.

One last, long look at the immense tidal wave of rot rolling his way—a moment's final hesitation, both to make sure beyond all doubt that the hotel was lost, and to again consider if he really was doing the right thing—and then he was gone.

5

Several hours passed, but it felt like it had been much longer. Driver remained sitting in the cab of one of the trucks blocking the junction at the end of the road leading up to the hotel, no more than a half mile away from the building and the people he'd left behind. He was still struggling with his conscience, unable to get past the fact that, just a short distance from where he was sitting, the people he'd left behind in the hotel were suffering. How many of them were still alive back there? He sat up in his already elevated seat and tried to look for them again, but it was no use. He could barely see anything, just a little of the angular outline of the roof of the building through the tops of the trees.

He'd had no choice, he kept telling himself, he'd had to do it. Even if he'd shown the rest of them the escape route he'd discovered, it wouldn't have done any of them any good. By the time they'd finished bickering about who was going and who should stay, the unstoppable avalanche of corpses would most likely have settled the matter for them. And even if, somehow, they'd still managed to get away, Driver knew exactly what they'd be doing right now. He could picture the lot of them, either standing in the middle of this junction or crammed into the back of one of the trucks, all arguing about whose fault it was the hotel had been lost. None of them would have accepted any responsibility; they'd all have been too busy pointing the finger at everyone else to take the blame.

No, as harsh as it seemed and as wrong as it felt, this was the best option for all concerned. He'd go back for what was left of the rest of them when he could.

Arming himself with a golf club he'd found stashed in the cab of the truck, Driver psyched himself up to move. He knew the disturbance around the hotel and the fires on the golf course would inevitably provide him with a brief pocket of freedom in which he could try to make his escape.

Short, sharp hops.

The key to getting away from here in one piece, he'd decided, was to move fast and stay exposed for brief periods at a time. And with so many thousands of corpses in the immediate vicinity, he had to stay on foot to remain quiet until he was more confident about his surroundings. He peered out through the truck window and surveyed the little of the landscape he could make out through the steadily increasing late-evening gloom. About fifty meters ahead was the outline of a lone house, and before the light had all but disappeared he'd seen that the front door had been left open invitingly. There were only two bodies that he could see between him and the house, and as far as he could tell, neither of them yet knew he was there.

Driver took a deep breath and carefully eased his unfit bulk down onto the road. He reached back up to grab his duffel bag and the golf club, then ran like hell. In his navy days he wouldn't even have broken a sweat covering a distance as short as this, but he was no longer in such good shape and the rigors of life since the end of the world—a poor diet and next to no exercise—definitely hadn't helped.

Already panting, and barely halfway there, he swung the golf putter around and caved in the side of the first corpse's skull, leaving a neat rectangular indentation which perfectly matched the head of the club. The corpse immediately collapsed at his feet as if he'd flicked an off switch, barely managing an untidy half-pirouette before it hit the deck, all arms and legs. Desperately wishing he was in better condition, Driver half-ducked, half-fell out of the way of the second creature as it made an uncoordinated grab for him. Picking himself up, he scrambled into the house and kicked the door shut. The remaining body was outside almost immediately, banging on the door. He knew he had to move fast before the noise brought countless others to the house.

There's something in here with me.

Before he'd even realized it was there, Driver caught the pint-sized cadaver of a small boy as it leaped up at him, holding onto it by the arm of its crusty, bloodstained sweater. Its arms and legs thrashed wildly as he shoved it into a cupboard in the corner of the kitchen, then wedged the back of a chair under the handle to stop the damn thing from getting out. Great—two of them filling the house with noise now. Why did there have to be so bloody many of them? As he made a mad thirty-second dash around the kitchen to check for food and other useful items, he realized the noise might actually help if he could get away from here without the dead realizing he'd gone. He paused by a side door and looked out. Another building about a hundred meters away, maybe a hundred and fifty. It looked like a used-car sales place. If he could get there without any of them noticing, he might still have a chance.

Several more corpses stumbled toward the house as Driver slipped out and ran toward the car lot for all he was worth.

He'd done eight or nine of these stop-start sprints to safety, and he was exhausted. The mad dashes were getting harder and the breath-catching gaps between them longer. It would be completely dark soon. Time to find somewhere to rest.

By the time he reached a shacklike roadside café, which appeared to be constructed almost entirely from sheets of corrugated metal nailed to a creaking wooden frame, he was doubled-over with effort. He let himself in and to his immense relief, as he didn't have the energy to fight again tonight, he found he was alone. He sat at a rickety table, swigging from his last bottle of water and looking out through the cobweb-covered window like any diner might. After the frantic, frightening events of the last days, this moment of silence and calm was both unexpected and blissful. And then, in this snatched moment of almost-normality, the enormity of recent events finally caught up with him. He wept openly, both for himself and for those he'd left behind, and again he struggled with his conscience, feeling a very real need to double-back to try and help the others. But he knew it wouldn't do them any good. Even if he made it back to the hotel, the seething crowds surrounding the building would make any attempt at rescue nigh on impossible. This was the very worst time to try and go back.

A lone female corpse stumbled in the road outside the café, its awkward, staccato movements illuminated by moonlight. The dead woman's shredded blouse rippled in the gentle wind, and the soft blue light on her ice-white skin gave her an unsettling, almost ghostlike appearance. She dropped heavily to her knees, and Driver watched as she awkwardly picked herself up again and carried on. Her tattered skirt was now just a strip of rag caught around one swollen foot, and she was otherwise naked, deformed and decayed almost beyond all recognition. She must have suffered some damage in the fall just now, because he noticed she was suddenly limping badly, barely able to keep walking. Driver stood up and moved closer to the window, hidden from view by a curtain of grime. The dead woman in the street outside looked so helpless and alone that, just for the very briefest of moments, he almost began to pity her. But then, without warning, she spotted something he couldn't see, and her pace quickened to an ominous, predatory speed.

Driver leaned back against the wall and screwed his eyes shut, not sure whether it was even worth trying to keep going.

He didn't move again until first light. Sufficiently rested, and having decided that if he was going to give up (and he still wasn't sure) there'd be countless better places to do it than here in this dingy little roadside café, he went back outside.

The long, straight road was clear in both directions, and this morning he could see for miles. Today he walked rather than ran, moving slowly and silently, hoping to mimic the slow crawl of the dead. Occasionally he slowed himself even further and dragged his feet along the ground when he thought he saw flashes of movement in the trees. At one point a particularly hideous monster, completely naked and with skin like a badly sewn-together patchwork quilt, crossed the width of the road just a few meters ahead of him, and yet he forced himself to keep moving and not make any sudden changes in direction. Even when it stumbled and then appeared to start coming toward him, he continued. To react in any way now would mark him out as different, and he didn't know if he could keep fighting these damn things today. He watched as it staggered past but he didn't flinch. He refused to react, even when his nostrils filled with its foul, decaying stench, even when it came close enough that he could hear its putrefied innards sloshing about inside its barrel-like gut. Driver didn't know how much longer he could keep on going like this.

After almost an hour—his progress painfully slow and frustratingly directionless—he reached the summit of a hill. It had been a deceptive, interminable slope to climb, and he'd resorted to using his golf-club weapon as a walking stick to help him get to the top. But once he was there, his mood had immediately changed for the better. On the other side of the slope there were three more bodies in the road, but that didn't matter because, just beyond them, parked neatly at what appeared to be a scheduled stop, was a bus. It was only a small, single-level bus—par for the course in these rural parts and nothing like the big, inner-city double-deckers he used to love to drive—but that didn't matter. Provided it had enough fuel and he could get it started, his fortune may well have just taken a turn for the better.

One of the three corpses moved to intercept him as he cantered down the hill. It had a gaping hole in the side of its face where insects and rot had eaten away much of its right cheek, and he could see into its mouth, its yellow teeth grinding and its lolling tongue clacking tirelessly. He stepped back out of the way as it lurched at him. Off-balance, it dropped to its knees. Before it could pick itself up, he smashed in the back of its skull like an egg with his golf club, then immediately swung the club around and knocked another one of them completely off its feet. He didn't even bother wasting any effort on the third, instead just shoving it out of the way as he climbed onto the bus.

One of the trapped passengers was still mobile. When it saw Driver it hurtled down the narrow aisle between the two rows of seats, the lack of space appearing to make it move faster than it actually was. It clipped its hip on the back of one of the chairs before it could reach him, then hit the deck heavily. Driver planted one of his boots between its shoulder blades to keep it down, then grabbed it by the scruff of its neck, dragged it along the bus, and manhandled it out of the door.

It was good to be back on a bus again, he thought to himself as he shifted several more dead (but thankfully immobile) passengers. One old crone was particularly difficult to budge from her seat. She'd been holding onto the handle of her shopping trolley when she'd died, and her wet decay had dried over time and welded her gnarled hands to the plastic grip like glue. He had to prise them apart to get her out.

The dried-up, eviscerated remains of the driver of the bus were far less awkward to remove. He peeled the dead man off his seat, then used the jacket which had been draped over the back of his chair to wipe it clear. He dashed out through a gap in the steadily increasing activity outside, and respectfully placed the body in the undergrowth at the side of the road, feeling strangely honor-bound to take a little more care with a fellow driver than any of the others. He returned to the bus, pushed the doors shut and then, finally, he was alone.

Driver walked the length of the long vehicle as he did at the beginning of every shift, picking up the odd discarded ticket and leaning across to open the high, vented windows and let the stale air circulate. Then, with an audience of eight corpses now watching him from outside, he took up his rightful position behind the wheel. It had only been a few days since he'd last driven, but it felt good to be sitting in a cab again: elevated, protected, untouchable. He took a deep, calming breath, closed his eyes, and started the engine. It took its time and rumbled and died several times, but eventually it caught and burst into life.

Driver made himself comfortable, put his newspaper in the gap between the windscreen and the back of the dashboard, and reveled in the sudden familiarity of the moment. He relaxed and imagined himself driving his old familiar routes around town, picturing himself anywhere but here.

6

Driver felt protected in his new bus, pleasingly isolated from the rest of the dead world through which he traveled, and yet he was no less directionless. He drove farther away from Bromwell, all the time having to swallow down his guilt, constantly ignoring the nagging voice which told him he should be driving in the opposite direction. He kept telling himself there was no point, that he couldn't yet risk trying to get to the others. If they managed to survive the hotel being surrounded and made it to safety, he reasoned, then as long as they had enough food to last a while, their situation wouldn't change. Best to wait until the dead were less of a threat.

For much of the last thirty or so years, Driver's time had been spent either taking orders or driving from point to point according to fixed schedules. Today he was finding driving aimlessly particularly difficult to handle. A few bad choices of direction made under pressure from the dead, and he soon found himself struggling to keep the bus moving forward along narrow country lanes for which this most urban of vehicles had definitely not been designed. With no obvious means of refueling, and in desperate need of something resembling a plan, he decided to park somewhere remote enough to be safe, yet not so far out as to risk being stranded. Late in the afternoon he shunted the bus through the narrow entrance to a National Trust car park, near to a farm and alongside the ruins of an ancient abbey, nestled deep in a valley between two moderately large hills. He turned the bus in a wide circle through the gravel, wheels crunching noisily, then stopped at the outermost edge of the car park at a point where he could sit and look out over a vast swathe of uninterrupted countryside.

For a while Driver sat and read his newspaper as he usually did. It was an instinctive reaction whenever the silence became too loud to stand. He'd held on to the same paper since that morning back in September when the world had gone to hell. Buying it had been the very last thing he'd done before people had started dropping dead all around him. He'd driven out of the bus depot as normal on that warm and sunny morning, and had then pulled up outside the same newsagents he stopped at every day to buy his regulation paper, cup of coffee, bottle of water and packet of gum. Since then this newspaper—those seventy-four precious, increasingly crumpled pages of smudged print—had taken on huge meaning. Apart from the obvious connections with the world which had been wrenched from him—the stories about once-familiar people and places, lying politicians and vacuous "celebrities" who were only famous for being famous, the weather forecast, the sports reports, the photographs of a normality now gone forever—the paper even smelled like the old world used to. It felt familiar, even sounded strangely reassuring as he rustled the pages and folded them back on themselves. Even the puzzle section—a part of the paper he rarely used to bother with—had helped him while away countless hours during the last two months, enabling him to temporarily fill his mind with pointless triviality. Concentrating on crosswords, Sudokus, anagrams and the like stopped him thinking about the relentless hell his life had become.

The paper wasn't having the same effect today. He threw it across the bus with frustration and it hit one of the windows opposite, pages spilling everywhere.

There was a small café and toilet block at the far end of the car park, and Driver decided to investigate. Inside the café he found the apron-wearing corpse of a young girl trapped in a meter-square of space behind the counter, penned in on every side and slumped against a wall. She began to move as soon as she saw him, clawing herself upright, brittle bones bursting into life. She threw herself forward and strained to reach out over the chest-height displays, lashing out at him. He looked deep into her pallid face for a moment, visible in a brief flash of space between her wildly flailing limbs. He tried to picture what she might have looked like before she'd died, but it was impossible. Patches of her badly discolored skin were dry; wrinkled and aged before time, covered in a layer of dust and the glistening silver traces of insect infestation. Several of her teeth appeared to have fallen out, dried-up gums no longer capable of holding them in place. There was something about the large black gaps in her mouth which filled Driver with sadness and disgust in equal measure. He remembered a young girl he'd known, Rachel, the daughter of a friend, who'd lost her front teeth in an accident. He remembered how it had shattered her confidence, and how important her appearance had been to her. He thought about Rachel as he gazed into the dead girl's eyes—milky-white, cataract-like. A large semicircular flap of skin covered with brittle, strawlike hair had peeled away from the side of her head and now hung down over one of her ears. This had once been a young girl with her whole life ahead of her, he thought, a girl like Rachel. Now look at her. What a cruel bastard of a disease.

The corpse swiped at him again and he took a step back with surprise. After studying her so closely, he now changed tack and did all he could to ignore her completely. He ducked down and used his elbow to smash the front of the outward-facing food display cabinets, then helped himself to everything he could find which was still edible, piling it all into his duffel bag. He reached in through the broken glass and quickly snatched up individual items between the dead girl's vicious, barely coordinated attacks.

After checking it was corpse-free, Driver used the toilet around the back of the café. He was desperate, and using the dark, unwelcoming building was a mildly more appealing option than squatting and crapping in the bushes. But he hated every second of it. It terrified him, made him feel as if he were suddenly a child again, afraid of the monster hiding in the corner. He didn't know which was the worst option—doing what he had to do in utter darkness, or propping all the doors open and sitting on the can, exposed to the world with his trousers around his ankles. Finally done, he wiped his hands on the dew-soaked grass next to the building, and there he found the remains of a small dog tied to a post. As dried-up as the empty water bowl it lay next to, the poor little creature's body looked as if it had been vacuum-packed in its own skin. Its ribs were visible, protruding through what was left of its short grey fur, and its dry eyes bulged. Its lips were drawn into a permanent snarl, almost as if it had died trying to ward off whatever it was that had killed its owner, wherever they were. The effect of seeing the dog took him by surprise, and for the second time since deciding to flee the hotel, he was reduced to tears. The thought of this poor little bugger waiting faithfully for its owner to return, and the long, slow, frightened, painful death from starvation it had inevitably endured was heartbreaking.

Driver curled up on the long seat at the very back of the bus, eating chocolate and listening to the never-ending silence. Alone for the first time in weeks, and suddenly given space to breathe, the true extent of what had happened to the world was only now hitting home.

The depth of the loss.

The extent of the damage.

How little remained untouched.

How everything had changed.

Time seemed to have slowed down to an almost undetectable crawl. Driver had taken a watch from one of the bodies he'd cleared out of the bus, and as he stared at its face he swore every second was taking twice as long to tick by as usual. Finally abandoning the idea of trying to get to sleep, he got up and walked to the front of the bus, where he looked out through the vast windscreen at the empty world outside. The land stretched out ahead of him forever, and he wondered how far he could actually see. Ten miles? Twenty? Farther? He knew little about his immediate area, and there were no obviously visible landmarks he could use to try and get his bearings. Not that it really mattered, of course, because one dead place was the same as the next now and there was nothing of any worth left anywhere.

Apart from one flicker of light.

Driver rubbed his eyes and leaned against the glass, convinced his mind was playing tricks. Was it just a reflection? A desert-less mirage? Whatever it was, he could still see it. It looked like the glow of a distant fire; a single bright interruption in the midst of the otherwise endless sea of darkness outside.

"Bugger me," he said out loud, surprising himself with the sound of his own voice.

Desperate not to lose sight of it, and still not entirely convinced there was actually anything there, Driver ferreted around in the pockets and alcoves around the dashboard, looking for a thick black marker pen he'd picked up on his travels. He used it to circle the position of the light on the windscreen, then drew a number of arrows all the way around it, all pointing inward to make sure that, when the morning came, he'd be able to locate it again.

Driver sat in the same position behind the wheel all night, waiting impatiently for morning to come and for the light levels to increase sufficiently so he could tell what it was he'd been looking at. More important, so he could find out where it was.

As gray light began to reluctantly edge across the ruined land, Driver returned to the café. He'd seen a selection of tourist guides in wall mounts behind the dead girl yesterday, but had paid them little attention at the time. The girl immediately sprung into action again as he approached her. Fighting to overcome his disgust, this time he grabbed hold of her left shoulder and spun her around. Feeling her soft, decayed flesh shift under the pressure of his grip like wet clay, he pushed her into the wall, face-first, and held her there. He reached up with his free hand and took as many maps, brochures, and leaflets as he could, then ran straight back to the bus.

Driver unfolded the largest map he'd got and spread it out over the steering wheel, flitting his eyes between the map and the view outside, trying to match them both up. For a while he was stumped, unable to orientate himself easily despite his naval training, distracted by the constant movement of the obnoxious, tireless husk of another dead woman which had, by chance, stumbled out of the trees and was now biting at the glass in front of him, moving from side to side, getting in the way and covering the window with greasy, cream-colored stains.

The map was simple and cartoonish and had few details. It was only when it dawned on Driver that the best landmarks to use

48

were the hills he was parked between, that everything finally began to click into place.

Got it.

He could see where the fire had been last night. There was a faint but steady wisp of smoke still rising up from it; a perilously thin trail of darker gray against the off-white clouds. Driver's eyes drifted back down toward ground level where he saw that the smoke seemed, bizarrely, to be coming from a castle. He picked up a tourist guide of the local area and flicked through the pages to find anything that looked even remotely similar.

And then he found it. Cheetham Castle.

7

Driver accelerated toward the castle, obliterating anything foolish enough to get in his way. The closer he'd got, the lighter the smoke trail hanging in the air had become to the point where he was now beginning to doubt he'd seen anything at all. Had he been hallucinating? Was it just a cloud formation he'd willed into being something else? He also knew there was a very real possibility that if there was a fire, it might well have started accidentally, and that this place was actually as dead as everywhere else. But whatever it was and whatever had or hadn't caused it, he was here now. For the first time he could remember, he was actually pleased to see a few more bodies around. Their numbers gave him some slight reassurance because the more of them he saw, the more likely he thought it that there might have been other survivors here recently. At best he might have stumbled upon a fully operational base camp. At worst, a damn good place to hide for a while. That was assuming, of course, that he could get in.

He followed the route of a road which roughly matched the curve of the castle wall, albeit at a considerable distance away. Between him and the fortress was a vast crowd of cadavers, perhaps even more than he'd seen approaching the hotel back in Bromwell, and close to the numbers he'd seen around the flats. The fact there were so many of them, so tightly packed in such a relatively confined space, was both a help and a hindrance. Those which had already noticed him were trapped and were finding it difficult to move, but their numbers were also preventing him from seeing much of the immediate area. Even from his elevated driving position it was difficult to see beyond the dead.

Driver forced himself to concentrate and watch the road again, steering hard around the back end of a burned-out car, and wiping out several stragglers in the process. He watched one he'd just plowed down in his mirror. He'd driven straight over it and had crushed its pelvis and spine (he knew that for a fact—he'd felt the crunch), and yet it was *still* coming after him. Dogged. Persistent. Only able to move its arms now, it seemed almost to be trying to swim along the tarmac.

The road climbed, and he was afforded a slightly better view of the land around the castle. With relief and surprise, he saw that the crowd of bodies didn't stretch all the way to the castle walls, and that was clearly because of the steep slope upwards. He also saw, a little farther ahead still, a bizarre queue of bodies stretching away from the bulk of the crowd and up toward the gatehouse entrance. They appeared to be following some kind of track, almost as if they were lining up to try and get inside. And that, he decided, would be his best chance of getting in too.

Driver continued forward, passing level with the snaking column of corpses. He could see the wooden gate of the castle up ahead now, shut fast, and a swollen bottleneck of dead flesh directly outside it. The turn onto the track from this direction was too tight an angle, so he continued farther down the road, then turned around in a large gravel car park which was only partially filled with corpses.

Some flung themselves at him, bouncing off the front of the bus like flies hitting the windscreen.

He accelerated back toward the castle, this time with a far better view of the approach road. He wrenched the steering wheel hard around and after misjudging his turn and driving through mud for a few seconds, fearing the bus might become mired, his wheels eventually gripped the tarmac and his speed increased as he began to climb. The bodies farther up the road were more spread out than they'd first appeared. It was no longer about them *wanting* to get to the castle which kept them moving, he realized, but a question of whether they were still physically able to keep climbing up. Some of them turned and started stumbling back down toward him, only to be obliterated on impact. Others now seemed to be trying to get farther up the road, almost as if they wanted to get out of the way, perhaps aware of the danger approaching them at speed.

A flash of movement higher up caught his eye. He looked down at the road when he lost control momentarily and clipped the curb, but then looked back and saw there was someone gesturing wildly at him from the top of the gatehouse. There were two of them now, a man and a woman, and they were pointing furiously at the wooden gate below.

Driver accelerated again, lining the bus up as best he could and hurtling toward the gate at optimum speed. On either side of the road now he saw that many of the dead were little more than piles of dismembered remains—heaps of broken bodies which looked to have been shunted out of the way in the same way a plow might clear a path through a fresh fall of winter snow. The bus juddered as he reached the wooden bridge before the gate, and he felt himself beginning to panic. What to do? Should he pull up and wait for the gate to open and risk being surrounded, or maintain this speed and just hope for the best? Up ahead, his question was answered as the two halves of the gate began to slowly part. Driver gripped the steering wheel tight, kept his foot down hard on the accelerator, and flew through the narrow gap before skidding to a halt in the middle of a vast courtyard filled with vehicles, caravans, equipment and . . . people! Healthy people. *Living* people!

He didn't move for a while. He couldn't. Exhausted, he switched off the engine and slumped forward over the steering wheel, his heart thumping so hard he thought it might be about to burst from his chest. Out of the corner of his eye he watched as a handful of corpses which had slipped through the gate with him were rounded up and destroyed. Some of the people he saw were hurriedly putting on hazmat suits; others wore leathers like Jas, Ian Harte, Greg Hollis and the rest of them used to wear. Some concentrated on getting the gate shut; others dealt with the disposal and removal of the dead. He was transfixed by this unexpected display of organization and cooperation.

A sudden knock on the door of the bus startled Driver. He sat up quickly and let a tall, clean, and remarkably well-presented man come on board.

"You okay?" the man asked.

"Think so," Driver mumbled, not entirely sure.

"My name's Jackson," he said, holding out his hand.

"Anthony Kent," he replied as they shook. "Tony. But most folks just call me Driver."

"Most folks? There's more of you?"

"There were. Probably still are."

"We'll get you some food, get you cleaned up, then you can tell me more," he said, gesturing for Driver to follow him off the bus. Driver did as he was told. He looked around him in disbelief.

"What is this place?"

"Home," Jackson replied.

8

Several hours later, Bob Wilkins ushered Driver into another part of the castle. Once part of a small museum space used as an onsite classroom by visiting schools, its size and relative comfort had resulted in it being adopted for use as a communal lounge by the current occupants of the ancient building. Driver waited in the doorway, feeling unexpectedly nervous, and Bob gently pushed him through. There were four other people in the room already, and he felt like a definite outsider.

"Come on in, love," Sue Preston said to him as she carried in a tray of food and drinks from the adjoining café and kitchen. "No standing on ceremony here."

Driver did as she said and walked a little farther, stopping again when he caught sight of his reflection in a window. He had to look twice to be sure it really was him. He'd almost forgotten what he looked like. Since arriving at the castle earlier he'd managed to shave for the first time in weeks, and one of the others—a lady called Shirley—had hacked at his long hair with a pair of scissors. He still wore his bus driver's uniform overcoat as he had almost every day since the beginning, partially because it was warm, but mainly because he didn't have anything else.

Jackson was sitting with another man in front of a paraffin heater which glowed a comforting orange. Even from here Driver could feel the heat it was producing. It was warmer than anything he'd felt in weeks. Jackson looked around, then beckoned him over, pulling up another chair. Driver sat down, still feeling unexpectedly uncomfortable.

"This is Kieran," Jackson said, introducing the man sitting on Driver's right. "Kieran, this is Tony."

"I prefer Driver."

"How're you doing?" Kieran asked as they shook hands.

"Been better, been worse," he replied, giving little away.

"Smoke?" Jackson offered.

"No thanks. Bad for you."

"Coffee?" Sue asked, leaning between them with a tray.

"Now that I won't say no to," Driver said quickly, taking a mug and reveling in its warmth and its bitter taste. He sipped the drink and stared at the glowing heater, trying to work out how he'd managed to get from yesterday's nightmare to here.

"Something wrong?"

Driver shook his head and glanced over at Jackson.

"Just doesn't feel right, that's all."

"What doesn't?"

"Sitting in a place like this, with people like you, enjoying a drink in front of the fire like nothing's happened."

"If there's somewhere else you'd rather be . . ."

"No," Driver said quickly, "of course not."

He drank more of his coffee—almost hiding behind it—and remembered the people he'd left behind at the hotel. He wondered what state they were in right now. Assuming, of course, they were still alive.

"It takes folks a few days to get used to being here," Jackson said. "It's a bit of a culture shock. Thing is, the castle is safer than most other places."

55

"I've heard that before."

"No, seriously, it is. The dead just can't get up here, apart from the few that make it up the road. The only downside of being somewhere as good as this, is it gives you time to think."

"Tell me about it," Driver said quietly. "I've been doing too much of that myself recently."

"Anything you want to share?"

Driver paused before answering.

"This time yesterday," he eventually said, feeling like he was confessing, "I was sitting in that bus out there, freezing cold, wondering if there was any point going on. I didn't have a bloody clue what I was going to do next. The night before that I spent hiding in a café. The night before that I spent sitting in a truck. Before that it was a hotel . . ."

"So what point are you making?"

"You just get used to running, don't you? You forget how to stop."

"Well, maybe it's time we all got used to stopping again," Jackson said, putting a reassuring hand on Driver's shoulder.

"It's been the best part of two months since all this started," Kieran said, his tone a little harsher than Jackson's, abrasive almost. "You've told us about the last few days. Where were you before that?"

"Spent most of the time in a block of flats."

"And why did you leave?"

"Same reason anyone leaves anywhere these days. A few thousand dead folk outside the front door that didn't want to leave us alone."

"Us?"

"That's right."

"So what happened to the others?"

Kieran's tone was almost accusatory now, and Jackson reeled him in quickly.

56

"Take it easy, mate. Driver here's had a tough day."

"They're all tough days now," Kieran said, unimpressed. "So what happened? Where are they?"

"We left the flats when the bodies got too close."

"How many of you?"

Driver paused as he tried to remember. Picturing the faces of each of the people he'd been at the flats with stretched the pause out a little longer still.

"Eight."

"And you're all that's left?"

"So where did you go?" Jackson asked, quickly taking over the questioning. "You said something about a hotel?"

"That's right. Over in Bromwell. We found more people there."

"How many more?"

Another endless pause. Jackson rocked back in his chair as he waited for Driver to answer. He was having trouble remembering. *Christ*, Jackson thought, *we've all been through a lot, but this is like getting blood out of a stone.*

"Five," he answered, finally. "And a dog."

"So that's thirteen of you altogether."

"And a dog," Kieran added sarcastically. Jackson shot him a withering glance.

"So where are they all?"

"Don't know for sure about all of them," Driver replied. "Things were getting bad, same as they always do. I knew the situation was most likely about to go shit-shaped, so I shut myself away in one of the rooms. Kept my distance from the rest of them."

"You hid?"

"If you like. You could say that. Thing is, sometimes it's better just to keep yourself to yourself, don't you think?"

That comment caught Jackson off-guard momentarily. He happened to agree.

"Okay, cut to the chase," he said, his patience wearing thin. "Just tell us what happened. What happened to all the others?"

"I'm not entirely sure. They'd been keeping the bodies out of the way for a while, distracting them with music."

"Smart move."

"But you probably know what it's been like. The bloody things started to get smarter and were working out what was what. Someone lost their nerve and screwed up and properly let the cat out of the bag, and the whole place was surrounded."

"So you just did a runner?" Kieran interrupted. He couldn't help himself.

"What else was I supposed to do? It didn't take a genius to work out what was going to happen next. All the escape routes were blocked. If I hadn't gone, no one would have got away."

"So you were just looking out for yourself," Kieran sneered. "Fuck the rest of them."

"No, it wasn't like that. I swear, I was planning to go back. I still am."

"Like hell."

"Go easy," Jackson warned. "Give the guy a break."

"You'd have done the same," Driver continued, sounding close to tears. "If I'd have stopped there with them, we'd have all been buggered. I thought I'd leave it a few days, maybe a couple of weeks, then try and get back and get them out. I know how it looks, but I swear I was going back."

The awkward conversation faltered. Although neither Kieran nor Jackson said as much, they both remained unsure about this strange little man.

"So let me see if I've got this straight," Jackson said. "Back at this hotel, there are potentially as many as twelve people stranded?"

"That's right."

"And this is in Bromwell."

"Yep."

"I know the place. It's not too far from here."

The other people in the room had been eavesdropping.

"Come on, Jackson," Bob protested, "we agreed. Surely you're not suggesting we should leave here and—"

"That's *exactly* what I'm suggesting," Jackson said, cutting across him. "We said we'd help other folks if we came across them. I'm not saying we should go today or tomorrow or even next week, but as soon as possible we should do all we can to try and reach those people. We can't afford not to. You know as well as I do, numbers are important now."

"Well I think it's a risk too far," Bob grumbled.

"Bob Hawkins," Sue Preston sighed. "Sometimes getting out of bed in the morning is a risk too far for you."

A few laughs punctuated the silence. Driver enjoyed the banter and soaked up the relaxed atmosphere. It had been a long time since he'd seen people getting on with each other like this. He watched Sue as she leaned against the window and sipped her drink.

"For what it's worth," she said to him, "I think Jackson's right. We should try and help your friends. You'll not find a better place than this, lover. We've got food, we're safe, there's room for everyone . . ."

"Well, I'm sold," Driver said, "but I do want to go back. I meant what I said, I didn't want to walk out on them like that. I just didn't have any choice."

"We understand," Jackson told him. "And like I said, the more people we have here, the better. Another twelve will take us up to almost thirty folks. As soon as the time's right we'll head on out to Bromwell and see what we can find."

Seventy-Six Days Since Infection

9

Driver had settled quickly into the routine—what little routine there was—of life within the crumbling walls of Cheetham Castle. In comparison to everywhere else he'd been recently, this was bliss. Okay, so he was having to work harder than he was used to, and sometimes Jackson's "all for the common good" ethos felt a little forced and hard to stomach, but he was safe and his mind was kept occupied and it was a small price to pay. He generally busied himself around the group's vehicles, particularly the comfortable backseat of his replacement bus. He was tasked with keeping them all in good working order but, as no one had ventured beyond the castle walls in all the time he'd been there, that hadn't required a huge amount of effort. But, Driver being Driver, he'd done all he could to make a little work last as long as possible. He always managed to make himself look busy when, in fact, none of them actually had very much to do at all.

He'd taken to living on the bus. It was as good a place as any: better than most parts of the castle itself—windproof and relatively warm—and as spacious as most of the caravans the others used (less crowded, too). This morning, however, it was particularly cold. Driver opened one eye, then quickly closed it. It was still dark, and he was nowhere near ready to start another day just yet. He snuggled down deeper into his sleeping bag and wrapped his arms around himself to try and retain as much precious heat as possible. He was on the verge of drifting off again when something slammed against the back end of the bus, close to where he was lying. He sat upright in an instant, heart pounding, expecting to see bodies surrounding him. He relaxed when he saw that it was just Jackson, wrapped up like an Arctic explorer. He gestured for Driver to let him in. Still in his sleeping bag, he grudgingly shuffled, jumped, and tripped the length of the bus to open the door.

"Bloody hell," he said, "do you know what time it is?"

"Do I look like I care what time it is?" Jackson replied, irritated. "Get yourself ready, Driver, we're going out."

"Out? Where?"

"Bromwell."

Within the hour, Driver found himself standing inside the prefabricated museum with a small team of volunteers. He looked around at them. Most people (himself included, if he was honest about it) did as little as they could to get by, content to leave the much of the work to the minority of folks. And here they were: the usual suspects—the same faces which tended to appear whenever anything important needed doing. Bob Wilkins was there, despite his frequent protestations about staying inside the castle walls and not taking risks, and next to him, wearing a grubby hazmat suit, was Steve Morecombe, another man who seemed to talk a lot but who said very little worth listening to.

Next to them, leaning up against the nearest wall, was Zoe, a tall, athletic-looking student. Driver liked Zoe, not that he'd had much to do with her so far. She was different from the others, and liked to keep herself to herself. He could identify with that. She was what Driver's ex-wife Sandra would have called "an individual." Much to the bemusement of the rest of the group, Zoe referred to herself as a student because that, technically, was what she still was. She could often be found alone in the corner of the classroom or the caravan where she lived, continuing to pore over the books and other texts she'd kept with her from university. *What good's all that going to do you now?* people asked her with infuriating regularity. Where was the point in studying a now-defunct subject such as criminal law, or in studying anything else for that matter? Driver knew they were missing the point entirely. He didn't need to ask Zoe why she studied, because he already knew. It was obvious. Like the newspaper he had read over and over, Zoe's studies were her coping mechanism. They were both a distraction and an occupation; a link to the past she wasn't yet ready to lose. "Just because you've all forgotten who you used to be," she'd sometimes tell them when she was feeling particularly frustrated, "doesn't mean I have to."

Kieran and Jackson marched across the courtyard toward the classroom, feet crunching through the gravel and frost. They'd barely got through the door before Bob was at them.

"Well?"

"Well what?" Jackson asked.

"Is it safe?"

"No way of knowing that for sure until we get out there, is there, Bob?"

"That's reassuring," Steve grumbled. Driver said nothing, but he shared their concern. This seemed like the most tenuous of plans.

"All I can tell you," Jackson said, "is that they're all pretty much frozen solid right now. The frost last night was particularly severe. I tried digging a hole just now, and I could barely get the spade to break the surface of the soil, so those things outside shouldn't be much more than chunks of ice. As long as we're back before they start to thaw out, we should be fine."

"*Should* be fine?" Bob said.

"*Will* be fine. Now, are we ready?"

There was a muted, barely audible response.

"I'm ready," Zoe said, keen to show she was willing and to kick the others up the backside a little.

"Good stuff," Jackson continued. "I know you all know what we're doing, but just so we're clear, I'll go through it again, okay?"

Nothing.

"Kieran's going out there first in the digger to clear those icy bastards off the road, Driver follows with the rest of us. He'll get us to the hotel, then it's in and out and back again as quick as we can. No messing around. Got it?"

"You make it sound so easy," Steve said.

"It *will* be easy," Jackson replied. "Trust me."

"Oh, we trust you, all right," Bob said, following Zoe as she walked out of the classroom. "It's what's left of the rest of the world we have a problem with."

Driver was the last to leave, his stomach knotted with nerves. He didn't know what scared him more—the prospect of leaving the safety of the castle walls, or what he might find back at the hotel.

10

Mark Ainsworth's fifteen minutes of fame had ended shortly before the rest of the world had died. He'd worked in a call center selling car insurance for eight years until just before last summer when a chance encounter on a busy high street had resulted in him appearing on a couple of episodes of a poorly rated, fashion-based reality TV show. Most people's professions had been rendered redundant by the apocalypse, none more so than Mark, but with the blissful ignorance of someone who thought that a brief appearance on TV suddenly promoted him from a nobody to a *somebody*, he refused to shut up about it. He still put gel in his hair every morning and used copious amounts of deodorant, still checked his appearance in the mirror whenever he left the caravan. But there were no TVs now. No fashion. No advertisers. None of it mattered—not that any of it ever had. Melanie was sick of hearing about it.

"Just give it a rest, Mark," she said, teeth chattering in the cold. "You've already told me."

"I know. Pretty cool though, eh?"

"If you say so."

"They were talking about getting me to do a few PAs at Oceania

67

in town. Now that would have been awesome. Did you ever go to that club?"

"Yeah. It was shit."

"You're kidding me. Oceania? That place was the dog's bollocks."

"Well it was bollocks," she said, "I'll give you that."

"You're a total dick, Mark," Will Bayliss said. "Shut up about your fucking TV and all that. You're doing my fucking head in."

Ainsworth finally shut up. Bayliss, several years his junior but with the offensive swagger of a wannabe bad boy, intimidated him. Bayliss tutted, and looked Ainsworth up and down dismissively. Paul Field, standing just behind him and doing all he could, as usual, to stay on the right side of Bayliss, shook his head and mumbled something that none of them could make out. For the first time she could remember, Melanie was actually pleased to see Jackson walking toward her.

"You lot ready with the gate?" he asked.

"We're ready," she said.

"Get it shut again as soon as Kieran gets the digger back inside, okay?"

"Okay," she said. Neither Ainsworth nor Bayliss made any comment, but he was used to their disrespect. He nodded his approval at Melanie, then walked back toward the digger and gave Kieran a thumbs-up. Kieran started the engine, filling the air with noise. Jackson looked around at the others—Sue Preston, Charlie Moorehouse, Shirley Brinksford, Phil Kent—all of them standing ready, armed with clubs and axes, poised to mop up any of the corpses which managed to avoid being crushed by the digger and squirm through while the gate was open.

Shirley's mouth was dry and her legs were heavy with nerves. She didn't know if she could do this. She glanced over her shoulder and saw Aiden's young face pressed up against the caravan window. *He shouldn't be watching this*, she thought. *He's too young. I should go back inside and look after him, leave all this violence to the boys.*

"Okay," Jackson shouted. "Open up!"

Ainsworth and Bayliss pulled their respective ropes and the two sides of the gate slowly opened. The nearest dead were immediately visible. *Here comes the flood*, thought Kieran, watching nervously from his elevated position. But they didn't move. A vast number of them had crowded up against the gate, melding together as a single gore-soaked mass, but they were completely frozen and were now stuck in position like someone had hit the pause button. The gate was fully open now, and still there was no movement. Perhaps there was a slight twitch now and then, a barely visible shudder, but that was all. The relief was palpable. Shirley dropped her ax and beckoned Kieran forward. He lowered the digger's heavy scoop and accelerated.

From up in his seat, Kieran had a clear and uninterrupted view of the frozen dead and the world beyond the castle walls. It truly was a bizarre sight; one of the strangest things he'd ever seen (and that was saying something, given everything he'd witnessed since September). It was impossible to even begin to estimate just how many bodies had crowded onto the road leading up to the castle gate. They were unrecognizable, having long since lost virtually all semblance of individual form, packed together like this. First the decay had deformed and distorted them, grossly altering their once-standard shapes in random ways, then the constant crowding had caused more damage, and now the bitter frost had welded them together. Their limbs and torsos were largely obscured by the general mass, but countless heads remained poking up above the bulk of the frozen flesh, their features delicately highlighted and given a strange, glassy sheen by a layer of ice.

Kieran stopped before the first impact, almost unable to comprehend what now lay ahead of him. It was, by turn, terrifying and pitiful. Terrifying because even though they remained motionless and unable to attack, the dead were still here in almost incalculable numbers. And pitiful because these damn things, which had caused him and everyone else so much pain, appeared to have been rendered utterly harmless by a sudden change in the weather. It was almost as if they'd been cut off midsentence, and he found it strangely reassuring, although he also felt uneasy knowing that a thaw would inevitably give some of them back their freedom. He almost laughed out loud at one of them. It had an arm raised and its head held high as if it was an athlete sprinting for the finishing line, caught in a freeze-frame photo with all the other corpses to decide the winner. When he thought he saw it tremble slightly—whether the result of vibrations from the digger, a slight increase in temperature, gravity, intent, or something else entirely—he shoved his foot down on the accelerator pedal and drove straight into it.

Jackson got onto the bus and stood next to Driver, both of them watching as Kieran powered along the road outside the castle, quickly carving a remarkably clean groove through the motionless ranks. He couldn't hear it, but he could imagine the noise of bits of the bodies crunching and snapping, the ice creaking, and he stared as random limbs were broken off like the dried-out branches of dead trees. He glanced across at Driver who remained looking forward, his face expressionless. *He's either focused or completely fucking terrified*, Jackson thought. *I can't tell which.*

When the curve of the road meant that Kieran disappeared from view, Jackson decided it was time to move. He nudged Driver sharply and he pulled away, following the almost perfect channel through the dead which the digger had left. There were steep banks of drifting decay on either side, and even as Jackson watched, he was sure he could see movement. It was subtle and slight, but it was definitely there. Some of the bodies buried deepest had been protected from the worst of the frost, and what was left of them was already starting to slowly inch back toward the area which had been cleared. He knew that if they waited long enough, the track would completely disappear. They had to get out and get back again before the corpses thawed out. The sun was beginning to climb. They didn't have long.

11

Driver's nervousness reached almost unbearable levels as they approached the hotel. His initial trepidation at being out in the open again had quickly faded and had been replaced with an even more uncomfortable feeling of apprehension. What were they going to find at the hotel? Either way he looked at it, it was going to be tough. Contrary to what Hollis, Lorna, and the others he'd left behind might have thought of him, he felt genuine affection for the people he'd been forced to abandon. He hoped they'd find them all safe. If they were dead, he knew he'd be riddled with guilt. And yet, conversely, the prospect of finding them alive made him feel equally nervous. How much would they all hate him for what he'd done? Even though he'd eventually returned for them—albeit a little over a fortnight later—would any of them ever be able to trust him again?

No time to think about that now. They were here. He could see the hotel up ahead.

"So does anyone have a plan for getting them out?" Zoe asked. She was standing just behind Jackson, holding onto a handrail as the bus clattered along.

"Sort of," Jackson replied, giving little away. "Difficult to plan much when you don't know what you're going to find."

"Great."

She knew Jackson was right. It was just her nerves talking. Making detailed preparations had been impossible from a distance. Driver had given them an overview of the basic geography of the area as best he could, explaining about the road between the hotel and the golf course, the fences and gates, the blocked road junction and the crashed vehicles (those he knew about, anyway).

They'd looped around and were now coming from the direction of Bromwell itself. Driver had deliberately chosen a route which would approach the hotel from this direction, because by coming this way, he'd explained to Jackson, they'd be able to get access to the hotel through the field below the golf course. That was where he thought Jas and the others had blown up their cars, and it seemed the most direct way to gain access to the building without having to waste time moving trucks or scrambling over the wreck of his poor old bus.

Driver stopped at the entrance to the field. The steep slope ahead was covered in remains, some standing upright, some decayed down to an almost unrecognizable mulch. Much like the hordes of bodies camped around the castle incessantly, the crowds here had been vast in number, and as a consequence it appeared that many of the dead had literally been trampled into the dirt. Much to the survivors' collective relief, the area remained almost entirely motionless. The bodies here were still frozen.

"I'll never get this bus up there," Driver said, looking at the gore-covered hill which climbed away in front of them. "Best not risk it."

"Let us out," Jackson said, barely acknowledging him. Driver did as instructed, and the four others disembarked.

Zoe, keen to get this done and get back, marched ahead. Her steel-capped boots crunched through the ice, then slid through the fleshy muck below as she stepped out onto the field, vile-smelling liquids splashing up her overtrousers. Bob followed close behind, carrying a screwdriver with a long shaft as a weapon. They walked along the bottom edge of the field to begin with, then began to climb when they reached the hedgerow nearest to the hotel building. A body which lay on its back beneath the hedge, shielded from the worst of the frost and still able to function to a limited extent, reached out for Bob and grabbed hold of his foot. Bob kicked it over, trod down on its neck, and plunged the screwdriver deep into one of its temples. He shook the screwdriver clean and looked over at Zoe. She was standing a short distance away, looking up into the sky.

"Problem?" he asked.

"Possibly," she replied. Since leaving the castle the skies overhead had cleared and were now relentlessly blue. Although it was still cold, the sun was fierce and where the light hit them, the bodies were beginning to defrost. Steam snaked away from them, carried on the gentlest of breezes, and now they could hear the *drip, drip, drip* which heralded the beginning of the thaw.

Steve and Jackson caught up. They were carrying two long ladders between them.

"We need to get on with this and get it done fast," Steve warned. "I don't fancy being stuck out here when those fuckers start moving around again."

Jackson agreed, although he didn't bother saying anything. Instead he continued to climb up the hill, dragging Steve behind on the other end of the ladders. Each step forward became increasingly difficult, the slope of the ground combining with the slush underfoot made it hard to get a grip. And the farther they climbed,

74

the more statuelike corpses they had to negotiate. Jackson watched them intently as he weaved around their frozen shapes. Maybe it was the way its face caught the light, but he was sure the one he was approaching now had just moved its eyes. Was it looking at him? Out of spite and for no other reason, he kicked out at it and it fell back into the icy mire like a felled tree.

"Gate," Zoe said, taking the lead again. There was a metal gate in the top right-hand corner of the field where the land leveled out slightly. She opened it fully, scraping away an arc of once-human remains. "Here's the road Driver was on about," she added, looking up and down the curving track which wound its way around the perimeter of the hotel grounds. Jackson caught up. Steve and Bob took the weight of one ladder, while he rested the other up the impenetrable hedgerow in front of them. He held it steady while Zoe climbed up. She lifted her hands to her face to shield her eyes from the brilliant winter sun.

"Bloody hell," she said to no one in particular.

"Trouble?" Steve asked anxiously.

"You could say that."

The other ladder appeared next to her, and Bob climbed up. "Fuck me," he said when he was alongside her.

"My sentiments exactly."

From this high vantage point, the hotel and much of the surrounding area were clearly visible. For as far as they could see in every direction around the building, the ground was covered in bodies. Like on the other side of the road, many of the dead had been crushed, but many more remained standing, a frozen forest of decay. Zoe looked back toward the bus on the road at the bottom of the hill. Sunlight reflected off the windscreen and she couldn't see Driver. She, like everyone else, had questioned his actions in abandoning his colleagues and getting away from this place by himself. Standing at the top of the ladder, however, soaking up the scale of what had happened here, what he'd done seemed eminently sensible. Even now, frozen, crushed, and wedged together as they all were, the immeasurable mass of dead flesh up ahead was large enough to make Zoe question what the hell *they* were doing here. She couldn't even begin to imagine what terror the people who'd been left behind here must have felt seeing this foul, germ-filled, unstoppable tidal wave of rot rolling toward them. Given the option, she had to admit she'd probably have done the same thing Driver did.

"See anything?" Steve yelled, casually kicking at a single hand which jutted up from the decay covering the road and which had begun to twitch as if trying to form a fist. Both Zoe and Bob were so overcome by the scale of what they could see that neither replied at first. Zoe had to force herself to divert her gaze from the slowly defrosting mass of corpses and start looking at the hotel instead. She scanned the building from right to left, catching her breath when she thought she saw people at a ground floor window. It was just more damn corpses, their faces shoved up hard against the glass by the force of countless others which had crowded into the same rooms behind them and pushed them forward.

"This is hopeless," she shouted down. "No one could have survived this."

"It's full of bodies," Bob added.

"What, the grounds or the hotel itself?" Jackson asked.

"Both," Bob replied. "The ground floor is definitely."

"Well, keep looking. It might be like when you capsize a boat."

"What are you on about?" Bob scowled, looking down at Jackson.

"You know how the air gets trapped and you can survive as long as you keep your head up at the top?"

"Yeah," Bob said, "but you haven't seen this place. There's no air here, only death."

"Wait!" Zoe yelled. "Look!"

She pointed at the hotel. Bob squinted to try and shut out the brightness and see what she'd seen.

"What?"

She paused momentarily, not sure herself now. But then she saw it again—movement on the first floor. And it was definite, controlled movement too. There were faces at the windows in two adjacent rooms.

"Bloody hell," she gasped, looking at Bob then down at Steve and Jackson. "We've found them."

The sudden euphoria at finding the survivors was quickly replaced by now familiar feelings of nervousness and unease. Getting the people out of the hotel took an uncomfortably long length of time, and with every extra minute that passed, so the dead around the building became increasingly animated.

Zoe had lifted Bob's ladder over the hedge and managed to drop it down the other side while keeping hold of the top rung. The two ladders interlocked at the top, forming an apex which, with a little careful negotiation, they could get over and climb down to the other side. Once they'd made it over, Zoe, Bob, and Steve waded through the semi-human mire with disgust. It was much deeper inside the perimeter fence of the hotel where the space was restricted. Thousands of bodies had managed to get in, yet none of them had got back out through the narrow gap. The decay ranged between ankle- and knee-deep, and their every footstep crunched ice and bone into the ground. Some corpses were still upright, standing like the dead stumps of trees after a forest fire, but most had simply collapsed over time and now lay on the ground in various stages of deterioration. Withered hands seemed to be constantly reaching up at them from the sea of fetid muck, fingers dripping with putrescence. And as they slowly thawed, so the appalling stench steadily worsened. Zoe gagged. Bob dry-heaved. It was only the desperate faces looking down and shouting at them from the first-floor windows which kept them moving forward. Zoe counted at least five people. How many more were there?

Bob tried to find a way to get inside the overrun building, but they quickly realized that that was impossible. Apart from the fact the entire ground floor appeared to be full to overflowing with rot, the comparative temperature inside the hotel had kept what remained of the dead in there marginally more animated than those outside, exposed to the elements. When they'd realized what he was trying to do, one of the trapped women had yelled down and explained that they'd also blocked the staircases to prevent the corpses from getting any closer. And as well as preventing the dead from getting up, their blockades also prevented them from getting down.

Zoe struggled to stay focused. Whenever she stood still for any length of time, those of the dead able to move began to gravitate toward her. Their speed was barely noticeable at first, but when she realized what was happening, it became hard to concentrate on anything else. They were like giant slugs; glistening with slime, moving almost undetectably slowly. You could try and ignore them if you wanted, but if you became distracted for any length of time, when you turned back they'd be right at you, poised to attack. It reminded Zoe of that game she'd played as a kid in the school playground. She could almost hear the dead shouting at her: *"What's the time, Mr. Wolf?"*

She fought her way over to stand directly beneath a first-floor window which one of the trapped men had opened. After talking to him for a couple of minutes, trying to work out the easiest way of getting them down, she stepped back, looked around, and saw that at least seven corpses were closing in on her, painfully slowly. Regardless of their lack of speed, she was grateful when Bob returned to watch her back.

Working together and trying to speed up as the sun climbed and the temperature increased, an escape route was quickly improvised. A number of mattresses were thrown down from the first floor and piled under one of the windows, both shielding the survivors from the dead below and creating a thick enough landing mat that they could risk jumping. And one by one, they threw themselves out. The drop was obviously of little concern in comparison to the prospect of remaining trapped in the morguelike hotel for even a minute longer. Their desperation to get away was clear. Three men and two women jumped down without hesitation. There was a momentary delay as a final man—potbellied but bedraggled and obviously starved—tried to coerce a dog to jump down. Bob yelled at him to "Just leave the fucking mutt" as he wrestled with a dripping corpse which had now completely shaken off its icy bonds and tried to attack. It was only when the dog's owner gave up and jumped from the window first that the hound almost immediately followed.

Questions and explanations were initially the furthest thing from anyone's mind. For a blissful few minutes, all that mattered to the people who had escaped the hotel was that, somehow, they were finally free. It felt unreal. Maybe it was? Their interminable incarceration had, until an hour or so ago, seemed set to continue until they'd each breathed their last. But now it was over.

Having managed to get back over the fence using the two ladders, they regrouped at the gate, then walked down the steep slope to the road. They moved quickly to avoid the dead which staggered and crawled toward them. Driver couldn't see anything from inside the bus, but the door was open and he could hear voices approaching.

"There's one thing I don't get," he heard a woman's voice say. Was that Caron? "How did you find us? This place is so isolated . . ."

"Got a mate of yours with us," he heard Jackson explain. "Go easy on him, though. The delay's not his fault. We couldn't risk coming back out to look for you until now."

Driver got off the bus, but he didn't go any farther. He was too nervous, and instead he waited for the others to come into view. They soon appeared, but the relentlessly bright sun made it difficult to see who was who. He tried to count heads, then stopped when he saw Harte. Their eyes met, and he felt his legs weaken with nerves. There was a brief and unexpected delay. Was it disbelief? Or maybe it was because they didn't recognize him. None of them had ever seen Driver clean-shaven before.

"Driver?" Harte said, his uncertainty clear. His tone was impossible to read. "Driver, you sly old bastard, is that you?"

"I'm sorry, Harte," Driver began to say, not knowing whether he should move farther forward or turn and run the other way. "I thought it was for the best. If I'd stuck with you lot, we'd have all been buggered . . ."

He braced himself as Harte moved closer, then relaxed as the man unexpectedly threw his arms around him and squeezed.

"Thanks, man," Harte said, almost in tears.

Driver looked up at the others who were approaching. There were more of them—more of his friends. He saw Hollis, Lorna, and Caron. And there was Howard Reece and that bloody dog of his. And there was Jas . . . Christ, he looked traumatized. He was barely interacting with any of the others.

Another corpse lying at the roadside managed to raise itself up by Jackson's feet. He booted it in what was left of its face.

"We need to get out of here," he said, and ushered the others onto the bus. Howard brought up the rear, carrying his dog.

"What about . . . ?" Driver started to ask. Howard shook his head, preempting his question.

"This is it, mate," he said. "This is all of us."

"But what about Webb and Gordon? Martin? The others . . ."

"We lost Amir and Sean out here," he explained, "and Webb and Martin bought it when the bodies got in." His voice became low and monotone, almost like it was an effort to remember. "Gordon and Ginnie just didn't want to keep going. We found them in their room one morning, a couple of weeks back, dead in bed together. Nicked a load of drugs from Caron, they had. I'd been starting to think they might have been the sensible ones."

"I'm sorry."

"Sorry? Bloody hell, what have you got to be sorry about?"

"Just seemed like the right thing to say."

"Believe me, you've got no need to be sorry, mate. This time yesterday I was close to giving up. You've done us all a favor."

12

Laura led Hollis up the spiral stairs of the gatehouse to where she'd left Harte and Jas earlier. They still hadn't moved. Both men were standing at the top of the tower, backs to each other, looking out over the battlements. It was getting dark, but she could see that Harte was looking down into the courtyard directly below. Jas's focus was clearly elsewhere.

"Hollis!" Harte said, turning around when he heard footsteps. "How are you, mate?"

"Good, thanks," he said quietly, his voice barely audible. "Really good."

"You had something to eat?"

"I didn't think he was ever going to stop eating," Lorna answered for him, tenderly squeezing his arm. "Howard's still down there, feeding his face."

"Where's Caron?"

"Asleep in one of the caravans, curled up with an empty bottle of wine. Did you really need to ask?"

"And Driver?"

"On his bus, I presume."

"The gang's all here, eh?" He grinned.

"Well, those of us who are left alive are," she said quietly. Hollis slowly sat down—moving like a man twice his age—and she sat next to him, checking he was okay. They'd all suffered during their imprisonment at the hotel, but Hollis had been affected more than most. He'd lost the hearing in one ear, and the associated loss of confidence had hit him hard. For a while after they'd become stranded in the besieged hotel, his behavior had become increasingly aggressive and unpredictable. Over the last couple of weeks he'd become withdrawn. Now he barely said anything to anyone, rarely even moved unless Lorna was there to help him up and drag him around. He was half the man he used to be.

The silence was getting to be too loud. "You okay, Jas?" Lorna asked, but he didn't even bother to turn around. He hadn't acknowledged her since she'd come up. "Much going on out there?" she asked, unperturbed.

Finally, a response.

"Nothing much," he said. "Nothing much going on anywhere anymore."

"Bloody hell," Harte sighed. "Cheer up, will you."

"Why should I?"

"Because this time yesterday we all thought our number was up. We were trapped. We were completely fucked."

"And this place is different because . . . ?"

Harte couldn't believe what he was hearing.

"This place couldn't be more different."

"And you're sure about that?"

"Yes."

"Well, I'm not. Not yet, anyway. Way I see it, it's just out of the frying pan, into the fire."

"You think?" Lorna said, disagreeing strongly. "It's way better than that. Way I see it, we're safely away from the dead. This is some-where we can live and breathe and walk outside and . . ."

"As long as we stay inside the castle walls."

"Yes, but—"

"Look, I'm not saying this place isn't better, I just don't think it's as good as you're making out."

"It's as good as it gets for now, I think," Hollis mumbled, but Jas still disagreed.

"They only came out for us today because the dead had fro-zen," he said, talking to the others more than Hollis. "It was a par-ticularly harsh frost. That's not going to happen every day. They're still trapped like we were."

"Yes, but we only have to worry about the dead for a few more months," Harte said. "Six months, that's what we've always said. We're almost halfway there now. It'll get easier."

"I've been hearing that kind of bullshit since day one," Jas in-terrupted, sounding increasingly angry. "I was talking to that guy Kieran when we got here. He said he cleared that road down there when Jackson and Driver went out looking for us."

"So?"

"So by the time we got back, it was blocked again, wasn't it? They had to get the digger back out and clear it before we could even get close to this place. And that's on a day when the condi-tions are in *our* favor."

"Oh just have a drink," Harte said, offering him a bottle of spirits. "Calm the fuck down."

Jas took a swig, winced, then passed the bottle back. Lorna watched him, concerned. Harte came over and sat down next to her in a corner of the tower. It was cold under his backside, but the strong walls shielded them from the icy wind. As uncomfortable as it was out here, they'd had enough of being trapped indoors recently.

Jas remained on the opposite side to the rest of them, staring out into space.

"What are you thinking?" Lorna asked him.

"I'm thinking how fucked-up everything still is," he replied, his voice wavering, "and how little of it I still understand. I'm asking myself why I'm stuck here in a bloody castle with you lot, when this time last year I'd have been at home with Harj and the kids and . . ."

His voice broke and he didn't finish his sentence, but it didn't matter. The point had already been made. Being here tonight felt like a hollow victory for Jas. It depressed him to think this might be as good as his life was going to get. It still hurt too much to think about his life before the apocalypse in any great detail, but now, strangely, thinking about more recent times was becoming equally painful. Standing out here tonight reminded him of the endless hours he'd spent out on the balcony back at the flats, drinking beer, looking out over the dead crowds and discussing the rigors and practicalities of daily survival with Hollis, Stokes and the others. He'd felt like the king of the world back then, like he and the rest of them were in almost total control. Christ, how things had changed. The flats were lost now, and the hotel too, and Stokes, Webb and many of the others were dead. Hollis was just a shell of a man . . . and as for the dead? Well, those fuckers continued to fight for all they were worth. Their decaying flesh may have been weak, but their intent was still clear.

"I was just thinking," he said, "how it feels like we've been here before."

"I've never been here before," Hollis said, mishearing him. Jas ignored him and continued speaking.

"Look down there," he said, gesturing out over the castle wall, "and what do you see? I'll tell you—a fucking huge crowd of dead bodies. Same as we saw when we looked out of the hotel windows every bloody morning. Same as we saw when we were back at the flats."

"But this is different." Lorna sighed. "Can't you see? Look at the condition they're in, Jas. Look at the state of them."

"Look at the state of *us*," he countered. "For fuck's sake, there's barely any of us left. Most of us are dead. Gordon, Ginnie, Martin, Webb, Ellie, Anita, Stokes . . . all gone."

"But we're still here," she protested. "We've survived."

"So far, yes."

"And all the other people Driver found here."

"What, all fifteen of them? Out of a population of something like sixty million people, there's only just over twenty of us left?"

"We don't know that. There could be hundreds more scattered all over the country."

"*Hundreds* more. Doesn't change the fact that *millions* have died."

"But this place is incredible," Harte said. "It's safe and it's strong. They've got a decent level of supplies and—"

"Spare me the bullshit," Jas interrupted.

"It's not bullshit."

"It is! We've heard it all before, again and again. Remember the early days back at the flats? You were walking around the place like the bloody cock of the roost, telling me how perfect it was, going on about how we were going to build this barrier to keep the bodies back, and how we'd do up the flats and make them inhabitable and—"

"And that's exactly what we did," Lorna said.

"Up to a point," Jas continued. "I believed it, though. We *all* believed it. But it didn't last. And when we got to that fucking hotel, it was the same again. Remember the first couple of days there?

How we were swanning around playing football, checking out the gym equipment, talking about draining the swimming pool and all that?"

"I know what you're saying, Jas, but nothing that happened there was because we did anything to—"

"What happened was avoidable," he yelled, the sudden raw emotion in his voice taking everyone by surprise. He picked up the bottle again and knocked back more booze. Lorna wondered whether this was just the drink talking. Maybe a combination of alcohol and relief that they'd finally escaped the hotel.

"This place is different," she said, risking his ire. He glared at her, but when he didn't immediately try shouting her down, she continued. "This place is different and the bodies are much weaker now. Give it a few more months and there won't be anything left of them but bones."

"A few months? I don't know if I can take a few more months of this. I don't know if I can take another day."

Jas knocked back the dregs at the bottom of the bottle and hurled it over the battlements. It was a few seconds before he heard it smash.

Lorna, Harte, and Hollis watched him with caution. Suddenly feeling the cold, Lorna wanted to go down. She stood up and helped Hollis to his feet. She was about to disappear down the spiral staircase when Jas turned and spoke to her again.

"You're right, Lorna," he said. "This place *is* going to be different and we will be okay here. And I'll tell you why—it's because I'm not going to have it any other way. I'm not letting you, Jackson, or any other fucker back me into a corner again. I'm not giving anyone control over what's left of my life now, understand?"

Eighty-Seven Days Since Infection

13

Within the castle walls now was a community of twenty-one: fifteen men and six women. Jackson, maintaining his position of unelected leader by virtue of the fact that no one complained and no one else seemed to want the role, was keen to try and keep everyone occupied. Boredom was an enemy—it gave people the unwelcome opportunity to think about how much they'd lost and how little they'd still got. Whether it was to keep them occupied, distracted, out of trouble . . . the reasons were unimportant. Most people willingly took on the duties assigned to them, and completed them to the best of their abilities, despite the blatantly obvious fact that much of the work didn't actually need to be done.

Caron was an intelligent woman, and she knew when to keep her mouth shut. This was definitely one of those times. She was less than pleased with the duties she'd been allocated, but she carried them out without complaint. Since arriving at Cheetham Castle, she'd done more cleaning than she had in the previous ten years combined. At least it was relatively warm and dry indoors, she thought. Winter had barely begun, but it felt like it had been like this forever.

Working in the museum was particularly sad. They were using parts of it as a storeroom now, and all the exhibits had been shoved into one end of the large, L-shaped space. For a while this morning she'd spent some time hidden around the corner, looking at them all. Valuable antiques now worth nothing. Beautifully restored and preserved artifacts now given less importance than food and water supplies, spare clothes and pretty much everything else. There were a number of wall-mounted displays which had been taken down and stacked against a wall. She flicked through them, avoiding doing any work for a little longer. There were paintings of the castle hundreds of years ago, newly built and full of people. Then there were pictures of the "second stage" buildings within the perimeter wall—a great hall, an armory, stables, living quarters, kitchens . . . all just ruins now. All those different eras and ages, the lords of the manor, the kings and the generals . . . all gone now. She couldn't help but think she was living through the last chapter of this once-great place. If she had any artistic talent—and she was under no illusions because she certainly *didn't*—then she'd have seriously considered painting a final frieze and hanging it on the museum wall. Twenty-one thin and frightened people. A handful of caravans. A basic smattering of supplies. An invading army of corpses waiting on the other side of the outer wall. Hardly a grand finale to the castle's hundreds of years of history.

This kind of physical work didn't come naturally to Caron anymore, but she bit her tongue and smiled when she needed to so as not to offend anyone. There were worse jobs to be had around here. She left the museum/storeroom and looked out across the courtyard as she walked. Elsewhere, Jackson had a group of people gathered around him, all trying to assemble some kind of bizarre construction out of wood and ropes close to where, according to some plans she'd been looking at, the kitchens had once been.

Elsewhere, people were chopping wooden pallets for firewood, making an industry out of something which probably didn't require such large amounts of effort, grading wood into large, medium, and small pieces and storing them in a dry shelter. Others were cleaning the caravans. Someone else was burning rubbish . . .

Too busy watching what was happening elsewhere and not concentrating on where she was going, she literally walked into Hollis. He jumped with surprise.

"Sorry, Greg."

"My fault," he mumbled apologetically. "I wasn't looking. You okay?"

"Fine."

"Been working hard?" he asked with a grin. He knew she hadn't.

"To all intents and purposes."

"What's that supposed to mean?"

She glanced around before putting down a bucketful of cleaning equipment. She moved a pair of unused yellow rubber gloves to reveal a well-thumbed paperback, half a bottle of wine, and some chocolate wrappers.

"Between you and me," she said secretively, "I've been taking it easy."

"I'm surprised at you," Hollis said, shaking his head with mock disappointment. "What would our Mr. Jackson say if he found out?"

"You're not going to rat on me, are you?" she asked, knowing full well that he wasn't. "Honestly, Greg, I know we didn't know each other before all this madness, but you know me well enough by now. Dirty, hard, physical work . . . it's just not my style."

"Caron," he said, grinning, "I know you well enough to understand that you're probably the person least suited to dirty, physical work I've ever met. Just keep your head down and get it done

93

though, eh? A few more months and we'll be able to stop hiding away like this and you can go wherever you want then. Let your new house get as dirty as you damn well please. Spend your life doing whatever you like. You could live like a pig in shit if it'd make you happy."

"Quite," she said, not sure how she was supposed to respond to that.

"Anyway," Hollis said, excusing himself, "speaking of shit, I'd best get to work myself."

"Oh, Greg, you're not?"

"And you thought you'd got it bad, eh?"

Caron laughed and picked up her stuff and walked on, leaving Hollis to head in the opposite direction. He'd have gladly swapped duties with Caron, but he knew she'd have balked at the very idea of slopping out. Someone had to do it, though, and at least working around the chemical toilets kept him away from everyone else. Right now, that was how he liked it.

14

Jackson was standing at the edge of the courtyard, near to where a number of interior walls had once stood. They were just crumbled ruins now, as dilapidated as everything else, but a single feature remained which still interested him—a well. They'd not yet managed to ascertain whether the water source was still there and accessible, but Jackson intended to find out. They had enough bottled water to see them through for a while longer, but having a steady supply on tap would make things immeasurably easier for everyone. Bob Wilkins had some engineering experience, and Charlie Moorehouse had been a Scout leader for a while. Between them they thought they'd be able to improvise a basic rope and pulley system to lower a bucket deep enough down and find out whether or not the well was dry.

A number of other people had been conscripted to help. Lorna, Mark Ainsworth, Paul Field, and Harte were busy digging a series of four holes around the well. Bob and Charlie were constructing two A-frames out of wood they'd taken from a working model of a catapult they'd found stored around the back of the museum, the feet of which were to be sunk into the four holes before the two frames were connected to make something that would hopefully resemble a child's swing. That was the plan, anyway.

"Want a hand?" Ainsworth asked Lorna.

"You've got your own hole to dig," she said. "No thanks."

"I'm almost done. You've barely started."

"I'm fine, thanks."

"We could swap sides if the ground's too hard over there. I don't mind."

"Did you not hear her?" Field sighed. "Fucking moron."

"I said I'm fine," Lorna snapped, panting with the effort of the dig.

"Just trying to help, that's all," Ainsworth said.

"Well, I don't need any help. Jesus Christ, this isn't the 1970s. Women are able to dig holes, you know."

"Bloody hell, you're touchy today, aren't you?"

"Leave her alone, Mark," Harte said.

"And what are you, her boyfriend?" Ainsworth sneered.

"Get a grip," Harte said and he carried on digging. Lorna dropped her shovel. "You okay?"

"Going to get a drink," she said. "Back in a minute."

The three men watched her disappear. Ainsworth caught Harte's eye and grinned at him.

"She's great, isn't she? Cracking pair of tits."

"Damn right," Field sniggered.

"For fuck's sake," Harte sighed, "is that all you've got to say about her? Lorna's got me out of more scrapes than I can remember. She's a fucking diamond. Bloody hell, the whole world's fallen apart and all you can say about her is she's got nice tits. There are better ways of assessing a person's worth, you know."

Jackson watched Harte and Ainsworth from a short distance away, feeling unexpectedly uneasy. Their conversation sounded alien and out of place. Ainsworth was talking the way people *used* to talk, back in the days when trivialities and appearances seemed to be all that mattered. The stakes were much higher now. There was no room here for petty arguments and superficial romances. Maybe in the future things would be different, but not yet. Not for a long time yet.

"Hold it steady," Charlie grumbled.

"Sorry."

Jackson had been supporting the top of one of the A-frames, trying to keep it steady as Charlie attempted to drill through a wooden post with a hand-drill which looked so old it could have come from the museum. They'd had to cannibalize and improvise to find enough materials, lashing the sections of wood together with tow ropes they'd found in the back of a truck.

Charlie grunted with effort, changed his grip and his stance, then began drilling again. His round, childlike face was an uncharacteristically flustered red, and sweat poured from him. He was almost through, though, and he kept working. Another few minutes' effort and the tip of the drill bit finally poked through the other side.

"Bloody hell," he said, wiping his brow. "Half an hour, that took."

"I know," said Jackson.

"Used to be able to cut a hole like that in seconds."

"I know," he said again. "We need to source some generators when we next get out of here. Try and get a decent power supply."

He looked up again and saw that Jas was walking past, heading in the direction of the kitchen. He stopped and looked at what they were doing—the digging and the frame building—then shook his head and walked on.

"You're not going to help then?" Jackson shouted after him.

"Nope," he replied, stopping again.

"But you'll be happy to use the water if we get this working."

"You won't get water out of there."

"We might."

"Come on, Jackson," he said, "get over yourself. You know as well as I do, you're only doing this to keep yourself busy. Same as all your bloody cleaning rotas."

"We have to start somewhere, Jas."

"Do we?"

"Of course we do."

"Well I think you're overcomplicating things. And I think you're doing it intentionally. Water flows down, not up. It's easier to collect rainwater than to try dragging it up from the ground. We need to build rain-catchers, not climbing frames."

"Okay, okay . . ." he said, walking up to Jas so their conversation couldn't easily be overheard. "So I'm trying to keep people busy. Nothing wrong with that."

"Except it looks like you're the one doing all the work." He nodded toward Harte, Field, and Ainsworth, who were now leaning up against their shovels, watching Lorna coming back toward them.

"Maybe I am. Anyway, it's not just me. I just want to keep everyone sharp and get us ready so we can clear out of here after the winter and make a fresh start."

"What's there to be ready for? What do you think's going to happen? I'm guessing we'll all just wander off in different directions and forget about all of this. That's what I'm planning. As soon as the bodies are gone I'm going to find myself a decent-sized house, get plenty of supplies in, then do as little as possible for as long as I can."

"And you'll be happy with that?"

"I reckon I will."

"There's got to be more to life than that, though."

"Has there? Sounds pretty idyllic to me."

"But we don't all have that freedom, do we? What about Aiden? He's only twelve. We can't leave him to fend for himself."

"He'll be okay. He won't have much choice. He'll grow up fast enough. Anyway, there's a few mother hens here who'd be more than willing to take him under their wings."

"There might be other kids."

"You think?"

"I don't know, and that's the point. We can't just split up and look after ourselves at the expense of everyone else. If we want the human race to survive then we—"

"Who said anything about that?"

"What?"

"All this 'human race' bullshit. It isn't my concern, mate. I've tried all that and it doesn't work. It's over. We're too far gone. You should stop stressing and get used to relaxing. We don't need to dig for water, 'cause there's millions of bottles of the stuff in the supermarkets up and down the country, just waiting to be taken. And there's plenty more besides—lakes, rivers, reservoirs . . ."

"So what about food?"

"Same. Just keep looting."

"But it'll all run out eventually and then—"

"—and then it won't be my problem. I'll be long gone. Dead and buried."

"Well, not buried, not if you're alone. You'll die in your armchair, feet up in front of your TV that doesn't work."

"Just dead, then. So what? I won't care. Point is, Jackson, I've already lost everything that mattered. I worked my bollocks off for my family, and I did everything I could for them. They meant more to me than anything else in the world, you know. But none of that meant anything because, in the end, there was fuck all I could do to help them. I couldn't save them. I couldn't ease the pain.

Bloody hell, I wasn't even there for them when they died. I was on my own. I was a security guard, looking after a new-built shopping center that wasn't even going to open for another month, and I should have been at home. Seems to me, the harder I've tried since then, the more fucked-up things have got.

"So I've made a decision and I've stopped. I'm not even going to try anymore. And if you want to waste your time doing stuff like this, then you go for it. Just don't expect me to help."

15

The small classroom had begun to resemble a sixth-form common room. Someone could be found in there most of the time, but the only person who used the room for its originally intended purpose now was Zoe, and the only reason she chose to work there was because it was the warmest place in the entire castle. She'd tried studying in her caravan, but it was nigh on impossible to concentrate there, even if she shut herself in the small, square bathroom and sat on the disconnected pan. As well as the subzero temperature, she was also having to share the confined space with Caron and Lorna, and with Melanie too now, who'd moved out of the caravan next door a few days earlier after an argument with Sue about something so trivial that neither of them could even remember what it was. And sharing with Melanie inevitably meant having to put up with either late-night visits from a stream of men (which drove Lorna crazy) or her coming in and out at all hours, usually having had more than a few drinks. Will Bayliss, Phil Kent, Paul Field . . . Zoe had lost count of all the different blokes Melanie had had through the door.

Zoe was beginning to despise this place. With six caravans all lined up in a row outside, it was starting to resemble the holiday park from hell. She had to keep reminding herself that this wasn't going to last forever, and that no matter how bad things were here, they were infinitely worse on the other side of the castle walls.

Ainsworth, Bayliss, Field, and Jas were sitting around the paraffin heater, blocking most of the heat and making a hell of a lot of noise. The light was beginning to fade, but Zoe was determined to finish the section of her study book she'd been working on all afternoon. It was a particularly complex, heavy-going section on the intricacies of one particular aspect of international commercial law, and it was quite possibly the most redundant topic she could have chosen to study. Much of it hadn't even made sense to her when there'd been a corporate world left to apply it to.

"Zoe, love," Sue called from the kitchen next door, "give us a hand, would you."

Zoe looked over her shoulder through the connecting doors between the classroom, café, and kitchen which Sue had left propped open with chairs. As usual, she'd been preparing an evening meal for anyone who could be bothered to drag themselves over to the café to eat.

"I'm busy," Zoe shouted back. "Ask someone else. There's four blokes in here all sat on their arses doing nothing. Ask one of them."

Sue walked over to the door. "I can't do that."

"Why not?"

She stumbled for an answer momentarily. "Because they've been working all day, that's why."

"So have I."

"Yes, but what you're doing is just for you. They've been doing stuff outside."

"So have I," she said again, "and I've been doing this since I came in. I'll ask them to help if you won't."

"No, don't. I'll just—"

It was too late.

"Oi, Will," Zoe shouted. "Sue needs a hand."

Ainsworth began a sarcastic slow clap.

"Why don't you help her, then?" Bayliss shouted back.

"Because I'm busy."

"So am I."

"Doing what?"

"Planning."

"Planning what?"

"Can't tell you."

"Doesn't matter," Sue said, sounding uncomfortable. "I'll do it myself."

The men turned their backs on Zoe and Sue again, and continued plotting and laughing. Frustrated, Zoe stood up and shoved her chair back. It scraped across the floor, filling the classroom with ugly noise as she grudgingly went to help.

Fifteen minutes later, Sue was standing outside the café, repeatedly hitting an empty saucepan with a wooden spoon, a makeshift dinner gong. It felt good to stand out in the open and make such noise, liberating almost. After weeks of silence, being able to scream was a blessed relief.

It took less than five minutes for virtually all of the people living within the castle walls to descend upon the café next door. Sue's food, although nothing special, was warm and filling and it was genuinely appreciated. She served up with a certain amount of pride.

With most people eating, the crowded room became relatively quiet. Jackson seized on the opportunity to speak.

"I've been thinking," he said, standing up. "Does anyone know anything about planting vegetables?"

"You dig a hole, chuck a seed in, and it grows," Ainsworth joked.

"Well I had an allotment," Bob began to say before he was interrupted by Jas groaning.

"Bloody hell, Jackson, what are you on about now? We'll be out of here by the time you can start planting."

"You might be, Jas, but some of us might decide to stay. I'm not sure what I'm doing yet. I'm just trying to start planning for the future. Looking ahead."

"Why would anybody want to stay here? And I've already told you, we don't have a future. Not like that, anyway."

"We'll have to agree to disagree, then, Jas," Jackson continued. "I just think we need to start thinking about these things sooner rather than later because if we don't we could end up missing planting dates and then—"

"—and then we'd just have to keep looting from the supermarkets for another year. No big deal. We'll be doing that anyway."

"But we need to think about our health. We'll need fresh fruit and vegetables."

"We can get by with tins for now. Bloody hell, how many times do we have to have this conversation?"

"Until we've found some answers. I don't think things are as black and white as you see them. The fact remains, at some point soon we're going to have to start fending for ourselves. You can put it off, but all you'll be doing is delaying the inevitable."

"Whatever," Jas grumbled, returning his attention to his food. "Depends on your definition of soon."

Jackson looked around the room, hopeful of catching someone's eye and finding a little support somewhere, but there was nothing. Bob had shut up and was concentrating on his dinner to avoid being drawn into the conversation. Even Hollis and Howard, two more mature men who'd both seemed keen to help and get involved since they'd arrived here, kept their heads bowed. Howard, as usual, seemed more interested in his dog than anything else. Jackson wondered if he really was the only one bothered about their survival. Surely that couldn't be the case. The rest of them would have given up long ago, wouldn't they? Why would any of them bother struggling through to today if none of them cared? Was it just some pointless and inevitable instinct, forcing them all to keep plodding on even when there was no longer any hope?

"For what it's worth," Lorna said quietly, almost as if she didn't want to be heard, "I think you're probably right. Thing is, though, this lot are going to need time before they start thinking about farming and stuff like that. Jas has got a point. There's enough to last us on the shelves for now."

Jackson sat down next to her, dejected. "But we've already had months."

"No, we haven't," she said. "We've had months to try and cope with all the shit that's been thrown at us constantly. But now the pressure seems to finally be easing off, and those dead fuckers outside are rotting away to nothing, so people are inevitably going to start asking themselves questions."

"Such as?"

"Such as . . . why did I lose everybody I gave a damn about? Is it worth going on? Do I want to live, if all I have to look forward to is people like these and places like this?"

Jackson didn't reply. He knew she was right. Since the very first day everything he'd done had been focused on surviving at all costs, without stopping to question why. And now, as Lorna had succinctly pointed out, things were beginning to change. Instead of just trying to instinctively cope and adapt, people now had the opportunity to see if they *wanted* to cope and adapt first. Asking stupid fucking questions about planting seeds to a group of people who clearly couldn't give a shit between them wasn't helping. It was his way of dealing with the pressure, but all it was doing was pissing everybody else off. Jas was clearly planning a different strategy, and right now it seemed there was hardly any common ground between them. Maybe he was right. Maybe Jackson was trying too hard.

"We're all going to need time," Lorna said, sensing his dejection and leaning closer again, "and this is the first opportunity most of us have had to think about the future. We need to make sense of what's left and remember how to be human again before we decide if it's worth trying to carry on. I know I do."

16

Hollis screwed up his face with concentration and disgust as he dragged over the last of the chemical toilets and emptied it into the vast cesspit which had been dug in the farthest corner of the enclosed castle grounds. He swilled the bottom of each of the four plastic tubs with a little reclaimed water, tipped them out, then added an inch or so of an acrid-smelling chemical to each before replacing the lids and taking them back over to the area of the castle designated as the lavatory. These few crumbling, half-height walls had apparently been a stable block, many hundreds of years ago. *All that progress we made*, Hollis thought, smiling wryly, *all those years and all those technological advances. Now look at us! Shitting in buckets behind a wall, and pissing into a narrow, foot-deep trench lined with stones for drainage. It's like the last five hundred years or so never happened.*

As basic as their conditions were, Hollis recognized the importance of maintaining good sanitation. It had become something of an obsession. After what had happened to Ellie and Anita back at the flats, he'd taken it upon himself to take charge of this side of things, not that anyone else had been vying with him to take on that particular responsibility. Their indifference didn't bother him. Whatever the cause of the disease which had killed the two girls, he knew they couldn't afford to take any similar risks here. No one was trapped inside the castle, but getting in or out of the place wasn't easy—it was practically impossible on foot while the dead outside still retained even the slightest spark of reanimation—and any such outbreak within these walls would inevitably be catastrophic. The risk of such a disease running rampant through these close confines didn't bare thinking about.

Hollis was preoccupied with his dark thoughts when he returned to the cesspit. It had been almost a day since his last visit here, and he decided to spread a little soil and lime on the pool of waste to try and neutralize the steadily worsening smell. Too tired to do it by hand—strange, he thought, how the less he did, the more tired he felt these days—he started up a small digger and drove it over. He picked up a scoop of earth from the huge pile made while digging the pit out, then swung the digger's extended arm across and emptied the dirt over the small lake of waste, spreading it as best he could.

After repeating the operation a couple more times, Hollis left the digger running and threw a couple of shovelfuls of pungent-smelling white powder onto the pit. He then returned to the digger, planning to drop another couple of scoops of soil. He swung the arm around, picked up more dirt, then swung back again and smacked it straight into someone walking the other way. It was Steve Morecombe, and the force of the impact knocked him off his feet. Morecombe collapsed to the ground, clutching his right arm and screaming in agony. He tried to get back up but his foot slipped off the edge of the pit and sunk into the foul-smelling waste. Hollis jumped off the digger and ran over to try and help. In his haste to get him away from the edge of the cesspit, he tried to pick Steve up but grabbed him under his injured arm, which made him scream twice as loud.

"Get off me, you fucking idiot!"

Hollis staggered back. Several people pushed past him. They were there before he'd even realized they were close. Jas and Kieran were first, closely followed by Howard and Zoe, then Jackson.

"What the hell happened here?" Jackson demanded, pushing his way to the front of the small crowd.

"*He* happened," Steve yelled, nodding at Hollis because he couldn't move either arm to point. The pain was excruciating. He was drenched with a sickly sweat and he felt nauseous, as if he was about to pass out. Zoe crouched down next to him and gingerly tried to examine his arm. He had on a number of layers of thick winter clothing, but from the unnatural angle of it she could see his arm was badly deformed. She looked into his face, overawed by the obvious seriousness of his injury. This was way past her limited first-aid skills. Steve's eyelids fluttered.

"It's shock, I think," Zoe said. Jackson took Steve's weight and lowered him onto his back as he drifted in and out of consciousness. Zoe looked up into the crowd of useless faces which stared back at her. "Well, don't just stand there," she shouted, "someone go and get Sue."

In the melting pot of mismatched skills and redundant past-life occupations within the castle community, Sue Preston had unwillingly found herself promoted to chief medical officer. She'd been a part-time nurse, working, on average, a couple of days a week for the last five years, but she had more medical knowledge than the rest of them put together. To her credit she was on the scene in seconds, more likely as a reaction to the noise and confusion she'd seen than as a result of any sense of duty.

Hollis was trying to get closer to Steve. He was distraught, overcome with guilt. Howard tried to pull him away from the others.

"It was an accident," Hollis said, tears in his eyes, his voice quieter than ever. "Honest, Howard, I didn't even know he was there. I just turned around and . . ."

"I know," Howard said, trying to lead him back toward the caravans. Jas caught Howard's arm as he passed him.

"Probably best to keep him away from machinery from now on," he said, talking to Howard rather than directly to Hollis. "Don't want to risk anything like this happening again."

"Bloody hell, Jas," Howard said, "he didn't mean for it to happen, you know."

"It was an accident," Hollis said, shaking himself free from Howard's grip.

"Well, we can't afford to have accidents anymore."

"I know that. Christ, you make it sound like I did it on purpose."

"I don't know what was going on here," Jas continued, "but there are a couple of things I *do* know. First, you can hardly hear anything anymore, so we can't risk having you operating machinery and—"

"I can hear," Hollis protested. "There's nothing wrong with my hearing."

"Spare me the bullshit," Jas sighed. "You're lip reading. I know it must be hard for you, but it doesn't take an idiot to work it out. Christ, I stood right behind you last night trying to get your attention and you didn't hear me."

"It's not that bad . . ."

"We all know that's not true."

Howard tried to drag Hollis away, but Hollis again shook him off.

"Come on, mate," Howard said.

"There's no reason why I can't do anything that—"

"There's a damn good reason why you can't be trusted with anything like this anymore," Jas interrupted, preempting Hollis's protest. "Thing is, if Steve's arm is as badly damaged as it looks, then he's fucked if no one here can fix it. No NHS anymore, no hospitals, remember? A little slip can become a big problem these days."

"He's not stupid, Jas," Howard said, speaking up for Hollis. "He understands."

"Thing is, I'm not going to risk my neck because your friend here likes playing with diggers."

"I wasn't playing," Hollis tried to say but they both ignored him.

"He was working here," Howard said. "He was keeping this place in order because no one else ever does. If it wasn't for Hollis slopping out, we'd all be ankle deep in shit by now."

"Not interested," Jas said, making it clear the discussion was over. "He stays away from machinery, right?"

"Who are you to say who does what? If he—"

Their voices were becoming raised. Zoe looked up disapprovingly as Sue tried to treat Steve's arm. Harte, who, along with several others, had come over to see what all the fuss was about, tried to position himself between Jas and Howard and defuse the tension. Jas simply turned, blocking him.

"You keep him away from machinery," he said again, pointing threateningly at Hollis, "or I will. Understand?"

Ninety-Eight Days Since Infection

17

Almost an entire week of bitter frosts followed—an unseasonably early cold snap. Beyond the walls of Cheetham Castle, the dead continued their relentless slow advance, impeded only by the extreme weather. Most mornings they remained frozen solid, only to slowly defrost as the temperature climbed. By midafternoon each day, some had regained the ability to move, only to be halted by the ice again a scant few hours later when the sun disappeared below the horizon.

The body of an eighteen-year-old boy made more progress than most by virtue of his position relative to the bulk of the rest of the dead crowds. Months ago he'd been on the verge of beginning a new chapter in his life when it had been cut short. He'd just left school, and had been less than a week away from starting his first proper job working as an office gopher for a firm of solicitors. Now he was barely even recognizable as human. He'd lost almost all of his clothing after weeks of dragging himself tirelessly around the dead world. What was left of his innards had slowly sunk down and had putrefied and escaped through the various holes which rot had eaten through his flesh. The gunk froze each night—tiny brown icicles of decay.

And yet, despite the appalling condition of the dead boy, whenever he was able to free himself from the grip of the ice, he still continued to move toward the castle, oblivious to his gradual demise. How much, if anything, he understood of what was happening was impossible to tell, but his ceaseless fascination with the faint light and noise made by the survivors remained undiminished.

The general mood within the castle was unexpectedly lifted one evening when heavy snow began to fall. By next morning the ground was covered in a layer several inches deep and when the people sheltering there looked outside the castle walls, for the first time in months, everything appeared relatively normal. Where yesterday there had been hordes of intermittently incessant, partially frozen, partially animated cadavers, today there was nothing but white. Pure, clean, and unspoiled.

From the top of the gatehouse, Lorna felt like she was looking at a greetings card picture from long ago. It made her think about Christmas, for what it was worth. Her head began to fill with carols and Christmas songs until she could think of something else to block them out and shut out the pain. It felt wrong even remembering Christmas; an unspoken taboo. The end of December was only a couple of weeks away, and there would be no celebrations this year, no presents, no gorging on food and drink. Just a hell of a lot of quiet introspection and, no doubt, vastly increased amounts of private hurt for each of them to deal with.

When she went back down, Lorna found almost everyone crammed into the classroom together to escape the cold. Jackson was talking to Jas and several of the others. Over the last week he'd made a conscious effort to lay off the future planning and sermons, and concentrate on just getting them all through to a time when such subjects might be discussed freely again.

The arrival of the rescued group from the hotel had put an unforeseen strain on the castle group's resources. Jackson, thinking ahead while also trying to appease Jas, had been planning a supply run for the last few days, and this morning's snow had suddenly made such a run a much more viable proposition. *"Remember how the snow used to slow us down,"* he'd said to Lorna when they'd spoken earlier. *"It'll be a hundred times worse for the dead."* As long as there was snow on the ground, he'd argued, they had a bigger physical advantage than usual over what remained of the corpses outside. And without the benefit of long-range weather forecasts—*any* weather forecasts, for that matter—it made sense to take advantage of the conditions now while they lasted. Lorna couldn't help thinking she'd heard this all before, back at the hotel: one last massive trip out for supplies to see us through . . .

Driver didn't look happy. He was uncharacteristically animated.

"What's up with him?" Lorna asked Caron as she sat down next to her.

"He doesn't want to go out," she replied.

"But why me?" Driver said. Jackson looked to the heavens.

"The clue's in your nickname, mate. You're the most experienced driver we've got. We need someone who knows what they're doing behind the wheel. Do you have any other pointless questions?"

"There must be someone else. They can do it."

"No," Jackson said, remaining unfailingly calm, "you can. Listen, for all your faults—of which there are more than a few—there's no one else can drive anything as big as a truck as well as you. And with the snow and everything else out there, I need your experience."

"Thanks for the compliments and all that, but I'm not going," he said defiantly.

"Yes, you are," Jas said firmly.

"Says who?"

"Says me."

"Driver," Jackson said, interrupting to try and defuse some of the unnecessary tension Jas's tone was clearly causing, "I know you better than you think. I know exactly what you do and what you don't do around here. I know you spend most of your time asleep at the back of your bus when you tell us you're out working on the vehicles. I've seen you wiping grease on your hands and trousers to make it look like you've been grafting for hours."

"I'm not the only one," he protested. "There are plenty of other folks around here who do the same. What about—"

"You're right," Jackson interrupted, "but my point is this: right now we need to play to all our strengths, and your strength is driving, so you're going out with us."

"Bollocks to that," Driver said, remaining unimpressed.

"Can't you just give the bloke a break?" Harte said from across the room. "*I'll* drive the bloody truck if it's that big a deal."

"The decision's made," Jackson said calmly. "Let's just get it done."

"Did you not hear me?" Harte protested.

"He heard you okay," Jas said. "Did you not hear him? We play to our strengths. Driver drives; Jackson, Kieran, you, me, Ainsworth, and Bayliss go out to loot."

Harte slumped back into his seat, knowing there was no point arguing further. Near to him, Caron leaned across to speak to Lorna.

"Surprised you're not going," she whispered.

"Don't even go there," Lorna said, crossing her arms defensively.

"Why?"

"Because as far as Jas is concerned," she explained, "playing to your strengths also means keeping us girls safely locked away in here to cook and clean up for the blokes. It's a bloody joke."

"And what about Jackson? He seems a more broad-minded kind of chap."

"You think? I spoke to him too, because bodies or no bodies, I'd actually love to get out of this fucking place for a while."

"And?"

"And he was as bad as Jas. Worse in some ways."

"Why? What did he say?"

"He said he doesn't want girls like me, Zoe, and Melanie going out and taking risks when there's plenty of men who can go."

"I don't understand," Caron said, confused. Lorna sighed. Was she being deliberately difficult?

"He didn't say as much," she explained, "but he's talking about babies. He was on one of his 'planning for the future' kicks again."

"Dirty old bugger."

"For Christ's sake, Caron, get a grip. He's not interested in any of us in *that* way, he's just trying to protect *the stock*."

"That's disgusting."

"Well, that's how it is. But I'll tell you something: if he thinks I'm going to sit here, pick a mate from this bunch of losers, then pop out a kid or five on demand, then he's got another think coming. Fuck that. I'll be over the wall and out of here before any bloke can lay a bloody finger on me."

18

The two-vehicle convoy crunched steadily through the ice and snow with an arrogant lack of speed. Kieran was up ahead, driving the digger with Jackson hanging on for the ride, while Driver followed behind, grudgingly steering the group's largest truck through the carnage. It was a box truck with enough room for several tons of food—if they could find that much—and it had been used for furniture deliveries before Jackson had acquired it shortly after arriving at the castle. On its sides there had been pictures of a family relaxing in their homes on their newly delivered sofas. Someone—he didn't know who—had painted over them with white emulsion a couple of weeks back, blocking out the past.

Jas and Ainsworth sat in the cab with Driver, Harte and Bayliss in the back with the roller shutter open, watching the world around them with wide, disbelieving eyes. For Ainsworth and Bayliss, this was their first trip outside the castle walls since they'd arrived there, and the difference between what they saw today and what they remembered was stark. In some ways they found it almost impossible to comprehend.

They were able to increase their speed slightly as they drove farther away from the castle. The hordes of bodies which had gravitated around their base over time, drawn there by the survivors' disproportionately amplified noise, had resulted in the rest of the surrounding area being left reassuringly empty. The blanket of snow helped perpetuate the illusion. Their passage was clear, although they were forced to stop occasionally when the route of the road ahead became unclear. Then Jas would order Harte and Bayliss to jump out of the back of the truck and shovel away the ice and the frozen once-human detritus which now seemed to cover everything.

After consulting with Kieran—a local—Jackson had decided to aim for Chadwick, a medium-sized port town and the nearest place of any substance in the immediate vicinity. Harte sat on the back of the truck, legs dangling, holding onto a securing strap fixed to the wall, and watched the dead world pass him by. He couldn't help comparing what he saw today with the scavenging trip he'd made into Bromwell with Jas, Hollis, and the others just before their incarceration at the besieged hotel had begun. That had been the last time he'd been anywhere even remotely urban, and, once he looked past the visible devastation, what he saw as they approached Chadwick today actually began to fill him with wholly unexpected optimism. He tried to explain as much to Bayliss, who barely said anything. Instead he just sat there, his face covered with a scarf, staring into space.

There were bodies on the way into the town. Why they were still there Harte couldn't even begin to hazard a guess, but that didn't matter. Like the rest of the dead he'd seen today, they were completely motionless. They stood like statues, trapped in bizarre poses. One looked as if it had been stopped midstride; another was slumped against a wall like a drunk. Some remained standing in the middle of open spaces, their lack of distinguishable colors and features almost making them look like standing stones. A clot of dead passengers were frozen in position inside a bus outside a station. They'd formed a bizarre plug of flesh at the driver's end as if they'd all been rushing to get off when first death, then the ice had caught them.

They skirted around the very center of town and approached the port from the south, driving up along the seafront first. The snow was thinner here, and those bodies they could make out appeared more substantially decayed. Harte assumed both of those factors were due to the level of salt spray in the air, eating through everything. He looked over to his left, out toward the ocean which appeared calm and inviting in comparison to the carnage so prevalent everywhere else. Apart from the wreck of a huge passenger ferry on the beach, tilted over at an almost impossible angle and showing the first telltale signs of corrosion, it all looked deceptively normal. Sunlight slipped through the gaps between increasingly broken clouds overhead, casting random shadows on the surface of the water.

The truck stopped, and Harte heard Jas yell for him and Bayliss to help. He grabbed his shovel and jumped down, then jogged up the road to see what the problem was. He was relieved to see it wasn't anything major—just a buildup of ice the digger had avoided but which the truck couldn't quite get through. He started digging; Bayliss did the same. When progress wasn't fast enough for his liking, Jas jumped down from the cab and pitched in. The collective noise of their three shovels scraping along the tarmac filled the air.

"Pretty grim, eh, Jas?" Harte said as they worked. Jas didn't reply. Instead he just made momentary eye contact, then returned his full attention back to digging. He looked apprehensive.

"That'll do," he said quietly when enough of the street had been cleared. He climbed back up to his seat. Harte walked around to the rear of the truck, all the time looking at their desolate surroundings. He'd never been to Chadwick, but he could picture what it must have been like before all of this had happened. He imagined it packed with people last summer, and then thought how unreal it still felt that those same people would almost certainly all be dead now, struck down a scant few weeks after returning home.

The main seafront was now a desperately sad affair. There were numerous cafés and amusement arcades with snow-covered children's rides still sitting outside, neglected and abandoned. On the other side of the road stood the remains of a fun fair, the distinctive outlines of the helter-skelter and carousels now blanketed in snow but with hints of their brightly painted surfaces peeking out from below the ice. Once again, the extent of the visible devastation was humbling; nothing had been left untouched. It made Harte question the point of staying at Cheetham Castle. Were they actually doing anything positive by being there, or were they just burying their heads in the sand, hiding away from all this decay?

Harte jumped back onto the truck as Driver pulled away. He was relieved when they turned a sharp left and drove deeper into town. Up ahead, the digger rumbled on down the main street, churning ice and decay away with its permanently lowered scoop. The sun disappeared behind a cloud, and the sudden low winter light combined with the shadows from the buildings which now surrounded them on either side to make the dead world appear increasingly frightening and bizarre. More of the occasional, random corpses were trapped here like glass-covered statues, caught in a literal freeze-frame.

The digger churned through the increasingly slushy snow with ease, scraping up a layer of decay also and combining the two into a foul paste full of unrecognizable shapes, all the colors reduced to ash-gray. Harte stared down into the mounds where bones now mixed freely with other rubbish. It left him in absolutely no doubt as to how misguided the human race as a whole had been about its importance in the overall scheme of things. When it came down to it, mankind had been discarded like empty bottles and used food wrappers, thrown onto a landfill site along with everything else. In time, he thought, all of this will be gone. When the snow's melted and spring comes, there will be green shoots everywhere—the aftermath of man. Weeds will begin to burst up through the gaps between what's left of the bodies, forcing their way between paving slabs and through cracks in walls. Wild animals will roam free, making dens and nests in empty houses. He knew that if he was to come back here in a couple of years, much of what he could see now would have disappeared. There was a part of him that actually wished he could see that.

The sudden hissing of brakes brought his idle daydreaming to an abrupt end. He leaned forward and peered around the back of the truck and saw that they'd pulled up outside the entrance to a small mall. A tattered, ice-covered sign read THE MINORIES. The mall's once-bright fascia was now dull and muted, posters and window displays having been bleached by the sun and stripped of color. Rows of icicles hung beneath every visible ledge and sill, and he noticed they were all dripping. Some of them looked big enough to cause real damage to anyone unfortunate enough to be underneath them if they fell. Imagine that, he thought, all too easily slipping into daydream mode again—surviving everything they'd got through to get to this stage, only to end up getting speared by a bloody icicle.

Now that the two engines had stopped, the silence was overpowering. Jackson called for the others to gather around the digger.

"Right," he said, "the plan's simple. Kieran says there's a few useful shops in here, and the more we can get in one place, the better.

So let's get inside and strip it clean. We don't stop until this truck is as full as we can get it, okay? Let's make sure this is the last trip out we have to make until winter's over. Got it?"

There were a few mumbles, little positive reaction. Harte looked around at the faces surrounding him. Strange how, just an hour or so ago back at the castle, they'd all been full of bravado and bull-shit.

"Got it," Kieran said, more out of duty than anything else, feeling obliged to at least say something.

"Our priority is food and water," Jackson continued. *Christ*, Harte thought, *as if we need this spelling out to us*. "Fuel, medicines, clothing, bedding . . . all that kind of stuff, okay?" He stopped talking momentarily and looked past the others towards Jas who was hanging back. "Everything all right, Jas?"

Jas didn't answer. Instead he remained staring toward the entrance to the mall. Will Bayliss, his scarf now lowered but much of his face still hidden behind an unruly mop of untidy blond hair, suddenly saw what the other man had seen. "Fuck me," he said, "would you look at that . . ."

"Bloody hell," Kieran added, unable to hide his unease when he saw it too. Jackson turned around to see what was happening be-hind him, just in time to see a lone body stumbling up through the interior of the mall, steadily coming into the light as if it was coming into focus. It slammed against the glass with a heavy slap, then stag-gered back into the shadows before coming at the door again.

"Thought you said they'd all be frozen," Jas said nervously.

"Well, most of them still are," Jackson replied quickly. "But come on, how naïve are you? There was always going to be a few of them trapped in buildings as long as they've been dead. It's not go-ing to be tropical in there, but it'll be a damn sight warmer than it is out here."

The corpse approached the glass again, even slower this time, almost as if it had learned from its initial mistake. Harte walked toward the entrance, studying the creature inside. He saw that there were several more of them, emerging from the darkness.

"They've been protected in there," Harte said. "There's no wind or rain indoors. Probably fewer insects too."

"Should we be doing this?" Bayliss asked. "I mean, is this a good idea? What if they—"

"This doesn't change anything," Jackson said quickly, immediately silencing him. "It just makes things a little more interesting, that's all. If we're careful and we take our time, we'll be okay."

"I'm not sure . . ."

"Then fuck off and start walking home," Kieran said.

Jackson walked around to the back of the truck. He climbed inside, then reemerged carrying a sledgehammer. The others watched him. No one moved. An icy gust of wind whipped down the otherwise silent street but no one even flinched, all eyes on Jackson. He marched over to the front of the mall, boots crunching through the snow, and shook the door. When it wouldn't open he swung the hammer around repeatedly, each time smashing a different pane of glass. The farthest forward corpse was showered with shards and then took a hammer-blow right to the center of its chest, sending it flying back into the darkness. Jackson turned his attention to the locks and began battering the top, bottom, and middle of the door-frame, quickly buckling it out of shape. He shoved the mangled door open, scraping it along the ground, then stepped back again and waited. A second corpse walked toward the light, tripping over the torso of the first and landing at Jackson's feet on all fours in the slush. Before it had a chance to move he attacked it, slamming the hammerhead down onto the back of its skull, squashing it almost paper-thin. The force, speed, and precision of his attack was such that the creature remained exactly where it was, hunched forward at his feet as if it was praying for mercy.

There were more of them coming. Jackson looked back over his shoulder at Jas and the others, then turned back and swung the hammer around again, shattering the pelvis of another cadaver.

"Let's move," he ordered. "I'm not doing this by myself."

The seven men—Driver included, despite his frantic attempts to stay behind the wheel—were standing in the middle of the mall, waiting for orders by a dried-up fountain. The sun had broken through again outside. There was a glass ceiling directly above them, but what was left of the snow prevented anything more than a fraction of the usual morning light from getting inside. There were bodies trapped in some of the shops around them—workers who'd died before trading had begun on the last day of their lives. Now they watched the living, clawing at the glass to be released, some even trying to bite at the windows, all of them desperate to get out and attack.

"We should split into two groups," Jackson suggested. "Me, Kieran, Driver, and Harte. Jas, you take the others."

Jas didn't move. He was staring into a nearby newsagent's where a dead woman wearing a red-and-white-checked apron tripped around the remains of a trashed window display; falling then picking herself back up, falling again, then getting up . . . again and again. Ainsworth, as nervous as hell and keen to get out, made the first move. As he approached the door of the shop, the woman became even more animated. She lurched forward, then took a few unsteady steps back.

"Go on, then," Bayliss said, egging him on but still holding back with Jas. Ainsworth didn't move. Neither did Jas. Bayliss barged past them both. "For fuck's sake, it can't be that difficult. She's dead."

He shoved the door open and grabbed at the woman as she came toward him. She managed to duck away from him at first—more through luck than anything else—but she had no way of matching his strength and speed. He caught her arm then pulled her closer and wrapped his gloved hand tight around her neck. He spun her around through almost a complete circle, then threw her back up against the window and let her drop. She slid down the dirty glass, leaving behind a thick but uneven trail of brown-black blood. Jas stepped over her sprawled legs and began clearing the shelves.

Harte, still standing by the fountain, watching events unfold in the newsagent's, realized he was alone. He looked around and saw that Jackson and the others were breaking into a small "metro" supermarket. As they smashed their way inside, a group of bodies fought their way out. They crowded on the other side of the glass, squabbling among themselves, baying for blood. He took a deep breath and readied himself for the fight.

19

The two groups of men worked with frantic speed to clear out their allotted stores. Each of them adopted the same simple strategy: break in, deal with any corpses still strong enough to cause problems, then strip the shelves. Once the initial trepidation at being this close to active bodies again had dissipated, the hard work began to feel unexpectedly cathartic. Being occupied like this—doing something inherently worthwhile for once—was a welcome break from the norm. When they stopped and regrouped at the truck almost two hours later, their nervousness immediately returned. Time had passed quickly while they'd been working, and the situation outside had changed.

"That one's moved," Bayliss said, pointing at the remains of a corpse lying in the middle of the street. Harte knew he was right. He couldn't remember having seen it before. As they watched, it slowly moved its legs, digging in with its feet, and half-crawled, half-shuffled a few inches farther. The level of its decay was such that it was difficult to make out any real detail. It glistened with water and patches of ice, and the entire corpse was a grotesque fecal brown. The damn thing looked like it had been dunked in tar.

"So what if it has moved?" Kieran said. "The temperature's rising. They're thawing out. We knew it would happen."

Harte stood still and listened. He was right. The bitter cold of early morning had eased and the intermittent dripping they'd heard earlier had now become a more constant noise. Water was dribbling down the fronts of buildings and running into the drains. The occasional creak and crack of thawing ice was more frequent than before, like faint gunshots ringing out from every direction. Most ominously, Harte could see slight movements from some of the otherwise still frozen, mannequin-like corpses: the twitch of a finger, a slight shuffle forward, the roll of a dead eye . . .

"We should think about getting out of here," Jackson said, hauling another box of food up onto the back of the truck.

"Not yet," Jas said, surprising everyone. He'd been quiet since they'd arrived in Chadwick. His voice now was lacking in emotion, but not intent. He wasn't throwing out a suggestion to the rest of the group for them to think about and discuss, he was giving an order.

"Bollocks," Bayliss said. "Let's go. The truck's half full. We've got enough to last us weeks."

"The truck is half empty, and we need to get more. I'm not coming back out here again."

"Jas is right," Kieran said. "Another half hour's not going to kill us. We're here now."

"We should go," Driver said, already heading back toward the cab. "They're thawing out. I don't want to be here when they're fully defrosted."

As if on cue, one of the cadavers nearest to Kieran managed to break its shoulder free and move a frozen arm up toward its face. It swung it up in an awkward, juddering movement like a puppet, then dropped it down again. Kieran didn't flinch. He looked directly at Jackson and Driver, then shoved the body over. It fell backward, clipping the edge of a bench on its way down, virtually snapping its right arm completely off. He picked up Jackson's hammer from where he'd left it leaning against the side of the truck, then thumped it down hard into the dead body's frustratingly expressionless face.

"Is this what you're scared of?" he asked, looking straight at Driver, then Bayliss, demanding an answer which never came. "Get over yourselves, for fuck's sake. I'm with Jas, we should do this right if we're going to do it at all."

"Come on," Harte said, "is it worth it? Seriously? Like Jackson said, we've probably got enough stuff."

"Probably isn't good enough," Jas said.

"Bollocks," Driver said. "I'm going."

He hauled himself up into his cab. Kieran walked around and stood in front of the truck.

"Where you gonna go? Don't fancy your chances of backing up in what's left of the snow, and you can't go forward."

He stood to one side and dangled the keys. The digger was blocking the road.

"There are two more decent-sized stores in there we should clear out before we leave," Jas said. "There's another food store, and a camping and outdoor place. We clear them, then we go."

For a moment no one moved. Driver remained in his seat. Harte took a very definite step out of the way, as did Ainsworth and Bayliss. Jackson felt like volunteers had just been asked to step forward, and everyone else had stepped back, volunteering him by default. His choice—and it suddenly felt like it *was* his choice—was stark: fight with Jas and Kieran, or fight with the dead.

131

The entire town was silent, save for the ice melting and the trickling of water running down the drains.

"Okay," he said. "Two more stores, then we're leaving."

By the time they'd managed to crowbar their way into a frozen-food store, they could already see several more bodies moving slowly but freely outside, gravitating around the truck and the entrance to the mall. Metal creaked and glass cracked and more of the dead staggered closer as Harte forced the door. He held it open as the outrageously unsteady corpse of a store worker lurched forward. It virtually fell out into the mall, straight into the path of Jackson, who caved its face in with his sledgehammer. It dropped at his feet, slumped against the wall in an untidy sitting position, dark blood slowly seeping down over its uniform.

More than anywhere else they'd so far been today, this particular shop was uncomfortably dark. Places like this always used to be permanently drenched in harsh white light, and the shadows felt unnatural, somehow wrong.

"What's the point of coming in here?" Driver nervously asked. The floor was covered in water, patches of it frozen. The contents of the numerous freezers had long since deteriorated into a mush of soggy cardboard and spoiled food.

"Get as many cans and packets as you can," Jas ordered. "And there's an aisle of drink back there. Clear that one out first."

The men began to move with renewed energy, buoyed up both by the prospect of booze and the thought of finally leaving Chadwick and returning to the castle. Harte left the rest of them and went out the back of the store, instinctively gravitating toward the loading bay and stock rooms where there was often more food stored in easy-to-shift crates. Another dead shop worker lurched at him from the shadows, taking him by surprise. He caught it mid-attack, then dragged it out in the open and began pounding it with his fist, the tension fuelling his overreaction. He held its collar in one hand and punched it repeatedly with the other, reducing its face to an almost unrecognizable mass of decay. It was only when it stopped moving and he dropped it that he even bothered to look at what it was he'd just destroyed. Even through the rot and the damage he'd inflicted, he could tell that the thing at his feet had once been a young girl. What was left of her hair was still tied up in a loose ponytail and she'd been wearing the kind of clothes the girls who'd hung around outside the school where he'd taught used to wear. That unexpected connection with the past took him by surprise for a moment. It made him stop and think about what he'd become. This time last year he was teaching kids like this and trying to help them grow. Now here he was, beating the shit out of one of them as he looted food from a mall.

He walked farther into the building, eventually leaving through a back door and finding himself in an outside delivery area shared with several of the neighboring retail units. He could hear water dripping all around him, amplified by the sudden closeness of this small enclosed area. There was a barrier across the road up ahead, and everything around him felt unexpectedly calm. This was a safe place, he realized. *An inaccessible place.* If only they'd found it earlier. It would have made looting a lot easier.

"Get it off me!"

When Harte heard Bayliss screaming for help, he immediately ran back to the others. Bayliss had been heading out through the mall back to the truck, and had been caught off-guard. A trio of freshly thawed corpses coming the other way had literally knocked him off his feet and were now crowding around him, attacking him in unison. And as Ainsworth and Kieran tried to help him up and collect the supplies he'd dropped, even more of them began to approach. They slipped and skidded through the slush both inside and outside the mall, barely able to stay upright on already unsteady feet. Though their capacity was clearly limited, their intentions were clear. They grabbed at Bayliss as he tried to scramble away. He was soaked through, and covered with dribbles of defrosted decay.

Outside the building, the truck had become surrounded. Driver, never happier to be behind the wheel, started the engine as he waited for the men to load their last armfuls of supplies and get onboard. Harte was last on, weaving his way around the slothful corpses converging on the truck. He squeezed into a gap in the back alongside Bayliss, then hammered on the side for Driver to start moving. He looked down into a sea of decay and tried to calm himself. He'd been in situations far worse than this with many more of the dead to contend with. The panic that he was feeling now was a gut reaction borne of nightmares he'd previously faced.

Driver accelerated. The engine whined with effort, but the truck wasn't going anywhere. Overloaded, the wheels couldn't get a grip. The harder he revved, the less success he seemed to be having. Harte could hear Jas screaming at him to get moving, but there was nothing he could do. He accelerated again, and this time the back end of the large, unwieldy vehicle slipped in the road, sliding over to one side but not moving forward. Harte stood up and looked around the side of the truck. Up ahead, Kieran had started the digger and turned it around, but what did he do first—clear the snow, clear the dead, or try and help move the truck?

"Get something under the wheels," Jas yelled. Jackson appeared and began trying to get rid of the nearest corpses, smacking them around the head with his shovel, then using its blade to decapitate them if they tried to get up again. Harte followed his lead and jumped back down. There were as many as forty corpses coming toward them now, maybe more, approaching from all angles, spurred on by the increasing activity and noise. He wondered if the dead were somehow picking up on the sudden panic in the air. Was the survivors' frantic and barely coordinated activity actually exciting them, increasing their desire to break free from the ice?

With Jackson dealing with the nearest corpses and Kieran doing what he could with the digger, Harte concentrated on trying to clear the slush away from the road around the truck's wheels. Some of it was compacted and he struggled to get the right angle to shift it. Jas reluctantly jumped back down onto the street, and Ainsworth followed Harte's lead and began to clear around the front tires. Jas was panicking. For all his aggression and the authority he frequently tried to impose upon the group, it was obvious to Harte that he was losing his nerve.

"Get that fucking digger over here," he yelled, his voice hoarse. "We need space. There's too many of them."

Kieran tried to do as he was told, but hit a piece of concrete street furniture on the pavement which had been hidden by the snow. He couldn't get through. He tried reversing, but he was wedged in, and all the digger's noise and stop-start movement was doing was attracting more and more of the dead. They were emerging from the shadows all around, dragging themselves around street corners and appearing from hitherto hidden places, the icy bonds which had previously held them captive seeming to weaken almost by the second.

As fast as Jackson was getting rid of the corpses, more seemed to be arriving. Harte wondered if he was the only one who could see what was happening. All the panic and bluster was causing their situation to rapidly worsen. Even if Driver was able to get the bus moving and Kieran managed to free the digger and get out of the way, there was a real danger that the sheer mass of dead flesh now advancing toward them might be enough to block the road and prevent them moving forward. The bodies were being channelled in their direction. He glanced up at Jas fighting near the front of the vehicle—the anger and desperation in his face, the effort he was continually having to exert just to stay alive—and he was immediately reminded of the time he'd spent trapped in the hotel. And in that split second he asked himself if being at the castle was any better. Different walls, a few different faces, but the same shit and the same problems. But it had to be better than being stuck out here, didn't it? He wasn't sure anymore.

He finished digging out the nearest wheel, then threw down his shovel, chucking it at a dripping corpse which seemed to have locked him in its sights, hitting it just above the pelvis and folding it in two. He checked the pockets of his thick winter jacket, patting himself up and down until he felt what he was looking for: his lighter. He grabbed hold of Ainsworth and spun him around. Ainsworth went for him, holding back at the last possible second when he realized it was Harte and not one of the dead.

"Tell Driver to kill the engine," Harte ordered, looking him straight in the eye. "All this noise is just making things worse. Get everyone on the truck, get out of sight, and wait until it's clear. I'm going to draw them away."

"But how . . . ?" Ainsworth started to say but Harte was already gone. He barged through the mass of corpses gravitating around the back of the truck, ducked down, and disappeared. Ainsworth did as he was told, working his way through the chaos to get close to Driver.

Harte pounded down the road, dodging the outstretched arms of a corpse in a crusty, blood-soaked blue hoodie, almost slipping on the ice. He picked himself up and carried on, veering over to the right and running toward a petrol station he'd spotted when they'd first arrived in Chadwick. *All I need to do,* he said to himself, *is give them something else to focus on.*

Way behind him the two engines had been silenced, but he could still hear those fucking idiots arguing. Jas was yelling pointless instructions at the others, Jackson was shouting equally pointless things back. Fucking morons.

There were two cars by the pumps on the petrol station forecourt, one facing in either direction, and a tanker parked a short distance away. Harte grabbed the handle of the nearest pump, distracted momentarily by the violently animated and remarkably well-preserved remains of the female passenger of a red Audi, and also by the wild thumping of a dead man wearing a gore-soaked polo shirt bearing the logo of the petrol company, who was trapped behind the thick kiosk glass. He could feel the coldness of the pump handle even through his thick glove. He squeezed and managed to get a dribble of fuel out, taking care to spill it down the front of the pump and over the back of the Audi. And then the next pump, then the next. He ran over to the blind side of the tanker, where a wide hosepipe remained connected to an inlet valve. With no way of knowing whether the tanker was empty or full, he forced the valve open and pulled the hose away. The stench of fuel was sudden and overpowering, compounding the nervousness he felt.

I just wish this would all stop for a while.

Moving so fast that he couldn't talk himself out of it, he reached into his pockets, pulled off his right glove with his teeth to get a better grip, and flicked his lighter.

The explosion was deafening; the heat and light it produced was enough to make it feel as if the sun had burst through the clouds again. There was a stunned silence inside the truck. No one moved. Jackson watched from the back of the digger as many of the dead began to turn and shuffle away, moving almost unbearably slowly, but moving away nonetheless.

"What the fuck did he just do?" Ainsworth said quietly, watching from the back of the truck with Jas and Bayliss. "I swear, he didn't say anything to me about blowing the place up."

Jas stared at the fireball. As if hypnotized, virtually all of the dead were now stumbling toward the flames, the men in the truck instantly forgotten. He scanned the street up ahead, but there was no sign of Harte.

"What do we do?" Bayliss asked. "We can't just leave him."

"Don't see we have any option," Jas replied. "No one could have survived that. What was the stupid fucker thinking?"

He was about to shout for Driver and Kieran to try moving again, to take full advantage of the distraction while it lasted, when Jackson sprinted past, hurtling toward the burning petrol station. Even from a distance he had to shield himself from the heat. The effects of the massive explosion had been devastating. Debris was scattered all around, smoking chunks of black surrounded by corresponding pools of space where the remaining snow had been melted away. The dead paid him little attention, even when they were close enough to attack. A few of them were burning—ignited by the intense heat even before they'd reached the flames, continuing to move until there was nothing left of them. With a deep, stomach-churning creak and crash, the forecourt roof collapsed, crushing everything below and fanning the flames still further. Great sheets of fire ate into it. Rolling clouds of toxic black smoke billowed up and drifted away.

Jackson tried to get closer but the heat was too intense. Jas jumped down and pulled him back, keen to get away. For the briefest of moments the two men squared off against each other.

"Leave it," Jas said. "Harte's had it. We need to get out of here."

"But what if he—"

"He's dead, and we will be too if we don't move."

He marched back to the truck, conversation over. Jackson stayed there a moment longer, trying to take in everything that had just happened. His eyes darted constantly around the devastation. More of the corpses, now almost completely ice-free, continued to stagger around him, moving toward the burning petrol station, their decay glistening in the bright, dancing light. Behind him, Driver started the truck.

"Let's go," Jas yelled. Jackson turned and ran back to the digger, which Kieran had managed to maneuver around to face the right way. He looked back over his shoulder one last time as they pulled away, long enough to be sure that Driver was finally able to follow. This time, with the road ahead clear, the heavy vehicle moved freely along the slush-covered tarmac.

PART II

One Hundred and Eleven Days
Since Infection

20

The helicopter skimmed over the surface of the ocean, its pilot and four passengers quiet and subdued. Without exception they were each too wrapped in their own thoughts to talk to the others. Sharing the feelings they were each experiencing was out of the question for now. The pain they felt coming back here was still too raw, harder that they'd imagined.

This cold, empty, desolate place had been where they'd each lived and loved, where they'd been born and where they'd grown up. The place where their families and friends had been. The place where they'd lived their very best and their very worst days. The place where, somewhere, lay the dust-covered memories of the lives they each used to lead and the people they used to be. A soldier, a computer consultant, an outdoor activities instructor, a student . . . what had happened to the world had stripped away those skills and experiences and left them all the same. Now they were just rank-and-file survivors, nothing more and nothing less. The last of a dying breed, perhaps.

The way they'd each lost everything was still impossible to even begin to try and understand. Their normal, relatively comfortable lives had been snatched from them in seconds and there hadn't been a damn thing any of them had been able to do about it, no way of retaliating or reclaiming what they'd lost. Since that first morning they'd been living through an all-consuming nightmare so intense they'd thought they'd never get through it. But they had. Against all the odds—and those odds were considerable—they'd somehow survived and come through the other side relatively unscathed. They'd begun to forge something resembling normal lives again on a small rocky island a short distance off the coast of the mainland. Nothing like the lives they'd led previously, but still infinitely better than anything they'd thought possible in those first dark, terrifying days after the rest of the world had died.

But now, for the first time since leaving, they were heading back, and it was a daunting prospect.

As the ocean below gave way to a once-familiar landscape, they slowly began to talk about what they could see. They flew relatively low, skirting over empty shops and houses, following the route of once busy roads which were now silent and led nowhere.

"What a fucking mess," Michael Collins said, barely able to comprehend the scale of the visible devastation below them. He didn't know what he'd expected to see here—he'd purposely tried not to think about it until now—but the reality was humbling. None of the streets were clear, all of them filled with decayed remains, litter which had been picked up and blown on the wind, and other waste which had been abandoned when the bulk of the human race had been brought to an abrupt end last September and accumulated ever since. There had been no cleanup. No emergency response. No international aid. Everything was just as it had been left that first morning—a little more rotted, rusted and ruined, that was all.

Richard Lawrence too was struggling to concentrate. He

made himself look up, not down, for fear of being distracted by the eerie chaos below. More than ever, today he was feeling the intense pressure of being the group's sole pilot—perhaps even the last pilot left alive anywhere—and it weighed heavily on his shoulders. It made him feel as if everything was down to him and him alone, that their continued survival was his sole responsibility, and that was a difficult cross to bear. A short shuttle run from the island to the mainland didn't sound like much, and in the overall scheme of things it wasn't, but what if something went wrong? The lives of the four people flying with him were in his hands. And what if something did happen and they couldn't make it back to the island? The consequences didn't bare thinking about. The people on Cormansey—such a small, fragile, and and isolated community—would struggle to stay alive. That was why they'd come back here today: to collect supplies and to find some alternative transport. The long-term plan had always been for the islanders to become self-sufficient over time, but that was still a way off yet. On a practical level they still had a huge amount to learn and emotionally . . . well, they hadn't even started. Their new lives were just beginning, but the wreckage of their old lives needed to be sorted out too. A period of adjustment and acceptance would inevitably be necessary before any of them could hope to start moving on.

Some of the people living on Cormansey had made a more successful start to island life than most. Others seemed almost to be there by default, having hidden in the shadows of university buildings, underground bunkers, and airfield control towers, being propped up and carried along by everyone else. Right place, right time. Michael had taken nothing for granted and had worked damn hard to stay alive. He knew he was luckier than most, because he'd already started to rebuild. He had a partner (girlfriend? wife? lover? None of those titles seemed to fit any more), and his relationship with Emma Mitchell was the most important thing left in his small and increasingly self-contained world. Some of the others had wanted him to stay on Cormansey and not make this trip back but he'd insisted. Emma was pregnant—the first pregnancy on the island—and Michael felt duty-bound to provide for his unborn child. He thought about Emma and the baby constantly. He and Emma said nothing to each other—because there was nothing either of them could do to affect the outcome—but they both knew the risks and uncertainties involved in childbirth. As well as the usual concerns, the lack of any decent medical facilities compounded their unease. To make matters worse, they'd been told about a baby born just after the infection had struck. The poor little thing had lived for only a matter of seconds outside its mother's womb before being killed by the same deadly germ which had wiped out everything else.

Sitting next to Michael in the back of the helicopter was Donna Yorke, and next to her was Mark Cooper. Emma had often talked about those two, idly gossiping about what a good couple she thought they'd make together. They spent a lot of time in each other's company and sometimes stopped over at each other's houses, but that was as far as it had gone. Michael wondered whether they were too scared to admit their feelings, not that it was any of his business, and not that he was particularly concerned. He remembered the risk he'd taken when he and Emma had first become close, and then intimate. Island life was too restrictive if things went wrong. It was impossible to escape if you fell out with anyone and he could only begin to imagine how awkward it would be for everyone if such a relationship soured, keeping their heads down in the midst of all the name-calling and blame. Cormansey often felt like a huge, open space when you were alone, walking miles from building to distant building along the silent, traffic-free roads, but you still saw the same few faces every day. Necessity had forced the community to become increasingly close-knit. They relied on each other, and it had been clear from the outset that their ongoing successful survival would require collective effort. Maybe Donna and Cooper did want to be closer, but the commitment was just too big a risk for them to take.

Harry Stayt sat next to Richard in the front of the helicopter, scanning the ground below.

"I think we should stick to the coast," he said to the pilot. "Things look as shitty as ever down there. Probably not worth risking going any further inland just yet."

Richard agreed. He banked right, taking them back toward the ocean. Michael looked out at the endless expanse of water again—the deceptive stillness, the sunlight glinting off the gently rolling waves—and wished they were anywhere but here. He wanted to be home again.

They set down in the next decent-sized port they reached, Richard skilfully maneuvering the helicopter and landing in a small patch of space on the open roof of a multistory car park, not wanting to risk leaving the precious machine down at ground level. Harry continued to look around as they descended, ticking boxes on his mental checklist: compact but decent-sized shopping area—*check*; easily accessible marinas with plenty of boats still moored there—*check*; a safe, remote place to land—*check*; no vast crowds of bodies baying for their blood—*check*.

"Nice day for it," he said as he got out of the helicopter. It was cold, but nowhere near as harsh as it had been recently. He stretched his back, yawned, then did up his jacket, thankful for the several layers of thin, insulated sports clothing he was wearing underneath. The air quality wasn't too bad up here. Not as good as they'd been used to on the island, but bearable nonetheless. He caught the odd trace of the immediately familiar stench of death they'd all become used to, but it was less prevalent than he remembered. The sea breeze carried it away before it outstayed its welcome.

Michael walked to the edge of the car park and peered over the wall, down into what, he presumed, had been the town's main shopping street. He'd once spent a couple of days hiding out on the roof of a car park like this with Emma. That had been right at the beginning of their nightmare—one of the worst days of the worst times, just after they'd lost their farmhouse hideout and their friend Carl Henshawe. He tried not to dwell on those memories. They'd been completely lost and directionless back then, not knowing how they were going to survive or even if they wanted to.

"Everything okay, Mike?" Cooper asked, disturbing his thoughts. He was glad of the interruption.

"Fine," he replied. "Just checking out the locals."

Cooper looked down. There was some stilted movement in the streets below, but nothing in comparison to what they'd been used to. There were just a few of the dead left here now, still restless and animated but moving with very little speed.

"Instead of just looking we could actually go down there and get this done," Harry sarcastically suggested. Michael looked back over his shoulder and saw the other man leaning up against the helicopter, casually cleaning his sword with a piece of cloth. The crazy bugger had made no secret of the fact he'd been itching for a chance to use it again. Michael had often seen him standing in the middle of a field just outside Danver's Lye—the small village at the heart of Cormansey life—practising his swordsmanship like a frustrated martial arts master without any pupils. Jack Baxter liked to wind Harry up, asking him if he cut hedges as well, because his needed a trim.

"What do we reckon, then?" Richard asked, returning from the far side of the car park roof, his hands buried deep in his pockets. "There's a decent-looking marina back there. Should find something suitable there."

"Sounds like a plan," Donna agreed. "Find ourselves a couple of boats, get them loaded up, then get out of here and get back home."

The five of them walked together down the access ramp which led down to ground level, pausing only to clamber over the wreck of a plum-colored Mini with a black-and-white-checked roof which had crashed into a barrier and blocked the way, midway down the corkscrew-like road. Michael rounded the final corner and stepped out onto the street, his pulse racing, feeling an uncomfortably familiar unease he'd not felt since he was last on the mainland. He gripped a crowbar tight, ready to fight, anticipating an attack. Nothing immediately came at him, but the tension didn't reduce. This didn't feel right. The living were conditioned to expect a battle with the dead now.

"Here we go," Harry said, quickening his pace and taking the lead, sword in hand. Up ahead, at the far end of a long, straight street otherwise devoid of all movement, a single corpse approached. He walked toward it purposefully but stopped a short distance away, feeling both curious and disgusted. The deterioration of the dead was remarkable.

In the months since this had all begun, everyone who'd survived had seen more than their fair share of horrific sights. Harry himself remembered several—like the time he'd found a still-moving man who'd been virtually cut in two by a broken plate-glass window, or that child he'd found trapped under the roof of an overturned car, its legs crushed but its arms still thrashing. Those grotesque memories paled in comparison to the creature stumbling toward

151

him now. From some angles he questioned whether or not it had ever been human, such was the extent of its deformity and decay. This was the stuff of nightmares, like nothing he'd ever seen before.

The reanimation of any of the dead was a bizarre impossibility, but it beggared belief that this thing was still able to keep moving. The clothing had been stripped from the bottom half of its body, leaving its spindly legs looking like brittle tree branches and its shrivelled penis and balls exposed. The color of the dead man's flesh was almost uniformly dark: greens and browns save for a few lighter blotches. The skin had been worn from the bottom of his feet because he no longer lifted them, rather he just dragged them along. Harry could see the bones of the foul thing's toes sticking out through what was left of the skin in the same way he could feel his own big toe poking through a hole in his sock. He wished the dead man would stop, because the closer he got, the more sickening detail was revealed and the more grotesque he became. His face was horrific. His nose had been eaten away, and decay and insect infestations had combined to alter the shape of his drooling mouth so it now looked like an uneven zigzag rip; a ghastly caricature of a long-gone smile. One of his eyes was completely missing, a hint of a trail of fibers and blood on his discolored cheek the only clue it had ever been there. His other eye still moved slightly, looking around but never seeming to settle on anything in particular, just doing enough to leave Harry in no doubt that the corpse knew he was there. The man's skull was covered in bald patches where much of his hair had simply fallen away in gooey clumps. The few remaining greasy strands were glued to his pock-marked scalp.

Harry took a step forward, but then stopped again, unnerved. He could see several more creatures in the distance now. While their appearance unsettled him, he forced himself to remember that that as foul as they were, they seemed to be mere shadows now of the vicious enemy he and the others had faced previously.

Without warning, the dead man took another step forward and lunged at Harry, who shoved him away with a single gloved hand, surprised by its lack of strength and weight. The corpse staggered back, then slowly came forward again. Each movement took it an age. Harry stood his ground, counting the seconds before it was close enough to attack again. *Christ*, he thought, *we don't even have to run from these things any longer. We can walk away fast enough to escape.*

"What's the hold up?" Cooper shouted.

"They're completely fucked," he yelled back. On hearing Harry's voice, the dead man became even more animated, desperately trying to move faster. Harry had had enough. He lifted his sword and flashed it in front of the corpse at neck height. Its head dropped from its shoulders and hit the ground with a wet thump. The rest of the man's diseased frame appeared about to take a final step forward, but it simply collapsed at Harry's feet. Normally he'd have immediately charged at the other corpses still moving closer, but he didn't bother. He was filled with a sudden newfound confidence.

"See that?" he asked as Cooper and the others finally caught up with him.

"Didn't put up much of a fight, did it?" Michael said.

"We can't get too cocky," Donna warned. "A couple of hundred will still cause us problems if we let them get too close."

"You think?" Harry asked. "I don't reckon there's even a couple of hundred left."

"You might be right, but I'm not taking any chances."

Cooper agreed. "Donna's right. Don't forget yourselves, and don't take anything for granted."

He led them down toward the marina, stepping over what was left of the decapitated corpse. Their footsteps echoed eerily.

"My dad brought me here when I was about nine," Richard

said. He was somewhat older than the others. Michael guessed he was fifty, maybe fifty-five. No one talked much about their ages anymore. It seemed irrelevant now. "He'd just lost his job," Richard continued to reminisce. "Mum was working all the hours she could, so he brought me and my sister here for a couple of days in the summer holidays."

"Changed much, has it?" Donna smiled.

"A little. The sea looks the same . . ."

". . . but everything else is fucked."

"Pretty much."

There were several more bodies around them now. Michael looked back and saw that a small crowd was moving in the general direction of the car park where they'd left the helicopter, no doubt still reacting to the aircraft's noisy and unexpected arrival. As long as they didn't make too much noise themselves, Michael realized, the dead didn't even seem to notice them. And those that did could easily be avoided. All they had to do was sidestep them or increase their speed slightly.

The car park was close to the town's large, once-busy station. Recently built, it was constructed mostly of glass and metal and they could see numerous wide-open spaces inside. Harry remained standing behind a set of automatic doors which, thankfully, were as useless as every other set of automatic doors in the country, staring at the appalling sight on the other side. Inside the station, the concourses were filled with bodies. Some were still trapped on buses and in shelters and waiting rooms.

"It was rush hour," Donna said quietly. "Remember that?"

Michael remembered the daily hell of the rush-hour grind all too well. Like the people who had died here, he'd once had to cram himself into overfull buses and trains to get to work and back each day. He remembered it with a kind of nostalgic fondness now, but another look into the desolation was enough to snap him out of his daze. The interior of the modern-looking building was like a mass grave, many bodies lying in the shadows on top of each other, many more still languidly moving through the dark. Some of them gravitated toward the glass, decaying hands pawing the windows and doors as if they were trying to attract his attention and get help. The time for that was long gone.

Leaving the others for a moment, Michael walked farther around the perimeter of the station, captivated by the succession of horrific sights which unfolded in front of him. A bus had become trapped in the station exit, hitting the wall on one side, becoming wedged and completely blocking the way out. Even now he could see a sticky mass of decay which was once its passengers, reduced to little more than a bone-filled soup as a result of several months' constant movement, grinding against each other in such a confined space. He couldn't see how many people had died on the bus, but their decay was sufficient that, even now, an offensive-smelling, yellow-brown bile was still dripping out from under the door.

Michael continued in the direction he'd been walking, and saw that this had been a railway station too, not just a bus depot. He stepped over the crumpled remains of a corpse lying at the bottom of a steep staircase, its neck broken by the fall, then climbed up onto an elevated walkway. This pedestrian bridge had obviously been necessary to get people over the train tracks which ran directly below, but it had also been designed as a viewing area of sorts, and from the midpoint he had a clear view over the entire station below: the tracks, the engines, the platforms, and the concourses. Jesus, he thought, this place had been packed when the world had been brought to an abrupt end last September. The station was heaving with decay. And as for the trains themselves . . . He could only look for a few seconds before turning away. At every window in every carriage there seemed to be countless dead faces staring out, still trying to escape after all this time.

Harry took out a few of the nearest corpses as they advanced toward the marina—it didn't feel right not to—but they simply walked past many of the others. It was almost as if time had stopped and everything had frozen. It felt impossible, surreal almost, and yet, bizarrely, it also felt *good*.

It's like we're in control again, Cooper thought as they walked— *walked!*—through the kind of open spaces which would have been impossible to cover on foot last time they were on the mainland. He crossed a miniature golf course nearer to the seafront, climbing over small hills and stepping over dried-up streams, weaving around wooden windmills with faded paint.

Today was a stark contrast to the last time he'd been on the mainland. He remembered his desperate escape back then after being stranded in the overrun airfield at Monkton with Emma, Juliet Appleby, and Steve Armitage. He never admitted as much, but he still had occasional nightmares about that day. Maybe his time back here now would change all that? It was a trendy expression he hated to use, but perhaps being here again would bring them all some closure.

21

They kept the car park and, more important, the helicopter in view as much as possible as they explored the rest of the town. After finding a small, industrial-looking boatyard first, they worked their way through increasingly exclusive-looking sections of the marina, eventually ending up in a more secluded landing area where a number of fantastically expensive boats had been moored. Most were empty. In one, a luxurious cruiser named *The BarJerr* (obviously a grotesque amalgamation of the owners' forenames, Cooper thought), Harry found a body preserved to an unfortunate degree by the dry conditions and relatively steady temperature inside the cabin. It still wore a pair of hideous shorts and sandals, and a shirt once pastel pink but now stained anything but. It threw itself at him with sudden speed—just like they used to, he thought—but it was no match for his strength. He cut it down with a few well-aimed strokes, leaving it hacked into two uneven halves on the deck, then moving on to the next boat.

After identifying a number of possibilities, they eventually found two boats moored next to each other which looked like they'd do the job: the *Duchess* and the *Summer Breeze*. They were both of a similar size, ten meters long, obviously strong and seaworthy, but more important they were in relatively good condition given the fact they'd been left in the water untended through the autumn and winter months, and looked easy enough to sail. Cooper and Harry both had a reasonable amount of experience with boats, albeit very different types of vessels they'd sailed in wildly different circumstances. But it would be enough to get them back to Cormansey.

Their objectives were straightforward—transport and supplies. They left Harry to secure this part of the marina, then check the two boats over and get them ready to sail. They took him at his word that he knew enough about electrics, propellers, waterproofing, outboards, and the like to get the job done.

Cooper, Richard, and Donna found a nearby supermarket. They broke in quickly and began looting, initially working at frantic speed, falling into old habits and grabbing whatever they could get their hands on as corpses began to crowd the building and slam up against the windows. After a while, however, their nervousness faded and they began to loot at a gentler pace. They took their time and collected food which would last and they could easily transport and distribute. Food which would keep the people on Cormansey healthy and strong. Medicines. Tools. Clothes. Cooper didn't find everything he was looking for. He made a mental note to try and find a garden center, DIY store, or farm shop before they returned to the island. *We need to start thinking ahead now*, he thought, realizing just how much their situation had changed since they'd last been on the mainland. *We need to start planning for the future, now that it looks like we might actually have one. We need to be able to plant and harvest crops, to grow as much of our own food as we can. We need to get ourselves into a position where everything we need can be found on the island and we never have to come back here again unless we want to.*

A short time later he found Donna standing in the middle of a clothing department, standing in silence, just looking up at the dust-covered mannequins. Jack Baxter had been moaning to her recently about all the clichés in the post-apocalyptic books he used to love to read. *"I don't want to end up looking like an idiot,"* he'd told her. *"I want to wear decent, comfortable clothes, not hand-knitted jumpers and coats made out of sewn-together animal skins!"*

Donna hadn't moved for a while. Cooper wondered what was wrong.

"You okay?" he asked, startling her. She caught her breath and turned around to face him, smiling briefly.

"I'm fine."

"You sure?"

"Sure."

"What were you looking at?"

She pointed at two female dummies directly in front of her. The wig had slipped off one of them, partially covering its face and leaving half of its head unflatteringly bald. The other had a beard of cobwebs stretching from its chin to its chest, and wore a short party dress; even now some of the thousands of sequins caught the afternoon light which trickled in through the window. It had a handbag slung over one frozen shoulder, and it was wearing a pair of gorgeous (Donna thought), yet completely impractical, stiletto heels.

"Love those shoes," she said.

"Have them, then."

"Are you having a laugh? I mean, I know I could take them, but what's the point? When am I going to get to wear them? When I'm walking into the village? Around the house? They're not that practical for trudging across fields."

159

"Sorry," Cooper said quickly, feeling unexpectedly embarrassed and insensitive.

"It's not your fault." Donna sighed, looking down with disappointment at the jeans and mud-splattered boots she was wearing, shoving her hands into the pockets of the same winter coat she'd worn every day for as long as she could remember. "I was just thinking, are we ever going to be able to dress like that again?"

"Well, I'm not," he joked, immediately regretting his ill-considered jibe when he saw the expression on her face.

"I can't believe we ever used to look like this," she said. "I used to love getting dressed up for a night out with the girls. Getting ready was half the fun. We were usually pissed before we'd even got out the front door."

"Bloody students," Cooper grumbled, but she didn't bite. Instead she thought more about what she'd just said, and tried to picture the others on Cormansey letting their hair down. Would any of them ever bother? Even if they did—all of them piling into the island's single pub, perhaps, finding a way to play music and glamming up for old times' sake—she knew it wouldn't be the same. It'd be like playacting, and would inevitably leave them all feeling emptier than ever. Such a night would only serve to highlight the fact that all of this was gone forever now. It was time to accept that that part of her life was over.

A few doors farther down the street, Michael was on his own in another store, collecting baby equipment from a list Emma had drawn up with help from some of the women on the island. She wasn't even halfway through her pregnancy yet, but he didn't know if or when he'd get another opportunity like this. He hadn't felt able to ask any of the other islanders to get this stuff for him—some people had lost kids, others assumed they'd now never have any—and that had been the main reason he'd agreed to come back here himself. Now he stood in the baby store, completely alone, the handwritten shopping list gripped tight in his hand, wishing he could feel even a fraction of the excitement he'd always imagined an expectant father should.

It was strange, he thought. Of all the silent, empty places he'd been since most of the world had died last September, this felt like the quietest, emptiest place of all. It was eerie. He was used to being alone—they all were—but being here took loneliness to another level entirely. Around him, the walls were covered with paintings of fairy-tale characters, oversized letters and numbers, and black-and-white photographs of the faces of innocent toddlers and expectant moms. He couldn't imagine that this place had ever been quiet like this before. On the rare occasions he'd had to come into stores like this, he'd always been driven out by the sounds of kids crying and the incessant nursery rhyme music being piped through the PA on repeat.

Michael had almost been looking forward to coming here—as much as he looked forward to anything these days—but the reality had proved to be disappointingly grim. He dutifully fetched himself a trolley and began to fill it, ticking items off the list: baby-grows, nappies, bottles, the odd toy, all the powdered milk and food he could find which was still in date with a decent shelf life . . . As he worked, disappointingly familiar doubts began to reappear. He'd managed to blank them out for a while, but here today on his own with Emma so far away, it was impossible not to think about the future his unborn child might or might not have. There remained a very real possibility—perhaps even a probability—that the baby would die almost immediately after birth. But even if it did survive, what kind of a life would it have to look forward to? He imagined the child growing up on Cormansey and outliving everyone else.

Suddenly it didn't seem too fantastic to believe that, all other things being equal, his and Emma's child might truly end up being the last person left alive on the face of the planet. How would he or she feel? Michael couldn't even begin to imagine the loneliness they might experience as their elders gradually passed away. Imagine knowing you were never going to see another person's face, that no one would ever come if you screamed for help . . .

Snap out of it, he told himself. *Get a fucking grip.*

Angry for allowing himself to sound so defeatist, and now moving with much more speed than before, Michael pushed the trolley around into another aisle and then stopped. Lying in front of him was the body of what he assumed had once been a young mom. Judging by the look of the stretched clothing which now hung like tent canvas, flapping over what remained of her emaciated frame, this woman had probably been pregnant when she'd died. Just ahead of her was a pushchair which had toppled over onto its side.

And it was empty.

Michael panicked, irrationally fearing that at any moment the dishevelled remains of a dead baby might be about to scuttle across the floor and attack him. He grabbed the rest of the things he needed and ran for the door, feeling like he was being watched.

When the four of them finally returned to the marina, they found that it had been surrounded. Harry had built a temporary blockade to keep the dead at bay, but they'd continued to advance. They moved almost too slowly to see, trickling forward like thick molasses.

22

It had always been their intention to spend at least one night on the mainland, probably two or three. After the emotional events of the day now ending, the group planned to make the most of their situation and relax. It actually seemed possible to do that now they realized how little a threat the dead posed in their pitifully weak condition. They lit a series of bonfires in metal dustbins and positioned them in open spaces around the marina and the closest parts of the town to distract the corpses and draw them away from the boats.

Harry had managed to get both of the boats' engines started while the others had been out looting. He'd even managed to rig up a basic radio in each boat. That had been unexpectedly unnerving, scanning the wavelengths and hearing nothing but unending static. For a while he'd wondered if he might find someone else transmitting, like he'd always seen happen in the movies. But he didn't. There was nothing.

It had taken a while to load up the boats, splitting the supplies equally between them, and yet there had still been plenty of space. Cooper suggested they should "shop" again in the morning, both to maximize the usefulness of this expedition, and to replace the food and booze he intended gorging himself on tonight.

Michael found another boat moored well away from all the others. It was an enormous luxury craft, so large it warranted a section of the marina almost to itself. He thought it would probably have cost more than his house, maybe even the entire street. They'd be back on Cormansey in a couple of days' time, and he suggested they spent their nights here. It would probably be their last opportunity to eat, drink, and relax in such relative comfort for a while, if not their last ever. There were rooms enough for all of them to sleep, and a large lounge. Harry managed to get the electrics working—he was proving bloody useful to have around—and the five of them settled down to an evening which, unexpectedly, began to echo the normality of their old lives.

Richard was in the galley, cooking. In times past he'd been a keen cook, to the point where he'd taken a couple of courses in the evenings after work. He'd initially gone along because he'd thought it might be a good place to meet women, before realizing that cooking was something he actually enjoyed. He'd long since tired of the bachelor life, but he'd never had much luck with relationships. A helicopter pilot who loved to cook: he used to joke with his friends that he couldn't understand how women could resist him. But there had been a serious side to his lighthearted moaning. He wasn't getting any younger, and he'd been actively looking for someone to settle down and share the rest of his life with. He'd even joined a couple of dating Web sites and had put one of those "last chance" (as he called them) lonely heart adverts in the local paper. It had all been academic, because the end of the world had come along and fucked everything up before he'd met anyone. Now he was damned like most of the rest of the men who'd survived to an enforced life of celibacy. It hadn't mattered until recently—until he'd been on the island for a while and had actually had a chance to start thinking about things like love and sex and relationships again—but it was beginning to really play on his mind now. He'd been daydreaming about finding a camp populated exclusively by nubile young female survivors, desperate for the company of men . . .

His idle thoughts were interrupted by a loud crash and a scream of protest from the other end of the boat. He quickly ran to the lounge but relaxed when he saw that it was nothing. Harry had knocked a bottle of beer over the table where he and Donna had been playing cards.

"Be careful, for Christ's sake," Richard said, acutely aware that he was starting to sound like an overzealous parent. Truth was, all he was worried about was the fact there were a finite number of bottles of beer left in the country, and he couldn't bear the thought of any drink being wasted.

"Food nearly done?" Harry asked, wiping the table with his sleeve, sounding slightly booze-slurred.

"Not yet," Richard said, already on his way back to the kitchen. "You can't rush perfection."

The meal was almost ready. He hadn't cooked much, but he'd enjoyed working in the galley with its equipment, which actually worked. In his house back on Cormansey he still used a portable gas burner which sat on the top of a perfectly good, but completely useless, electric oven. Other people cooked on open fires. In the early days on the island, there had been a spontaneous, almost ceremonial disposal of pretty much anything electrical. Telephones, computers, TVs . . . they'd all been thrown on a huge fire in the middle of Danver's Lye. There hadn't seemed to be any point keeping anything like that.

Richard opened the oven and sniffed the cottage pie he'd

cooked. Bloody hell, it smelled good. The meat and vegetables were tinned, the sauce was out of a jar, and the mashed potato on top was from a packet mix, but it didn't matter. What he'd have given for some fresh ingredients though. *Imagine that*, he thought, his mouth watering. *Steak . . . a bacon sandwich for breakfast . . . a mug of tea first thing in the morning made with real milk . . .*

He was giving semi-serious consideration to the practicalities of finding a couple of dairy cows and winching them over the ocean to Cormansey when he heard something outside which made him freeze with apprehension. It was a definite noise close to the galley window. And now movement too. The starboard side of the boat dipped down slightly.

Cooper was already onto it. He ran for the door to the deck, a fire ax held ready to attack.

"Bodies?" Donna asked.

"Must be," Michael said, moving to one side as Harry also pushed past him, carrying his sword, immediately sober. Cooper paused and listened before going outside. The boat rocked again. There was something moving around the stern. They could hear it scrambling around the hatch now, trying to get inside.

"Many of them?" Harry asked as Cooper peered out through a porthole window.

"Can't see much out there," he said. "We could do with some deck lights. Probably just a couple that have managed to get down here."

"It's the noise Harry's been making," Richard suggested, semi-seriously.

"Or the smell of your cooking," Harry replied. "I'm surprised, though. The temperature's dropped out there. I'd have thought they—"

He stopped speaking midsentence as the door onto the deck

166

began to rattle. He stood ready with his sword as Cooper moved to open it, but it flew open before he could get anywhere near. A single bedraggled figure fell into the room and immediately scrambled back to its feet. It lurched toward Donna, arms outstretched. In spite of the drink, her reactions were razor sharp. She grabbed it by the collar and slammed it up against the nearest wall, then threw it down, dragging it over onto its back and holding it ready for Harry to attack and finish it off.

"Don't . . ." the body on the floor said.

Stunned, Donna stood up and staggered back, struggling to comprehend the fact that, lying on the floor in the middle of the room, was another survivor. His face was gaunt and unshaven, although he certainly didn't look like he was starving.

"Food smells good," he said as he picked himself up and brushed himself down.

"Where the fuck did you come from?" Michael asked.

"I've been here for a couple weeks," the man replied. "My name's Ian. Ian Harte."

23

For a time Harte's unannounced arrival was distraction enough to defer the interrogation he might naturally have expected. Harte offered little information, save that he'd been hiding out in an apartment block just north of Chadwick since he'd arrived in the town two weeks earlier. Despite the fact there were five of them and only one of him, he asked so many questions that he began to monopolize the conversation.

"You say you're from an island?"

"That's right," Michael said.

"And there's more than fifty of you."

"Yep."

"Jesus."

"What?"

"Doesn't seem possible, that's all."

"None of what's happened since last September seems possible," Cooper said. "If you think about it, fifty-odd people flying over to an island is one of the more believable aspects."

"Suppose. It's just that until I heard your helicopter this morning, I thought I was going to be on my own forever. You know what it's like, I thought I was imagining things. By the time I got here I couldn't hear the helicopter, but I decided to head for the center of town just in case. I saw it up on top of that car park. I waited up there for you to come back, but then I saw the fires you'd lit around the marina . . ."

"And you're on your own?"

"I was," Harte replied. "Look, this is a bit of a long shot, but when you first went over to this island, did you use a plane as well as a helicopter?"

"How the hell did you know that?" Richard said. Harte grinned broadly and sank the remains of a bottle of beer before continuing.

"I knew it! Couple of months back," he explained, "I was hiding out in a hotel with a group of others. We saw a helicopter flying backwards and forwards, day after day, and later there was a plane. It must have been you lot. We tried everything to get your attention. We wrote messages on the ground with sheets, started fires . . ."

"I didn't see any messages," Richard said. "I'd have investigated if I had. And as for your fires, if you'd seen what I'd seen from up there since all of this kicked off, you'd know not to give fires a second glance. There's always something burning somewhere. Unless it's a bloody big blaze I probably wouldn't even bother with it."

"Bit of a long shot, though," Harry mumbled, not yet sure whether or not he trusted Harte. "I mean, what are the chances of you hearing us all the way back then, then finding us again today."

"Pretty bloody astronomical," Harte agreed.

"Probably not as far-fetched as you'd think," Richard said. "Think about it. How many hundreds of other people like Harte might we have missed? The skies are clear and as far as we know, we're the only ones still flying. The chopper would have been visible for miles. It's not unreasonable to believe that—"

"Never mind all that," Donna interrupted, cutting across

him. "Whether he heard us or not isn't important." She turned to face Harte. "You said something about a hotel and other people. What happened to them?"

Harte's face dropped. He helped himself to another bottle.

"We made a few mistakes," he admitted, "most of them trying to get your attention, as it happens. We ended up cut off from everything else by a few thousand of those dead fuckers outside. We were stranded. Took us weeks to get out."

"So how did you get out?" she pressed. "And was it just you, or did others get away too?"

Harte was beginning to feel uncomfortable. "What is this? The fucking Spanish Inquisition?"

"We just need to know, that's all."

He was outnumbered and he knew it. He continued with his reluctant explanation.

"Before we got to the hotel, we were based in some flats. A couple of the girls there got sick. We didn't know what it was or how they caught it, but it killed the pair of them. That's how we ended up on the run, and that's how we ended up at the hotel. We'd been there a while when one of our guys, Driver, started complaining that he was feeling sick too."

"So what did you do?"

"We quarantined him."

"Sensible."

"That's what we thought."

"All well and good, but what's this got to do with anything?" Michael asked.

"The crafty bastard was having us on. There was nothing wrong with him. As soon as the shit hit the fan and the bodies got too close, he bailed out on us without anyone realizing. He came back weeks later when the dead first froze."

Cooper stared intently at Harte. "So what are you not telling us? There's got to be more to it than that."

"Nothing," he answered quickly, drinking more of his beer and doing all he could not to make eye contact.

"Bollocks."

"Give the guy a break, Cooper," Harry said.

"I mean, this is all well and good," Cooper continued, "but there are a lot of gaps in your story. How many of you were trapped in the hotel, and what happened to the rest of them? How comes you're out here on your own now?"

The silence while they waited for his answer was deafening.

"I screwed up," he eventually admitted.

"How?"

Harte took a deep breath, resigned to the fact he was going to have to stop beating around the bush and explain what had happened to him since leaving the hotel.

"While Driver was on the run, he found another group, based out of a castle about fifteen miles or so from here."

"How many?" Michael asked.

"Twenty-one once we'd all turned up. They'd been there from the start. The place is rough and basic, but it's rock solid. The dead have never been able to get near enough to cause any real problems."

"So why would you leave a place like that and come out here on your own?" Donna asked. She glared at him, seeming to demand an answer.

"Remember that cold snap just before Christmas? Really bloody cold, it was. Loads of snow."

"We remember," Michael said, casting his mind back to the difficult conditions they too had endured a couple weeks earlier. It had been hard going on the island back then. They'd almost run

171

out of firewood and fuel, and had resorted to cramming everyone into a couple of homes temporarily to try and conserve supplies. The difficulties they'd experienced back then were one of the main reasons they'd decided to come back to the mainland so soon.

"I came out to this place with a truckload of blokes from the castle," Harte continued. "Broke into a shopping center. We'd been collecting stuff for hours, but they kept trying to get more so they didn't have to come back again. By the time we were ready to move out, the thaw had started and we were surrounded."

"The Minories," Richard said.

"What?" Cooper asked.

"That's it," Harte said.

"The Minories," Richard repeated. "We passed it when we were looting earlier. I thought it looked like it had been done over. All the doors were buckled and the glass was smashed. It was by the station, remember?"

"The station. You want to stay away from that place," Harte warned.

"And you didn't think to say anything about this at the time?" Cooper asked Richard, ignoring Harte.

"Didn't see there was very much point. We were looking for food, not empty shops. And anyway, there was no way of knowing how long it had been since it was cleared out. I couldn't tell if the damage had been done two days ago or three months. I didn't bother saying anything because I assumed all the good stuff would already have been taken."

"And you also assumed no one else was around?" Donna said, surprised by Richard's apparent belligerence.

"They'd have heard the helicopter if they were," he answered quickly. "Anyway," he continued, pointing at Harte, "he turned up, didn't he."

172

"So why are you still here?" Cooper asked, keen to get the conversation back on track.

"Did you see the petrol station?"

"What petrol station?"

"Exactly. I torched a petrol station to distract the dead so that the truck could get away. Only I did the job a little too well. Blew the fuck out of the place. The size of the explosion took me by surprise, and I got caught on the wrong side of it. By the time I'd come around and managed to get back to the mall, the rest of them were long gone."

"Jesus," Richard said under his breath. "So you were stuck out here?"

"That's about it. I found a safe place in what was left of the mall, so I stayed there for a while. Eventually I moved on."

"And it never crossed your mind to try and get back to the castle?" Cooper asked, sounding less than convinced.

"It crossed my mind," Harte answered quickly, "of course it did, but it wasn't that easy. There was the weather for a start, then the bodies. And the distance too. You couldn't walk it."

"You could have taken a car, there are plenty lying around. You could have cycled there, come to that."

"I didn't want to take the risk. I figured that even if I managed to make it back to the castle, there was no guarantee they'd let me in. They probably wouldn't even see me for a start."

"You could have yelled at them to open up. Surely they'd have heard you with everything else so quiet."

"Yeah, and so would the dead. They couldn't get right up to the castle walls, but there were still thousands of them hanging around back there. Tens of thousands, probably. I couldn't have fought my way through that lot on my own."

The conversation faltered. For a moment the only sounds

were occasional creaks from the vessel and the lapping of the waves against its hull. Michael had been quiet, watching the conversation from across the cabin.

"Forgive me, Ian," he said. "I know we've only just met, and I might be making a hell of a presumption here, but everything you've just told us is a load of bollocks, isn't it?"

"Come on, Mike," Harry protested. "That's a bit harsh, isn't it?"

"You think?"

"No," Harte said, "I swear. We were here looting, I blew up the petrol station and—"

"Oh, I don't doubt that," Michael interrupted. "It's everything since then that I have a problem with. How long ago did all this happen?"

"About two weeks ago, why?"

"Because you would have got back by now if you'd really wanted to, I know I would. You planned to stay out here on your own, didn't you?"

Harte looked down into his beer, then up at the others again.

"So what if I did? What difference does it make? I made a choice, that's all."

"What choice?" Donna asked.

Another hesitation.

"Okay, I'll admit it. There was never a plan. I don't know if I really made a conscious decision or whether I bottled it or just made a stupid mistake. I'd been stuck with those fuckers for weeks, and I was sick of all the fighting and arguing. I don't know what you lot are like, but even though there are hardly any of us left alive, the group mentality gets a bit suffocating, you know? Whether you're with five people or five hundred, you always seem to end up with some cocky fucker who thinks they're in charge, and you know it's only a matter of time before things turn ugly. That's why

174

we were fucked over at the hotel, and that's what I could see happening again at the castle."

"So there's a cocky fucker like that back there?"

"At least two, with a few more waiting in the wings. There's Jackson, the guy who found the place, then there's Jas."

"Jas?"

"I'd been with him virtually since day one. He was always a good guy, but I'd been starting to think our time trapped in the hotel sent him a little stir-crazy. Him and Jackson were constantly at each other's throats, and I could just see things heading down that same old slippery slope again. So I took a leaf out of Driver's book and did a runner."

"So what's it actually like at this castle?" Cooper asked.

"Basic, but pretty good, all things considered," Harte admitted.

"Twenty-one people, you say?"

"Twenty now."

"Supplies?"

"They should have enough to get them through the winter, assuming the truck got back, that is."

"And the bodies are held at a safe distance?"

"The place is built on a rise, so they physically can't get up to it. There's an access road leading up to the main gate that some of them manage to get up, but they're nothing that can't be handled with a couple of vehicles and a little brute force. Anyway, what about this island of yours?" he asked, keen to redirect the conversation. "Many bodies left there?"

"None," Richard told him. "We cleared them all out when we first arrived."

"You cleared them out? *All* of them? Jesus, how many was that?"

"Three or four hundred, give or take."

"So you've got plenty of room?"

"Loads of space. Why, are you trying to hitch a lift now?"

"Wouldn't say no," Harte immediately said, needing no time to think about his answer.

"Just one thing before you get too carried away," Cooper said ominously, "and I don't want to piss on your parade or anything, but this is important. Whatever your real reasons for being out here alone are, we can't ignore the people back at the castle. There's no reason why you can't come back with us, but we need to make the same offer to them too."

"Sounds reasonable," Michael said. "The more the merrier."

"I'm not sure about this," Harte said. "They think I'm dead. When they find out I ran out on them, they'll have my balls. Jas will go fucking mental."

"You reckon?" Cooper asked. "I think you're the one holding all the trump cards. From where I'm sitting, you're in a much better position than you think."

"And how do you work that out?"

"Well, when you turn up there tomorrow morning in a helicopter and offer to help whisk them all away to a place where there are no bodies and where they'll be completely safe, they'll think you're the best fucking thing since sliced bread."

"Sliced bread—remember that?" Richard said to himself, laughing sadly.

"You don't know that," Harte protested, sounding increasingly nervous. "You don't know how they'll react."

"True," Cooper admitted. "You're absolutely right, I don't know for sure. But here's the deal: we'll give it a try and if things don't work out, I promise we'll get you out of there and over to Cormansey with us. It's either that or you go back to wherever you've been hiding in the morning and crawl back under your rock. You'll end up spending the rest of your life on your own, though, picking through the bones of what's left of this place."

Harte didn't say anything. He sank farther back into his seat and reached for another bottle of beer, knowing full well that he had little choice but to go back to the castle in the morning.

24

Harte's guts were churning. It could have been for any number of reasons: the fact he was in a helicopter, hundreds of meters above the ground, perhaps? Or maybe it was because he was hungover from all the beer and wine he'd drunk last night. Then again, it might have just been the nervousness he felt at the prospect of returning to the castle—returning from the grave—and facing Jas and the others again after being away from them for weeks. Most likely it was a combination of all those factors. He kept his head bowed and focused on the floor between his feet, trying not to think about anything.

"That it?" Richard asked, shouting to make himself heard over the helicopter noise. Harte looked up, then looked down. There was the castle: an ugly gray scar surrounded by a narrow band of green, then another dark circle of land where the remains of tens of thousands of bodies gathered ominously, still looking like they were poised to make their deadly assault. Within the castle walls he could see the off-white roofs of the six caravans and several trucks too. Smoke rose up from the remains of fires. One or two people appeared, cautiously reacting to the noise. The longer he watched, the more of them he saw coming out into the open.

"That's it," he answered.

It had only been two weeks since he'd last been at Cheetham Castle, but Harte thought it looked very different to how he'd left it. As Richard took the helicopter down, he was able to make out more detail. The number of bodies waiting around the elevated settlement seemed to have increased, but that may have been because he'd never approached from this angle before. From up here they seemed to have combined to form a single, virtually uninterrupted rotting mass—a ring of dead flesh—and that was consistent with what he'd seen elsewhere. Where there were fewer bodies, they sometimes lasted longer. When they were crammed together like this, the way they crowded and constantly jostled for position, grinding against each other, caused their fragile flesh to deteriorate much faster. Even now more of them were still moving toward the castle. They walked alone now, whereas they would have been in larger packs before, and they were painfully slow, but still they came. It beggared belief that these creatures had probably been walking aimlessly like this for weeks, maybe even months, and were only now reaching the castle. From up here they looked like stick figures, and their speed was barely visible. That they were still drawn to the living after all this time was both terrifying and remarkable.

The road leading up to the castle entrance was full of bodies as he'd expected. There were mounds of dead flesh on either side where the corpses had previously been shoveled away, but by the looks of things no one had been outside in some time. As they drifted downward, Harte saw that there were several people on the top of the gatehouse. He couldn't see who it was from here.

"You ready for this?" Donna asked, sitting next to him.

"I guess," he replied, sounding less than convinced. He looked at the other three traveling in the helicopter with him; all of them appeared much calmer and more relaxed than he felt. Cooper was watching the ground intently, surveying the scene. They'd left Harry and Michael back at the marina to look after the boats. Michael, in particular, had also remained behind because he had more to lose than the others. Harte would gladly have traded places with either of them now. What he'd have given to be back in his seafront apartment just north of Chadwick, bored out of his brain as usual but without a damn care. *You're a fucking idiot*, he said to himself. *You should have stopped where you were.* Suddenly the loneliness and the frequent guilt he'd struggled with intermittently over the past weeks all seemed preferable to what he was feeling now.

Donna picked up on his obvious unease.

"You'll be all right," she said. "They'll understand why you didn't come back."

"You think?"

"Stick to your story and you'll be okay," Cooper agreed from the front. "You fucked up and got yourself in trouble when you torched the petrol station. You came around and they'd gone. Fifteen miles is a long way, these days. The snow stopped you getting back."

"Yeah, but the snow was gone a couple of days after that."

"Then improvise, for crying out loud. Seriously, they're not going to care what happened. Like I said last night, you turning up in a bloody helicopter will give them plenty to think about. They'll have more important things to ask than why you disappeared."

Harte said nothing. He leaned against the glass and watched the ground below come closer and the faces come into focus as Richard lowered them toward the castle courtyard.

"Clear the ground," Lorna ordered, doing her best to spur some of the others into action and clear enough space for the helicopter to land. Around her, most of the others stood in dumbstruck silence, staring up into the air and watching the aircraft descend. *Christ,* she thought, *you'd think they'd never seen a bloody helicopter* before.

She kicked over the remains of a fire from last night, sending clouds of smoke and still-warm ash up into the air, then dragged away several partially burnt lumps of wood. Between them, Bob Wilkins and Howard pushed a broken-down car out of the way, straining with effort as the noise and downwind from the helicopter rapidly increased, and cursing Bayliss, the lazy bastard who'd been promising to get it fixed and shifted for the last fortnight but who'd done nothing.

The ground was clear. The crowd which gathered to watch the helicopter now shuffled farther and farther back as it came in to land.

"It *must* be the same one that kept flying over the hotel," Caron shouted to Lorna over the noise.

"How could it be? What are the chances of that happening?"

"I don't know, but how many other helicopters have you seen since everyone died?"

"Well if it is the same people," she said, "then they're a few months late."

"But still very welcome."

The helicopter seemed to pause slightly before gently dropping the last few feet down. Dust filled the air. No one moved. The engine stopped and when the noise had faded away to nothing, the expectant silence which replaced it was strangely unsettling. A man disembarked, then a woman, then the pilot. Jackson walked out to meet them. He confidently strode up to the nearest of the two men, and offered his hand.

"I'm Jackson," he announced, smiling broadly.

"Cooper."

"Good to meet you, Cooper."

"This is Richard and Donna," he said, introducing the others.

Harte was watching from the back of the helicopter, his heart thumping. Thankfully no one seemed to have noticed him yet. He wanted to stay in here and hide but he knew that, as the only person who knew everyone, he should be the one right in the middle of the conversation, not watching from a distance like a naughty kid sitting on the stairs, eavesdropping on his parents. *Oh, grow some bollocks*, he ordered himself, and he jumped down and landed on the gravel, directly in Jackson's line of vision.

"Hello," was all he could say. Jackson looked at him and grinned, but he couldn't speak either.

"Where the fuck have you been?" Jas demanded, storming over.

"You must be Jas," Cooper said perceptively, but he was ignored.

"We thought you were dead . . ." Jackson said, still struggling to take everything in.

"Obviously not," Jas said. Harte's eyes flickered from face to face.

"I'm sorry," he said, not quite sure why he was apologizing. His mind was swimming—all the reasons why and excuses he'd remembered suddenly becoming confused. "I must have been too close to the petrol station when it went up. Didn't know anything until I came around later. You'd all gone by then and I . . ."

"Bollocks," Jas said. "You'd have been burnt to a crisp."

"Give it a rest, Jas, it doesn't matter," Jackson said. "What's done is done." He pointed at the helicopter. "Don't you think we have a few more important issues to discuss right now?"

25

"Drink?"

Jackson ushered the new arrivals into the caravan he shared with Howard and Bob, then carried on through into one of the bedrooms. Jas, the last one in, pulled the door closed behind him, shutting everyone else out. Jackson returned carrying bottles of water, Coke, and beer. He gestured for everyone to sit. They squeezed onto a cluttered U-shaped sofa at the end of the caravan, having to move various piles of belongings out of the way to find enough space.

"Decent setup you have here," Richard said.

"We shouldn't complain," Jackson replied, "though Christ alone knows we do. We're all fortunate just to be alive. The fact we found this spot is a real bonus."

"Wise move, setting yourself up in a castle," Cooper said.

"You're not wrong," Jackson agreed. "Think about it logically—places like this have already been standing for hundreds of years. They've survived wars and who knows what else. A few thousand dead bodies was never going to be that much of a threat to them."

"Well, it's thanks to Harte here that we found you," Cooper

said, deliberately involving Harte and giving him credit to try and deflect any bad feelings the others might be harboring against him.

"I just did what anybody else would have done," Harte said, sounding less than confident. Would everybody else really have faked their own death for an easy life? he wondered. Jackson just nodded and grinned. He looked genuinely pleased to see him.

"So you're all getting by here?" Cooper asked.

"We're doing okay," Jas said, sitting opposite. "Things will get a lot easier when we've seen the last of the dead."

"I don't think you'll have long to wait," Donna said. "From what we saw in the air just now, there's not a lot of activity out there."

"*Any* activity is too much activity," Jas replied, sounding surprisingly forceful. "We've lasted here until now without any problems. Another couple of months and maybe we'll look at moving on."

"Why wait?" Cooper asked. "Seriously, from what we've seen since we've been back on the mainland, things aren't as bad out there as you probably think."

"What do you mean, since you've been back on the mainland?" Jackson asked. "Where the hell did you come from to get here?"

"They're from an island," Harte said enthusiastically, answering for the others.

"An island?" Jackson repeated in disbelief.

"And you haven't heard the best of it," Harte continued. "There are no bodies there. They cleared them all out."

"It's a lot easier to do in such a small and concentrated area," Cooper explained. "It's nothing like the situation you've had here."

"The dead are less of a problem than they used to be," Jackson said.

"But they are still a problem," Jas quickly added. "I'm sure

Harte's told you about the day he left us. Those things were frozen solid when we set out. By the time we were ready to head back, they were all over us."

"It wasn't that bad," Harte said. "And you forget, Jas, I've been out there since then. They're becoming less and less of a threat each day."

"They were all over us," Jas repeated, laboring the point. "And I for one am not going out there again until every last one of those fuckers has rolled over and given up the ghost for good."

"So you've not been out again since that day?"

"We brought enough stuff back with us. There was no need to go out again. And if we're sensible, we can make what we've got left last until the dead are finished."

"Seriously," Cooper said, "you might want to reconsider your strategy. There were still bodies walking around Chadwick yesterday and today. We just walked past them. Seriously, you can outrun them now without even having to run. The threat is over."

"Then why don't you go up to the gatehouse and watch them on the road and on the bridge? They're still coming, friend, and they won't stop until they're physically unable to move. We're still surrounded here. The threat is *far* from over."

Richard sensed a sudden tension in the air and changed tack to try and diffuse it.

"Harte says you've got about twenty people here."

"That's right," Jackson answered. "What about you? How many of you are on this island of yours?"

"Over fifty, including the five of us."

"Five of you?"

"We left a couple of men back at the port. Apart from the lack of seats in the helicopter, we didn't want to risk bringing Michael over here until we'd checked the place out, no offense."

"None taken. But why? What's different about this Michael chap?"

"He's going to be a dad."

The caravan fell silent. Jackson, taken by surprise, wasn't sure what to say.

"How . . . ?"

"Jesus, how d'you think?" Donna mumbled.

"I mean, was it before everyone died or . . . ?"

"After," she answered. "Emma and Michael got together after it had happened."

"Bloody hell."

"It's not that incredible," Richard said. "Women used to have kids all the time."

"I know that, but since the world fell apart . . . I don't know what I'm trying to say. An hour ago it felt like everything was coming to an end, then you turn up here out of the blue in your bloody helicopter, telling us about your island where there are no dead bodies, and then that you've got a woman who's pregnant and . . . and it's like you've come here from another world. Truly amazing."

"I wouldn't go that far," Jas said.

"Well, I would. It sounds like these folks have achieved a huge amount. There's a lot we could learn from them."

"With the greatest respect," Jas interrupted, looking at each of the new arrivals before turning toward Jackson, "we don't have anything to learn from anyone. All this lot is doing is what we *used* to do, and it's what we'll do again once the bodies are gone and we're out of here."

"No one has to learn anything from anyone," Donna said. "You make it sound like we're from different tribes. We might be all that's left, and that's the main reason we came back here with Harte. We think it makes sense for us all to group together. We think you should all come over to the island."

"I'm not sure . . ." Jas began to say before Jackson spoke over him.

"Makes sense, providing we can all get there."

"We've got a couple of boats ready in Chadwick," Cooper explained. "That's one of the reasons we came back, to get some alternative transport and take the pressure off Richard here."

"Sounds good."

"Just wait," Jas said, his voice louder and more forceful this time. "You can't make a blanket decision on behalf of all the people here, not without consulting them and not without thinking it through. There might be some who don't want to go to an island. Not sure I do, if I'm honest. It sounds a little risky to me, a little cut off and exposed."

"It's not perfect," Cooper admitted, "but I've yet to find a better place. As good as this castle looks to have been for you all, I think the island is better. You've still not got your freedom here."

"Doesn't matter if we're surrounded by sea of dead flesh or by the ocean itself, sounds to me like we're all still prisoners."

"Jas is right about one thing," Jackson said. "I was wrong to assume. Everyone has the right to make their own choices. We'll get everybody together and give them the options. We're talking about decisions which will affect the rest of everybody's lives."

26

"Harte? Harte, is that you?"

The voice caught him by surprise. He didn't think anyone else was out here. He'd been sitting in a quiet corner where he could see the helicopter, not wanting to stray too far in case Cooper and the others upped and left without him.

"Lorna?"

He got up and walked over to her. It was getting dark, and he followed the noise her boots made crunching through the gravel. When he saw her he grabbed hold of her and held her tight. He hadn't realized how much he'd missed her. She led him over toward the row of caravans and sat down with him on a pile of discarded wooden pallets. In the light coming from the window of the nearest caravan, he thought she looked tired, old even. Her face appeared angular and stark in the gloom and her hair was scraped back. She looked pensive, and it was out of character from the Lorna he remembered. Previously she'd always seemed relaxed and comfortable in herself, regardless of how bad everything else was around her.

"I looked for you earlier," Harte said. "You okay?"

"Fine," she replied, sounding less than convinced. "I was working. I'm on my break right now."

"On your break? From what?"

"Cooking rota."

"You on a cooking rota! Bloody hell, Lor!"

"It's not funny."

"I didn't say it was. Just a surprise, that's all."

"Tell me about it."

"So Jackson's cracking the whip around here now is he?"

"Jackson and Jas. I swear, they're like a double act sometimes."

"Good cop, bad cop."

"Bad cop, worse cop."

"Well, all that might be about to change. You've heard about the island."

"I've heard rumblings. You don't tend to hear much news in the kitchen, not that there's usually any news to hear."

"Are things really that bad?"

"No, I'm making it sound worse than it is. But I can see things going downhill if we're not careful. The fewer people there are left, the more narrow-minded some of them seem to be becoming. I swear, it's like we've gone back fifty years. Sexual equality and all that stuff's a thing of the past now."

"It must be grim if they've got you cooking."

"Cheeky bastard. You're right, though. Us *ladies* are politely excused from doing anything physical or even remotely dangerous. Most of them are happy with that because they're old maids like Caron, Sue, and Shirley. Zoe's a stubborn bugger who just locks herself in her caravan and refuses to come out unless it suits her . . ."

"So most of the work is down to you."

"Pretty much."

"What about Melanie? She still here?"

"Oh, she's here all right. Dirty bitch."

"That's a bit harsh."

"Is it? Dirty cow's just a communal fuck-buddy. Whenever she wants anything she just flashes her tits and flutters her eyelids at one of the blokes and they cover for her."

"You could try that."

"You could fuck off! I've got more self-respect. Anyway, I'd destroy the piss-poor men here. I'd eat you alive for starters."

"Look, I'm not arguing. I know you would!" He paused, then asked her if she was going to leave for the island.

"I'm planning to," she answered quietly. "I don't like the way things are going here."

"Why? What's happened?"

"Ah, it's just all the usual bollocks you get when there are too many dumb blokes stuck in the same place together with limited options. They stop thinking sensibly and spend all their time playing bloody stupid mind games with each other."

"Jas and Jackson?"

"Jackson tries to keep Jas in check, but from where I'm sitting it looks like Jas is the one with more influence these days. You've heard about Howard, haven't you?"

"I haven't heard anything. Haven't seen much of him, come to that. I tried to talk to him earlier, but he was in a right fucking foul mood."

"He lost his dog last week."

"Shit. What happened? Did it get sick or . . . ?"

"Mark Ainsworth happened. Apparently Jas had said something to him about Dog using up food which was meant for us. So Ainsworth threw the dog out. Middle of the night he just opened the gates and kicked the poor little bastard out. Howard was in bits, and they wouldn't let him out to look for her."

"Fuck me."

"And that's not the worst of it."

"There's worse?"

"Hollis."

"Yeah, where is he? I was looking for him . . ."

"Gone," she said, sounding subdued.

"Gone where?"

"No idea. They kicked him out too."

"Why?"

"Were you here when he had that accident?"

"The shit pit? When he busted Steve Morecombe's arm up? That's a point, I haven't seen Steve either."

"You wouldn't have. He's dead."

"Dead? How?"

"How d'you think? His broken arm got infected. Sue's supposed to be a nurse, but if you need anything more than a fucking headache tablet, she's next to useless. I swear, it was like when Ellie and Anita died. All we could do was watch the poor sod fade away. Happened last week. Fucking horrible, it was."

"But Hollis . . . it was just an accident. It wasn't like he meant to do it."

"I know, but you know what he's like. He takes it all so personally. The toilets hadn't been emptied, so he went back again to sort them out. Jas caught him on the digger and they ended up fighting. He practically threw him out. He gave him a choice—spend all his time in his caravan, virtually under lock and key, or leave. So he walked."

"Fuck . . ."

"To be honest, I think Hollis was happy to go. And have you seen the state of the shit pit since you've been back?"

"I went to use it earlier but couldn't face it. The stink was terrible. Found a quiet bit of wall and took a piss up that instead."

"Exactly. The toilets are overflowing, the pit reeks, there's flies everywhere . . . Hollis was the only one who kept on top of the waste, so to speak. Now he's gone, no one else is willing to get their hands dirty. Jas has just shot himself in the foot. Well, all of us, really. I swear, Harte, it's getting to be like the Dark Ages here."

"Everything all right?" a voice asked from behind them, startling them both. Harte spun around. He couldn't immediately see who it was, but Lorna knew straightaway. It was Mark Ainsworth.

"Have you met my stalker?" she whispered before raising her voice to answer Ainsworth. "We're fine, thanks. Just catching up on a little gossip."

"You sure?"

"I'm sure."

"Just be careful what you're gossiping about, right?"

"Will do. Thanks, Mark."

Harte listened carefully until he was sure that Ainsworth had gone again.

"What's his problem?" he whispered.

"Where do I start? A guilty conscience, for one thing. That and the fact he's probably jealous."

"Jealous of what?"

"Us talking. He's taken quite a shine to me, unfortunately. He's setting his sights a little higher than a quick fumble around the back of a caravan with Melanie now."

"Are you serious?"

"Deadly."

"You've changed, Lor. When I first met you, you'd have eaten blokes like Mark Ainsworth for breakfast. Christ, I remember how you used to run rings around Webb and the others back at the flats."

"I'm still the same," she said quietly, "it's the situation that's changed. I'm keeping the blokes sweet while I have to, that's all. I'll do their cooking and a little bit of cleaning and I might even flutter my eyelids at them when it suits, but if they fuck around with me or overstep the mark, I'll break their balls."

"I don't doubt you. I'm not going to argue."

"I wouldn't. Anyway, it won't be for much longer. I've just been biding my time until I get out of here, and you bringing that helicopter here has just changed everything."

27

In an ideal world, Cooper thought, which this place was most definitely not, he'd have been in and out of the castle in a matter of hours. As it was, they'd already been hanging around for most of the day and he expected to be around for a little longer still, probably overnight. He'd been to some hellish, war-torn places during his years of service, and he'd had more than his fair share of awkward situations to try and resolve through diplomacy, and this was no different. Although Jackson was keen to leave the castle, Jas most definitely was yet to be convinced. Cooper thought it better to spend a little time trying to get all of them onside rather than going in heavy-handed and screwing everything up. But even Cooper's patience was being tested tonight. He felt like they were going around in circles, and he had to keep reminding himself they were actually trying to help these people. Every time he made a suggestion, he felt like it was being shot down by Jas and a few others without any consideration. He was on the verge of getting the others together and flying back to Chadwick.

The small classroom was packed and stiflingly hot, overheated by a paraffin heater at one end. It was brightly lit by lamps running off a series of connected extension cords which were, in turn, connected to a small but bloody noisy petrol generator outside. Condensation was running down the windows. Harte felt increasingly uncomfortable, and not just because of the heat. He'd been shocked by the things he'd seen and heard since returning to the castle. The atmosphere had changed markedly, and it seemed to be continually changing still, almost from minute to minute depending on who he was talking to.

He'd already learned that the looting expedition to Chadwick he'd been a part of had been the last time anyone had left the castle. It seemed that, since then, some of the direction Jackson had previously provided had been ignored. The wooden construction to investigate the well, which he himself had helped put together many weeks ago, remained in exactly the same unfinished state as when he'd last seen it. There were huge piles of waste gathered around the edges of the courtyard and, as he'd already discovered, the cesspit and toilets were full to overflowing. There'd also been a fire in one of the caravans; he'd noticed after talking to Lorna earlier. There was smoke damage and black scorch marks around several of the windows, but no attempt had been made to do anything about the wreck.

Harte positioned himself at the edge of the group, quite near the front, not completely sure where he should be sitting. He took comfort in some of the familiar faces he could see—Lorna, Caron, Driver, and Howard—but he now found himself aligning more with Donna, Richard, and Cooper. He hadn't seen it, didn't even know for sure if it really existed, but their idyllic island of Cormansey, despite its apparent bleakness and basic lifestyle, seemed his idea of heaven tonight. Too bad a vociferous handful didn't seem to share his opinion. He could tell that Cooper was getting annoyed.

"I don't see what the problem is. We're offering you a place that's safe and free from walking bodies and all the complications they bring."

"Well, why don't you just fuck off back there, then?" Jas said unhelpfully. He'd been increasingly obstructive since this "town hall" meeting had begun what felt like hours ago now. Unfortunately he seemed to have plenty of vocal support. "Listen, I agree with what you're saying in principle, but this island of yours is completely the wrong place. You're cutting yourself off."

"Cutting ourselves off from what?" Donna demanded, unable to believe what she was hearing. "There's fuck all else left."

Jas continued. "I think it's better to stay here and wait a little longer. Here we've got access to what's left of the entire country. Better than some barren little island with half a dozen houses."

"But can't you see? The island is much more than that. It's the best bet for all of us. I'll be honest, there's still plenty more work to be done, but with more of us there it'll be finished quicker and we'll be self-sufficient. It's clean and safe."

"I don't want to spend the rest of my life living in some hippie-loving, new-age commune," Kieran said.

"Seems to me we're all going to have to become self-sufficient whether we like it or not," Jackson interrupted, beginning to sound as frustrated as Cooper. "There's no alternative now, is there? There's no government anymore, no benefits system, no McDonalds, no utility companies, no Internet . . ."

"No government." Ainsworth smirked. "Sounds pretty good to me when you put it like that."

Jackson sighed. "Come on, grow up."

"All we're trying to do is be realistic, that's all," Donna said, exasperated. "The supplies here on the mainland will run out eventually and—"

"—and by then we'll *all* be dead and buried," Jas said. "With only this many of us left, we'll be picking meat off the bones for years yet. There's nothing you've got on your island that we haven't got here, but there's plenty here that you'll go without. You're isolating yourselves unnecessarily. Cutting yourselves off like this seems bloody futile."

"I think you're looking at this completely the wrong way," Donna said, refusing to give up. "You're still thinking about things in terms of your old life and all the stuff you *used* to need. All that's gone now. Everything's changed. Here's an example—cars and roads. We don't need them anymore to any great extent, because you can walk the entire length of the island in a couple of hours."

"I understand that, but why *should* I do without cars? There are millions of them just lying around. I could have any car I could ever dream of, it's just a question of finding it and getting it started. What you're suggesting is limiting yourselves to some kind of medieval lifestyle."

"You're the one living in a castle," Richard said under his breath.

"No, we're not limiting ourselves," Donna protested. "Bloody hell, Jas, what do you think's going to happen when the bodies are completely finished and you finally pluck up courage to go back outside? Are you just going to flick a few switches and turn the world back on again? You won't get the power working, or the gas. What happens when all the batteries in all the cars finally run flat, or when all the fuel's used up and you've drained every tank dry? What do you do then? You're going to end up building yourself an island of your own, and you'll be as stranded and cut off as we are."

"Bollocks."

"She's right," Jackson said, speaking just to Jas initially, but then turning around so that he could address everyone in the room. "It's all about economies of scale now. The world's too far gone to pull back from the brink. We've got no choice but to go right back to basics, and no matter what you say, Jas, Donna's right. Your world is going to keep getting smaller and smaller until it's just you. They've already anticipated that on the island. And because of their location and their attitude, they're going to try and build something from the ruins instead of just picking meat off the bones, as you put it. I don't know about the rest of you lot, but I think our best bet is to leave here with these people and head for the island."

"I don't," Jas said, his voice loud enough for everyone to hear, but also strangely unemotional and detached. In the expectant pause before he spoke again, the only sound was the steady low thumping of the generator outside. It sounded like a headache felt. "Leaving the mainland would be a mistake," he continued, "and it's a mistake you'll find hard to put right. They're not going to operate charter helicopter flights to fly you back if things don't work out, are they? Anyone who leaves here will be risking everything. We'd be completely cut off. What happens if things go wrong? Where's the escape plan?"

"If we do it right we won't need to escape," Lorna said. Jas looked at her with disappointment.

"I thought you'd understand, Lorna. You should know better than most that you *always* need an escape plan. Do you remember what happened when we were at the flats, or have you already forgotten about Ellie and Anita?"

She shook her head. Several low and uneasy sounding conversations began to spring up.

"Of course I haven't forgotten them," Lorna said. "You're just scaremongering."

"No, I'm not," he said. "This is an important and valid point. For those of you who don't know, Ellie and Anita were with us a long time back, right at the beginning. They both got sick and died. We don't know what killed them or why it didn't finish the rest of us off, we just packed up and moved on rather than hang around and find out. So tell me, if there's an outbreak of something like the disease that killed Ellie and Anita on the island, where are you going to run to?"

"What do you think the source was?" Cooper asked.

"Don't know," Jas replied. "We assumed it was the bodies. We were surrounded by masses of them."

"Problem solved, then. We don't have any bodies on Cormansey. Nothing to worry about."

"We *assumed* it was the bodies," Jas said again, "but I've long wondered if that really was the case. No one else got sick after them, and we were all exposed, some of us considerably more so, in fact. It might have been something else—something they both ate, something they smoked, something naturally occurring. Don't forget, we're moving into an age now where our chances of getting ill are going to increase. Smallpox, TB, the Black Death . . . who knows what might make a reappearance to bite our arses."

"Donna's right—now you *are* just scaremongering," Cooper said. "The risks of getting contagious diseases are hardly going to increase when there's no one else left to catch them from. Look, I still don't understand why you're doing this. We came here to offer a solution, not to cause more problems."

Jas stood up and pointed accusingly at him.

"Have you not listened to anything I've said? Your bloody solution might well turn out to be the cause of the problems. The bottom line is, isolating ourselves on an island is just too big a chance to take. We can't risk it. *I* won't risk it, and if anyone else here has got any sense, they won't either."

Jackson also got to his feet. He'd had enough.

"We're not going to get anywhere like this. I suggest we all sleep on it. Make your decisions overnight. Those who want to leave can go first thing. The rest of you can stay."

Jas nodded his agreement. He remained where he was for a few moments longer, but there was nothing left to say. He left the room, meeting over. Several others—Kieran, Bayliss, Ainsworth, Paul Field, and Melanie among them—left with him.

Cooper helped himself to a can of lager and downed it at once. Around him, other people began drifting away until just a handful remained. Donna pulled up a chair next to him, a drink in her hand too. Richard remained dry—their designated driver, ready to take the controls of the helicopter in a hurry if they needed him to. And although it was looking increasingly likely they were going to be spending the night here, he wasn't taking any chances.

Caron was still sitting at the back of the classroom with Driver. Harte walked over and sat down next to her.

"You okay?" he asked.

"Fine," she replied, before adding, "all things considered. It's a little stifling in here tonight, don't you think? Bit too much testosterone for my liking."

Harte smirked. Good old caustic Caron. Hers was the wine-addled voice of reason. He'd forgotten her uncanny ability to cut through the bullshit and see things for what they were.

"That helicopter guy," she whispered, "he said they've got a girl on this island of theirs that's pregnant."

"They have. I met the father."

"He's here?"

"Back in Chadwick. They didn't let him come here. Didn't want him to risk butting heads with Jas and his mates."

"Sensible. Shame, though."

"What's a shame?"

"The pregnant girl. Having a kid born into all this mess."

"And that's half the problem, I think. No one knows if it'll be born at all. Providing it doesn't come out coughing up blood, it should be okay . . . I guess."

"Suppose. I don't fancy its chances, though. Poor little thing will probably grow up wild. Doesn't bear thinking about really."

"So what are you going to do, Caron? Stay here or leave?"

"I'm not sure yet," she answered honestly. "There are plenty of aspects which appeal, but you know me. All that hard work and physical graft? I'll always get my hands dirty when I have to, but I'm no cleaner and I'm certainly not a farmer. My childbearing days are long over, so I'm not a lot of use to anyone anymore. Mind you, that's how I like it. I just want to retire quietly. All I need is a decent supply of food, a few bottles of wine, and a library. I'm happy just reading and drinking until I drop."

"I know you too well. You say that, but I think you want more than that."

"I quite like the look of that helicopter pilot," she half joked.

"You know what I mean."

"A little peace and quiet and some booze, that'll do me nicely, thank you very much."

"The island sounds peaceful. Mind you, try finding somewhere that *isn't* quiet these days."

"I know. Truth is, I'm really not sure what I want to do yet. I need a good night's sleep to try and help me decide. I can see plenty of reasons for staying, but I can find as many good reasons to go."

"Well, I'm going," Driver said, eavesdropping on their conversation. "I'll tell you this for nothing, first chance I get I'm buggering off to this island. Always fancied retiring to the country, I did."

28

Harte hardly slept all night. He'd laid awake on a spare sofa bed in one of the caravans, the trailer next to Jackson's, where Kieran and Jas slept—along with Ainsworth and Field, who'd both moved in after the "accident" with a wastepaper bin, a bottle of booze, and a box of matches which had caused the fire. He'd seen Donna, Cooper, and Richard go into Jackson's caravan late last night, and they hadn't yet come out. His restless night had mostly been spent looking out of windows. He watched the caravan next door for a while, then turned the other way to check on the helicopter in the middle of the courtyard, desperate for it not to leave without him.

After tossing and turning restlessly for hours, he finally fell into a relatively deep sleep around four. Noises outside woke him later and he got up with a start. He was out of bed so fast it made him feel nauseous. He pressed his face against the window and saw that there were people gathered around the helicopter. He ran outside, frantically pulling his clothes on as he went.

"Morning," Richard said casually as Harte blustered toward him, all arms and legs and panic. "All right, are you?"

"Thought I was going to miss my flight," he answered breathlessly.

"You are," Cooper said from behind him, startling him. He spun around. Jackson was there too.

"What are you talking about?" he asked. He turned to look at Jackson. "What's he on about?"

"We were talking in the caravan after the meeting," Jackson explained. "Some of the things Jas said last night were right. This is a big decision for people to make, and we can't rush them. Cooper here has kindly agreed to give us all a little more time to make up our minds about what we want to do."

"We're flying back to Chadwick this morning," Cooper began. "We're going to—"

"I'm coming with you," Harte interrupted. "You said."

Cooper shook his head. "We need you here. Look, we need to get back to the marina to let Harry and Michael know what's going on. In the meantime, you and Jackson will be organizing this end of things, finding out who's going and who's staying and getting things packed up."

"But why me? You don't need me for that. Anyone could do it."

"You know the area better than most," he explained. "You've spent a couple of weeks scavenging around Chadwick, and you know where to find the boats we're planning to take. Your man Driver has agreed to transport everyone, but he needs your help to get there. This is important, Harte."

Harte just looked at him, feeling deflated and unexpectedly angry.

"This is bullshit," he spat, turning his ire on Cooper. "I agreed to come back here on the condition you'd get me out again."

"And that's still going to happen. It's just that you'll be leaving here by bus, not helicopter, that's all. What difference does it make? We're going to wait for you in Chadwick until midday tomorrow, so come the end of the week you should still be on Cormansey. These people need you, Harte; Jackson and Driver most of all. I think it's the least you can do after running out on them like that."

Harte tried to argue with Cooper but he couldn't. There was no point.

Just past midday. A clear sky and a cool breeze. Jas was standing on the top of the gatehouse with Kieran. Below them the rotor blades on top of the helicopter had just started to spin. Their noise and speed increased rapidly, blowing clouds of dust across the courtyard and sending people scattering, looking for cover. The aircraft rose majestically, and Jas watched it effortlessly climb.

It was gone in a matter of minutes. All the noise and bluster disappeared in a remarkably short period of time.

"So what do you think?" he said to Kieran. Kieran stared into the distance, looking as far as he could see in the general direction the helicopter had taken.

"I'm guessing fifty-fifty," he answered. "Maybe more will want to go than stay. The grass is always greener, and all that shite."

"And that's all it is," Jas said, "shite. Most of the people here are just sheep, following the rest of the herd. If you told them to swim the Channel because there's no dead bodies in France, most of them probably would."

"They're not that bad."

"Some of them are."

Kieran thought for a moment before asking, "So what are we going to do?"

Jas walked to the other side of the gatehouse roof and looked out between the battlements over the dead world beyond the wall. Kieran followed him. Down below he could see what was left of the dead, still drawing ever closer even after all this time, the noise of the helicopter piquing their unwanted interest this morning. Christ, they were pitiful-looking creatures now. He watched one of them, one leg broken, the other missing, as it lay on its belly and slowly dragged itself across the muddy grass. Another tried to move past one which had expired against the trunk of a tree. In its clumsiness the two rib cages had become entangled, and now the corpse which still moved was dragging the other behind it.

The dead appalled Jas. He didn't admit as much to anyone else, but they still scared the hell out of him too. How could anyone not be afraid of monsters such as these? Foul and hideous, ungodly beasts which would stop at nothing to reach the living. Detestable fuckers with no consideration for their own physical condition, less anyone or anything else's. Even today, months after death when their physical bodies had deteriorated to such a repulsive extent, they were still a threat. There was nothing human about them now. They were evil: driven to keep attacking until they could no longer function. He wondered how anything could be filled with such relentless, remorseless hate.

"We can't let anyone leave," Jas said, finally responding to Kieran's question. "Can't they see what they're doing? They're making a huge mistake."

"We could try talking to them again," Kieran suggested. "Maybe now they've had time to think they'll see things differently."

"I doubt it."

The two men remained looking over the battlements for a while longer. Eventually increasing noises from around the courtyard distracted Kieran.

"I'm going to see what's going on down there, okay?"

"Okay," Jas said.

Suddenly alone, Jas leaned against the wall, then sank down to the floor. He held his head in his hands and tried to make sense of the whirlpool of emotions he was feeling. He thought about everything he'd gone through to get to this point—that first morning when he'd lost his family, the time he'd spent with the others at the flats and the circumstances under which they'd been forced to leave, their nightmare incarceration at the besieged hotel . . .

It was the weeks he'd spent trapped in the hotel which still troubled him most. Just the thought of those dark, endless hours was enough to bring a tidal wave of uncomfortably familiar feelings of helplessness, panic, and dread crashing over him. He'd found it almost impossible to deal with the cruel finality of their imprisonment there—the fact there wasn't a damn thing he could do to help himself—and the prospect of being backed into a corner like that again now terrified him. And despite all the assurances he'd heard over and over, that was how this island seemed. He'd be giving up control if he went there. He'd be trapped unless he could persuade Richard Lawrence to fly him back or find someone who could sail a boat back to the mainland. And travel to and from the island was inevitably going to get harder with time, not easier.

Cheetham Castle wasn't perfect. It was an ill-equipped, uncomfortable place, but that didn't matter. It was just a staging point—a stepping stone, a shelter where they could weather the final days of this tumultuous storm—and it had served its purpose adequately. It would soon be time to move on, but not yet. And definitely not to Cormansey.

Without thinking, Jas slipped his hand into his inside pocket and pulled out the wallet he'd carried with him constantly since before his nightmare had begun. In it was the last remaining photograph of his family. It had become increasingly ragged and dog-eared over time, more so recently because he seemed to be looking at it more than ever. He gazed deep into the last image of his wife's beautiful brown eyes—still sparkling and intense in spite of the wear to the picture—and then, as he did whenever he felt his options were reducing, he asked her what she thought he should do.

Tell me, Harj . . . do I stay or do I go?

29

Short winter days and long nights conspired against all of them. In Chadwick, Cooper and the others spent much of the rest of the day collecting additional supplies, mindful that more than ever, they needed to maximize the usefulness of their time on the mainland. Taking more people back would inevitably reduce the space they had available, but at the same time, the potential increase to the size of Cormansey's population also meant they needed to take as much as possible. They unpacked and repacked the boats, discarding anything unnecessary and loading the bulk of the supplies onto the *Summer Breeze*, the slightly smaller of the two. Both of the boats could carry ten people each, maybe more at a push. Working on the assumption that Jas and his inner circle wouldn't be leaving with them, and with four spare seats in the helicopter, they worked out that they should easily be able to fit all their passengers and their belongings on board the *Duchess*.

They spent their third night on the mainland on the luxury cruiser again, as comfortable as before but, strangely, more subdued. Maybe the people back at the castle hadn't shared their enthusiasm for island life? Donna was surprised. She thought a few of them would have turned up by now, at least.

"They'll be here," Cooper said, seeming to read her thoughts. "You know what it's like when you're leaving somewhere," he half joked. "There's always more to sort out than you expect."

She smiled.

"I know," she said. "I just want to get going, that's all. I want to go home."

At the castle, Driver had moved his tired old bus for the first time in weeks. He drove it out into the center of the courtyard where the helicopter had been standing hours earlier. He checked it over thoroughly, keen to satisfy himself that the vehicle would be able to get them all the fifteen miles or so into Chadwick. The distance was strangely daunting. In times past he'd have covered it in barely any time at all, but things were different now.

Another reason for shifting the bus into a more central position was to allow all those who wanted to leave to get their belongings (and any supplies they could half-hitch in the process) loaded up. There had been a steady stream of people getting on and off the bus for as long as it had been out in the open.

Jackson and Harte watched from a distance.

"First light and we'll be off, okay?"

"Okay," Harte said. "The sooner the better. Got any idea how many are leaving?"

"Thirteen or fourteen, I think," he replied, "including you and me."

"Good. Just Jas and his mates staying behind, then?"

"Looks that way. Jas, Kieran, Melanie, Ainsworth, and Bayliss, I think. Phil Kent's undecided."

"It's probably for the best. No point in them coming if they're not committed. Jas does have a point, but we're all taking risks whatever we do now, and I know where I'd rather be."

"As long as we're all happy with our own personal decisions, that's all that matters."

Out of sight on the far side of the bus, Ainsworth, Kieran, and Jas were shifting boxes of supplies from the café kitchen and the back of two trucks and a van, stashing them away, locking them in the gift shop and museum.

"You sure we should be doing this?" Ainsworth asked.

"We need this stuff," Kieran replied quickly. "There'll be plenty more where they're going tomorrow. It's different for us. We're not leaving here, so we have to make this last. This is our share. We worked for it and we're entitled to it. We're just making sure they don't take what's ours."

"Get as much as you can move," Jas said. "The more we lock away, the less there is for them to take."

30

It was after eight before the sun rose fully, but as soon as there was enough light for people to see, the castle courtyard quickly became a hive of frantic activity. Those who were leaving grabbed the last of their belongings and stashed them on the bus.

By just after ten they were ready to load up the remaining food and other supplies. Jackson, Bob, Howard, and Harte walked over to the kitchen to start, but where they'd expected to find large stocks of provisions, they instead found just an empty space.

When she heard what had happened, Lorna began checking around the rest of the castle. She spotted the bulk of the missing supplies in the gift shop, hidden behind display racks and the counter.

"Over here," she yelled, her voice loud enough to alert everyone who was awake. "I've found it all."

Jackson and the others ran over to the gift shop.

"Who has the keys for this lock?" Harte asked.

"There are only two keys, I think," Howard answered.

"I didn't ask you how many there were, I asked you who has them."

"Jas has got one," Bob said.

"And I'm pretty sure Kieran has the other," Howard added.

"Let's get this door open. Some of that's our stuff in there. I'm sure as hell not going to leave it all in there for Jas and his cronies to gorge themselves on when we're gone."

"That's exactly what you're going to do," Jas said. Unnoticed, he'd walked up behind them, flanked by Ainsworth and Bayliss.

"Come on, Jas, this is stupid," Jackson protested. "We won't take it all, but we're entitled to some of this stuff. It's *ours*."

"It's staying here. You're going back into Chadwick, aren't you, so you can get more. Remember, we're stopping here for a while longer yet. We need this more than you do."

"Yes, but not all of it. Christ, there's only going to be a handful of you staying behind. And anyway, just a couple of days back you were telling us all how you were going to rape and pillage the whole country."

"That's in the future. Until then, we need those supplies."

"And so do *we*!"

Jackson turned his back on Jas and shook the door but it wouldn't open. He took a knife from his belt and started trying to force the lock.

"Go and find Kieran," he said under his breath to Harte. "Talk some sense into him. See if you can get the other key off him."

Before Harte could move, Jas grabbed hold of Jackson and threw him away from the gift shop entrance. Jas had a clear strength advantage, and Jackson was sent flying. He landed on the floor then got up, brushed himself down and ran at the door, trying to shoulder-charge it open. It was stronger than it looked and he simply bounced back off it, but he tried again, regardless.

"You'll never do it, you fucking idiot," Jas said. He was about to speak again when someone shouted behind him.

211

"Stop her!"

Jas spun around and saw that Lorna was helping herself to more supplies from the back of one of the trucks. She scooped up as much as she could carry and sprinted over to the bus. Following her lead, several others did the same.

For a moment longer Jackson tried to force the door. When Jas didn't come at him again, he looked back and saw him running off toward the truck which was rapidly being emptied by Lorna and the others. Driver was standing in the middle of the courtyard, watching the chaos unfolding all around him, dumbstruck.

"Get the fucking bus started," Jackson screamed at him as he ran past. "Let's get out of here."

Lorna weaved around Jas, slipping down onto one knee momentarily, just managing to hold on to everything she was carrying. She threw herself forward and scrambled up onto the bus, barely getting through the open door before Driver came storming up behind her. He clambered into his cab and started the engine, sinking into his seat with relief. He looked behind and saw that there were only a handful of people onboard. More were running over from the caravans, terrified that they were going to be left behind. Howard stumbled up the steps, his arms overloaded.

Outside, Jas positioned himself directly between the front of the bus and the gate. Charlie Moorehouse tripped while carrying two heavy cellophane-wrapped packs of bottled water, and while he was off-balance Ainsworth shoved him right over and put a boot between his shoulder blades, preventing him from getting up. Elsewhere, Zoe fought to get past Will Bayliss, who was blocking her way back to the bus. She tried to barge him out of the way but he stood his ground. She went to slap him but he was too fast. He caught her wrist and twisted her arm around so her position was reversed. He shoved her up onto the bus, empty-handed.

"You can fuck off," he spat at her. "I'll be glad to see the back of you."

"Don't do this, Jas," Jackson said, refusing to show any anger or malice as he approached the other man, arms open but still carrying the knife he'd been using to try and force the gift shop door open. He sheathed it to show his peaceful intentions.

"Unload the supplies," Jas said, "and I'll let you leave."

"You'll let us leave!" Jackson laughed. "Come on, Jas, grow up. What do you think this is, a movie? We've all made our individual decisions, just like you insisted. Everyone's had their say and made their choice, now you have to respect those choices."

"I can't. I've got a conscience."

"What are you talking about? You could come with us. You *should* come with us."

"How many times do we need to have this argument? The island is a dead end. A full stop. Going there won't do anybody any favors."

"I think you're wrong."

"I know I'm right."

"Come on, Jas, it doesn't have to be like this."

All around Jas and Jackson, the furious activity had suddenly stopped. Many of the people who wanted to leave had made it onto the bus, but several more hadn't. They now stood a cautious distance away, unsure what to do next, too afraid to move. Driver inched the bus forward slightly, and that small movement was enough to cause panic again. The remaining would-be escapees ran toward the noisy vehicle, too many for Ainsworth and Bayliss to stop. Paul Field caught Bob Wilkins, rugby-tackling him as he tried to run past. He held him facedown in the gravel, virtually sitting on him to keep him down.

"No one's going anywhere," Jas announced.

"He's got a gun!" Shirley Brinksford screamed as she tried to get onto the bus. Jackson looked up and saw that Kieran had appeared, brandishing the same rifle he'd shoved into his face when he'd first arrived at the castle.

"Get them out of here!" Jackson bellowed to Driver, who immediately responded. Caron hauled Shirley up onto the bus just as the doors closed with a hiss of hydraulics. The bus juddered forward, then began to pick up speed. Driver saw that Jackson had suddenly started running toward the gate. Jas turned around and realized what was happening, but Driver managed to drive forward and position the bus directly between the two of them to give Jackson a brief but necessary advantage. Jackson reached up and lifted the heavy wooden crossbar which secured the gate from its brackets, then threw it to one side. He grabbed one of the thick ropes hanging from either side of the gate and pulled it open. A clot of dead flesh, which had been pushed up hard against the outside of the barrier by the force of many more pushing from behind, immediately freed itself and fell forward. Almost completely unrecognizable as the remains of the teenage boy it had once been, the putrescence-dripping shadow of a man took a few staggering steps before more of the foul things overtook and trampled over it. Everyone, Jas and Jackson included, was transfixed momentarily by the hideous sight. How any of these things could continue to function in such a pitiful condition was beyond anyone's comprehension.

Jackson was the first to move again. He jumped the decaying body lying in front of him and ran over to the other side of the gate. He'd only managed to half open it when Jas came at him again. He viciously grabbed Jackson around the waist and wrestled him away. Beside them, more of the dead spilled forward, moving together like a viscous, disease-filled sludge, a slowly spreading pool of decay.

Driver tried to get through, but the gap ahead wasn't wide

enough. In response to the sudden movement of the bus, Kieran fired a warning shot. The recoil took Kieran by surprise—he'd only had cause to fire a couple of times previously—and he misfired and shattered the windscreen, only just missing Driver. The air was immediately filled with panicked screams. People who were even now still trying to get onto the bus hammered on the door at the same time as those trying to get off. Kieran reloaded and moved around to the other side, firing twice more at close range, each time hitting one of the bus's massive tires, leaving the heavy vehicle listing to one side.

Jackson freed himself from Jas's grip and ran to try and stop Kieran firing. Jas—too fast for him—caught hold of him again before he was anywhere near. He dragged Jackson back and slammed him down into several inches of the foul-smelling, once-human slurry that continued to spread across the courtyard like an oil slick. Jackson gagged at the overpowering stench and the feel of the ice-cold muck on his skin. Winded, he spat out splashes of flesh and struggled to speak.

"Why, Jas?" he wheezed, his voice little more than a whisper. Jas stood up and walked a few paces away. Jackson slowly picked himself up, slipping in the decay, every bone in his body aching. He managed only a few steps before dropping to his knees again. With his energy fading, he stood up straight once more and took the knife from his belt. "You have to let them make their own decisions, and you have to abide by what they decide. You can't decide for them."

He ran at Jas again. His back turned, Jas heard his heavy footsteps and turned at the last possible moment. He grabbed hold of Jackson's arm as he lunged at him, then flipped him over onto his stomach and dropped down onto his back. Jackson groaned with pain, but this time he didn't fight back. He didn't move.

"You're wrong," Jas hissed in his ear, crouching down so no one else could hear. "You've got this all wrong. If we want to survive, then we've got to work together and we need to base ourselves here. There's nothing to be gained from going to this bloody island. You hear me, Jackson?"

When Jackson didn't react, Jas grabbed his shoulder, still soaked with glistening decay, and rolled him over onto his back. He staggered away in shock. Jackson's knife had sunk hilt-deep into his belly. Sue Preston forced her way off the now useless bus—followed by a flood of others—and ran over to help Jackson, but there was nothing she could do. He was already dead. The courtyard emptied as people ran for cover. Kieran walked forward and looked down at Jackson's body, a flood of deep-red blood pulsing steadily from his wound.

On the other side of the castle grounds, another engine was started. Hidden from Jas and Kieran's view by the wrecked bus, neither of them saw the black Ford Fiesta until it skidded out into the open and accelerated toward the gate, churning up gravel.

"Get the fucking gate shut!" Jas yelled, his voice hoarse with anger and shock. Kieran and Bayliss ran to close up the barrier. Kieran weaved around an abhorrent corpse which had just enough muscle remaining to be able to walk unsteadily. It reached out for him and he recoiled, slipping over in the greasy decay which continued to spill forward in a slow-motion flood of filth. He got up, then dived out of the way again as the Fiesta powered past, skidding through the sludge between him and Bayliss. It squeezed through the gap by the barest of margins, clipping the gate and losing the driver's wing mirror in the process.

Kieran picked himself up and pushed his side of the gate shut, gagging at the low wave of putrefied gunk and driftwood-like bones which rippled back as he did so. Bayliss closed the other side and between them they dropped the crossbar back into place.

"Who the hell was that?" Jas demanded.

"That was my car," Melanie whined.

"Never mind that, who was driving it?"

"Harte," Kieran replied.

31

Eleven o'clock came and went. The waiting at the marina in Chadwick was interminable. As each minute passed by, the likelihood that they'd be returning to Cormansey without anyone else seemed to be increasing.

"So what happens if they don't get here?" Donna asked, her anxiety mounting. "We can't just leave them."

"What else are we supposed to do?" Cooper replied. "We gave them a decent timescale with plenty of opportunity. We said we'd wait until midday and we will. If none of them are here by then, we leave."

"Anything could have happened," Harry said. "Absolutely anything."

"My money's on Jas," Richard sighed. "He's a troubled soul, that one. Scared to death of putting a foot outside the castle wall, he is. He'll have been putting pressure on all of the rest of them not to leave, you mark my words. They'll have agreed to stay there just to pacify him."

"We've done what we said we would," Cooper said. "We've given them more than enough time. There's still the best part of an hour to go."

"Like Cooper says, they've had plenty long enough. If they were coming, you'd have thought they'd have virtually followed you back. Maybe they just decided they didn't want to go with us after all," Michael suggested.

"Or someone suggested for them," Richard said.

"Whatever the reason, it's out of our hands now," Cooper said. "Our priority is the people on Cormansey, and we need to get back to them with these supplies. Whether the others stay at the castle or not, they'll be okay. One thing Jas was right about is the amount of stuff they're going to be able to help themselves to once the dead are finished. It's not the same back on the island. They need the stuff we've collected. *We* need it. This is about people's lives."

"I'll be honest," Richard said. "Whether we take anyone else back or not, I just want out of here now. This is a dead place. I've left too many bad memories here for my liking."

Harte raced toward Chadwick, struggling to find his way into the town along mazelike roads which all looked the same. Although he'd spent more time than anyone else around the port and its surroundings, most of the time he'd been on foot and he'd never actually driven this route from the castle himself. He'd only been this way once before, and that was on the ill-fated looting expedition from which he'd failed to return. Everywhere looked depressingly featureless: a confusion of chaos, littered with debris and the remains of endless bodies. He knew he was against the clock but he'd screwed up and wasted fifteen minutes driving the wrong way before he'd realized, and that had just added to the pressure. He'd been desperately disorientated—almost completely lost—and it was only when he saw the names of a couple of nearby places he remembered hearing Jas, Kieran, and Jackson talk about that he knew he was finally heading in the right direction.

For what felt like mile after endless mile there was nothing but trees, hedges, and the occasional building on either side of the road. His speed was restricted by the appalling carnage all around, the remnants of a world untended for almost four months. Nothing was where it should be anymore. The roads themselves were becoming harder to distinguish: winding tracks covered in sludge-like decay, the curbs disappearing into the undergrowth. Exposed bones were becoming increasingly visible through the abhorrent mire, looking like the fallen branches of trees after a particularly violent storm.

After reaching the top of a hill, Harte caught a glimpse of the ocean in the distance. Twenty minutes to go, give or take, and only a few miles left to cover. The sight of the water gave him renewed hope that he'd get to the marina in time, and that he'd be able to tell Cooper and the others what had happened back at the castle. A bend in the road obscured his view momentarily, but within seconds he could see the ocean again, and this time he could see the town too. He accelerated, arms locked as he struggled to keep control down a steep incline and then, just before it disappeared below the treetops, he saw it. Perched back on top of the multistory car park was the helicopter.

Another long, straight climb and an equally long and frantic descent, and he'd finally reached a part of the road network he was sure he recognized. He'd definitely driven into Chadwick this way with Jas, Driver, and the others on that ice-cold, snow-covered morning just before he'd taken leave of them all and disappeared. Part of him wished he'd stayed where he'd been hiding in the apartment a little farther up the coast. Much as the isolation had been becoming increasingly hard to handle, staying there alone would have been infinitely easier than the brief return to Cheetham Castle he'd made yesterday. He couldn't help thinking he was to blame for the chaos he'd left back there. If he hadn't led the helicopter to them, they'd have been none the wiser. Maybe the people at the castle would have been okay without him. Perhaps they'd have lasted through the final days of the dead without incident as Jas had wanted. Sure, they wouldn't have had an easy time of it, but maybe they'd have coped. They had so far—well, most of them, anyway. He thought he'd been doing the right thing, but all he'd done was put other people in danger.

The right thing for who? he asked himself as he struggled to keep the car moving at speed. *Me or everyone else?*

Harte swung the car around a tight corner, a little over a mile short of the very center of town now, maybe a mile and a half from the marina. His wheels skidded on a greasy sheen of frost and compacted decay, and for a heart-stopping moment the back end of the souped-up Fiesta threatened to slide out of control. Harte recovered and kept his foot down on the accelerator. And then, as he drove the wrong way around a roundabout to aim toward the marina, he saw something which made him accelerate again. He had to look twice, unsure if it was just his mind playing tricks.

It wasn't.

The rotor blades on top of the helicopter were spinning.

He pressed down hard on the gas, gripping the steering wheel tighter as he plowed into and drove straight through two corpses. There were more bodies around here—a sure sign he was close. When he next looked up, he could see that the helicopter had taken off and was hovering above the car park roof.

Harte looked down at the road again and instinctively slammed on his brakes. One of the remaining dead had dragged itself into the middle of the tarmac. It was crawling along on its hands and knees, too weak now to stand up straight, and because of its low height he almost didn't see it in time. He wrenched the

221

wheel hard left, skidded around the crawling corpse, then threw the car back the other way.

Now the helicopter was definitely climbing. He could see it rising up above the rest of the buildings. A flash of light distracted him—the sun glinting off a window—and he looked down and saw another corpse in the road directly ahead. This one was upright, arms outstretched in a clichéd pose, brown rags of soiled clothing and saggy flaps of skin hanging off what was left of its emaciated frame like sticky robes. It was too late to avoid it, so he simply kept driving. The body dissolved on impact, showering the car with a gutful of wet yellow-black gore, and the foul distraction was such that Harte didn't see a small pedestrian crossing in the middle of the road. He reacted late and hit a concrete traffic island at full speed, the impact with the front driver's-side wheel hard enough to send the car spinning around through a complete 360-degree turn. Thrown back in his seat, his feet slipped off the pedals and the engine stalled. When he tried to start it again, it wouldn't turn over, and the only engine noise he could still hear was that of the rapidly disappearing helicopter.

Frantically, Harte scrambled out of the car and ran, briefly glancing back to see a flat front tire, a badly damaged wing, and a flood of oil or power-steering fluid or something similar dribbling out along the road after him.

He ran through the streets as fast as he could, dividing his attention between weaving through the grotesque corpses and watching the helicopter overhead. It continued to hover above the town, and just for a second he allowed himself to believe that Richard and whoever else was up there with him might have seen him. Maybe they were going back to the castle again to see what had happened to the others? He glanced at his watch. It was past midday. His only option now was to try and get to the marina in time.

The roads along which he now sprinted were increasingly filled with dead flesh, drawn here over the last couple of days by the presence of the survivors and their activity in and around the marina. He moved so fast that they were of little threat and even lesser consequence. Some of them went to grab at him as he hurtled past, but most didn't even realize he was there until he'd already gone. He darted down along the slope which led to the water, still watching the helicopter as it moved out over the ocean, flying extraordinarily low now.

Harte broke right to avoid another cadaver, and ran straight into one of the still-smoldering dustbin fires which had first guided him here in the darkness a couple of nights ago. He knocked it over, sending sparks and ash spilling out over the cold ground, just managing to jump over the rolling dustbin. Up ahead now he could see the luxury cruiser where he'd first found the others. He pounded along the jetty and climbed on board but it was too late—there was no one here, just the remains of the meal he'd shared with them that night and a few more empty beer bottles. But wait, they'd never intended to leave the mainland in this vessel, he remembered. Cooper had told him they'd loaded all their supplies onto another boat elsewhere.

Back the other way.

It was hard to see much of anything through the mass of masts and the countless moored boats of various classes. He ran back toward the marina entrance, barely able to keep moving now, soaked with sweat, and then dragged himself out along another jetty. He ran out to the end of the narrow wooden decking which stretched beyond the last of the boats, and looked out over the water. He sank to his knees. Out there, rapidly disappearing toward the horizon, the helicopter gracefully drifted away. And below it on the water, a single boat.

223

What did he do now? He ruled out the most obvious two answers in order of impossibility: go back to the castle and try and salvage something from the chaos there, or get into a boat and try to find the island on his own. If he could just find a map and compass, then remember the name of the damn island, then teach himself to navigate, then learn how to sail a bloody boat . . .

Who was he kidding? Everything was completely fucked. His best option—probably the only real option remaining—was to either go back to the cruiser or the flat he'd previously occupied, lock the fucking door behind him, and never take a single step outside again.

"Harte, what the hell is going on?" a voice shouted from out of nowhere. He scrambled back to his feet, then spun around and saw Michael standing at the other end of the jetty.

32

"You're bloody lucky. Another couple of minutes and we'd have been gone," Harry said as he passed Harte a bottle of water and a towel. Harte wiped his face dry and drank thirstily, then tried to ask the first of the hundreds of questions which had flooded into his brain. He could barely speak, let alone think straight.

"Why . . . ?" was all he could manage.

"Why what? Why are we still here?" Michael asked. Harte nodded. "Like Harry said," he explained, "we weren't planning on hanging around much longer. Did you see Cooper and Richard? We were supposed to be following them."

"We put the supplies on the other boat and left this one empty for all the passengers we were supposed to be taking," Harry said. "We stopped back to try and load up a few more things before we left. I swear, mate, you caught us by the skin of your teeth."

"Anyway," Michael said, leaning back against the cabin wall and watching Harte intently, "more to the point, why are *you* here?"

"You're making a habit of abandoning your mates, aren't you?" Harry added unnecessarily.

Harte finished his water, wiped his face again, and tried to explain.

"It's Jas," he said. "The fucker's completely lost the plot. We were getting ready to clear out and he went ape-shit. We were just trying to get our share of the supplies and he flew off the handle. Before we knew what was happening there were guns going off and he was fighting with Jackson and all sorts."

Michael looked at Harry. "Sounds about right from what Cooper and Donna said. That's the guy who thought living on an island was a bad idea? Cooper said there'd probably be some trouble with him."

"You can say that again."

"So what exactly happened?"

"I didn't see it all—"

"Too busy plotting your escape?"

Harte ignored Harry's cheap jibe and continued. "Jas reckons the island is too restrictive. Thinks it's too cut off."

"Doesn't make any difference these days," Michael said quickly. "Where you are is far less important than—"

"Listen, you don't have to convince me," Harte interrupted, "I've already had this argument. I was planning to go with you, remember? Look, no one really knows what the best long-term option is anymore, no one can, but most folks seemed to have decided that going with you guys was the safer option."

"And this Jas wouldn't let them?"

"That's about it."

"So what do we do now?" Harry asked. "Just head back home like we agreed?"

"You can't," Harte said, an uncharacteristic urgency in his voice. "The only reason people aren't here is because they *couldn't* get away, not because they didn't want to."

"And what about you? Are you just here because you were still hoping to catch a lift?"

Harte shook his head and looked at both of the other two men. He wasn't sure what they thought of him. Did they believe anything he said?

"I came back because I want your help," he said. "I know I ran away before and yes, I did it because I was a coward and I didn't want to go back to the castle. But you've got to believe me, this is different. My friends are trapped back there, and I want to get them out."

33

The castle was a hive of frightened activity. The beaten-up bus sat useless in the middle of the courtyard like a beached whale. Its other tires had been slashed to make sure it wasn't going anywhere, and all the supplies which had been loaded onboard had been removed. All around, people carried out Jas's orders, passed to them by Kieran, Bayliss, Ainsworth, and Field. Field himself stood guard in front of the gate, a rifle held where everyone could see it, his presence alone enough to deter anyone from trying to get out. He occasionally barked instructions at Howard and Bob, who were shoveling the remains of the dead into wheelbarrows, then dumping them into the overfull cesspit. They were both exhausted, too tired to even think about rebelling now. Jackson's body had been taken over to the cesspit area too. His corpse had been left by the outside wall, wrapped in a tarpaulin and dumped next to where Steve Morecombe had been buried a week and a half earlier. No one would notice the stink over there, Field had said.

Jas watched the proceedings alone from the top of the gatehouse, keen to put as much distance as possible between himself and everyone else. It had taken him more than an hour and two cans of lager to stop shaking after Jackson's death. He was overwhelmed by a raft of unexpected emotions: guilt, fear, anger, remorse . . . but there was nothing he could do. *It wasn't my fault. What's done is done*, he kept telling himself. *I need to get this lot back on track now. Let them forget about the helicopter and that bloody island and all that bullshit. Another few weeks and we can move out of here.*

But he kept coming back to one dark thought.

I've killed a man.

He tried to focus on something—anything—else, but it was impossible. He hadn't actually sunk the knife into the other man's chest, but he may as well have. Over the months he'd destroyed untold hundreds of those wretched cadavers which walked the dead world outside, dispatching even the least decayed, most human of them without a second's thought—but this was different. Completely different.

Less than a hundred people left alive that I know of, and I killed one of them . . .

"What do you want me to do with them?"

Jas, startled by the unexpected voice, quickly turned around. It was Kieran.

"What?"

"I asked you what you want me to do with them. Do we just keep them locked up in the caravans for now?"

Jas thought for a moment. "Might as well," he replied, trying not to sound as distracted and nervous as he felt. "Use the vans nearest the gatehouse. Let them calm down. We need to get everything back to how it was before those fuckers turned up here and screwed everything up."

Kieran paused before answering. "Okay. You're the boss."

He turned to go back downstairs, but Jas called to him before he disappeared.

"We're doing the right thing, you know," he said. Kieran nodded. "Look, no one meant for any of this to happen. Fact is, they'll have fucked off back to their island again by now, so what's done is done." He walked over to the other man. "Get some food going. Get a couple of the girls working in the kitchen, and crack open a few bottles of booze, the best stuff you can find. Keep the people safe and warm and give them what they want within reason. Let's not give them any excuses to try anything we might all end up regretting."

34

The basic communications Harry had rigged up between the two boats and the helicopter worked intermittently, their efficiency steadily fading away with range. Between the frequent bursts of static and the increasingly long radio silences, Harry managed to get sufficient information to Richard, Donna, and Cooper so that everyone knew what was happening.

With the *Summer Breeze* full of supplies, Donna and Cooper had little option but to continue back to Cormansey. There was nothing to be gained from them turning back. Richard stayed with them for a while, flying close and remaining in contact until he was sure they could reach the small port close to Danver's Lye. He then flew back to the mainland, cursing the fact that, yet again, everything seemed to be down to him.

Harry, Harte, and Michael watched the helicopter land on top of the car park. About twenty minutes later Richard returned to the marina, breathless.

"Bloody hell, I hate being out there on my own," he admitted. "It's a ghost town. You turn any corner and there are still those things waiting for you. Good job they're so slow. They scare the shit out of me, they do." He stopped talking and looked at the others. "What?"

"You finished?" Harry asked.

"Sorry," he mumbled. "Bit nervous, that's all."

He followed them onto the virtually empty *Duchess*, feeling self-conscious.

"Donna and Cooper get back to Cormansey okay?" Harry asked.

"I left them a few miles short. They'll be there by now."

"Did you stop and land . . . ?" Michael started to ask. Richard shook his head.

"Wasn't any point. I turned around and came straight back. They'll explain to the others as soon as they've moored. So what's the plan? I'm assuming that we *do* have a plan?"

"Get back to the castle and get those who want out, out," Harry flippantly replied.

"Simple," Richard said, equally flippantly. "I'll just land in the middle of the castle and ship them out in threes and fours. No one will mind."

"How the hell *are* we going to do it?" Harte asked, nervously chewing his fingers. "Because you're right, we're not going to be able to just fly in. Jas is going to be seriously pissed off. He's not going to let anyone in or out without a fight."

"Then we'll have to find another way," Michael said, stating the obvious.

"Whoa . . . *you're* not going anywhere," Richard interrupted. "You can't. You've got Emma and the baby to think about."

"I think about them all the time," he said, suddenly sounding subdued. "Thing is, I'm here now, and it doesn't look like I'm going anywhere until we've got Harte's people out of this castle. There's no way I *can't* get involved, is there?"

"But you should stay out of trouble. Wait here for the rest of us to get back . . ."

Michael was shaking his head. "There's no point. I told you, I've been doing a lot of thinking. Things are different now. Believe me, there's nowhere I'd rather be than back on the island with Emma. I fall asleep thinking about her and the baby at night, and I wake up every morning still thinking about them. But at the end of the day, me not being there isn't going to make a massive amount of difference. It wouldn't be the end of the world."

"You've missed that," Harry mumbled. "That's already been and gone."

Michael ignored him. This was serious.

"What I'm saying is, there's nothing I can do to help the baby be born, is there? I mean, I can do all the practical stuff and run errands and all that, but me being around won't make a huge difference to Emma giving birth, will it?"

"I think you're doing yourself a huge disservice," Richard said. "Your missus and your kid will need you. There's another fifty bods back on Cormansey who can do chores and run errands, but you're the only one Emma actually needs. You shouldn't take any risks you don't need to, that's all I'm saying."

"But these are risks we *do* need to take," Michael said. "Imagine the difference another ten or so folks will make on Cormansey."

"I understand what you're saying, but I still don't agree."

"Well, that's how it is. I've made my decision. You'd all probably do the same thing if you were in my shoes."

"This is all very lovely," Harte said cynically, "but it's all academic anyway. How the hell are we going to get them out of the castle? Are we just going to stroll up to the front door and knock and ask if Jas will let them out?"

"He's right," Richard agreed. "This is a fool's errand."

"No, it isn't," Harry said from the corner. "I know exactly how we'll do it."

35

Caron and Lorna had been locked in the café kitchen to prepare the food Jas had ordered.

"I'd piss in this if I wasn't going to have to eat it myself," Lorna said, seething with anger, barely able to keep calm. "Who the fuck does Jas think he is?"

She stirred a vast pot of soup they'd bulked up with tinned vegetables. Caron was busy steaming a job lot of chocolate puddings they'd found in the stores. She hunted through various crates and trays for a box of catering–size packets of custard powder she was sure she'd seen recently.

"Have you seen the custard powder?" she asked.

"No, I haven't seen any fucking custard powder," Lorna yelled at her. "Fucking hell, Caron, there are more important things to think about right now than pudding."

Unfazed by Lorna's outburst, Caron found what she'd been looking for. She dropped the box onto the table next to the gas burner she was using.

"This should be nice," she said.

"Nice! For fuck's sake, who gives a damn if the food tastes

nice? Are you completely fucking stupid? Haven't you seen what's been happening around here? Jackson's dead, in case you hadn't noticed."

"Of course I've noticed," Caron snapped, finally showing a little emotion. "Stupid thing to say."

"Then why are you talking about custard and things tasting nice? Our last decent chance to get out of this place disappeared this afternoon."

"I'm well aware of that, thank you very much."

"You don't act like you are."

Caron stopped and stared at Lorna.

"Getting shitty with me isn't going to make any difference," she said, instantly slipping back into "mother mode" and talking to Lorna the same way she used to try reasoning with Matthew, her late son. "I know exactly what's going on. We are where we are, Lorna, and there's absolutely nothing you or I can do about it for the moment. We need to make the most of what we've still got, because the way things are going, we might lose that tomorrow. Now, have you seen any clean bowls?"

"No," Lorna grunted.

"I don't know what's wrong with these people," Caron continued, conveniently forgetting the blatantly obvious fact that what was wrong with these people was that, through no fault of their own, their lives had been destroyed and that even now, several months further down the line, many of them were still completely fucking traumatized. Trivializing everything seemed to be helping Caron cope tonight. "I don't know," she grumbled to herself, "people help themselves, leave their dirty cups and plates all over the place, then moan at us when there's none left."

"Am I supposed to care, Caron? Fuck 'em. I'll ladle this shit into their bare fucking hands if they complain."

"I'm going to see what I can find outside, okay?"

"Whatever."

Caron picked up an empty washing-up bowl with which she could carry back any dirty crockery she found lying around the site. She knocked on the door between the kitchen and the café to get the attention of Mark Ainsworth, who was standing guard outside. He was leaning up against a wall, his head drooping, half asleep. Caron's knocking woke him up.

"Got to go and collect up some dishes, okay?" she shouted at him through a window. He didn't say anything, he just yawned, nodded, and let her out.

The door slammed shut and Lorna continued to work, trying to concentrate on the food and block out everything else. It was all an effort. Her arm ached, her back ached, her head ached . . . She cursed herself, wishing she'd been as selfish as Harte. If she'd been more with it then she'd have been out of here by now, and maybe some of the others would have got away with her too. As it was, she was stuck. And Jackson was dead. Had Jas meant to kill him? The same Jas she'd spent the last few months with . . .

This was like something out of a bad dream, and yet it was frighteningly real. Caron's words rattled around her head: make the most of what you've got today, because you might lose it tomorrow. Christ, how right she was. The fact that Jas had committed an act so foul and out of character just served to confirm something she'd suspected for a long time now: the farther they got from their old lives, the less they resembled the people they used to be. What would be the end result? Would they manage to stop the rot and salvage some semblance of normality, or this time next year would they all be running around like savages? She continued to stir the soup as she thought about the world beyond the castle walls, emptier than ever, with all the previously enforced

236

restrictions about where you could and couldn't go and what you could or couldn't do now removed. Theoretically she was free to roam wherever she wanted, provided she could get out of this fucking place and—

Lorna froze rigid when a hand touched her shoulder. She spun around, heart pounding, ready to attack with the ladle she'd been using to stir the soup.

It was Mark Ainsworth. She relaxed slightly. Only slightly.

"Sorry, love," he said. "I didn't mean to startle you."

"Then why did you creep up on me like that, you idiot?" she yelled back at him. "And I'm not your 'love,' okay? I'm not anybody's love."

He backed away, hands held up in submission.

"Sorry," he said again.

"What do you want, anyway?"

"Cup of tea would nice, if you're offering."

"I'm not. You know where everything is, make it yourself."

"No need to be like that . . ."

"Piss off."

"You want one?"

"No."

Ainsworth fetched himself a mug and made his drink with hot water from the steamer Caron had been using, all the time watching Lorna. She sensed him staring at her but refused to make eye contact. *Just ignore him and he'll go away.*

But Ainsworth wasn't going anywhere.

"Look," he said, "I think we both got off on the wrong foot. I don't want any trouble. I just want us to get along."

"We'll get along fine if you fuck off and stay out of my face, understand?"

"That's not going to be so easy now we're all stuck here."

237

"You've got your mate Jas to thank for that."

"I thought he was *your* mate?"

"He's no friend of mine. Not after today."

"Don't let him hear you talking like that, eh?"

"Why, what's he going to do? Kill me?"

"I won't let him hurt you, Lorna. I'll look out for you."

"You come anywhere near me and I'll have your balls."

"You can have my balls anytime, lover," he said, slipping into sleaze mode with uncomfortable ease and immediately regretting it.

"Come anywhere near me and I swear I'll cut them off and shove them down your bloody throat."

He was about to make some stupid, insensitive quip about Lorna's kinks and vices when he stopped himself. She looked angry enough to carry out her threats. He paused, knowing he should probably leave, but still wanting to say more.

"Look, Lorna, I'm sorry," he said. "It's just my humor. I don't mean anything by it, it's just the way I deal with all of this." He watched her for a moment longer. When she didn't react, he decided to risk talking again. "You're right, we are all stuck here. I don't want to fight with you."

"Then like I said, stay away."

"Things are going to get difficult around here, I'm sure they are. I'll watch out for you."

"Don't bother."

"I want to. I like you, Lorna. I think we could—"

He immediately shut up when the door behind him flew open. Caron barged in to the kitchen, carrying a rattling bowl full of dirty washing-up. She sensed something was wrong and looked at Lorna, concerned.

"Everything all right?"

"Everything's fine," Lorna said, not looking up.

"I was just leaving," said Ainsworth.

"Good," Lorna mumbled. She glanced over her shoulder and watched him leave.

"I'll catch you later, ladies."

"Hope not," Caron said, just loud enough for him to hear.

36

Cooper wasn't a natural captain, and Donna freely admitted she
didn't have a clue. Richard had guided them close enough so that
they could see Cormansey in the near distance—a beautiful, inspir-
ing sight, a few fires and the first lights of early evening burning
through the endless darkness of absolutely everything else—but it
had taken several hours longer for them to navigate around to the
small port near Danver's Lye. By the time they were finally ready to
disembark, a large crowd of villagers was already waiting on the jetty.

Jackie Soames and Jack Baxter were near the front of the
group. Jack caught the landing rope Cooper threw to him, and tied
up the boat.

"Good to see you back," Jackie said, helping Donna onto dry
land, then hugging her affectionately. "We were starting to get
worried. What's with the helicopter turning back again?"

"There's nothing to worry about," Cooper said, sounding
subdued.

"Nothing to worry about?" Donna yelled at him.

"What's wrong?" Jack asked. "Where's Michael and Harry?"

"We need to get the boat emptied so we can head back,"
Donna said, ignoring his question.

"We're not going back," Cooper told her. It was clear from the tone of his voice there would be no negotiation.

"I am. I'll take someone else if you won't go."

Donna and Cooper stood on the jetty meters apart, barely able to maintain eye contact with each other. Jackie pushed her way between them.

"Look, will one of you please tell us what the hell is going on?"

"Michael, Harry, and Richard are fine," Cooper explained. "We found more survivors. We were hoping to bring them back with us, but there was a complication."

"A complication?"

"A couple of egos facing off against each other. Nothing too serious."

"Nothing serious?" Donna protested. "Fuck, were you listening to the same radio message as me? Harry said someone had been killed."

A ripple of low noise spread through the crowd gathered on the jetty.

"So where exactly are the others?" Jackie asked.

"They've gone back to try and get them out," Cooper replied. "There's no point us going back to help. There's nothing we can do. They've got enough room and by the time we get there they'll be on their way over."

"Jesus," Jackie said. "And Michael's gone too? Bloody hell, what will poor Emma say?"

"Do we have to tell her? I mean, they should be back sometime tomorrow and—"

"Of course we have to tell her," Donna yelled at him, barely able to believe what she was hearing. "Michael's the father of her child. She's got a right to know."

"Did you bring me back any fags, Cooper?" Jackie asked.

"Plenty, why?"

241

"And booze?"

"Loads, as ordered."

"Good, because I think I need a drink. Anybody care to join me?"

"Not for me," Cooper said. "You're right, Donna, I'll go and see Emma and let her know what—"

"You stay away from her," Donna interrupted, pushing past Cooper and moving through the crowd on the jetty. "Leave her alone. *I'll* go."

37

It was dark and cold. A full moon illuminated far too much of Chadwick and its dead population for Michael's liking. He was standing on the car park roof, looking out toward the ocean and doing his best to ignore everything that lay between him and the edge of the water.

"We ready?" Richard asked, hanging out of the helicopter door.

"Go for it," Harry said, and he climbed into the seat next to the pilot's. Harte was already in the back. Michael got in, sat down next to him and buckled up.

"You're all completely sure about this?" Richard said as he ran through his preflight checks and started the powerful machine. "Hell of a risk, this."

"I don't see we have much choice," Michael said as the noise and vibration increased. "We have to try."

"Fair enough."

Richard pulled back on the controls and took off. The helicopter rapidly climbed up into the night.

The helicopter was over the castle in no time at all. Richard banked around and peered down into the courtyard. He could already see people down there, looking up, following the aircraft as it circled. He switched on his searchlight, both to help him and make it more difficult for those on the ground to track his movements. There weren't as many people out in the open as he'd expected to see. Where were the rest of them? They'd already ruled out trying to touch down within the castle wall, but that was academic now because much of the courtyard below was filled with rubbish and clutter. The bus occupied the area where he'd set down previously. He couldn't land there even if he wanted to.

He completed another circuit, a little lower this time, sweeping around the castle and trying to distract and confuse the people down below. He could see figures up on the top of the gatehouse. When he saw one of them lift a rifle then fire it, he knew it was time to leave. He broke off from his flight path and flew back toward Chadwick, climbing rapidly, not about to risk being hit.

In an overgrown field a mile and a half farther north, Michael, Harte, and Harry stood and watched the lights of the helicopter disappear. Between them they carried a mass of mountaineering equipment which had been looted from Chadwick in the hours prior to them setting out again. Harry already had much of it prepared. While most people who had survived had cast off virtually all remnants of the lives they used to lead, others had found new outlets for the skills they'd previously employed. As an outdoor activities instructor, many of the things Harry had spent his time teaching to school kids and corporate employees on team building weekends were still proving useful. Sailing for one. Mountain craft and rock climbing another.

They clambered over a low dry-stone wall which ran around the perimeter of the field where Richard had set them down before flying over the castle. The moon highlighted everything with its ice-white light, but Michael wished it would disappear as they approached the outermost edge of part of the vast crowd of bodies which had encircled the castle. Although the immediate threat the dead once posed had now been substantially reduced, and the plummeting temperature had restricted them further tonight, crossing this immense sea of decay was still a daunting prospect. The three men stood together on the last patch of clear grass they could find, each of them looking for reasons to delay the next step forward.

Harry hoisted a long coil of heavy climbing rope up onto his shoulder and looked toward the castle up ahead.

"There's nothing much in the way of cover out here," he said, "but I don't think anyone's going to be expecting us to walk through this lot."

"I don't think they're expecting anything," Michael said, sounding more confident than he felt. "I think they'll have fallen for Richard's little bluff. They'll think we're all still in the helicopter."

"Is this going to work?" Harte mumbled, far less confident than the others. Everything had made sense back at the port, but the nearer they'd got to the castle, the more uncertain he'd begun to feel.

"If we're careful it should," Michael replied. "Like I said, Jas won't be expecting this. And if you're right and more of them want to leave than want to stay, then he's going to be well outnumbered too."

"Suppose," he said, still not convinced.

"Come on, ladies," Harry said, tired of dawdling, "let's just get this done, shall we? Opposite end to the gatehouse, you reckon?"

"That's our best bet," Harte replied. "No caravans or anything else around there as far as I can remember. There's the cesspit, but that's all. The bloody stink from that keeps most folk away."

"That'll do, then."

Harry took his hesitant first step into the remains of the dead. His boot cracked a thin sheen of ice, then sank into a layer of mud and decay that was several inches thick. The ground—what he could see of it—was unexpectedly uneven. The mulch they were going to have to walk through was filled with buried bones and other less obvious obstacles. He stopped walking as suddenly as he'd started, and tried to work out the physics of the crowd. There were shapes that were more recognizable as human up ahead, but out here on the fringes everything appeared to have been reduced to a featureless sludge. That made sense. New arrivals to the massive gathering would have been less restricted and, over time, would have crushed their weaker brethren under their feet as they'd advanced toward the castle, creating a compacted layer of dirt and gore. The situation would no doubt change as they got deeper into the decay.

They walked in single file. Harry attempted to lead them in a relatively straight line through the unending muck, but it was next to impossible given what they were trying to walk through. Michael brought up the rear, the gruesome mire making his stomach churn. It was ankle-deep now, and there were more recognisable remains around them: a half-buried corpse still trying to crawl, another stood upright with its foot stuck, unable to get free, another lying flat on its back, spindly arms occasionally thrashing like a drowning swimmer. Their boots snapped bones like twigs, and whenever Michael lifted a foot and looked down, he saw teeming movement where his boot had just been. The viscous sludge was alive with worms, maggots, and all manner of other creatures which gorged themselves on this proliferation of putrefying flesh. He was thankful it had hardly rained over the last few days. A couple of heavy downpours was all it would have taken to turn this place into an impassable quagmire.

Progress was slow, their footing constantly unsteady. Obstructions had been hidden by the blanket of decay. Walls, fences, streams . . . everything remained invisible until they were virtually on top of them. Up ahead now was a dark, featureless mound—it looked like a glistening heap of rot—and for a time the men were unable to work out what it was or why it was there.

"It's a car," Harte said. "Fuck me, look at that."

He took another sliding step closer, then gingerly grabbed a cadaver's shoulder with one gloved hand. He tried to pull the corpse away, but its level of decay was severe and where he expected the whole body to move away, instead its legs remained fused. He pulled it harder still and it snapped, folding back on itself near the base of its spine. The creature's head was now upside down, its skull almost touching the back of its heels, and as he stared into its disease-ravaged face, he thought he saw its mouth move.

Harte moved another corpse to try and uncover more. He was right, it was definitely a car, and he pushed several bodies away to reveal almost the full width of its windshield. The make, model, even the color of the vehicle was impossible to make out such was the amount of rot piled up all over it, but he could see that the dead driver remained behind the wheel, held in position by his safety belt. Preserved by the relatively dry air inside the car, the corpse was less decayed than most others. As they watched, it lifted its head to look at them, then raised a single bony hand and slapped it against the window. Harte jumped back with surprise. To Michael's right, another body tried to lift itself up and separate itself from the rest of the upright mass it was glued to. Even now after months of decay and all that it had been through, the creature still seemed to immediately identify Michael and the others as a threat and tried to attack.

"Keep moving," he said. "Try not to look and just keep moving."

The gruesome, sticky sea through which they were still slipping (and frequently wading now) seemed to constantly be changing in

247

texture and depth. Knee-deep in some places, shallow in others, every single footstep was unpredictable. They'd been walking for what felt like an eternity. Harry estimated they'd crossed almost a mile of dead-packed land, but it was virtually impossible in the low night light to see how far they still had to go. While more bodies remained upright the deeper the three men went, the constant shifting and grinding of so many of them in such close proximity for so long meant there was little more left than bone. Occasionally one still had enough muscle and nerve remaining to manage a clumsy swipe at the men as they trudged past, but such attacks were easily avoided.

"Cut right," Harry said suddenly. Harte moved too far too soon and took a misstep, one of his boots crunching through the exposed rib cage of a creature which lay on the ground with its back arched. Michael steadied him as he shook himself free.

"Fucking things," he complained pointlessly as he shook all manner of foul gunk off his shoe.

Harry continued to walk forward, and he suddenly began to sink. For a moment he panicked, terrified that he was about to be sucked down into a foul quicksand-like pit of decay. He fought against his instincts and did all he could to remain calm and not thrash wildly, and his feet eventually made contact with solid ground again.

"It's okay," he said, feeling his way forward. "Some kind of furrow, I think. Maybe what's left of the moat."

Michael and Harte followed cautiously, matching his footsteps and speed as best they could. Michael continued to sink—the mire reaching his thighs, then almost up to his belt—and he found himself gripping onto the remains of occasional corpses stranded upright so that he could keep his balance. Harte gagged when he slipped and found his face just inches away from the slurry, and his retching and dry heaves made Michael taste bile too. Christ, he hoped this was going to work. He didn't think he could face the prospect of having to walk back the same way if they couldn't get into the castle. He glanced down when he almost lost his footing, but when he saw an ear floating on top of the slop, then the fingers of a hand, then half a face, he made himself look anywhere else. He breathed hard, each time taking in a lungful of germ-filled, foul-smelling air, but it was either that or he'd vomit and he didn't want to lose control. With his head spinning and his entire body drenched in a cold, sticky sweat, he made himself look dead ahead and focus on Harry's back. And then, finally, he saw that the other man was climbing again. Harry changed direction slightly to avoid another corpse—he couldn't see its face, but he could swear it had started turning towards him—then led the three of them toward clearer ground. Before long they'd made it through the slurry and away from the last of the corpses.

Despite now climbing a steep and steady rise up toward the base of the castle walls, Harry didn't let his pace drop. He only dared stop when he'd reached the very top and could stand with his back up against the ancient masonry, safe in the knowledge no one inside the castle could see him from here.

Michael reached the top of the climb about thirty seconds later, Harte another minute after that.

"You both okay?" Harry asked.

"Think so," Michael said. Harte just nodded, too tired to answer. Michael took his rucksack off his shoulders and emptied it. There were three smaller bags of clean clothing inside, one each. The men took their allotted bags and began to change, peeling off their sodden, stinking gear and dumping it. Harte passed around towels and they cleaned themselves up as best they could. It was bitterly cold, but each of them preferred to freeze than to keep wearing their soiled clothes. The rot had even seeped through to their underwear. Michael's inner trousers, long johns, and boxers all had to be discarded.

It took an age for them to change, but eventually they stood together in the shadows of the castle wall, numb with cold.

"What do you think then, Harte?" Harry asked. "Is this the right spot?"

Harte looked up and down the length of the massive, gently curving wall.

"It'll do I think," he said. "Should be fine here . . ."

Harry looked at him. Did he have more to say? He looked unsure. "But . . . ?" he pressed.

"Nothing . . . it's just that the wall looks fucking huge now we're stood next to it. Are we going to get over it?"

"We're going to have to," Michael said. "Desperate times call for desperate actions."

"Where d'you get that little gem from?" Harry grinned.

"Can't remember. Some film or other, I expect. It's true, though."

"Bloody hell," Harte continued nervously, "climbing over castle walls in the middle of the night. It's all a bit James Bond, isn't it?"

"Give us an alternative and we'll listen," Harry said.

"We gave up on the idea of a helicopter rescue, remember?" Michael said. "Now *that* was more like James Bond."

Harte was too anxious to see the funny side. Truth was, he wasn't even listening anymore.

"It's fine," Harry said, trying to reassure him. "I did a lot of climbing. I've been up rock faces far worse than this in my time."

With that he began to get himself ready. He took various pieces of kit from the bag Harte had been carrying—carabiners, harnesses, and the like—and issued the same to both of the others.

"What am I supposed to do with this?" Harte asked.

"Nothing. Leave it to Michael. You remember what to do, don't you Mike?"

Michael nodded and hoped that he did. Harry had given him the briefest instruction before they'd started out, but after all they'd been through to get here, he thought he'd probably forgotten most of it.

"I remember," he said, sounding less than convincing.

Harry laid out the climbing rope, unspooling it carefully along the ground, then attached one end to his belt. "I'll get up and over," he explained, "get the rope fastened to something on the other side, then you two follow when you hear my signal, okay?"

"Okay," Harte said. "What's the signal?"

"It's the middle of the fucking night," Harry said. "If you hear anything out of the ordinary, take that as your cue to start climbing."

"Got it," Michael said. "Get going."

Harry stood at the foot of the wall and looked up to find his first handholds. He reached up, dug his fingers into the narrow gaps between the huge, ancient stones, and lifted himself off the ground. Michael watched as he hauled himself up, impressed by his dexterity and speed. He'd climbed several meters in no time at all.

"I'll never be able to do that," Harte complained.

"You don't have to. You'll have the rope to help you, re-member?"

Harte looked up at Harry, way above both of them now, scrambling up the sheer face of the wall at lizard-like speed and without a damn care. It had all sounded deceptively simple when they were back in Chadwick making plans—get across the dead by foot, scale the wall and get into the castle, round up everyone who wants to leave, find a vehicle big enough for them all, then get the fuck out of the castle before anyone notices. *But plans like this always sound okay until you're there*, he said to himself. Crossing the dead had been a nightmare in itself, and as for climbing the wall . . . he honestly didn't know if he could make it. If Harry slipped and fell . . . it didn't bear thinking about. There'd be no way he could survive and no way they could help him. He remembered Steve Morecombe who'd died as a result of an accident he should have made a full recovery from.

Bloody hell, and this was the *easy* part of the plan. He was seriously doubting if they were going to make this.

Harry was more than two-thirds of the way up now. His arms ached—he hadn't done anything like this for a while—but he was able to ignore the pain because he knew it wouldn't last much longer. He felt for another handhold, and managed to find a narrow gap between two huge chunks of stone which had been carved and dropped into position hundreds of years ago. *Now's not the time to get distracted*, he told himself as he thought about how many years these massive blocks had remained in place and all that had happened to the world around them in that time. Even if he made it through tonight and lasted another fifty years, his entire life would be little more than the blink of an eye in comparison to the centuries this place had been here.

He eventually reached the top of the wall, peering over at first, then pulling his legs over, keeping low so that he wouldn't be spotted from inside. He lay flat on his stomach and looked down into the castle grounds. There was the cesspit Harte had told him about—he could smell it from up here—and near to it lay an unmistakable shape wrapped in a tarpaulin. It was a body, no question about it. He glanced back in the other direction and gave Michael and Harte a quick thumbs-up to let them know he was okay and he hadn't been seen. Bloody hell, all that talk of James Bond . . . he was actually starting to feel like a spy. But spying was yet another redundant profession now there were so few people left alive.

Harry looked along the inside of the wall in both directions. Several trucks had been parked a short distance behind him. They'd make this immeasurably easier. As well as giving him something at a convenient height to lower himself onto, one of the trucks would also be a perfect anchor for him to tie the rope to. More than that, if he could get hold of the keys, any of the vehicles he could see would be perfect for getting people out of the castle compound. He looked back at Michael and Harte again, still standing in the same place, still waiting for his signal, then gestured in the direction in which he planned to move.

38

Between them, Harry and Michael helped Harte down onto the roof of the truck. The three of them lay flat, so as not to be seen. It was past eight, although the day had been long and tumultuous and it felt like the middle of the night. The moon was still out, but vast swathes of the camp inside the castle remained hidden in shadow, the tall encircling wall blocking out what little light there was. The only other illumination came from the windows of a couple of the caravans at the far end by the gatehouse, and from the glowing remains of a small, untended fire. Fortunately the bitter cold seemed to have kept everyone inside their shelters tonight, hiding away like hibernating animals.

"Do you know who wants out and can you make them known to us somehow?" Michael whispered. "Problem is, we don't know who's who."

"I've got a good idea."

"So where are they likely to be? In those caravans?"

"I guess so," he replied. "There's a classroom, a café, and a few other rooms over by the gatehouse, but I don't see much activity up there. They must be in the vans. We need to be careful, though. Don't want to find ourselves knocking on Jas's door by mistake."

"We should split up," Harry suggested. "Go recce the place out, then meet back up over here and decide on a plan of action when we know where everyone is. Just stay out of sight and don't get caught."

"Wasn't planning on it," Harte mumbled. Did they think he was stupid?

The three men climbed down off the truck, lowering themselves as far as they could then dropping the last meter or so onto the gravel. Dressed in dark clothes, and with hats and scarves intentionally obscuring their faces, they moved off in different directions. Michael took the long way around to the various prefabricated rooms near to the gatehouse, but found no one there as Harte had suspected. He thought the place looked surprisingly well organized. If it hadn't been for the wreck of the bus in the middle of the courtyard and the signs of fire damage to one of the caravans, all would have seemed well.

Harry went in the opposite direction, checking out the area around the cesspit. He noticed there were two bodies—the one wrapped in cloth he'd seen from the top of the wall, and another buried in a shallow grave with a rudimentary wooden cross hammered into the ground at one end. *So despite everything I've heard,* Harry thought, *these people aren't total savages.* He ducked out of sight when he thought he heard someone coming, hiding behind a wall where a trench urinal had been dug, the smell so strong it made his eyes water. Satisfied no one was there, he crept back out into the open and worked his way back around to the trucks where he'd first come in.

Harte made a quick dash across a patch of open space and slipped between two of the caravans. Inside one he could hear voices—it sounded like Kieran and several others, but he couldn't be sure. He turned his attention to the van next door and stood up on tiptoes. Through a crack in the curtains he could see Lorna curled up on a narrow bed, but this wasn't the van she usually slept

255

in. And there was Zoe, sitting in a corner with her back against the wall. There was Sue, and Driver too. Bingo. This was what he was after. He turned and ran back to find the others.

Harte found Harry hiding in the back of one of the trucks. Michael returned seconds later.

"Well?" Harry asked.

"They're in the caravans like we thought," Harte explained.

"Easy to get to?"

"Don't know yet."

"So once we've got them," Michael said, "how do we get them out of here."

Harry tapped the side of the truck and dangled a set of keys in front of him. "They were left in the ignition," he explained. "Very convenient."

"So what's the plan? Just get everyone we can loaded into this truck and drive out of here?"

"It'll work as long as they don't start shooting this time."

"Shooting?" Harry said. "What kind of weapons have they got."

"A couple of hunting rifles," Harte explained. "Nothing too serious."

"Nothing too serious? Jesus."

"All right," Michael said, "there's nothing we can do about it, just be on the lookout. So assuming we get everyone together, how do we get out of this place? I didn't want to get too close to the gate. I thought they'd have guards there."

"There probably is someone watching," Harte agreed. "Up in the gatehouse, I expect. We should leave it till the last minute. There's no lock or anything like that, just a wooden crossbeam. Get rid of that, then you just pull the two sides of the gate open."

"Cool," Harry said. "Sounds straightforward. Are we ready then?"

Harte immediately began to backpedal. "What, now?"

"Yes, now," Michael sighed. "What did you think we were going to do? Wait for the sun to come up so we can see what we're doing? Bloody hell, Harte."

"Okay, okay . . ."

"You and I will go and see if we can get these people out. Harry, you get in the front of the truck and wait for us."

Harry nodded.

Michael pushed Harte back out of the truck, then followed him along the castle wall until they were level with the back of the caravan where he'd seen Lorna.

"This the one?"

"Yep, in here," Harte said. He gestured for Michael to stay back in the shadows, then crept across and lightly tapped on the window next to where Lorna was lying. At first she didn't respond. He wrapped his knuckles on the glass a little harder, cringing at the noise, and after a couple of seconds she sat up and looked around. She moved with more urgency when she saw his face at the window. He gestured for her to come outside.

"Wait there," she mouthed. She disappeared, and Harte could hear her talking to someone inside. After a delay, the caravan door opened. He could hear her voice more clearly now, telling someone she needed to go for a piss. The other person—it sounded like Mark Ainsworth, he thought—gave her permission but told her to be quick. If he was supposed to be acting as a guard, then he was a pretty ineffectual one. Lorna shut the door behind her then ran around to the back of the caravan and dragged Harte over into the shadows behind the remains of another crumbled interior castle wall. Michael followed.

"Bloody hell," she said, "did you parachute back in here, Harte? I thought you'd run out on us again."

"Just taking a leaf out of Driver's book. Best to slip away and wait until it's safe to come back."

"It's hardly safe now."

"I know that, but this was the right time to do this."

"That's not what you said earlier," Michael interrupted. "He's been whinging like an old woman. I'm Michael, by the way."

"Lorna," she said. "Hey, are you the one with the baby?"

"Hopefully."

"Save the small talk," Harte said, his stomach still churning with nerves. "We need to get everybody out of here."

"And how exactly are we going to do that?"

"Our man Harry's waiting in a truck over the way," Michael explained. "We'll get everyone who wants to leave loaded into the back of it, then get the gates open and get the hell out of here, hopefully before anyone else has realized what's going on."

"Simple as that?"

"Hopefully."

"Are you all in this caravan?" Harte asked.

"Mostly," Lorna replied, "there are a few more next door. But there's a problem."

"What's that?"

"Guard dogs. At least one in each caravan."

Harte looked at Michael anxiously. "Do we take them out?"

Michael looked equally unsure. Dealing with dead bodies was one thing, but fighting a fellow survivor was a different matter altogether.

"Stay back here and give me a couple of minutes," Lorna said. "I've got an idea."

39

"You took your time," Ainsworth said as Lorna returned to the caravan. He sounded half asleep. Maybe if she'd waited a little longer he'd have drifted off completely and they might have all been able to walk out unchallenged, she thought, regretting her clumsy entrance. Her heart was pounding and the palms of her hands were clammy. She didn't know if she could go through with this.

"Sorry," she said, slipping back into character. "I didn't mean to take so long. I was just thinking . . ."

"What about?"

"About you, actually. I was thinking about how rude I've been to you recently. How rude I was in the kitchen earlier. I'm sorry."

"You've got nothing to apologize for," he said, sounding shocked and yet surprisingly honest. "It was me. I can be a real dick at times. I kind of forget myself sometimes, you know, especially with all this shit going on around us."

"I know."

"So you don't need to apologize. Okay?"

"Okay. Thanks."

She watched him watching her. Poor dumb bugger didn't

have a clue what to say next. He could talk the talk when it mattered, boring everyone senseless with stories about his irrelevant fifteen minutes (more like fifteen seconds) of fame on TV last year, but he wasn't the sharpest tool in the box by any means. Lorna knew that Ainsworth wanted her—she'd known it for ages. She also knew that he'd never expected to be having a conversation like this with her in a hundred years.

"Look," she said, "I feel really bad. I want to make it up to you, but there are too many people in here. Do you think we could go somewhere else and talk?"

"Sure."

"I think I got the wrong impression earlier."

"I think I gave you the wrong impression."

"It's just that it's hard to know what to do for the best these days, isn't it? And like you say, with everything that's happened here today, everyone's on a knife edge. The stakes are so much higher now, you know? You put a foot out of place or say the wrong thing to the wrong person at the wrong time and . . ."

"I know," Mark said. "I feel the same. Especially with Jas. It's like I'm treading on eggshells all the time. Don't say anything, but I'm starting to think he's losing the plot."

"He's struggling, just like the rest of us," Lorna agreed. "Hey, I kept a bottle of wine hidden away in the kitchen. It won't help against the cold, but if you fancy a glass . . . ?"

"Or two?"

"Or three?"

He moved toward her and she started back down the steps. She led him quickly across the courtyard, both of them frantically looking from side to side, checking no one else was around like a pair of kids sneaking out after being grounded by their parents. They stopped outside the café door.

"Have you still got the keys?" she asked. He rummaged in his trouser pockets and pulled out a bunch of keys. He started looking through them, holding up one at a time until he found the one which fitted the lock. Hands trembling with nervous excitement, he unlocked the door and pushed it open, then did the same with the door into the kitchen.

They'd barely got inside before she was on him. She shut the door behind her, then wrapped her arms around him and kissed him hard. Dumbstruck, for a moment he forgot how to react. It had been so long since he'd had any physical contact like this. The kiss took Lorna by surprise too, and for a few seconds she forgot herself. The warmth of holding another person close . . . the softness of their lips . . . the moisture and heat which passed between them . . . Basic pleasures had all but been completely neglected since the day everyone had died. How long had it been since either of them had felt anything like this?

"Bloody hell, Lorna," he said in a momentary gap between her frantic kisses, barely able to control himself.

"Put something up at the window," she told him. "We don't want anyone looking in on us."

He kissed her again, then reluctantly pulled away and did as she asked. He was hard and he adjusted himself, struggling to think straight, his belly burning with desire. He managed to block the narrow strip windows with dish cloths, chopping boards and empty boxes, doing all he could to cover up the gaps as quickly as possible.

"I wasn't expecting this," he said as he worked, suddenly feeling incredibly emotional but doing all he could not to show it. "I didn't think you felt this way . . ."

"Funny how things work out," she replied, leaning up against a stainless steel work unit and watching him. He looked back over

261

his shoulder as she undid the zip on the heavy winter coat she seemed to be permanently wearing these days. With no real heating anywhere in the castle other than the classroom, everyone wore as many layers of clothing as they could comfortably get on. She took off her coat and a sweatshirt, already struggling with the cold, then slowly started to undo the buttons on her shirt. Ainsworth couldn't take his eyes off her. "Are you ready for that drink now?" she asked.

"Sure . . . thanks . . ."

Lorna moved forward and kissed him again, a gentle peck on his unshaven cheek this time. He felt her breasts brush against him and he thought he might be about to pass out from the sudden strength of the previously supressed emotions which washed over him. She turned her back on him and bent over. Was she being deliberately provocative for his benefit? He studied the curves of her body, buried for so long under all those layers. She reached down into a narrow gap between two work units where she and Caron had stashed several bottles of drink earlier in the week.

"Hope you like red," she said.

"I'm not bothered," Ainsworth replied quickly, a definite and unexpected vulnerability evident in his voice. Lorna wrapped the fingers of her outstretched hand around the neck of the closest bottle and gripped it tight.

Moving with sudden, unexpected speed, she stood up, swung around, and smacked him across the face. Ainsworth fell at her feet. She looked down at him sprawled out over the floor, and nudged him with her foot. Nothing. Whether she'd just knocked him out or killed him, she didn't have time to care. She took his keys, locked him in the kitchen, then disappeared back out into the shadows.

40

Harte, who'd been waiting just outside the unguarded caravan for Lorna to return, saw that she was running back toward him. He immediately opened the door and began to usher the other people who'd been in there over to the truck. There was another seven of them crammed in there. Five emerged immediately and without question: Bob, Zoe, Phil Kent, Charlie Moorehouse, and Driver, quickly followed by young Aiden, holding on to Sue's hand as they ran together across the gravel courtyard.

"There's room for a couple of you up front with me," Harry hissed at them as they reached the truck.

"Are they going to be all right in there?" Harte asked, watching as the last of them disappeared into the back.

"They're going to have to be."

"There are more people up in one of the other caravans," Lorna explained. "I'm going to get them out."

"I'll go with her," Harte told him. "Michael's waiting up by the gate. He'll open it as soon as you start the engine."

Michael stood by the gate, squinting into the gloom, trying to make sense of everything he couldn't see. He pressed himself up against the wall, doing all he could to melt into the shadows. Once he was satisfied the coast was clear, he reached up and ran his hands across the heavy wooden barrier until he found the crossbar Harte had told him about. It didn't seem to be secured at all—just resting in a pair of metal brackets, one at either end. After checking again that he wasn't being watched, he lifted it up and moved it away. He then grabbed one of the ropes on either side of the gate and pulled it gently, just to see if it would open. The bottom of the gate moved slightly, scraping along the gravel. He cringed at the noise it made and froze again until he was sure he hadn't been heard. Nothing. No sign of any movement. He looked back across the courtyard toward the caravans. The ends of the long white metal boxes were clearly visible in the moonlight, and he could just about see a couple of figures moving between them.

But then the fragile silence of the night was shattered.

A sudden burst of noise came from one of the buildings close to where he was standing: someone hammering on the door to be let out, screaming with anger. The door of another of the caravans flew open almost instantly, and several men sprinted out into the open, illuminated by the light flooding out from behind them. They ran toward the source of the noise. Michael stood his ground and remained perfectly still, watching as Lorna and Harte slipped into the open van.

"What's going on?" Caron demanded as Harte shook her shoulder. "Harte, is that you? I thought you'd gone again . . ."

He dragged her up but she lolled back onto the sofa where she'd been sleeping, an empty bottle of wine rolling around on the floor below her. Howard, by contrast, was immediately up and ready.

"What's happening?" he asked.

"We're going."

"Where?"

"Day trip to Blackpool," Harte answered sarcastically. "Where d'you think we're going? This bloody island we've been hearing about, I hope." He leaned out the door, hoping to see either Michael or the headlights of the truck, but he quickly pulled his head back in again when he saw Will Bayliss running across the courtyard from the direction of the gift shop, carrying Kieran's rifle and pulling on his clothes. Melanie followed close behind, hoisting up her knickers.

Lorna had gone down to the far end of the caravan and had worked her way back up, checking the bedrooms and small bathroom for others. She'd found Shirley cowering in one of the bedrooms, no one else.

"This it?" she asked.

"Just me, Shirley, and Caron," Howard replied. "Are you surprised? Don't forget, Jas, Kieran, and Paul were in here. Funny how most folks preferred the van next door."

The noise coming from the prefabricated rooms nearby and the excitement it had caused was enough to make Michael decide to change his plans. He'd managed to get both sides of the gate open without being noticed. A handful of corpses had attempted to stagger in, but the frost was gripping and they were so badly decayed that they only lasted a couple of paces before collapsing. In fact, he realized, their forward movement was due more to the fact the gate they'd been leaning up against had moved than anything else.

Michael started to run toward the caravan but then turned back and tucked himself in against the wall when an armed, half-dressed man he didn't recognize thundered past.

Over in the farthest corner of the castle grounds, Harry sensed that something was wrong. He could see people crisscrossing the courtyard in the moonlight, but from here he couldn't tell if Michael or Harte were among them.

"Anyone you recognize?" he said to Bob Wilkins who was sitting next to him in the front of the truck.

"I don't know what's going on," Bob whispered, "but that looks like Kieran. He's one of Jas's lot."

Harry waited a few seconds longer before deciding he had to move. He started the engine and accelerated out into the open, trying to get close enough to the caravans so that Harte and the others could make the quick short dash to safety. He could already see that the gates were open.

Shirley barged closer to the caravan door.

"Is that for us?" she asked, pushing past Howard and Harte when she saw the truck's headlights approaching. Harte tried to grab her but she was too fast, slipping between them and running outside before stopping in front of the truck and waving her arms wildly. Harry slammed on the brakes and she ran around to the back where Sue was calling out to her. Lorna ran out to follow her but then ducked down and turned back when a gunshot rang out. In the emptiness of the night it sounded close but unnervingly directionless and she dived for cover, falling back into the caravan.

"We've got to run for it," Harte said, helping her up. "We've got to get on that truck."

Outside he could see Bayliss trying to head off the truck now, reloading the rifle as he marched toward it.

"Go!" Howard yelled, trying to push them all forward. "Just get out of here!"

Another gunshot echoed around the castle courtyard, this time hitting the front of the truck and smashing a headlamp. Howard tried to lead them out of the caravan but Kieran appeared and blocked him, pushing them all back inside. He was armed too.

266

"Stay here," he warned, making sure they all saw his gun. "Don't any of you move a bloody muscle."

Under fire, Harry had to make a split-second decision: get some of them out, or none. He accelerated toward the open gate, churning up plumes of gravel and dust behind him, swerving around Bayliss, who was struggling to reload again. He headed straight for the exit, then ploughed deep into the sea of semi-liquid flesh outside the entrance to the castle. Fighting to keep control and struggling to see anything with only one headlamp, Harry drove out into the dark.

Lorna pressed her face against the caravan window and watched the truck's taillights disappear from view. Behind her, Kieran blocked the door.

That's it now, she thought sadly. *We're truly fucked.*

41

"One of you get the gates closed," Jas ordered as he tried to force the kitchen door open, "and put a fucking van in front of it to stop any other fucker getting out."

Paul Field immediately jumped into action, keen to get away from Jas more than anything else. Melanie watched from a cautious distance as Jas shoulder-charged the door again and again. Inside the kitchen, Ainsworth tried to kick his way out in the gaps between Jas's attempts to batter his way in. Eventually, between them, they'd done enough damage to the door to be able to get it open. Ainsworth staggered out into the café, as unsteady on his legs as any of the dead. Melanie shone a torch in his face and grimaced. He was badly bruised, one eye swollen shut. He dropped to his knees in front of Jas and spat out blood.

"What the hell happened to you?" Jas demanded. "Who did this?"

"Lorna," he replied, barely able to speak her name.

Jas turned and glared at Melanie. "Find her."

"But she's probably gone—" Melanie started to say.

"They can't have all got out. Get the rest of them rounded up."

"So that all went well," Kieran said. "Nice rescue attempt."

"Fuck you," Harte spat at him. "We got most people away."

"But not all."

"There's still time," Lorna said. "Jas can't keep us locked up in here."

"Seems to me like he's going to try," Kieran replied, looking through the window over Lorna's shoulder. "See that? He's got someone blocking the gate with a van."

"Well, that's us screwed then, isn't it," Howard moaned.

"Not quite," Kieran said. "There's another way out."

"Bullshit. You're taking the piss," Harte said quickly. Forgetting himself, he squared up to Kieran, who didn't react.

"How do we know you're not pulling a fast one on us?" asked Howard.

"You don't. Now shut up and get out of sight. Someone's coming."

There was a sudden scramble as people disappeared into other rooms in the caravan and hid under beds. Lorna crouched under a melamine table in a cluttered dining area and listened as Kieran went outside. She could hear him talking, and she could hear Melanie's voice too.

"Nah, I've checked in here," he said, "it's empty. They must have got away in that truck."

"Jas is going mental. He's scaring me, Kieran."

"He's been scaring me since it all kicked off this morning. Stick with Paul and Will and you might be okay."

"You sure they're not in there?"

"I'm telling you, Mel, this caravan's empty. I was going to try around the cesspit next. Thought I heard people around there just now."

Lorna heard footsteps moving away, then Kieran returned to the caravan. She poked her head above the table and he beckoned her out. She hissed for the others to come out from their hiding places too.

"So where's this other exit?" Lorna asked. "I've never seen it."

"How did you get in?" Howard asked Harte.

"We came in over the wall. Harry, the guy who just took off in the truck, was into rock climbing and all that stuff. The rope's probably still there if you fancy it."

"No need for that," Kieran said. "There is another way."

"Why should we believe you?" Lorna said. "You've been up Jas's backside for days. You're just bluffing . . ."

"I know how it must look, but I was just covering my back, that's all. It seemed to make sense to stick close to the guy who was making most noise."

"We can argue about this later," Harte said. "Where's this way out?"

"I've been here since the start," Kieran explained. "I found this place on the morning everyone died and I decided to stay here. I didn't think you could get anywhere much safer than a bloody castle."

"So? Get to the point."

"So there were only a few of us here to begin with, and we thought we'd got the place completely sealed off. But we were just sitting there one day, and Jackson appeared from out of nowhere."

"How?"

"That's what I'm trying to tell you. He found another way in. He got in through the bloody dungeons."

"Okay, so how do we get out?"

"The exit's at the back of the gift shop. Follow me and I'll show you."

42

Kieran led the others across the courtyard in darkness. Harte had barely taken two steps out of the caravan when someone grabbed him by the shoulder and spun him around. It was Michael.

"Thought you might have been on that truck."

"No such luck," Michael replied. "What's going on?"

"The guy up front is Kieran," Harte explained. "He says he knows another way out of here."

"And can we trust him?"

"Don't see as we have much choice right now."

The small group—four men and two women now—walked across the courtyard rather than ran, taking a wide, indirect route to avoid Jas, Ainsworth, and the others, most of whom were gravitating around the van now blocking the gate. The door to the gift shop had been left open by Bayliss and Melanie when the sudden movement of the truck had abruptly interrupted their lovemaking.

"Who the fuck's this?" Kieran asked as they crowded into the gift shop, Michael bringing up the rear and closing the door behind him.

"I'm Michael," he said. "Pleasure to meet you too."

"Michael's the dad-to-be from the island," Harte explained.

"Then what are you doing here, you muppet?"

"I've been asking myself the same question," he replied. "Now where's this exit?"

"In here, somewhere," Kieran said unhelpfully as he began searching through the few boxes of supplies which had been left in the gift shop. He found what he was looking for on a shelf—torches. It didn't matter that they were novelty kid's torches made in the shape of castle turrets, as long as they worked. He handed them around, then distributed packs of batteries from a wall display behind a long-unused till. Lorna was the first to get hers working. She shone it around the various faces.

"Michael, this is Howard, Caron, and Kieran."

"And you're all that's left here now? Harry got the rest of you away?"

"As far as we can tell. I think everyone's accounted for."

"Too late now if they're not," he mumbled as he went deeper into the shop. "Now what exactly are we looking for?"

"Some kind of door, I guess," Kieran explained. "All I know is that Jackson got in this way."

"And you never bothered to look for it before?"

"There wasn't any need. No one was trying to get out of the castle until your lot turned up in your bloody helicopter."

"Fair point."

They split up and scoured the walls of the cluttered room. In the months since the castle had first been used as a base by survivors, the gift shop had been used for a variety of reasons. Bayliss and Melanie's love nest apart, people had dumped rubbish here, used it to store less useful items which had been scavenged (Michael noticed a couple of flat-screen TVs) and, judging from the smell, someone had used this place in favor of the chemical toilets too.

"There are catacombs and dungeons here, you know," Caron said suddenly.

"What?" Michael asked.

"Ignore her," Howard said, "she's half-pissed."

"I might well be," she continued, "but I'm not stupid. I tell you, there are dungeons and all sorts under this place."

"How would you know?"

"Because I've spent hours and hours pretending to clean the museum, remember? I saw some displays."

"And you didn't think to mention this?" Lorna said in disbelief.

"I didn't think it mattered. Like Kieran said, we weren't planning on leaving until a couple of days ago."

"Wait," Michael said, "this guy Jackson. You said he came *into* the castle through here?"

"Yes," Kieran replied. "Why?"

"Because if that's the case he probably got in this way."

Michael flashed his torch at a door he was standing next to. It had a large NO EXIT sign in the middle of it. They'd all glanced at it, but the penny hadn't dropped. They'd been looking for a way out, not a way in. Jackson had been coming the other way. His entrance was their "no exit."

"Must be it," Kieran said, reaching for the emergency access bar right across the middle of the door. He pushed it down and the latches opened. Michael slipped his fingers around the edges and between them they pulled the door open. A blast of cold, musty air hit them. Michael shone his torch into a small room which looked like it had been carved out of rock.

"We need to get moving," Howard said nervously. "I think they're coming this way."

"Go for it," Michael suggested. "Even if we just end up hiding in here for a couple of hours, it'll do."

He led them down into the confined space; Harte and Kieran close behind, Howard, Lorna, and Caron bringing up the rear. The temperature felt ice-cold.

"Fuck me!" Harte cursed. "Jesus!"

Michael turned around quickly to see what it was that Harte had seen. It made him catch his breath too. A painfully thin, ghostly white body was shackled to the wall. Lorna sighed.

"Harte, you're bloody useless," she said. "It's a bloody dummy."

"How was I supposed to know? Christ, what kind of place has fake dead bodies chained to the walls?"

"Castles with dungeons," Caron said. "I told you I saw displays. It was part of some kind of 'be a smuggler' attraction, I think."

"Be quiet and keep moving," Michael said, leading them toward another door.

"Go through?" Kieran asked, pointlessly.

"Unless you've got a better idea?"

Kieran tried the door and it opened. He cautiously entered a narrow passageway which sloped downward and which curved away to the left. He kept walking, suddenly a reluctant leader, shuffling his feet along the ground, unsure of the slope. This passage too appeared to have been carved out of the rock and supported with rudimentary brickwork. The miserable light from their torches now illuminated only a fraction of the narrow space around them, just a patch of the walls and the low ceiling. It felt almost unbearably claustrophobic; even sound felt restricted and trapped here, echoing quickly, unable to escape. Kieran's already slow pace slowed further as nerves set in. He held his torch in one hand and groped his way forward with the other.

"Shh . . ." Harte said suddenly, grabbing Michael's shoulder. "Stop!"

They immediately froze, walking into each other and bunching up in the narrow confines. They all became completely still, their collective breathing the only sound.

"What is it?" Lorna asked anxiously. He shone his torch into her face.

"I thought I heard something."

"You think Jas is following us?"

"I thought I heard it too," Kieran said. "It wasn't behind us, it was up ahead."

"Just keep moving," Michael said, squeezing through and taking the lead. "The sooner we get out of here, the better."

Kieran was about to follow when he stopped. There it was again. A definite noise.

"Wait . . ." he said.

"He's trying it on," Howard said. "Fucker's brought us down here and told Jas to follow. I'm betting it's a bloody dead end up ahead."

"And do you think I'd want to get myself trapped too? Get real, Howard. No, I swear, there's something down here."

"I'm going back," Caron started to moan, trying to get past Howard and get back up the slope. "We never should have come here."

"You're not going anywhere," Michael told her, the tone of his voice immediately silencing her. "Whatever's down here can't be any worse than your friends back in the castle."

"You reckon?" Harte mumbled.

"It's probably just rats or something like that," Howard said, doing his best to find a rational explanation for the noise but causing more panic in the process. At the mention of rats Caron began to wail with fear. Lorna felt her starting to move again and she grabbed hold of her.

"Get off me!" she screamed, trying to beat her off.

"Leave it out, you silly cow," Lorna cursed, pushing Caron up against the damp, cold wall and preventing her from getting out.

"Will you two keep it down," Michael ordered from the front. He started moving again, following the curve of the passage around until it opened out into another, much larger space. He paused in the entrance to the chamber. There were colorful displays hanging on the walls, and another dummy had been chained to the rock for its sins. Harte and Kieran stood on either side of him. Harte took another couple of steps forward, then froze.

"Fucking hell!" he yelled. "Bodies!"

"It's all right," Michael said quickly, loud enough for those behind to hear him. "It's just another dummy."

"No, it isn't," Kieran said, grabbing his arm and turning him around. "Look."

Harte's torch had picked out a single corpse which began walking toward him. Keeping the light focused on the creature's grotesque face, he desperately searched his pockets for anything he could use as a weapon.

"There are more of them," Kieran said. "Oh fuck, there are loads of them."

Michael watched in abject terror as more and more bodies emerged into the light. Drawn like moths to the torchlight, they staggered ever closer.

"What do we do?" Caron asked anxiously, sandwiched between Michael, Kieran and Harte on one side, Howard and Lorna on the other.

"Go back," Harte said, already trying to move away. "We need to get ourselves back behind one of those doors we came through."

"But they're just going to keep coming," Lorna said, stating the obvious. "Fuck this, we might as well head all the way back out and take our chances with Jas and the others."

The dead continued their approach. There were at least five of them now that Michael could see, maybe even more behind. He didn't want to look, but at the same time he wished their torches were brighter. The thought of what he couldn't see in the shadows beyond this chamber was even more frightening than what he could. How many more were there?

The farthest forward of the corpses seemed to have locked onto him now, and he felt the hairs on the back of his neck stand on end as it raised its haggard face to look directly at him with mournful, sunken eyes. Someone clumsily knocked into him from behind, and he grabbed at the walls in panic, desperate to find something to hold onto. And still the corpse came . . .

"Use this," Howard said from close behind him. Michael looked around and the other man shoved a screwdriver into his hand. "Found it in the gift shop. Thought I'd bring it along just in case. Now kill the damn thing!"

Michael still didn't attack. It had been a long time since he'd seen one of the dead in this kind of condition: nowhere near as decayed as those outside the castle, still capable of moving with relative strength and speed . . . This was like those they'd cleared off the island when they'd first arrived there. But that was months ago . . .

Michael knew he had no option. The rest of these pathetic shysters weren't going to be any help. Despite his still-considerable bulk, Howard had managed to force himself away and was now cowering back in the passageway with Lorna and Caron. Lorna was hanging onto Caron's arm. Caron was trying to drag her back toward the castle. He knew that if he wanted out of here, he'd have to take control. He gripped the screwdriver like a dagger and then, still holding the torch in his other hand so he could see what he was doing, he ran toward the approaching corpse, screaming with rage.

The creature stopped. Michael stopped too, mid-attack, surprised by its unexpected and very definite response. It staggered back a couple of unsteady steps and raised its arm like it was trying to defend itself. The bloody thing seemed to be cowering from him.

"What the hell's going on?" he said as he moved forward. The corpse moved farther away, clumsily backing into the others which were hovering behind it now. "Look at this thing. This isn't right."

"Who cares," Howard yelled from a safe distance away. "Finish them! Just get rid of them."

Harte found his nerve and moved toward the dead, determined to do what Michael wouldn't, but Michael shot out his arm and held him back.

"We don't have time for this," Lorna said. "What the hell are you waiting for?"

Michael wasn't listening. He moved closer again, and this time the corpse had nowhere left to go.

"Look at it," he said, studying its decayed face. He ran the torchlight over it, revealing the full extent of its horrific deterioration. Its skin—the little remaining which hadn't been eaten or rotted away—seemed to have slipped down like an ill-fitting mask, leaving heavy, sagging bags beneath its clouded eyes. He could see burrowing things moving in the holes which had been worn through its flesh. Its drooping mouth hung open, occasionally half closing as if it was chuntering something unintelligible.

"What about it?" Harte asked.

"Compare it to the bodies you've seen outside recently. How does it match up?"

"It's still solid," Harte said, calmer now, creeping a little closer. "It's still got some meat on its bones. Some of those things outside are little more than liquid now."

"Exactly. It's like the one we saw trapped in that car."

"What are you talking about?" Kieran asked, hovering just behind him.

"On the way to get in here tonight," Harte explained, "we walked across the dead outside. We found a great mound of them all stacked up, and we dug down to find out why. There was a car buried underneath them, and the driver was like this one. It had been preserved, I guess."

"Can't you just get rid of them?" Caron asked. Michael ignored her.

"It looks like they all did about a month ago," Lorna said.

"Kieran, how long's it been since anyone came through here?"

"We'd been here a few weeks when Jackson first got in," he replied, "and as far as I know no one's been down here since. Why?"

"Because these bodies have probably been down here since then, haven't they."

"So?"

"So Harte's right. They've been preserved. Think about it, there's probably a pretty constant temperature down here, no wind or rain . . . they used to keep food and stuff in cellars like this, didn't they? These things managed to get themselves trapped. Remarkable."

"Just bloody well kill them," Caron demanded again, shining her torch around into every corner she could in case more of the dead were close.

Much as she'd rather they battered this particularly foul aberration into oblivion, Lorna was beginning to appreciate the significance of Michael's comments. She watched as he moved toward the group of bodies again, and they all tried to get out of the way, as if they knew he was going to attack. But when he stopped and didn't advance any farther, the creature at the front seemed to visibly relax, slouching its shoulders and rocking back slightly on what was left of its heels. Michael remained a cautious half-meter away, and shone his torch directly into its wizened face once again. It didn't react. Its wide, dark, emotionless eyes slowly moved around Michael's face.

"Poor thing," Lorna said, surprising everyone.

"What do you mean, poor thing?" Howard said, unable to believe what he was hearing. "You sound like you pity it! You know what these bastards have done, how much pain and grief they've caused us."

"Yes, but none of it was their fault, was it? They had no control over what was happening to them. Same as we didn't."

"We should just get rid of them," Howard suggested. "Finish them off and put them out of our misery."

The corpse seemed to react to his words. It immediately became more animated and reached out for the torch Michael was still holding. He pulled it back and stepped out of the way, concerned it was about to lash out at him, but it didn't. It made a second clumsy grab at the torch, but it was definitely the torch it was going for, not Michael. Not sure what he was doing, and with the light from all the other torches now focused on this one particular figure, he handed it over. It tried to grip but it couldn't and its bony hands simply slipped off the handle. The torch dropped to the ground. Michael picked it up again. The corpse's shoulders slumped forward and it dropped its head and its hand in what Michael presumed was a bizarre approximation of frustration.

"What's it doing now?" Howard asked.

"Giving up, I think," Michael said. "Bloody hell, it's like they've come full circle."

"Full circle? What are you talking about?"

"Just look at it. It's helpless. It hasn't attacked me, and I don't even think it wants to. What I mean is, I think it's got more self-control than any others I've seen before. It doesn't seem to want to fight anymore."

The creature moved, correcting its balance, and Michael flinched nervously. It tried once again to grab the torch, but it still couldn't get a strong enough grip. Perhaps sensing the futility of its actions and the limitations of its physical shell, it instead raised its hand up to its head, almost seeming to be pointing at its skull.

"What's it doing now?" Lorna asked, transfixed, all thoughts of what was happening elsewhere in the castle temporarily forgotten. Michael couldn't believe what he was seeing. He sounded stupid when he tried to give them his interpretation of the dead man's behavior.

"I think it wants me to kill it."

"You're out of your bloody mind," Harte said, trying to get past so that he could finish the damn thing off. Michael blocked him again.

"I'm serious."

He looked at several of the other decaying faces crowding behind the first corpse. They all seemed as passive as it was. Michael remained cautious.

"How many are here?" Howard nervously mumbled, asking an obviously unanswerable question.

"There could be hundreds," Kieran said. "I don't expect Jackson stopped to shut the door behind him when he was trying to get in here. That's if there even *is* a door."

"Well, there must be something," Lorna said, tracking the irregular movement of another corpse with her torch, "otherwise they'd probably have filled this place, wouldn't they?"

"Only one way to find out," Michael said. He began to move again, edging around the first body, doing all he could not to make direct contact with it. It watched him as well as it was able, following his movements with its entire head, not just its eyes, having long since lost anything resembling fine motor skills.

He moved toward the far end of this chamber, and the bodies there dropped back, appearing to try and get out of his way. Beyond this room was another sloping passageway, narrow and steep. A corpse was crawling toward him on its hands and knees, its pitifully slow and awkward progress going someway to explain why so few of the dead had made it this far up into the dungeons. He continued down the slope, the rest of the group following close behind, and entered another sudden swell of space, a chamber similar to the one they'd just left. He saw that this area too was filled with the dead. They lined the edges of the large space, most of them appearing to do all they could to keep their distance from the living. One of them, Michael noticed, looked like it was sitting in a corner, and several more were lying down. Were these intentional movements, or were the bodies now so weak, their limbs so emaciated, that they were no longer physically able to support what was left of their own weight?

"I don't like this," Howard moaned from close behind his shoulder. Michael too felt increasingly uneasy. The stench in here was appalling, and to all intents and purposes, they were now surrounded by the dead.

"But if they were going to attack us, wouldn't they have done it by now?" he said, trying to reassure himself as much as anyone else. "As long as they don't think we're threatening them, there's no reason why they should go for us."

"It's never stopped them before, or maybe you've spent too long on your bloody island and you've forgotten what they're like."

The mention of the island made Michael stop and check himself momentarily. What the hell was he doing wasting time here? He should be back home on Cormansey with Emma, not buried underground with only a handful of idiots and several dungeons full of corpses for company.

"This is different," he said. "*They're different.* I don't know what your experience has been, Howard, but I've watched the dead steadily changing—*constantly changing*—since the very beginning of all of this. Their self-control has improved as their bodies have decayed. It doesn't make a lot of sense and I can't explain it, but that's what's happened. You must have seen it too."

"Of course we've seen it," Harte said, "but why should the ones down here be any different?"

One of the corpses lining the wall nearest to him twitched involuntarily and Harte flinched. His sudden movement caused another reaction which, in turn, caused another then another. In a matter of moments virtually an entire wall of rotting flesh had become uncomfortably animated. Michael positioned himself in front of Harte and held his arms out at either side, forming a barrier between the living and the dead. It was hard to believe, but after a few seconds the bodies in front of him seemed to become calmer again.

"You see," he said, "they don't want a fight any more than you do. They're long past that stage now."

"I don't understand," Caron said, worming her way right into the center of the group of six so that she was surrounded on all sides. She didn't want her back to any of the dead without someone else there to cover her. "This doesn't make any sense at all."

"It makes perfect sense," Michael explained. "Like I said, when your man Jackson forced his way in through here, he must have allowed this lot to get in too. The conditions here are different from outside: the air's drier, the temperature's steady, there's barely any moisture, no light . . . They're being preserved. What's going on in their brains has continued at the same rate it has done since they all died, but down here their physical decay has been much, much slower."

"Bollocks," Howard said. Michael ignored him. He knew he was right.

"Watch," he said. He'd seen more than enough corpses up close over the last few months to know beyond any shadow of a doubt that there was something very different about these. He shone his torch at the nearest few, working his way along as if he was inspecting an identity parade, moving slowly and shining the light at their chests rather than directly into their faces to avoid provoking another spontaneous reaction as Harte very nearly had done a few moments earlier. One of the creatures over to his right was dressed differently from the others. It was wearing a nurse's uniform. He had to look twice to be sure that was what it was, such was the level of discoloration caused by seepage from its body. Much of the heavily stained material had dried hard like cardboard. He carefully moved a flap of clothing out of the way, the remains of a cardigan or some kind of light jacket, he couldn't tell which.

The corpse had an identity badge clipped to its breast pocket. He looked into its wizened face for a moment, almost as if he was asking permission, then he unclipped the badge. He wiped away a layer of grime to reveal an inch-square picture of a woman's face beneath. The little visible detail was reduced even further in the poor light. He squinted to try and make her out. She looked beautiful—the first preapocalypse face he'd seen in some time— and her smile took him by surprise. Hers was a face unspoiled by disease; an expression free of rot and also free from the strain of having to endure the living hell which he and the others had been trying to survive through since day one. Her short, dark hair was cut into a neat bob, her fringe tucked out of the way behind her ear. She wore a pair of angular, heavy-rimmed glasses which perfectly suited the shape of her soft, delicately square-jawed face. But it was her lips he couldn't stop looking at. Gorgeous, full, dark red lips. The fact she was wearing makeup took him by surprise, even though it shouldn't have. Her vivid, painted smile immediately took him back to a time now long gone, when appearances felt like they'd mattered. Emma and the rest of the women on Cormansey never wore makeup, mainly because they hardly had any, but also because there didn't seem to be any point anymore. There was no longer any desire, let alone any need, to spend time trying to conform to society's idea of beauty when that society lay in tatters, thirty miles or so over the ocean. Michael couldn't take his eyes off those lips. It saddened him to think he'd probably never see Emma dressed to the nines for a night out. That was if he ever saw Emma again. He had a long way to go before he'd be anywhere near the woman he—

"You okay?" Harte asked, nudging him gently.

"What? Oh, sorry," he said, feeling both sad and embarrassed, and also annoyed with himself for getting so easily distracted. Regardless of his assumptions, just because he hadn't been attacked so far, it didn't mean he was completely safe. He wiped the rest of the identity badge clear and then looked up into the dead face it belonged to. After seeing what she used to look like, he almost couldn't bare to look at what was left of this woman now. Her dry, discolored skin, patchy hair, misshapen face and unnaturally prominent bones left her looking like a grotesque caricature of the person she'd once been. A large circle of skin around her top lip had been eaten away. Despite the obvious individuality of each corpse's decay, in some ways they all looked the same as each other now, strangely featureless. "This is Michelle Bright," he announced.

One of the men said something flippant and unnecessary, but

the others paid him no attention because their sole focus was now the dead woman standing in front of Michael. At the mention of her name she'd reacted. She moved forward slightly, then lifted a tired arm up closer to her face. Barely able to control her awkward movements, she lightly placed what was left of one of her hands against her hollow-sounding chest. "Me," she seemed to be saying.

"Fuck me," Howard said.

"I'd rather fuck her," Harte mumbled. Michael turned around and scowled at them both.

"This is all well and good," Caron said, completely sober now, "but it's not actually getting us anywhere, is it?"

"Depends on your perspective," Michael said. She was about to ask him what he meant when Lorna distracted her.

"Look at that," she said. "Where the hell are they going?"

They watched as a slowly moving queue of corpses traipsed away in the direction from which the living had entered the dungeons, back toward the center of the castle.

"They're trying to get out, aren't they?" Kieran said. "They're trying to get into the castle."

"I think that's exactly what they're trying to do," Michael agreed. "They know they can't go the other way because it must be blocked, so they're trying to get out the way we came in."

"Then we should let them," Lorna suggested. "It'll get them out of our way . . ."

". . . and give the fuckers up there something else to worry about. Good thinking."

"But when Jas and the others see them, they'll go crazy," Harte said. "They'll probably batter hell out of them."

"Look at the state they're in," Michael said quietly, almost as if he didn't want the dead to hear him. "It'd probably be for the best."

He was about to talk to Lorna again but it was too late, she was already gone. He watched her disappear back in the direction from which they'd just come, and by the sounds of things she was opening both doors they'd come through too, clearing the way back out to the gift shop. She quickly returned to the chamber where the others were waiting and snatched Caron's torch. She took Michelle Bright's corpse by the arm and gently led it up the slope into the other chamber. The dead girl walked slowly forward, then stopped. Lorna let go and pushed her forward again. She began to walk toward a dull patch of light in the distance where Lorna had left her torch, following an unsteady queue of other corpses which had already started to move. She left Caron's torch on the ground too, hoping to help guide the dead along.

Following Lorna's lead, Howard, Harte, and Kieran began to do the same, pushing lethargic bodies up toward the dull lights. They followed each other out of the caverns in a bizarre and surreal parade; a horrendously overdue funeral procession.

"Let's get moving," Michael said, pushing still more of the creatures away, ready to go deeper into the darkness.

"Wait," Caron said, holding on to his arm. "What did you mean about perspective just now?"

"All those thousands of bodies outside this place," he explained, continuing to watch the dead march. "We assumed all they wanted to do was attack."

"That's because they did. We all saw more than enough of that. Nasty, vicious things."

"All I'm saying is, that might well be what they did do, but the real question is, *why* did they do it? Why did they constantly herd around us in massive numbers? We assumed it was because they saw us as a threat to them and they wanted us dead, but like I said, it's all about perspective. Having seen what I've seen in here today, I think we might have been misreading the situation. They wanted our help, that's why they wouldn't leave us alone."

"That's preposterous," she scoffed.

"Is it? I'm not sure. They wanted our help, but they couldn't control themselves sufficiently to make that clear. We misread their actions as being all about anger and hate. Maybe they were just scared? I think they knew a lot more about who they were and what they'd become than we gave them credit for. I think they wanted our help, they just didn't have any way of showing it."

43

"What do you mean, you can't find them?" Jas demanded. Ainsworth was standing in front of him, his face aching, his mouth dry with nerves, not knowing what else he was supposed to say.

"We've checked everywhere . . . all the caravans, all the rooms. We've been twice around the ruins. They've disappeared."

"They can't have. Look again."

"But Jas, it's pitch black, mate. We've blocked the gates. Let's wait until morning. They're probably hiding around that well Jackson was working on, or somewhere near the toilets. If we wait until the sun's up we'll have a better chance of—"

"Keep looking," Jas ordered. Ainsworth just stared at him. *What the fuck is wrong with you?* He wanted to ask the question out loud but couldn't. To his relief, Will Bayliss and Paul Field came running over. Hopefully they'd found something.

"Mel found a climbing rope," Bayliss said, breathless.

"Where?"

"Hanging over the wall, over by the shit-pit."

"So is that how they got out?"

"I doubt it. It's too high."

"Where the hell did they get a climbing rope from?"

"There was other stuff as well," field continued. "Harnesses, belts, stuff like that."

"So what are you saying?"

Field shrugged his shoulders. It was starting to make sense to Ainsworth.

"That's not how they got out," he said. "It's how they got *in*. Someone must have come in over the wall, then tried to get them all together in one truck and get them out."

"Those fuckers from the island? I thought they'd have long gone."

"The helicopter was back earlier, don't forget," Bayliss said. "It must have been them."

"With a little help," Ainsworth said.

"Your girlfriend Lorna?" Jas sneered. Ainsworth didn't bite.

"I was thinking more about your friend Harte."

"Well, at least we know where they'll be heading," Jas continued. "They'll be on their way to Chadwick. We can cut them off."

"What's the point?" Bayliss said.

"What?"

"Why bother?"

"Because they've got our supplies."

"Then we'll get more."

"Are you fucking stupid? I thought he was the dumb one," Jas said, pointing at Ainsworth, who stared back at him, doing all he could to stop his bottom lip from quivering. All he could think about was Lorna, and how empty and foolish he felt at having let her take advantage of him like that.

But the worst part of all, he thought sadly, *is that I'd let it happen again in a heartbeat. I'd give anything to be close to her like that again. All the pain and the grief I've had since from Jas was worth it for that one kiss . . .*

Melanie jogged over.

"Can't find any of them," she said. "They've all cleared out. Looks like Kieran's gone too."

"Bastard," Jas yelled, kicking the ground with frustration. "That little shit has sold me out."

"But if they didn't get out over the wall," Bayliss said, "and we know they didn't all get out in the truck, then they must still be here."

"Check the caravans again," Jas ordered.

"What for? We've checked them already."

"Just fucking do it!"

They grudgingly headed over to the caravans and split up, happy to put some distance between themselves and Jas. Ainsworth checked the caravan he'd been guarding once more, staring at the bed where Lorna had been lying and wishing he could turn the clock back so that none of this had happened. And not just tonight, either. He wanted to go further back . . . back to when he'd first arrived here. Maybe he'd have chosen his friends differently if he had his time again.

"Anything?" Jas said, standing in the doorway behind him.

"Nothing," he replied dejectedly, trying to get back out. Jas was blocking the door, and Ainsworth was relieved when he moved on to the next caravan. He sat down on the step, held his head in his hands, and listened as Jas yelled at the others when they also reported back that they'd found nothing.

44

Michael led the others deeper into the cavernous spaces underground. After several minutes of slow, shuffling movement, all of those corpses which still had a degree of mobility had been herded back in the direction from which the living had just come, back toward the gift shop and the interior of the castle, leaving just those which could no longer move.

The progress of Michael and the rest of the small group was painfully slow, such was the level of decay which had suddenly begun to accumulate around them. The farther they traveled from the center of the castle, the fewer complete bodies they found. With each footstep Michael took, it seemed, so the condition of the dead around him was rapidly worsening. It was now like the mile or so of compacted decay he'd earlier had to walk through with Harry and Harte, although this was somehow worse because of the increasingly close confines and the complete absence of fresh air. Caron had vomited as a result of the inescapable stench. She'd seen more than her fair share of gore over the last few months, but this had proved too much for her. Howard and Kieran now helped her along between them, one on either arm, or one in front and one behind if the way forward became too restrictive. The air was filled with the fetid stink of the gases produced by the putrefaction of the dead. *Just don't anyone dare light a match*, Michael thought. *The whole fucking place could go up.*

"Dead end," he announced as his outstretched hands made contact with another cold, rock-carved wall.

"Maybe we should just turn back," Howard suggested for about the hundredth time.

"Bit late for that now," Michael replied. "Besides, if Jackson got in this way, then we must be able to get out."

He looked around, his feet slipping in the decay. He felt disorientated. Problem was, everything looked the same down here, particularly with such limited light from so few torches remaining. Kieran, he noticed, had switched his off now, perhaps figuring he'd still have a chance if they hadn't escaped by the time everyone else's batteries died. Michael didn't want to be stuck down here without any light. Actually, he didn't want to be stuck down here at all. There had to be a way out.

He shuffled back toward the others, scraping his feet along the floor to feel his way, moving inch by slow inch through the slurry. And then it occurred to him that he might be able to use the depth of the mire as a kind of primitive gauge.

"What are you thinking?" Lorna asked, concerned that he'd stopped.

"Just trying to work out how the dead would have moved through here."

"Me too," she said. "Those bodies back there . . ."

". . . must have been some of the first to get through. They must have followed Jackson in. Presumably he would have had quite a crowd behind him."

"If they were in large enough numbers," Harte said, "then there's a chance some of them would have been trampled like we saw outside."

"That's what I was thinking," Michael agreed.

"So the deeper the shite," Lorna said, "the better?"

"Exactly."

Caron was still green. Her stomach rolled at the thought of more dead flesh. "You want to go deeper?"

Michael didn't say anything. Instead he shone his torch down and began feeling around with his boots. He tried to picture Jackson's arrival, how his bluster and noise would inevitably have caused a huge swell of the dead to try and follow him into the castle. He worked his way around the edge of the room, torch in one hand, feeling the wall with the other. The rest of the group remained still and watched him as he kept moving, prodding the ground, taking one tentative step at a time. He knew he was onto something, because the depth of the muck was increasing now. He'd barely been splashing in it initially, but it was already up over the toes of his boots. And now it had almost reached his ankles. He moved again, and now it was halfway up his shin.

And then the hard wall Michael was holding onto for support disappeared. He stopped and felt his way around the edges of the entrance to another passageway, initially obscured by shadow. He shuffled closer, feeling the unimaginably foul gloop around his feet rising with virtually every step.

"This is it," he said. "It has to be."

"Can you see anything?" Lorna asked from close behind. He shone the torch deeper into the passage.

"Not a damn thing, but we have to be close now."

"I can't keep going," Caron whined from the back.

"Shut her up, would you?" Michael said wearily. "She's doing my bloody head in."

"Give it a rest, Caron," Lorna yelled at her before lowering her voice and adding. "You don't have any choice."

"Everybody ready?" Michael asked. Absolute silence.

"Just do it," Kieran reluctantly said.

"Single file. Hold onto the back of the person in front, okay?" Michael didn't wait for anyone to reply. As soon as Harte grabbed his shoulder he began to move along the passageway he'd uncovered, his boots crunching and slipping through the rapidly deepening mess. He frequently lost his footing when he trod on submerged bones and he did his best to sweep them away to either side. He crunched through rib cages and pushed skulls away like footballs.

"Shit," Howard cursed when he tripped and almost dragged half the group over. His frightened voice was amplified by the narrowness of the corridor they now followed. "This is madness. We should turn back."

"You can if you like," Michael said, finding it increasingly hard to concentrate, almost having to wade through the decay now, "but I'm getting out of here."

Lorna gagged at the ice-cold mire which was now close to reaching her waist. The stench was all-consuming. It felt like it was coating the insides of her nostrils and throat.

"We don't even know if this is the way Jackson came," Howard said, continuing to complain. "There might have been another way. We might have missed a turning or something . . ."

"He's right," Harte reluctantly admitted, almost losing his balance again. "Maybe we should think about going back? Those bodies will cause a distraction up there and we can—"

"As long as I can keep moving forward," Michael said through gritted teeth, "then there's still a chance we're going the right way."

Still feeling his way ahead with outstretched hands, Michael suddenly stopped. The rest of the group bunched up behind him.

"What is it?" Lorna nervously asked. He didn't answer. His legs felt weak. Was it a dead end?

"Michael? What is it? What's the problem?"

"Wait a second," he said. In front of him he could feel another huge mound of decay. He turned around and passed his torch to Harte. "Do me a favor, try and give me some light."

Harte and the others who still carried torches obliged, but by the time they'd all got their lights aimed toward him, Michael had disappeared. He ducked down, his chin almost scraping the surface of the mire, and stretched out his arms. Moments later he stood up again, dripping with decay.

"Did you slip?" Lorna asked. She held out her hand to him. "Come on, let's go back . . ."

Michael was grinning. "I think this is it. I think I can feel a way through. Has anybody got anything I can dig with?"

He realized as soon as he'd said it that that was a stupid question as none of them had anything with them other than torches and Howard's screwdriver. He sunk both hands into the decay and pulled out a limb. At first he thought it was an arm, but he realized it was a leg and he stripped away what little muscles and nerves remained, then snapped off what was left of a flapping foot. Using the ankle end of the leg as a prod, he tried to feel and push his way through. He tried to dig frantically and, after a few seconds of concerted effort, he discarded the leg and shoved his arm into the gap he'd made in the offensive gloop. Working blind, he grabbed at whatever he could get hold of now and tried to drag it all back toward him. Sucking, squelching noises filled the narrow space as more and more of the mess came away in large congealed chunks. He pushed his weight forward against the blockage, and more of the decay toppled away. And then he felt cold, relatively fresh air on his face.

"I don't think there's a door," he said, "just a hole. Everyone ready?"

No one answered but he didn't care. He took a deep breath, dropped his shoulder, and charged forward, throwing himself at the clog of remains which was blocking their way out. It gave way with surprisingly little effort and then, suddenly, he was outside. A huge mass of death came spilling out after him, as if he'd burst an enormous spot on the side of the castle. The rest of the group staggered out, glistening with decay in the faint light of the moon. They stood together, soaked and stinking but not giving a damn, just relieved to be outside the castle walls again.

45

How the hell had he missed that?

Will Bayliss looked across the castle courtyard. It was pitch black—still the middle of the night—but he was sure he'd seen something moving over by the prefabricated buildings. Jas, Mel, Paul Field, and Ainsworth were in one of the caravans, trying to keep warm and arguing about what they were going to do next. Jas, who seemed to rapidly be losing touch with the rest of them, was trying to lay down the law and tell them exactly how things were going to be—how they were going to leave the castle before morning and track Kieran and the rest of those fuckers down. Bayliss had had enough. Who the hell did Jas think he was? About twenty minutes ago he'd used the excuse of going for a piss to get out of the caravan for a while. He'd have stayed out longer if it hadn't been so bloody cold.

He was about to go back inside, but the glimpse of movement over the way had stopped him in his tracks. That was them, it had to be. The dumb bastards hadn't seen him either. He slipped back into the caravan.

"Where've you been?" Mel asked. Bayliss ignored her.

"Found them, Jas," he said, grinning. "They're in the gift shop."

The five of them crept slowly around the perimeter wall, two coming from one side, three from the other.

"Stupid fuckers," Jas said. "What were they thinking? Why go to all that effort, then just hide in the bloody gift shop? Fucking morons."

Ainsworth crept along behind him. He desperately wanted to see her again. There were just a handful of people left alive now, and all he wanted was to see just one of them. He wanted to tell Lorna how sorry he was and how he'd understood why she'd done what she had.

Jas stopped just short of the gift shop door, and gestured for Bayliss, Field, and Melanie to stop on the other side. He had one of the rifles with him, and by God, this time he thought he might actually use it. He rushed forward, pumped full of adrenaline, and kicked the door open.

Then he stopped.

Corpses began lurching toward him, and he backed away in horror as they spilled out of the open door and flooded into the courtyard. Even in the pitifully low light the full extent of their danger was immediately apparent. These creatures were stronger than all the others he'd seen on the other side of the castle wall, less decayed and more controlled. Had they been hiding? Waiting for him?

"The dead!" he screamed. "The dead are inside!"

Ainsworth tried to drag him away. "Let's get out of here."

Jas remained rooted to the spot, the corpses drawing ever closer. Ainsworth looked up and saw the other three running for cover. Were they heading back to the caravans? No, it looked like they had other plans. They were heading for the van which had been parked across the gate to block the entrance. And now someone was opening the gate . . .

"Wait!" he yelled, but they ignored him. He started to run, but then looked back at Jas, who had hardly moved. The nearest of the dead had lifted their arms and were almost upon him now, ready to attack. He looked back again when he heard an engine starting. The van moved with sudden speed, skidding around in a tight circle, then driving straight out through the open gate and into the decay outside. It was impossible to see what was happening from here, but Ainsworth knew the dead would no doubt be pouring in through the gate too. After standing strong for so long, the castle was about to be overthrown.

He grabbed Jas by the arm and pulled him away. Jas was terrified. Ainsworth couldn't remember ever seeing anyone look so scared. "Come on, Jas. We have to get out of here."

46

Freezing cold and disorientated, Michael, Lorna, Harte, and the others were struggling to keep moving.

"Where now?" Howard asked, teeth chattering.

"We need to find somewhere to shelter and get some fresh clothes. We're going to get hypothermia if we don't," Kieran said.

"You know the area better than the rest of us," Harte said. "Where do you suggest?"

"I'm not sure," he replied unhelpfully. "I need to work out where we've come out in relation to the front of the castle. There are a couple of villages nearby. A few other places, maybe. But we don't want to be walking all night in the wrong direction and . . ."

Kieran's voice trailed away. Michael was immediately concerned. "Problem?"

"Shh . . ." he said. "Listen."

Everyone became completely silent. In the near distance they could hear an engine.

"Who's that?" Caron asked.

"More of your lot coming back for us?" Lorna suggested.

"I doubt it," Michael replied, wishing he could be more positive. "Even if it is, fat lot of good it's going to do us. They'll check out the castle, but they won't bother searching the area, will they? It'll be like looking for a needle in a haystack. If I know Harry, he'll be doing exactly what he said he'd do, and that's getting those people over to Cormansey."

"What if it's Jas?" Caron asked anxiously.

"Do you really think he'll still be interested in us?"

"I don't know. But what if he is?"

"Then we'll deal with it. Right now we've got a more pressing problem."

"What's that?"

"Getting back across a mile or so of dead bodies."

47

When Harry arrived back in Chadwick, he was relieved to see the silhouette of the helicopter perched on top of the multistory car park. He drove the truck along increasingly familiar roads toward the marina. His passengers remained almost completely silent.

Zoe, sitting up front between Harry and Bob, stared in disbelief at the dead world they were traveling through, a stream of tears rolling down her cheeks. She knew Chadwick well—she'd had digs in the town since starting at university—and she could make out more than enough of it tonight to be able to appreciate the full extent of its remarkable deterioration. Being back in Chadwick hurt.

She hadn't left the confines of the castle since the rescue of the others from the hotel near Bromwell. On that first morning when everyone else had died, she'd been stopping at the house of a friend who'd lived a couple of miles from the castle, and this was the first time she'd been back anywhere near home since her nightmare had begun. She'd been too scared to try getting back to her flat back then, and so had remained in her friend Sally's house, with only Sally's corpse for company. She'd tried phoning family and other friends tirelessly, but no one had answered and then the line had stopped connecting, and then her mobile signal had died. She'd stayed where she was for a while—unaware that there were other survivors so close—until she'd woken up one morning and found dead Sally standing over her. She'd thrown the body of her dead friend out of her own home and barricaded herself in for weeks until she'd heard Kieran and Jackson out looting and tracked them back to the castle.

It had been obvious from the very beginning that there would have been no point trying to get home because all that Zoe would have found would have been the bodies of her loved ones, but that didn't stop her suddenly feeling as guilty as hell today.

Zoe remembered back to the Saturday before all of this had begun. She'd been to the gym first thing, and had then met up with Sally and Trish, a friend from uni. Sally had picked her up in her cool little red Peugeot, and they'd parked in the multistory where the helicopter had landed today. The three of them had walked through town together to the marina where they'd had lunch in one of the waterfront cafés. They'd spent the whole afternoon talking about nothing—stuff so trivial and inconsequential that she couldn't even begin to remember any of it now. Nothing had mattered back then. The biggest stresses in her life had been getting her assignments finished, turning up to lectures on time, and trying to make her overdraft last until the next installment of her student loan came in.

The truck turned a familiar corner. On the opposite side of the road to them now was a billboard advertising some new hair product Zoe had long since forgotten about. Christ, she'd had such a laugh when she'd last been here. Trish had been such a gullible cow, she remembered. She used to believe anything anyone told her. She'd been babbling constantly about how the shampoo she used was better than the one being advertised on the hoarding, because 72 percent of women said they preferred it according to what it said on the bottle. Silly sod had always been suckered in by adverts, but she'd never have it. It's *science*, she kept trying to convince them, science and statistics. You can't argue with facts!

The billboard advert was still there—just—but it had faded quite badly. The edges had curled, and one vertical strip of paper had been torn away, half of the model's face now missing. *Got to try and forget about all that now,* she told herself. *It's all gone.* Zoe shook her head and tried to look anywhere but at the street she'd walked along with her friends that last Saturday afternoon. It was covered with the remains of dead people now—some of the people she'd walked alongside that day, perhaps—and some of them were still moving ever so slowly forward. *Everything you remember is gone, and you're never going to get it back again.*

What was left of the population of Chadwick caused Harry little concern this morning. They were too slow and too badly decayed to pose any real threat anymore. Beyond what looked like a low hillock formed entirely of body parts—the remains of the crowd which had been drawn to the marina by the sounds of the living—he could see the road which would take them down to the edge of the water. He swerved around what was left of the corpses and continued until he was as close as he could get to where the Duchess was moored. At the sound of the approaching engine, Richard appeared on the jetty.

Harry stopped and his frightened, bewildered passengers piled out.

"Well done, mate," Richard said, shaking Harry's hand. He could immediately tell from Harry's expression and his less than enthusiastic response that all was not well. "Problem?"

"This isn't everyone," he said. "We got in okay, got this lot loaded into the truck, then it all went shit-shaped. There was nothing I could do. They were firing at us. I had to get out."

Richard looked anxiously along the expectant faces which had gathered on the jetty. "Michael?"

Harry shook his head. "Don't know what happened to him. Harte too. I lost the pair of them."

The two men stood and stared at each other in silence for a moment longer, both thinking the same thing.

"We talked about this," Richard said. "We knew there was a chance it might happen."

"I know that, but it doesn't make it any easier, does it?"

"What do we do now?" Zoe asked. Harry took her arm and pointed out their boat.

"Get everything and everybody loaded up onto the *Duchess*."

"What about . . . ?" she started to ask, not bothering to finish her obvious question.

"What do you think?" Harry asked Richard. "We can't just give up on them and ship out."

"I don't like it any more than you do," Richard said, "but we both know that's exactly what we have to do. It's what we agreed last night. It's what we *all* agreed."

"I know, but—"

"But nothing. *We agreed*."

Harry knew he was right. "Do me a favor before we ship out, though," he said hopefully.

"What?"

"One last flyover. Just a quick look. It's the least we owe Emma."

Richard thought carefully before answering.

"Okay. It'll be dawn in a few more hours. We'll wait until the light breaks."

48

Over the months the castle had been completely encircled with dead flesh. The thought of having to hike back across it had filled both Michael and Harte with dread, but the reality had proved to be less of an ordeal than they'd expected, certainly no worse than what they'd just been through underneath the castle. That had actually proved to be good preparation for trudging through the ankle-deep, frost-encrusted, once-human slime outside. It was somehow easier the second time around.

They felt strangely invisible—a good thing if Jas did decide to come looking for them. In the low light of early morning, the living were hard to distinguish from the decayed remains they were walking through. And they were all still soaked with decay from their castle escape too. All they needed to do, should Jas or any of his cronies appear, was stand still and wait until they disappeared again.

Michael looked back over his shoulder at the castle they'd somehow managed to escape from, then at the ragtag group of people who were following him, picking their way through the carnage. He could tell a lot about each of them by the way they were dealing with what they were walking through tonight. Harte and Kieran were stomping through the slime, exhausted and just desperate to get across to the other side in the shortest time possible. Howard was constantly grumbling. Seriously unfit, he spent more time looking for a dog he'd told Michael he'd lost than he did trying to get away from the remains of the dead. He placed the two women at opposite extremes. Caron was infuriating; the slowest of all, she was constantly moaning about the dirt under her nails and asking how long they had left to go, like an irritating kid stuck in the back seat of the family car. Lorna, on the other hand, was strong and unflappable and kept Caron in check. She was clearly tough, so much so that he wouldn't have fancied his chances against her in a fistfight.

Michael caught her eye, then looked away. He turned back when he realized she'd stopped. Something had caught her attention. Her head was raised and she remained perfectly still, like an animal sniffing the air for a scent.

"Problem?" he asked.

"Don't think so."

"What, then?"

"See that house over there?"

Michael squinted into the dark. It took him a few seconds to spot the building she was referring to. In the predawn gloom, it was just another dark shape among many. He was soon able to make out its walls and roof. Harte was too.

"I see it," he said. "What's the problem?"

"Oh, there's no problem," she casually replied. "There's a light on in one of the windows, that's all."

Suddenly revitalized, the group moved at speed toward the house in the distance. The nearer they got, the clearer the light in the downstairs window became.

Caron was still complaining as they approached it.

"These bloody bodies," she said. "Are we ever going to get away from them? You said we only had to walk a mile or so and we'd be through them."

Michael stopped and looked down at his feet, thinking about what she'd just said. "We are through them."

"But how can we be? There are still loads of them around—look."

She was right, there was still an unexpectedly high number of corpses nearby. More to the point, most of them were on their feet, and some were still moving—an indication that, perhaps, these creatures had never made it as far as the crowd around the castle. The ground they were now walking over was clear, and they'd long since made it through most of the sea of decay which had surrounded the castle.

"This is something else, isn't it?" Lorna said, clearly coming to the same conclusion as Michael. "These bodies are here because of whatever's in that house."

She started running toward the building. Harte called for her to be careful, but she wasn't listening. The front lawn was over-grown, and the windows were covered in thick curtains of cobwebs and dust. Before she'd made it even halfway down the garden path, the front door opened inwards.

"Hello, you," said Hollis.

49

It hadn't taken long for the *Duchess*' prospective passengers to empty the supplies from the back of the truck and get ready to leave. They were loading the last few scraps and searching around the jetty for extra lifejackets when a noise distracted them. It was another truck approaching.

"Michael and the others?" Harry wondered.

"Must be," Richard said.

"I'm not so sure," Zoe said. They both looked at her and she explained. "I assume he knows his way around here?"

"Yes, why . . . ?"

"Because whoever that is," she continued, "they don't have a fucking clue. Listen. They're driving up and down the main roads, probably trying to find this place."

"Shit," Harry cursed. He knew she was probably right. "We need to get going."

"You get the boat moving, I'll get back to the helicopter," Richard said. "I'll take a couple with me, just in case."

With that he turned and started to run. Harry watched him go, people suddenly crisscrossing around him, being marshaled by Zoe.

"One last flyover first," he shouted, "remember?"

Richard stopped. "There's no point while it's still dark."

Harry knew he was right. There was no chance of seeing anything yet. "But you *will* come back."

"Once I've got you lot safely on your way."

With that Richard ran on, closely followed by two others.

Zoe and Charlie Moorehouse remained on the jetty as the others boarded the *Duchess*. They were both armed with batons, although neither knew if they'd be able to fight. Harry wished he had his sword. Bloody hell, he couldn't even remember where he'd left it. He was about to do a final head count and check everyone was accounted for when a van sped down the sloping road which led into the marina. It skidded to a halt just short of the *Duchess*.

"Let's go," Harry said, pushing Moorehouse onto the boat. "Get out of here before they start shooting at us."

"Wait!" a woman shouted from over by the truck. Zoe took a few steps forward. It wasn't Jas. It was Melanie, Bayliss, and Paul Field.

"Let us on, Zoe," she said. "Please."

"Where's Jas?"

"He's coming. He's probably not far behind us. Please!"

Field and Bayliss approached, their arms loaded with more stuff from the back of their truck.

"There's a few more boxes in there," Bayliss said. "We should take as much as we can."

Harry looked up. He could hear another engine approaching now. Was this another trick? An attempt to delay them so Jas could get his precious supplies back?

"Fuck the food," he said. "We've got enough."

"Please let us on," Melanie said, tears streaking her face.

"Don't trust them," Zoe said. "They're with Jas."

311

"Not anymore," she sobbed. "We just want to get away from here, same as you do. Please, Zoe . . ."

What choice do we have? Harry asked himself. *I don't know any of these people. But I know one thing: if any of them try anything, I'll kick the fuckers overboard.*

"Get on," he said, and all three of them pushed past, clearly desperate to get away. Harry undid the mooring rope, then jumped back onto the boat. The *Duchess* felt uncomfortably low in the water. He pushed his way through to the cabin and took the controls. He fired up the engine and the noise and sudden movement was reassuring.

"He's coming!" someone shouted from the stern of the boat. Harry looked back and through the sea of heads filling almost every available square inch of deck space behind him, he saw another vehicle driving down toward the jetty.

Jas jumped out of the beaten-up old Renault which had once belonged to Shirley Brinksford's husband, and screamed with frustration and anger as the boat sailed away from the jetty. Ainsworth stood a short distance behind him, too scared to run.

They looked up as the helicopter flew overhead, guiding the *Duchess* away from the mainland and out toward Cormansey.

50

"Fuck me, it's cold," Michael said, wrapping his arms around himself before heading upstairs to check the bedrooms for some clean and dry clothes. Caron was in the kitchen looking for food, while Howard and Kieran were busy exploring the rest of the building, each of them finding the situation they were in unexpectedly strange. This sudden return to something almost resembling normality was jarring.

Lorna was in the living room with Hollis. By the looks of things he'd barely used the rest of the house, preferring to remain in this one room.

"I didn't want to go far," he explained. "I knew I wasn't welcome in the castle anymore, but I still didn't want to cut myself off completely so I decided to stay close. You can see the castle gate from upstairs. I thought you'd all leave at some point, and I thought I might be able to tag on with some of you."

"We *are* leaving," she said. "You heard the helicopter, didn't you?"

"Thought I was imagining it at first," he said, sounding close to tears. "What with all the grief I've been having with my ears,

313

I didn't think it was real. I thought I'd got tinnitus or something like that."

"Did you see the truck leave?"

"What truck?"

"A few hours after the helicopter, some of them got away in a truck."

"Didn't see it. Tell you the truth, I fell asleep. I mean, I kept watch for a while after the helicopter had gone, but I figured that was probably it."

"You daft bugger."

He shrugged his shoulders. "If I'm honest, I felt so bad about what happened to Steve that getting away was the important part. That's all I was really bothered about."

"What happened to Steve wasn't your fault."

"I didn't help matters, though."

"Don't beat yourself up about it. Anyway, like I said, we are getting away. We're going to an island."

Harte stood in the doorway, watching the two of them talking. It saddened him to see Hollis like this: a shell of the man he used to be. Irrespective of the low light, the expression on his face was hard to read. He didn't seem to show any emotion when Lorna told him about the island. He either hadn't heard properly, he didn't believe her, or he just didn't care anymore. Feeling like he was intruding, Harte walked away to look around the rest of the house again.

He'd found no bodies since they'd been here, save for a single motionless corpse he'd seen by torchlight outside, curled around the bottom of a rotary washing line. Whoever it was, it looked like hanging out the laundry had been the very last thing they'd done before their life had been brutally truncated. They'd managed to peg out a few items of clothing, and there they'd remained hanging for months: a couple of towels, a floral summer dress, a few items of children's underwear . . . The clothes were little more than rags now, weather-beaten and faded. Before he'd even realised what he was doing, Harte found himself trying to fit together the pieces of the family which might have lived here. A little girl, seven or eight years old, perhaps living with her mom (surely that was who it was lying dead in the garden). On a worktop in the kitchen he found an opened letter addressed to Mr. John Prentice. He wondered what John used to do for a living . . . tried to imagine where he might have been when he'd died. Had he been one of the tens of thousands of corpses decaying outside the castle wall? Even more concerning, Harte found himself wondering what had happened to the little girl. The thought of turning a corner and running into a waist-high, three-months-dead child's corpse unsettled him more than it ever should have.

It had been a long time since he'd spent any time in a house like this. The last house he'd visited, he remembered, was the semi-detached that he and Jas had torched to provide a distraction so that Webb, Hollis, and several of the others could massacre some of the endless hordes of bodies which had gathered around the flats. Fat lot of good that had done them. Christ, that all seemed so long ago now. Almost as long ago as the days when he'd taught in a school and lived in a home not too dissimilar to this one . . .

He passed Kieran, who was in a small study, sitting in front of a computer, shining his torch around the room. He naturally held the mouse in his hand and leaned back in the chair, as if he was about to browse the Web or send an e-mail. He looked up and saw Harte watching him.

"Funny how things work out, eh?" he said.

"What do you mean?"

"My life used to revolve around these bloody things, now there's not even any power to turn them on."

He threw down the mouse and shoved the keyboard away, then got up and walked out.

Caron had taken off her dirty clothes and thrown them outside. She was now sitting on a sofa at one end of a long and narrow conservatory which ran across almost the full width of the back of the house. It was cold, but she appreciated the view through the glass walls and ceiling: close to being outside, but still safe and protected. All around her were potted plants, shriveled up and yellow, sitting in tubs of bone-dry dirt. She wore a dressing gown and pajamas which had most probably once belonged to the woman lying dead in the middle of the back lawn, but even that didn't seem to matter now.

"So how long have we got?" Caron shouted, addressing her question to no one in particular.

"Long enough to catch our breath and get cleaned up," Lorna shouted back.

"I say we should wait until it's lighter before moving on," Harte suggested. "Give us a couple of hours to get our heads together."

"Doesn't seem much point racing anywhere, really," Michael said, sounding hopelessly dejected.

"I thought you'd be desperate to get back to your island."

"I am."

"So what's the problem?"

"There's no problem getting back to Chadwick," he explained, "but that's probably as far as we're going to get. Unless any of us can sail, that is."

"Harry will have waited, won't he?"

"For as long as he could, but I expect he'll have long gone by now."

"So what are you saying?"

"That I don't know how to sail a boat," he admitted, shrugging his shoulders dejectedly, "so I don't know how I'm going to get home."

"It can't be that difficult," Howard said.

"You might be right, sailing might be a piece of piss. But can you navigate? Can any of us read a bloody map?"

"Won't the helicopter come back?" Lorna wondered.

"He might."

"But we can't just give up," she said. "You especially."

Michael held his head in his hands, close to tears. The sudden futility of his situation was beginning to sink in. Being away from Emma like this was tearing him in two. Until now he'd been distracted, and before tonight he'd been confident that he'd either be flying back to the island or sailing there alongside Cooper or Harry. All those options had steadily disappeared and now he was stranded. The narrow strip of water which separated Cormansey from the mainland might as well have been a thousand nautical miles wide.

"So when do we leave?" Howard asked, feeling guilty at having given Michael's situation such little consideration.

"Like Harte says, let's give it a few hours," Michael said. "We should head out just before dawn, I reckon. Things might look better in the morning."

Caron went to bed in a child's room. Thankfully the child must have been on its way to school when it had died, because its body wasn't there. The room was just as it had been left. Untidy. Lived in. Bed unmade. A pile of clothes dumped on the floor outside the wardrobe door. Perfect.

Unlike most of the others, Caron had been sheltered from much of the looting and devastation since everything had fallen apart. She'd been content to play homemaker initially, taking comfort in the mundane familiarity of chores and only going out into the open when she had absolutely no choice but to do so. Since then she'd been little more than a passenger, ferried about and protected from the madness by whoever else she'd been around at the time. It was surprising, quite reassuring actually, just how easy she'd found it to slip back into the routine of all she'd lost. Little things she'd forgotten about suddenly began to feel like they mattered again, albeit only temporarily. On a dressing table in another bedroom she'd found some makeup and moisturizing cream which she'd sat in front of a mirror and applied to her face. Even that most insignificant of acts had a disproportionate effect, filling her with a whole raft of bittersweet memories. The coldness of the cream in her hand, working it into her skin with the tips of her fingers, the smell . . . In a world filled with cesspits, rotting flesh, and germs, the delicate, flowery scent seemed unnaturally strong now, almost overpowering.

She went into an en suite bathroom off the main bedroom which none of the others seemed to have used, and there she allowed herself the luxury of using the toilet. So sad that she had been reduced to this—that having a real, ceramic lavatory seat to sit on should feel like such a blessing. There was enough water left in the cistern for a single flush, and she pressed down the handle and listened to every second of that beautiful and instantly familiar crashing, running, swirling noise which she hadn't heard in months. She'd become accustomed to using buckets and chemical toilets and to slopping out, not flushing.

Caron wondered what life on this island would actually be like, should they ever get there. Would it be any better than this strange, backward world she'd almost begun to get used to? Would it be anything like she'd experienced in this house tonight, or might it be like some strange hybrid of what she knew now and what she remembered? Steampunk, she'd heard someone jokingly call it, not that she knew what that meant. She imagined things wouldn't be quite as rough and ready as the things she'd experienced (and endured) in the early days at the flats, then the hotel, then the castle, but she knew the future wasn't going to be anywhere near as refined as the life she used to lead. The possibilities were endless, and all her questions were unanswerable.

She climbed onto the little girl's bed and covered herself with the dressing gown she'd been wearing. The mattress was so comfortable. *So normal.* She stretched out in the darkness and listened to the instantly familiar sounds which surrounded her. Someone talking downstairs. The house groaning as the temperature changed and pipes expanded and contracted. Floorboards creaking as someone else looked for a place to sleep. She could even hear snoring from the room next door.

It was just like it used to be.

51

"What do you mean, he's not here?" Emma demanded, cradling her belly. She was standing in the lounge of The Fox—Cormansey's only pub—surrounded by several other folks who'd spent the night there with her, waiting. The hours between the arrival of Donna and Cooper on the first boat and the second boat captained by Harry had felt endless. The return of the helicopter had signaled their arrival. Along with his passengers, Harry, exhausted and barely able to stay standing, could do little to defend himself as she assailed him.

"I'm sorry," he said, "I don't know what happened. It was chaotic back there. It was pitch black and there were people running everywhere. Some of them were shooting at us, for Christ's sake. We had to get away."

Donna tried to pull Emma away from him but she was having none of it.

"But you just *abandoned* him?"

"You tell me what else I was supposed to do then, Emma. Michael would have done exactly the same thing. It was what we both agreed before we set out. Getting as many people away and over to the island was what mattered most."

"I don't believe this," Emma sobbed, finally relenting and sitting down. She looked around the dark room, illuminated by oil lamps and several candles which had almost burned down to stumps, desperately staring at each of the new faces she could make out, hoping she'd just made a mistake and missed him. But she hadn't. He wasn't there. She watched the new arrivals watching her, keeping their distance and looking at her as if she was some kind of freak with her distended belly and swollen ankles. Donna crouched down beside her, holding her hand.

Richard Lawrence waited in the doorway, not sure if he dared get any closer. He cleared his throat, feeling duty bound to say something. As it was, Emma spoke first.

"Are you going to go back, Richard?"

"In the morning."

"Why not now?"

"Because I'm bloody exhausted, that's why. I need to rest a while first, otherwise I'll end up pitching in the sea. I'll go back tomorrow."

"Please, Richard, go tonight."

He shook his head and looked away, barely able to face her.

"I can't. And anyway, there's no point. I'll never be able to see them in the dark. We have to wait for daylight. It would be stupid not to."

52

Lorna was the first one awake. She woke everyone up, turfing them out of their beds and rolling them off the sofas they'd been sleeping on. There was the usual early morning reluctance to take that first step of the day, but then memories of what had happened last night quickly returned, acting like smelling salts and forcing them all into action. Michael moved with more determination than any of them. His circumstances were the same, but his motives were wholly different. To the rest of them, getting to the island would be an unexpected bonus. To him it was all that mattered.

They heard the wind and rain before any of them had taken even a single step outside. The relative calm of yesterday's weather had gone, and the conditions outside now were atrocious. Dense gray clouds filled the sky, low enough to hide the tops of trees and the castle turret in the distance.

After stripping the house of anything worthwhile (mostly clean clothes and coats—Hollis had already used virtually everything else), they walked out onto the street. The wind was fierce, seeming almost to want to push them back inside the house. Michael took the lead and walked to the edge of the small front garden, and then he stopped. All around the house were the remains of more bodies. There hadn't been as many as this here when they'd arrived in the early hours. Some were just about able to still walk, others weren't even whole, just broken pieces of things which had once been people.

Lorna turned around and saw that Hollis had retreated. She went back to him.

"They're always here," he said, "but never this many. It's like they knew where I was."

"It's not what you think," she told him. "They're not a threat anymore. They won't attack—look."

She led him forward and they watched as Kieran approached the nearest of the dead. On the ground near his feet laid a head and torso which repeatedly stretched out its arms and attempted to pull itself along, moving only inches at a time. Across the road was another rain-soaked creature which crawled forward on all fours, its limbs frequently buckling under its negligible weight.

"But they're *still* coming," Hollis said.

Kieran watched them with a heavy heart. He'd barely slept, and had instead spent the time thinking about the corpses they'd found under the castle. He knew why they were here now, probably better than they knew themselves. They wanted help. They wanted release from the endless torment of feeling themselves decaying and being unable to do anything about it. The kindest thing, he decided, was to put them out of their misery. He crouched down closer to the one at his feet, and he looked at it and remembered the hundreds he'd killed before today, picturing all the frantic and violent battles he'd been involved in. Could it be that they'd been wrong about the dead all along? Had they always wanted help, but just weren't able to show it?

Using a crowbar he'd taken from the garage of the house they'd just left, he worked his way around the small group of cadavers, finishing each one of them off in turn. It didn't feel like when he'd killed them before . . . today there was no flourish, no satisfaction, no relief, just a strange sadness as each of the corpses slumped and finally became still. The last one, he thought, seemed to have moved its head to watch him as he approached. For a split second it was almost as if it had tried to make eye contact. It had been standing directly ahead of him, rainwater running down its broken, uneven skin, dripping off the last few wisps of hair which clung to its pockmarked scalp. It didn't react when he raised the crowbar. He put a hand on its shoulder to steady it, then plunged the weapon deep into its left temple. Instinctively, he caught the body as it fell.

Howard had found a map in the house. He unfolded and refolded it, struggling with the creases in the squally wind which turned the map inside out whenever he was close to getting it to a manageable size. Distracted, he tripped over a curbstone and growled with frustration. Following close behind, Kieran caught up and looked over his shoulder.

"That's north," he said, pointing over to their left. "So we're west of Chadwick, I think."

"Southwest," Howard corrected him, finally making sense of the map. "We can either follow this road, or try heading cross-country."

"Whichever's shortest," Michael said, "but we need to try and stay visible in case Richard comes back."

"You think he will?" Lorna shouted, fighting to make herself heard over the wind.

"If this weather lets up he might."

Kieran and Howard had already stopped again to recheck the map. "Shortcut," Howard said, pointing toward a small park on the opposite side of the road before marching off, head down into the rain. The others followed him into a sad and lifeless place. The once well-tended grass was overgrown, the flower beds choked with weeds. Winter seemed to have bleached the color from everything: where they would have expected to see lush greens, they instead saw only sickly yellows and browns.

The group of seven walked in silence and in single file along the edge of a children's playground outside a small school on the other side of the park. Each of them individually did all they could to avoid looking too closely, but it was hard not to stare. Even now the remains of several tiny bodies lay about the place, as if they were chicks which had all fallen from the same nest. Farther ahead, at the edge of a field on the other side of a narrow service road, one small corpse had become entangled with a barbed wire fence. How long had it been there? Rags matching the color of the uniform worn by the other dead children flapped around what was left of its skeletal frame. It was a safe assumption that this poor little creature had died, then reanimated, then stumbled away and had only made it as far as here before becoming trapped. Its small, unexpectedly white skull had been pecked clean of flesh, the dead child unable to protect itself from the birds, insects, and other scavengers which had found it. Kieran tried not to, but he couldn't help imagining what the poor little thing might have been thinking as it had stood there, trapped, feeling itself being steadily eaten away. In light of what he now believed the bodies understood, how self-aware they actually might have been, had this one been scared? Had it spent the last months of its time waiting here for its parents to come and take it home, wondering why it had been abandoned?

After following the service road between the school and the field to its end, then walking a mile or so down a steep and narrow but still relatively clear lane, they reached a farm. The place was deserted, save for a handful of chickens which still clucked around

the muddy yard as if nothing had ever happened. A number of untended animals had died in sheds, and they found what was left of
six cows dead from starvation in their caged milking stalls. Dotted
around several of the fields nearby, Michael could see wisps of sheep
fleeces. He couldn't tell from this distance whether they were
healthy animals or carcasses. It didn't matter. This place was as dead
as everywhere else.

53

"River coming up ahead," Howard said, "and we need to be on the other side of it."

"Just keep walking till we find a bridge, then," Lorna said.

"No shit, Lorna," Howard sighed. "Why didn't I think of that?"

There had been no let up in the atrocious conditions since they'd first set out. It was late morning now, and the sky still looked equally black and heavy with rain in every direction. Soaked through, they trudged across a muddy field of ruined crops which should have been harvested months ago. How many millions of pounds' worth of food like this has gone to ruin, Harte wondered. He corrected himself. It wasn't right to think about the financial value of things any more: pounds, dollars, euros . . . none of those counted for anything today. Anyway, he decided, trying to make himself feel more optimistic, crops can be regrown. There was no reason this couldn't be turned around in the future, albeit on a much smaller scale, of course. After all, he thought, remembering his late parents with fond sadness, Mom and Dad grew their own vegetables for years. He cursed himself for having constantly mocked his parents' attempts to be self-sufficient. There's no point doing all this, he used to regularly tell his dad as he watched him struggling to tend the hard soil in the vegetable patch at the bottom of his garden. Food's so cheap these days, and you can get pretty much everything you want from any supermarket. There's no need to work yourself into the ground like this.

You were right, Dad, Harte admitted silently as he marched on through the cloying mud, skirting around a scarecrow-like corpse which had sunk to its knees in the mire. Harte wished his old man was here to witness him eating humble pie. He would have loved that. *"You bloody teachers,"* Dad always used to say, *"you think you know everything about everything. But all you do is tell kids about life when you haven't even lived it yourself. You go to school, go to university, then go straight back to school again. Where's the sense in that? There's a whole world out there you're missing out on."*

Fair point, Dad, he thought, *but would anything have equipped any of us for this?*

Before they reached the river, they came across a collection of buildings at the roadside. It was the smallest of villages, hidden by the hissing rain until they were almost right upon it. Howard gazed around him at the old, tired-looking cottages and shops. What was this place, and how long had it been here? Who cared? He used to be interested in local history, but not anymore. The story of this place was probably still accessible, buried deep in some book in a dust-filled, permanently silent library somewhere, but it was irrelevant now. Standing, as they were, on the cusp of what increasingly felt like mankind's last days, what had gone before them now mattered not one iota. Who'd lived in the house they were now passing, who'd built it, who'd designed it, who'd owned the land, who'd sold it to them . . . all pointless, forgotten details now, never to be recalled. And it was worse than that, he realized, continuing along a train of thought he was beginning to wish he'd never started, *hardly anything that ever happened matters anymore.* Every war that had been fought, every deal that had been brokered, every discovery made . . . all irrelevant. From the flat-screen TV in the window of the shop opposite to the Large Hadron Collider— none of it counted for anything today.

In spite of the appalling conditions and all the pressures and uncertainties they each individually felt, being out in the open like this was surprisingly liberating. It was, Lorna realized, the first time they'd been beyond the walls of their various hideouts since "the death of the dead," as she'd heard one of the others call it. It was by no means a comfortable experience, but it was definitely preferable to how they'd been forced to spend the previous three months or so.

"It's like a bloody ghost town," Kieran said as they walked together through the village. Without realizing, they'd bunched up close to each other.

"It *is* a ghost town," Caron said, holding onto Hollis's arm. "They all are."

She looked from side to side, squinting through the rain to make out the shapes which surrounded them. There were few bodies left here. She saw one couple in a parked car, sitting bolt upright together. Their mutual decay had rendered them bizarrely ageless and sexless, and a host of ferociously active spiders had weaved a grey connective bridge of webs between their heads. She imagined that if she opened the car and touched either one of them—not that she would—they'd both crumble to dust.

"Aye aye," Harte said, quickening his pace slightly and crossing over toward a small general store. "I don't think we're the first ones here."

"How can you tell?" Caron asked, trying to look over his

shoulder into the shop but at the same time not wanting to get too close.

"Some of the shelves have been stripped," he explained. "And look, they've cleared out the fags too."

She took another couple of steps nearer and saw that he was right. Behind the counter, a wall display had been stripped of every last packet of cigarettes.

"Was it recent?" Lorna wondered.

"Don't think so," Harte replied from just inside the store. "There's plenty of dust in here. I can't see footprints or anything like that. I guess they just took what they needed and moved on."

"Makes you wonder, though, doesn't it?" she said to him as they carried on down the road again.

"What does?"

"That place. It makes you wonder how many other people there were like us."

"They might still be alive. There might be hundreds of them. In the major cities, maybe? You never know, things might be better elsewhere."

"Yeah, right. I don't think that's really likely, do you?"

"You never know," he said again, the tone of his voice giving the impression that even he was struggling to believe what he was saying. "Some folks might have fared better on their own."

"They might," Lorna said, "but I don't think I'd have wanted to be on my own through all of this. Would you?"

"No way."

She walked a little farther before speaking again.

"You know, that's what makes what Jas did even harder to accept. There's hardly any of us left alive now, and yet we're still busy trying to score points and fuck each other over. It's fucking heartbreaking."

They found the person they presumed had been the cigarette looter a short while later. Michael made the grim discovery around the back of a single detached house about half a mile outside the village. There were signs that there had been huge amounts of corpse activity all around the place—vegetation which had been crushed underfoot, collapsed fencing, a gummy brown residue coating everything, bones in the undergrowth. And right at the bottom of the back garden, hanging by its neck from the bow of a gnarled, ancient-looking oak tree with a huge trunk, was another corpse. Despite the level of its decay, in comparison to the countless others they'd seen they could tell this person had only died a few weeks ago—a month or so at most. This poor soul had probably cracked under the strain of trying to stay alive while being under siege from the dead. And the cruelest irony of all? From a little farther down the road you could see the castle. If that poor bastard had had the courage to look out and look up, he might have seen that he wasn't alone.

54

The group was standing at the side of the road, sheltering under a tree and watching Michael and Kieran trying to get a dark blue Volkswagen van started. The wind whipped through the branches, giving them little protection and seeming to almost increase the ferocity of the rain, but they were past caring now. They were all soaked and numb with cold, every layer of clothing drenched.

The van refused to turn over.

"This is bloody stupid," Howard moaned. "Give it up and try another car. Or let's just keep walking. Anything but stand out here like this."

Michael kicked the wheel of the Volkswagen with frustration.

"Howard's right," Lorna said. "We should keep moving. This isn't helping anyone."

Michael kicked the car again.

"How am I supposed to get back home when I can't even get a bloody car started?"

Howard emerged from under the tree, covering his head with the map. He pointed farther down the road. "Look, there are some buildings up ahead. We could stop there for a while. Warm up. Get some food inside us. Try and dry out a little . . ."

Michael reluctantly accepted he was right. This wasn't doing them any good. At least getting under cover for a short while would allow them to take stock and build up a little much needed energy for the final push toward Chadwick later today. Howard had checked the map just before they'd tried to get the van started, and had given them all the bad news that they'd probably covered less than half the distance they needed to. As desperate as Michael was to reach the port, the thought of walking as far again made his heart sink. And that was before they'd even thought about what they were going to do when they got there. No boat. No means of getting back to the island. No fucking point.

Michael was too tired and dejected to discuss the situation any farther. He looked down at the ground, irrationally angry both with himself and everybody else, doing all he could to avoid making eye contact with anyone. In the undergrowth just ahead of him was a skull. It was yellow-white, every trace of flesh worn away, and as he watched a large, well-gorged, glistening worm crawled out of one eye socket, then slithered down and disappeared into its gaping mouth, like something off the cover of the cheap horror novels he used to keep hidden under his bed when he was a kid. His mom used to try and stop him reading them, concerned that he was too young and that they were a bad influence. If only she could see him now. In comparison to the world he'd been living in since last September, nothing he'd ever read or seen in any horror film felt even remotely frightening anymore. Just behind the skull was another one, lying on its side. And ahead of that, an arm or a leg, he couldn't immediately tell which. And there was the distinctive curved shape of a spine and a butterfly-like pelvis, then the upright parallel bones of a rib cage . . . the closer he looked, the more it seemed the entire world had become one vast, never-ending graveyard. Did he and the others even have any place here any more?

"Come on, mate," Howard said, gripping his shoulder, trying to sound enthusiastic but failing miserably. "Not far now."

The factory had produced car parts back in the day. There was a smattering of cars parked outside the gray, warehouse-like building, but none of the group had enough energy left to even think about trying to get any of them started. For now all they wanted was a little shelter and warmth. Getting inside was easy. Everyone here had died toward the end of the early shift, and the main doors were closed but unlocked.

They stood there together, dripping wet, in a small reception area. To their left a dead receptionist still sat at her desk, her skeletal face resting peacefully on her keyboard. Hollis pushed the door shut behind them, and as it closed it finally shut out the noise of the howling gale and driving rain outside. The silence was welcome, but short-lived.

"What's that?" Caron asked, although she already knew full well what it was. There were noises coming from elsewhere in the building—the sounds of the dead. What remained of the early shift had been stirred up by the unexpected arrival of the living.

"What do we do?"

Michael looked at her. Stupid bloody question, he thought. "We get rid of them, I guess."

He dumped most of his stuff by the reception desk—his sodden overcoat and a small bag of supplies he'd managed to loot along the way—and then walked deeper into the factory. Kieran and Harte followed close behind.

Before going through the main door which led out onto the factory floor, they came upon a small office. Harte looked inside and saw that it was empty. He beckoned for the other two to follow him. No doubt an office which had once belonged to a foreman or shift manager, it had a wide safety-glass window which afforded them a full view over the entire shop floor. The office itself was dark, but the rest of the factory was illuminated by the light which trickled in through dirty Perspex panes in the corrugated roof above.

"Fuck," Kieran said under his breath.

There were numerous large machines and workbenches dotted all around the working area: lathes and presses and other less immediately recognizable things. On the ground around them were bodies, withered away, wrapped in raglike clothes which appeared several sizes too big. And then, from all sides, other corpses which could still move and which had been trapped in the factory since the very beginning, started to drag themselves toward the faces watching them from the office window. Michael felt like he was watching these creatures in some kind of bizarre zoo, as if they'd been held in captivity here. The three men were transfixed, unable to look away as the dead drew closer and closer. They behaved in much the same way they always had done, staggering awkwardly on legs powered by muscles which were now brittle and wasted away, occasionally lurching into the path of others and being pushed back. The farthest forward of them slammed up against the glass and began clawing it with numb, slow-moving fingers. And yet, for all the familiarity, there was something undeniably different about this encounter.

"Look at them, poor fuckers," Harte said quietly. "I know we've had it bad, but they must have been going through hell, stuck here all this time."

Kieran said nothing, but he knew that Harte was right. "All they want is for it to be over," he said. "They've changed. They just want us to end it for them, don't they?"

"I don't think they've changed," Michael said. "There's nothing to say they haven't been like this all along, they just couldn't control themselves enough to show it. If anyone's changed, it's us."

"What are you on about?" Harte sneered.

335

"It's our attitude to them that's different now. I've hated these things since day one and I've done all I could to get rid of as many of them as possible. And it makes me feel bad that all this time, all they wanted was to die."

"So you helped them. Nothing to feel bad about. We had no way of knowing."

"Suppose. Doesn't make me feel any better, though."

"Get a grip. You're talking crap."

"Maybe I am," he said, looking at the mass of constantly shifting, horrifically disfigured creatures which crowded in front of the office window now, blocking out the light. They slid from side to side, covering the glass with stains of their decay. They each wore matching overalls, originally dark blue and marked with patches of grease and oil, now also covered in the remains of themselves. "They just came to work one day and never went home again," he said under his breath. "They're just people. Just people like us. We've *all* lost everything."

Kieran left the office and went out onto the shop floor. The bodies around the window reacted, immediately trying to move closer toward him. Michael watched Kieran as he walked into a central area of relatively clear space and waited. One by one, those corpses which could still move gradually made their way toward him. And, one by one, he destroyed them.

Howard found a van in a dry shelter around the back of the building, half-loaded with car parts, ready for a delivery run which never happened. He carefully removed the driver—who had died half-in and half-out of his vehicle—then turned the key in the ignition, expecting nothing. When the engine burst into life he yelled out with delight, surprising even himself with the uninhibited volume of his voice after so many weeks of enforced silence. The beautiful mechanical sound had an immediate revitalising effect on the others.

"There's still a few hours before dark," Lorna said as they grouped around the van. "We could be at the port and away before long."

No one replied. No one needed to. Within minutes they were ready to leave.

55

The constant wind and rain refused to let up, battering everything, buffeting the sides of the van as Harte drove them toward the center of Chadwick.

"Head straight for the marina," Michael said, nervously stating the obvious.

"What else was I going to do?" Harte quickly replied. "Stop for a pizza?"

He was struggling to see out through the rain, windscreen wipers on full speed. Michael sat in the seat next to him, his stomach churning with nerves. Had the others got away safely before the weather had broken? Had they got away at all? If they'd delayed leaving for any reason, then there was a strong possibility they'd still be here, under cover somewhere, waiting out the storm. Worse still, what if the storm had hit during their crossing? That didn't bear thinking about.

Harte drove down roads he'd followed many times before, past things he recognized and which sparked strong memories: the petrol station he'd used as cover to make his escape from Jas and the others, and The Minories—the shopping mall they'd been looting that day. And as they approached the town, he looked out into the distance toward the apartments where he'd spent a couple of weeks alone in the midst of all this chaos. Strange now, he thought, how he almost felt a kind of fondness for those days. Things had generally been easier while he'd been on his own, much less complicated, but it hadn't been an easy ride. The solitude had been alternately stimulating and soul-destroying. It was by no means perfect, but there was a lot to be said for the isolation. He could also see that the helicopter had gone. That had to be a good sign, didn't it?

Harte tried to drive down the route he knew best to get down to the marina, but he couldn't get through. The roads were blocked. Many more slow-moving corpses had dragged themselves down the narrow streets than had been here last time.

"We might as well leave the van," Michael suggested. "It's not far now. We'll get there quicker on foot."

Harte stopped the van and before anyone else had chance to move or say anything, Michael was out and running toward the marina. He sprinted down the road, skidding in gore, occasionally changing direction to avoid the odd corpse which desperately reached out for him. The others followed as best they could, their line becoming spaced out as large gaps appeared between the fittest and the slowest. Caron, Hollis, and Lorna brought up the rear. Lorna refused to leave the other two behind, and they were the last to reach the water's edge. There they found the others. Howard, Kieran, and Harte had stopped short of Michael, who stood alone at the end of the jetty, hands on his knees, doubled-over with effort and breathing hard. Even from a distance they could sense his pain.

The marina had been destroyed.

Every boat—every single boat, no matter how large or small— had been damaged beyond repair. And this wasn't storm damage: everywhere they looked they saw ruptured hulls, broken masts, slashed sails . . . several smaller vessels had been burned out and were now just floating wrecks. Others had sunk, parts of them still jutting out of the water, reminiscent of the way the bones of the dead now littered the land.

Michael slowly stood up straight, turned around and walked back towards the others. He looked beaten, disconsolate.

"Who did this?" Caron asked as he pushed past her.

"Who do you think?" he replied. "Your bloody friend Jas and his lackeys."

"Are you sure? It might have been—"

"I'm sure," he said angrily, turning back to face her. "No one else would have done anything like this. Such a fucking pointless waste. No one from the island would have done this."

"But why?"

"To stop us getting away," Howard suggested.

"Either that or it's to stop the others getting back," Kieran said. He looked around the boatyard, trying to take it all in. In spite of everything he'd witnessed since last September, what they'd found here was unexpectedly shocking. It was the sheer senseless, wanton destruction that was eating at him. He felt ashamed to have ever had any allegiance to Jas. He'd always thought he was better than this.

"So what do we do now?" Lorna asked. "There's no way we're getting off the mainland now."

"And there's no way Richard will be able to bring the helicopter back in this weather either," Michael said.

"We should wait until the storm passes," Howard said. "Maybe there's another boat . . ."

"We've already been through this. Even if there is, who's going to navigate?"

"Okay, but we can't just sit here feeling sorry for ourselves."

"You give me an alternative and I'll listen."

"What about the castle?"

"What, go back there? No thanks," Harte said quickly.

"What, then? Stay here? This place is a ruin."

"Isn't everywhere?" said Caron.

"So what exactly are you saying?" Lorna demanded, looking directly toward Michael for an answer. "After surviving everything we've been through, are we just supposed to roll over now and play dead?" Her outburst was met with silence from the others but she continued, unabated. "I'm not going to give up now, and neither should any of you." She pointed at Michael. "For fuck's sake, you've got a baby coming. You can't stay here. Your missus is going to need you."

"You think I don't already know that?"

"I think you're missing the point, Lor," Caron said, holding her arm against the wind. "It's not that he doesn't want to go back, he can't. *We* can't."

"Not now, perhaps, but there's always tomorrow. We can find another port, find a boat that's still seaworthy, *learn* to navigate if we have to. But I don't think it's going to come to that."

"Why not?" Kieran asked.

"Surely the helicopter will come back at some point?"

Everyone looked at Michael.

"Richard might come back, I guess. I hope he will, but I can't assume that he'll—"

"I don't think we can do anything *but* assume. We've got to hope he flies back over."

"So what if he does," Harte said. "Don't tell me, we'll try and attract his attention from the ground."

"Haven't we been through this before?" Hollis said, an increasingly rare interjection from the exhausted, beaten man.

"Bloody hell," Howard sighed "How many times have we tried that?"

"Yes, but things are different now," Lorna said.

"Are they?"

"The stakes are higher, for a start. This is absolutely our last chance. And the bodies are different too. We don't have to worry about them like we used to."

"So?"

"So all we have to do now is concentrate on doing something big enough that he can't miss from the air."

"It won't work," Harte said, sounding dejected. "Richard told me. He said there's always something burning somewhere, those were his exact words. We'd have to burn the whole bloody town for him to see us."

"Then let's do that," she quickly replied. "Let's torch the whole place if we have to. Because there's another thing you're not considering here."

"And what's that?" Michael asked.

"This time Richard knows we're here. If he does come back, he'll actually be looking for us."

56

"This one," Kieran said, stopping outside a modern-looking block of seafront apartments. The building was on the edge of a fairly new development not far from the marina, probably thrown up in the last property boom and left half-empty as a result of the property bust which had followed. "Look at it. It's perfect. Beach-facing location, not far from the center of town, and it's fucking huge."

He was right. If they were going to set fire to any building, Michael thought, realizing how weird that sounded, then this was definitely the right one. The group of seven huddled together under a concrete canopy which ran above a series of small shops, protecting the pavement.

"When do we do it, then?" Howard asked.

"We're too late now," Michael said, "it's almost dark. And like I said, Richard's not going to come out while the weather's this bad."

"We should wait until morning," Lorna suggested. "And as soon as the storm passes, we'll do it."

The building they'd earmarked for destruction seemed the logical place to stay and sit out the night. They took over a well-appointed

343

ground-floor flat, glad to have a chance to finally shut the door on the foul conditions outside and rest a while. They used their torches to investigate some of the shops nearby where they found enough food and drink to last the evening, more dry clothes and some brighter lights. It felt strange sitting in a place they were planning to destroy. Surreal, almost. Kieran thought it felt like their last night on Earth.

They found the owner of the flat in the bathroom, spread-eagled in the tray at the bottom of the shower cubicle, naked and still moving but unable to get out. The temptation had been to just leave her there, but that didn't feel right. Lorna picked her up and draped a soft toweling wrap over what was left of her body. The shower tray was filled with a disgusting sludge: the remnants of the girl's decay. Strands of hair, teeth, fingernails, and other less recognizable items lay in an inch-deep, semi-dry gunk of putrefied flesh.

Before removing her from her flat, Lorna had found out a little more about the girl. She was virtually mummified now, but they could see from the pictures in frames around the dusty, open-plan living space that she'd been a young and very beautiful woman before she'd died last September. Her name was Jenna Walker, according to the bank cards Lorna found in her purse. Bizarrely, she felt uneasy looking through the dead girl's things while she was still in the house, but it felt equally wrong to think about her as an *it* and ignore the person she'd once been.

Lorna tried to piece together her past from the clues lying around the flat. Jenna had died young—only a couple of years older than she herself was now—and she'd worked in the research department of a large petrochemical company which operated a plant a little farther down the coast. She'd lived alone, but by the looks of the calendar hanging in the kitchen, she'd had an active social life. Lorna wondered if she'd had a boyfriend. Had she been close to her parents? Had she read all of the hundreds of paperback books piled up in her bedroom and on shelves around the living room? Had she enjoyed the DVD she'd left next to the TV?

Getting to know Jenna felt like a necessity, but it also made what Lorna knew she had to do that much harder. The more she knew about the dead girl, the harder it was to think of her as just another corpse. Giving her back her name and something of her history, and finishing her time with a little care and dignity, all combined to give the whole experience a melancholic, funereal feel which Lorna hadn't expected. She took the corpse by the arm and slowly pulled it along the corridor into another apartment. She could feel the girl's bones under her fingers as she shuffled along, much of the meat now rotted away.

She looked down into Jenna's decayed face, her features still just about recognizable from certain angles and in a certain light, and remembered the girl in the pictures as she finished her time with a bread knife through the temple. Shame it had to be so brutal, she thought, but there was no other way. She couldn't asphyxiate her or give her an overdose of pills. Couldn't strangle or drown her. When she'd finished Jenna she felt like she'd just carried out a gangland killing.

Lorna returned to the flat and sat down with the others, tired and subdued, but more determined than ever to get away from this hellish place at the earliest opportunity. Even if they ended up drifting out to sea on a boat loaded up with food, destined never to find Cormansey, then that would surely be preferable to spending what was left of her life in this desolate tomb of a country.

She slept intermittently, but never relaxed fully. It felt like only minutes had passed when Michael woke them all.

"It's time," he said, pulling back the blinds and letting bright daylight flood into the room. "Storm's passed."

57

The air outside was unexpectedly clear and fresh. A strong wind blew in off the sea, temporarily dispersing the decay-filled tang which was usually so prominent. The ground was still wet from the rain, but the storm had completely cleared and the angry gray clouds which had clogged the skies all day yesterday had now disappeared.

There was a handful of bodies outside when they left the apartment. They must either have followed the survivors last night or been drawn here subsequently by their activity and noise. They continued to converge on the building as the small group worked to get things ready. No one bothered to do anything about the dead: they simply worked around them knowing the fire would bring an end to them all soon enough.

All seven of the small group worked individually and without complaint, finding it infinitely easier to be outside now that the dead were no longer the threat they'd originally perceived them to be. Several cars had been left in the car park outside the apartment block, and Harte rolled some of them closer to the building. His plan was simple: crowd the base of the apartments with enough vehicles so that, when the heat from the fire they intended starting indoors was fierce enough, the fuel in the cars would explode and fan the flames.

While Harte shifted the cars, Michael, Kieran, and Hollis disappeared into the town and siphoned fuel from more vehicles into petrol cans and buckets, then carried them back to the flats. Lorna and Howard drenched the ground floor of the building with petrol and opened all the windows and interior doors. After working for a while, Caron sat herself down on a low stone wall on the other side of the road and watched.

When all the fuel had been used up, they were ready to start the fire. Kieran splashed fuel around the entrance to the apartments, Harte remained standing a short distance back from him, holding a Molotov cocktail, and watched.

"You done?" he asked as Kieran jogged back over to where the others were waiting. They'd all taken cover on the other side of the stone wall now, leaving him on his own.

"We're done," Kieran shouted.

Harte nervously held a lighter in one hand, the petrol bomb in the other. The fumes from the fuel were stinging his eyes and nose; he wasn't sure if they were coming from the bottle or the apartments. The stench reminded him of when he'd burned down the petrol station, and the memory of the blast back then seemed to increase his nervousness tenfold.

"Get on with it," Hollis yelled at him. He flicked the lighter before he could talk himself out of it. The petrol-soaked rag caught immediately. He threw the bottle and turned and sprinted back toward the others in a single, barely coordinated movement. Kieran grinned at him as he ran back.

"Crap shot!" he laughed. Harte dived over the wall, then scrambled back up again. He was right, it had been a bad shot—the bottle had smashed against the side of the front entrance, missing the door completely—but it didn't matter. They'd drenched the place in more than enough petrol and the fumes caught light almost instantly. Flames filled the air like a scorching mist, billowing left and right, then racing inside and tearing up through the apartment block. It wasn't as dramatic as he'd been expecting, but it was enough. He stood back, arms folded, and watched with satisfaction as the fire began to take grip.

"Quite therapeutic, actually," Howard said, and Harte thought back to those days at the flats when Webb used to spend his time beating the shit out of random corpses and calling that therapy. He knew exactly how he felt now. A little wanton destruction of property wasn't doing anyone any harm, but Christ, it made him feel a lot better. Even if they didn't make it off the mainland, maybe he could fill his time smashing things up to try and vent his numerous frustrations.

Less than a minute had passed, but the fire had already begun to take a substantial hold. Dancing orange-and-yellow light was visible through many of the first-floor windows, illuminating the insides of the individual flats which had, until now, remained shadow-filled and unlit. He watched through one particular window, directly ahead of him. The fire snaked in through the open doorway, then furniture toward the back of the room caught light, seeming to burst into flames spontaneously. The fire moved quickly, its pace accelerated by the copious amounts of petrol with which everything had been doused. A couple of seconds later and the curtains were alight, then flames began to lick up against the window as if they were trying to escape. Somewhere else another window shattered, exploding outward, flying glass followed by a belch of white-hot flame. And then another, then another. Within minutes a couple of the cars were alight too. They all knew it wouldn't be long before fuel tanks caught and the raging firestorm they'd started would be burning out of control.

Several bodies were already moving toward the growing inferno. Lorna thought she was imagining it, but their speed seemed to have increased slightly. She watched as one walked right up to the apartment building, seemingly oblivious to the flames which now surrounded it. A loose rag of clothing caught light, and in an instant the whole body was consumed. It staggered on for a few more seconds, completely enveloped by fire now, before collapsing. The same thing happened to several more. Another one walked toward a part of the building where the flames were particularly ferocious. It caught light before it had even made contact with anything which was burning, the intensity of the heat enough to cause it to spontaneously combust.

"So what do we do now? Just sit here and wait?" Caron asked. She looked at the others, their faces bathed in the strangely soothing flickering orange glow.

"It's going to get too dangerous here," Michael said. Almost on cue, there came a series of quick, successive explosions like gunshots; aerosols or something equally flammable detonating inside. The noises seemed to spur on even more of the dead to get closer.

"So where do we go?"

"There's only one place to go, isn't there?" he said. "If Richard does come back for us, he's going to head straight for the car park."

"The car park?" Caron said, confused. Michael was about to explain but another blast stopped him from speaking. The fuel in the tank of one of the cars had exploded, sending the vehicle up onto its nose, pirouetting, then crashing back down against the side of the burning apartment block. When the noise had subsided, Michael tried to speak again. He pointed out across town.

"See that multistory car park over there? That's where he lands, so that's where we need to be."

Without waiting for any of them to respond, he started walking.

58

The noise coming from the burning building they were moving away from was astonishing. Frequent explosions continued to ring out, making the otherwise silent town sound like a battlefield. Although it was dry today, the fierce wind continued to blow, whipping off the sea now, gusting along the streets and fanning the flames.

There were more bodies coming toward them. Despite all they'd seen over the last day, there was still a moment of instinctive, nervous hesitation whenever they were this close to any of the dead—the split-second fear of attack—but it was clear that the attention of these corpses was now completely focused elsewhere. They weren't interested in the living any longer, probably weren't even aware they were there. The fire in the near distance was acting like a call to the faithful and the longer it burns, Harte thought to himself, the more of them will be drawn away from the rest of town. In a bizarre way, it felt like they'd begun cleansing Chadwick.

"Look at that," Hollis said. Harte immediately turned around, and what he saw took him by surprise. They'd reached a modern-looking office block, the front of which was almost completely made up of huge panes of glass, most of which were now filled with bodies. A huge mass of dead workers who'd been trapped in the building since September were now crowding against the glass, unable to go anywhere but still desperately trying to get closer to the distant flames. Even from here the blaze was clearly visible, burning bright against the muted colors of everything else. Harte stopped and watched them watching the fire. When another explosion echoed around the town, the dead became even more animated and began hammering against the window to get out. Like the bodies beneath the castle, these people had been sheltered from the worst of the elements by virtue of the fact they'd died indoors, and their decay appeared much less advanced than many of those left out on the streets. Harte caught his breath when one of the corpses stumbled forward and clattered against the other side of a glass door next to where he was standing. Even now his instinctive reaction was either to run or fight, and it took great effort for him to maintain control and not do either. The corpse flinched again, reacting to another flash of flame, and Harte saw that it still had a name badge clipped to the pocket of its crusted, gore-streaked shirt. Ryan Fleming: Head of Research. And like Michelle Bright—the corpse of the nurse under the castle—and Jenna Walker, the young, dead chemist whose home they'd just torched, Ryan Fleming suddenly mattered.

Apart from Kieran, the others had all continued walking. The street was filling with drifting smoke, making it increasingly difficult to differentiate between the movements of the living and the dead.

"What the hell are you doing?" Kieran asked.

"Letting them out," Harte shouted back at him and then, without stopping to consider the consequences, he forced the door to the building open. He guided Ryan Fleming's dishevelled shell out onto the street, still half-expecting it to turn on him and attack, but it didn't. It simply lifted its tired, diseased head to look up at the light in the distance, then lethargically walked away in the general direction of the fire. He watched it go, and was gently pushed away to the side as more corpses followed and began to spill out of the office building, clumsily barging past him.

"What's the point of doing that?" Kieran asked.

"Makes me feel better," he replied with a nonchalant shrug of his shoulders.

In the next property along—a coffee shop—he could see more of them now, tripping over the tables and chairs where they'd drunk their last coffees, colliding with the bodies of the last people they'd seen and spoken to; the last human interactions they'd had before they'd died. Harte released them all. And in the building next to the coffee shop there were even more corpses pawing to get out. In a gym a short distance further down the street, crowds of the dead clamored around the dirty windows, stumbling over dust- and cobweb-covered exercise equipment to get closer to the light. Even though he'd seen thousands of them before, Harte continued to be distracted by their grotesque appearance. Several of them were still dressed in figure-hugging Lycra outfits. Their heavily stained exercise clothing still clung to their figures, but their shapes had altered dramatically since they'd first put on their outfits months earlier, stretching and bulging with decay. Some of them were imprisoned by the fitness machines they'd been using at the moment of death. He could see at least two of them who'd died midpress and who were now pinned down by bars and weights. Keen to catch up with the others who had now disappeared out of sight around a corner, Harte wedged the door open, then hurried after them. There were three steps down onto the street. He looked back as the dead began to stumble out after him, some of them losing their footing and falling, then being trampled by others before picking themselves up again and carrying on.

Kieran had waited for him. "Do you think they know what they're doing?" he asked.

"I have no idea," Harte admitted. "But like I say, it makes me feel better."

The two men ran on. Kieran stepped to one side to let another rancid corpse crawl past. Behind them now the street was full of corpses disappearing into the ever-increasing clouds of smoke.

Michael glanced over his shoulder but he couldn't see Kieran or Harte. No matter. They all knew where they were supposed to be heading. He recognized the street they were walking along now. Over to his right was the road which led to the baby store, and up ahead was the supermarket Donna, Richard, and Cooper had looted on their first day back on the mainland. That felt like it had been weeks ago now. He looked up into the narrow strip of sky visible between the roofs of the buildings on either side of the road as he walked, wishing he could see the helicopter, willing it to be there. The sky was a beautiful deep blue this morning, but it was increasingly hard to see through the clouds of smoke which were being blown in their direction.

"Where the hell did you come from?" he heard Howard say. He walked into the back of Lorna who'd stopped suddenly. Michael wafted smoke out of his eyes to see.

"Same place as you, you fucking idiot," a voice he didn't know replied.

"Then why don't you fuck off back there again, Jas," Lorna shouted angrily. Michael could see more clearly now. There were two men he didn't recognize standing in the street directly ahead of them. One of them, Jas he presumed, was carrying a rifle. He moved forward menacingly. Caron, Howard, and Hollis moved away. The other man held back.

"Why did you do it?" Jas demanded. "You idiots, you fucked everything up."

"*We* fucked everything up?" Lorna said, pushing her way to the front of the group again. "Last time I checked, *you* were the one causing all the grief. You were the one who tried to keep us locked up. You're the one who killed Jackson."

There was a hint of emotion in Jas's face. A momentary flicker.

"I didn't kill him," he said, sounding marginally less aggressive. "He fell on his knife."

"And you expect us to believe that?"

"I don't really care what you believe. I'm not interested."

"Then why are you here?"

"Would somebody tell me what the hell is going on?" Michael said. "Who are these jokers?"

"This is Jas," Lorna replied, confirming his suspicions and almost having to force herself to spit out his name. "And this other useless strip of piss is Mark Ainsworth."

Another explosion came from the direction of the burning apartment block, this time so loud and violent that Michael felt the ground shake beneath his feet.

"So where are your playmates, Jas?" Caron asked, being deliberately antagonistic. "Are you two all on your own now? Have they all abandoned you?"

She didn't realize how close to the truth she was.

"They've gone, useless bastards," Jas admitted before adding, "and it looks like they've taken your places on the last boat out to your precious bloody island."

Michael reeled from what he'd just heard. He felt like he'd been punched in the gut. It was bad enough that he was left stranded here, but the thought that this callous, murdering wanker's associates—probably the same fuckers who were responsible for all the grief back at the castle earlier, putting everyone's lives in danger—had made it back to Cormansey when he hadn't was unbearable. He pushed his way through the others and lunged at Jas, taking him by surprise. He grabbed him by the collar and smacked him up against the window of a health food shop. Inside, a corpse immediately began hammering at the glass to be set free. For a moment Jas seemed more concerned by the dead body behind him than by Michael.

"Was that all your doing down at the marina?" Michael demanded. "Did you wreck all the boats?"

"So what if I did?"

Michael didn't have a chance to speak again. Jas was too strong for him. Powerfully built and fired-up, he forced Michael back, shoved him to the ground, and aimed the rifle into his face.

"Don't be stupid, Jas," Lorna yelled, trying to pull him away. Michael scrambled back up onto his feet, but Jas came at him again, this time kicking his legs out from under him. He hit the ground hard, flat on his back, all the air knocked out of him. Lorna forced herself between the two men as Jas went for him a third time.

"Stop, Jas," Ainsworth said, but his words had no effect.

"Leave him," Lorna ordered. "You stupid bastard, Jas. He's got a kid waiting to be born on that island. You've taken away his last chance of getting back there."

"He's better off here," Jas replied as Ainsworth tried to pull him away. "The kid's as good as dead, anyway."

Michael groaned with anger and pain and stood back up. Lorna blocked him, stopping him from getting any closer.

A corpse brushed past Jas. He tried to load the rifle but his hands were shaking. Instead he swung it around and clubbed the stumbling body away.

"You all think I'm some kind of villain," he said, trying again to load and now looking around at the frightened faces staring back at him—people he'd called friends at one time or other before now. "I'm not. I didn't want for any of this to happen. Contrary to what you might think, I didn't kill Jackson either, I swear . . ."

He stopped talking when the air was filled with another thunderous noise. For a second several of them thought it might be the helicopter returning, but it was quickly clear that this was something else entirely. Howard took a few steps back toward the main street, sidestepping several more cadavers, and saw that a billowing cloud of dust and smoke was rolling steadily toward them. The air felt hot and dry. Had part of the apartment building collapsed? It was impossible to tell, but the flames were spreading fast. Through the haze he could see more of the dead continuing to stagger forward, the farthest advanced of them catching fire long before they reached the burning apartments.

Harte and Kieran came running out of the chaos toward him. "We need to get out of here," Harte shouted, wiping tears from his stinging eyes. "The whole bloody town's going to go up in flames."

He stopped speaking when he saw the expression on Howard's face.

"Harte . . ." Howard started to say.

"What is it?" Harte demanded. He continued around the corner and saw Jas. Jas saw him too, and immediately raised the rifle and aimed it at him. And then Kieran appeared, and Harte was immediately forgotten. Jas directed the full force of his anger at him instead.

"You sold me out, you fucker!" he screamed, charging into Kieran and sending him flying. He aimed the rifle at him and Kieran staggered back, tripping on the curb and landing on his backside.

"You were wrong, Jas," he said, barely able to get the words out.

"Jesus," Lorna shouted, "is there anyone you're not pissed off with? Doesn't that tell you something? Like, that *you* might be the one who's got this wrong?"

Jas glared at her, but was distracted as another random body collided with him. He recoiled, shoving the foul thing away. It continued to try and move toward him, trying to get to the fire in the distance, but Jas misinterpreted its actions as an attack. He forced the rifle up into the creatures gaping mouth and fired, splattering what was left of its brains over the pavement in a firework-like shower of dark brown gore. He spun around and saw another cadaver walking listlessly toward him, and fired again. This time he hit the cadaver in the right shoulder. It collapsed, but immediately tried to drag itself forward with its one remaining good arm. He clubbed the back of its head with the butt of his rifle.

"Jas, stop!" Harte shouted, but his words had no effect.

"They're coming!" he screamed, the panic in his voice now clearly evident. The collapsing building had clearly attracted the attention of many more of the creatures, and another surge of dead flesh was now advancing toward them.

"They might be coming," Harte said, still trying to stop him, "but they're not coming for you, you idiot. Haven't you worked it out yet? The dead aren't our enemy. They're as scared and as lost as we are."

Jas spun around again. Another corpse, and another shot to the face. This time Ainsworth tried to stop him, grabbing the barrel of the rifle. In Jas's panic and confusion, his trigger finger tightened and

357

he fired. Ainsworth was blown backward. He collided with a corpse, then dropped to the ground, a bloody gaping hole in his chest.

"What the hell have you done?" Lorna demanded, standing over Ainsworth's twitching body, barely able to comprehend what had just happened. Wisps of smoke rose from around the edges of his wound. She didn't need to get any closer to know he was dead. She looked up and saw the others moving farther away from Jas, who was reloading the rifle with another handful of shells from his pocket. "What happened to you, Jas?"

"The last three months happened," he replied, still looking for his next target. He aimed and fired at another cadaver, then another and another . . . The rest of the living scattered as he reloaded again, regrouping around the back of a garbage truck. Harte tried to call to Lorna from the truck, but she wasn't listening. She was still crouched next to Ainsworth's lifeless body. Jas fired at yet another cadaver.

"The last three months have fucked us all up," she said, "but I thought you were better than this. It didn't have to be this way. You, me, the dead . . . we're all victims, you know. It's not about us versus them or you versus me, it's just about us all trying to survive."

"I know that," he said, lowering the rifle momentarily. "I know that better than anyone. I've been trying to tell you, you won't survive on that island, it's a dead end. You should stay here. You should stay here with me."

Lorna stood up and walked over, terrified that at any moment he was going to lift his weapon and start firing again, but still feeling a need to try and talk to him. She thought he sounded desperate. She glanced back along the street, and in the distance she could see the glow of the flames. The warm wind continued to gust toward them, fanning the fire and helping it spread with remarkable speed.

"We have to go," she said, gently putting her hand on his arm. "It's not safe here."

His voice cracked. "It's not safe anywhere. Don't go to the island, Lorna. Please don't."

He pushed her away, his sudden, unexpected movement taking her by surprise, and then fired another shot into the smoke. She saw a body go down, visible only when it hit the ground.

"I know you're scared," she said, hiding behind him now as yet more of the dead approached in greater numbers, "and I don't pretend to understand why you did what you did, but your best chance is to come with us now and try to get to Cormansey. There's no future for any of us here, but there might still be on the island."

"You think?" he said, taking aim again. "You all think I killed Jackson. You *know* I killed Ainsworth. But I didn't mean for any of it to happen . . ."

"I know that, and we can put it behind us. It might be a struggle on the island, but—"

"I'm not going," he said abruptly. He fired once more.

"But this is madness. Come on, Jas, you're confused. Think about Michael . . . he's going to be a dad. What would you be doing if your kids were still alive? Would you have wanted them to stay here, or would you have wanted them to go to the island?"

Jas instinctively pressed his palm to his chest, feeling for the outline of his precious wallet under several layers of clothing. But then another group of bodies stumbled into view and he tried to fire again. The rifle was empty. Lorna tried to pull him away but he shrugged her off and marched toward the nearest corpse and clubbed it to the ground. Then another. Then another. And now he was surrounded. The slow trickle of bodies emerging had become an unsteady flood, more and more of them approaching all the time, attracted both by the distant flames and by Jas's bluster.

Once more Lorna tried to pull him back but he just pushed her away, desperate to destroy every last one of the foul, disease-ridden cadavers which now seemed to be converging on him. There were scores of them everywhere he looked now: some limping, some crawling, some barely moving at all. Some were still nearly recognizable as people, others were little more than gelatinous heaps of decay that were somehow still able to function. Jas felt his legs weaken. He was surrounded, more of them approaching than he could deal with alone. He glanced back over his shoulder, looking for help, but even more bodies had sealed him off, preventing him from seeing Lorna now. She could still see him—just—and was poised to run deeper into the crowd to try and drag him away when Harte grabbed her from behind and pulled her to safety behind the garbage truck.

"Leave him," he said.

"We can't . . ."

"We can. We've got more important things to worry about."

He stood back and she saw that Hollis was slumped on the floor, resting up against a grubby shop window. His clothes were soaked with blood. Lorna couldn't process what she was seeing. She tried to talk, but no words came out. Caron was sitting by Hollis's side, gently stroking his arm. She stood up and held Lorna.

"He got caught in the shooting," she explained. "We didn't even realize he'd been hit . . ."

Lorna crouched down next to Hollis. He looked up at her, his filthy face streaked with tears. There was blood on his lips.

"I know I don't look so good these days," he said, his voice hard to hear, "but I didn't think Jas would mistake me for one of them."

"Oh, Greg . . ." she said.

"You lot go on," he mumbled, blood bubbling. "I'll never make it."

"He's right," Harte said. "We need to go."

"What's the point?" Lorna demanded, sobbing. The tears carved clean lines through the dirt and soot on her cheeks. "Let's face it, we're fucked."

"Bloody hell," Hollis said, forcing a grin. "Things must be bad if you reckon we're fucked."

"Just being realistic, that's all."

"Realistic!" Harte protested. "Christ, Lor, we've spent three months trying to avoid the walking dead, hiding in castles and hotels and the like, and you decide today's the day to start talking about being *realistic*!"

"He's got a point," Kieran agreed.

"But we can't just leave Hollis . . ."

"Yes, you can," Hollis said. "Go, Lorna. Get out of here."

"No . . ."

Hollis managed to lift his head slightly and looked up at Harte, who acknowledged his friend.

"Come on," Harte said, gently picking Lorna up. She shook him off, wanting to say good-bye to Hollis, but she realized it was too late. She'd seen enough death to know there was no life left in his tired, glassy eyes.

Harte peered out around the front of the garbage truck. There were more corpses now—an incalculable number. The mass of dead bodies still trudging down the street toward the fire in the distance was undiminished, an unstoppable thick brown river of decay now. There was no sign of Jas; he'd long since been swallowed up. The bulk of the corpses seemed to be coming from the direction of the station, and the road to the car park was still relatively clear.

"What do you reckon?" Howard asked.

"Sprint for the car park," he replied. "It's our only option. Got to get up there and hope Richard turns up before the whole bloody town burns down."

They grouped together, ready to move.

"Wait," Caron said, looking around. "Where's Michael?"

59

Michael was waiting for them at the entrance to the car park.

"Where the hell have you been?" Kieran asked.

Michael answered with his own question. "Who's missing?"

"Hollis is dead," Lorna replied. "Shot."

"And Jas?"

"He's dead too, presumably. We lost him in all those bodies."
Michael nodded.

"Did you have something to do with that?" Howard asked.
"What did you do?"

"It wasn't just about him, you know," he explained. "All I did
was open up the station. I saw hundreds of them trapped there
when I first came to this place. Figured I should let them out before we leave."

"*If* we leave," Kieran said.

"I just wanted your friend Jas to get an idea of what he would
really be up against if he stayed here."

Lorna shook her head and started to climb, not sure whether
she believed Michael. She took Caron's hand and led her up the
corkscrew-shaped road. What they were going to do when they
reached the roof, however, she had no idea.

They climbed over a plum-colored Mini which had crashed into a barrier, then stopped on the third floor of five and peered down into the streets below. The town was steadily filling with fire, building after building being eaten up by the heat and light. But somehow the position didn't look as bad from up here as it had down at ground level. The fire hadn't made as much progress as they'd feared. Michael was relieved; they'd have a good few hours before they'd need to move again.

Howard peered over the edge and looked directly down. Closer to the entrance to the car park he could see the station which Michael had opened up. Even now there was a massive column of bodies trying to escape. They played a bizarre game of follow-the-leader as they spilled out onto the street and walked toward the red-hot devastation in the distance.

And then, just for a second, he thought he caught a glimpse of Jas, still fighting in the midst of the chaos. It was impossible to be sure from up here, such was the extent of the dead masses which filled the street outside the car park. Was it really him, or had it just been more corpses reacting to each other? It was gone again in just a few seconds.

In the distance Kieran could see the farthest advanced of the bodies burning up, and he watched them with an unexpected mix of emotions: relief, first and foremost, that the time of the dead was finally coming to an end. These were undoubtedly their final days, their final hours perhaps. He also felt an undeniable sense of achievement that he'd made it through to see this moment—that he'd survived when so many millions of others hadn't. And, strangely, he also felt pleased that, one way or another, everyone's suffering would soon be over—living and dead alike. He understood why Michael had done what he'd done.

The others had left him behind. Kieran looked around, then

started to run again, half the climb still to complete. His lungs felt as if they were full of smoke, and every step took a massive amount of effort. His thighs burned but he kept on moving, refusing to stop.

He eventually reached the roof and crossed the tarmac to stand with the others who were looking out over the burning town. Heavy palls of black smoke continued to rise up from the area along the sea front which was on fire. The dark, billowing clouds were blowing this way, almost blocking out the sun. From up here the world looked decidedly apocalyptic—like Judgment Day. *What am I thinking?* he asked himself wryly. *This can't be Armageddon. The world ended months ago.*

"You lot took your time," a voice said. Kieran spun around, his heart thumping, and found himself face-to-face with a familiar, scruffy-looking figure with a duffel bag over one shoulder and a newspaper tucked under his arm.

"Fuck me," he gasped. "Hello, Driver."

"What the hell are you doing here?" Lorna demanded.

"What do you think I'm doing here? I heard there might still be people around who needed a lift."

"But what about the others? Didn't they get to the island?"

"I presume. I volunteered to stay back here."

"You volunteered? Why?"

"Because I knew there'd be more of you to come. There's times recently when you've been almost as slippery as me," he said, pointing at Harte. "I thought if anyone could get away from that castle again, it'd be you."

"But why here?"

"Harry said it'd be the safest bet. He said you'd probably end up back here looking for the helicopter, and he was right."

"So where is it?"

"What, the helicopter?"

"Yes, the helicopter. What did you think I meant?"

"Oh, it's still on the island as far as I'm aware."

"So what are we going to do? Are you planning to bus us all over there?"

"Something like that. I've got another way out."

Caron walked toward Driver, her mind a whirlpool of conflicting emotions.

"I could kiss you . . ." she said.

"Maybe later," he said, quietly pleased, as he led them back toward ground level.

60

The descent took less than half the time it had taken them to reach the top of the car park. Introductions and explanations were quickly completed on the way back down. Once they'd reached ground level the mayhem out on the streets immediately refocused Michael.

"So what's the plan?"

"We head for the boats," Driver replied.

"No use going down there," Kieran said, "Jas totaled the place."

"I know, I watched him. Can't abide vandalism like that. Now I know you lot have just torched half the town, but I'm guessing you did that for a reason. What he did was just plain stupid."

"So where are we going?"

"I had a word with your mates Richard and Harry before they left," Driver said to Michael. "There's another option, providing we can get past this lot."

He watched the nearest of the corpses with the same nervous distrust they'd seen Jas display.

"They won't hurt you," Caron said.

"And you expect me to believe that after everything we've been through?"

"We wouldn't be here if it wasn't true," Michael said.

"Fair point," Driver agreed, knowing he'd no choice now anyway. "Right, this way."

He led them down toward the marina, carefully skirting around the edge of the vast crowd of corpses which were still swarming out of the station, all of them moving in the direction of the fire. They paid no attention to the living, the fire now their only focus. The air was dry, the smoke increasingly dense.

Less than ten minutes' walking and they entered the marina, quickly making their way past the ruined boatyard they'd seen yesterday on their return to the town. Michael thought he knew where they were going. Driver led them past the gap in the moorings where the *Summer Breeze* and the *Duchess* had been moored, then into the more exclusive area where he'd spent his first night here on the luxury cruiser. *Surely he can't have got that started?* he thought as he ran toward it.

"Not that one," Driver said, gesturing a little farther along the jetty. "That one."

He pointed at a boat just a fraction of the size of the first. It was beautifully appointed, but barely looked big enough to take the seven of them.

"Lovely," Harte said sarcastically. He turned to look at Michael. "Think we can get it going?"

"We can give it a go," Michael replied, sounding less than confident. He didn't see they had any alternative.

"Your friend Harry's already sorted out the engine," Driver told them. "He said you lot left him here on his own for a day. He said this boat was in pretty good working order but he didn't bother doing anything with it because it wasn't big enough. Didn't think he'd need it so he didn't say anything, but he had it ready as a backup."

"Good man, Harry," Michael said under his breath.

"This is all well and good," Caron said, eyeing the small vessel up with some unease, "but we've still got the little problem of trying to sail."

"And then we've got to find the island," Kieran added. "Are there any maps or . . . ?"

He let his words trail away and looked at Driver, who was standing opposite them all, looking back at the burning town they were so desperate to leave.

"Have any of you lot ever heard of a bloke called Tony Kent?" he asked. Six blank faces returned six blank expressions.

"Was he someone you used to know who sailed boats?" Howard suggested.

"Something like that," he replied. He tried another question. "Do any of you know what I used to do?"

"You drove buses," Harte said quickly.

"Correct. Before that?" No answer. "I'll tell you," he explained. "Before I drove buses I was a tour guide. Before that, I studied."

"Well done, you," Lorna mumbled.

"And before that," he continued, "I did fifteen years service in the navy."

"You never said."

"You never asked."

It took a few seconds for the importance of what he was telling them to sink in. Michael was the first to twig.

"So you think you can . . . ?" he started to say, too afraid to finish his question.

"What? Get you to the island? I'm a little rusty, but I think we'll be okay."

Harte grinned. "Bloody hell. I always said you were a dark horse."

"When?" Michael asked. "Now?"

"Well, I've no reason to be hanging around here. Don't know about you lot."

The fact that Caron, Kieran, Howard, and Michael were already rushing to board the boat immediately answered Driver's question. Lorna and Harte remained where they were for a moment longer.

"So who is Tony Kent?" Lorna remembered to ask just before she stepped off dry land.

"Who do you think?" Driver replied, thumping his chest. "It's me, you daft bugger."

She wrapped her arms around him and squeezed. Taken aback by the sudden show of affection, he wiped a tear away from the corner of his eye and hoped she hadn't noticed.

"So what are we supposed to call you now?" Harte asked, determined not to let his emotions get the better of him. "Is it Tony now, or still Driver?"

"Tony would be nice once we get to this island," he said. "I've done all the driving I'm going to, I think."

"What about Sailor?" Harte laughed. Driver just glared.

Lorna and Harte got onto the boat. It looked like it was going to be as tight a squeeze as he'd predicted. Driver shoved his well-read newspaper into his bag, then left it on the side of the jetty.

61

This was a boat which had never been designed for making sea crossings. More at home pottering along rivers or drifting along the Norfolk Broads and similar gentle waterways, the overloaded little vessel was clearly struggling. The group's euphoria at having finally made it off the mainland disappeared quickly, replaced with an undeniable unease. They felt uncomfortably low in the water, and despite the relatively clear sky overhead, the vicious wind continued to whip up the waves and repeatedly knock them off course. The seven survivors crammed onto the boat were cold, wet, and afraid.

But it could have been worse.

They could have died last September along with everyone else, Lorna thought. They could have got sick like Ellie and Anita and ended their time alone, desperately frightened, wallowing in their own waste. They could have cracked under the pressure of everything that had happened like Webb and Martin Priest and, most recently, Jas, or died senselessly like Ainsworth, Hollis, or Jackson. They could have fallen apart in any one of a hundred thousand different ways but they hadn't, not yet. They could have been trapped in the burning chaos of Chadwick, or buried under the castle, or they might still be trapped on the first floor of the besieged hotel, but they weren't. Unlike most people she'd come across since the end of the world, the seven of them still had a chance, albeit a small one. No matter how positive she tried to make herself feel, however, the endless gray water which surrounded them now made their situation feel increasingly hopeless again.

Driver used a compass and a map to navigate, doing his best to hide the fact that he was struggling from the others. Although shielded from the worst of the sea spray which soaked everyone and everything else, the rolling waves were making it increasingly difficult to concentrate. And they'd just reached a psychologically important point, he realized as he looked up and around for inspiration. His last visual reference point had disappeared far behind them, the faintest trace of the smoke hanging over Chadwick still remained like a smudge on the horizon, but otherwise there was absolutely nothing. He turned back around to face the bow again, trying to avoid catching the eye of any of the others for fear of starting another uncomfortable, slightly panic-tinged conversation which, inevitably, wouldn't do them any good. Instead, he just looked into the rolling waves; port, starboard, aft, bow . . . all he could see in every direction was water now.

Another hour, maybe slightly longer, and the silent nervousness in the boat had reached new levels. Conditions were deteriorating. The wind had picked up markedly, and although the sea wasn't particularly wild, to the seven people in the inappropriately small boat being knocked around by the waves, it certainly felt that way.

Caron was beginning to panic. Lorna, despite feeling increasingly anxious herself, did what she could to calm her. Michael squeezed through the others to reach Driver. Harte did the same, his sudden movements far less subtle than Michael's.

"How much longer?" he demanded as the boat swayed to one side, lurching sickeningly.

"How am I supposed to know?" Driver grumbled.

"You must have some idea."

"Forgot my sat nav."

"Don't take the piss."

"Don't talk bollocks, then. You can get out and walk if you like."

"Do we have any life jackets?" Caron wailed from close behind.

"Do we look like we have any life jackets?" Harte angrily protested. "Wouldn't we be wearing them?"

"Would you all just shut up and let me concentrate," Driver shouted. "All this noise is doing my bloody head in."

"You mean you haven't been concentrating so far?" Howard asked, semi-seriously. The pointless bickering continued, and Michael took the opportunity to try and find out how much of it was justified. He clung to the side of the boat as a wave crashed against the starboard side. Bigger than any of the waves they'd so far seen, it splashed over the deck, soaking everyone, filling the bottom of the boat with about an inch of water and cranking Caron's nervousness up to another level.

"Do you have any idea?" he asked quietly. Driver looked at him.

"I'm not going to lie to you," he said. "I'm not completely sure. I mean, I have a bearing and I've been sticking to it as best I can, but it's difficult. This boat's not ideal, you know, and the weather's getting worse."

"So what's the prognosis?"

"Keep heading in this direction for about another hour if we can. Then start with the flares."

"Flares?"

Driver looked down and kicked the door of a waterproof cupboard with the toe of his boot.

"That was the plan," he explained. "Richard said sail as close as you can to where you think the island is, then set off a flare. Put one up every hour."

"And then?"

"And then he'll hopefully see us at some point, then come out and guide us in."

Michael nodded thoughtfully. It sounded like a pretty piss-poor plan, but it was still slightly better than he'd expected. At worst they could keep setting off flares all night until someone on the island saw them. "So how many flares do you have down there?"

Driver looked at him before reluctantly answering. "Three."

62

The rising panic of Driver's passengers had been muted slightly by a number of factors. Caron's continual wailing and complaining seemed to have worn her out and she was now quieter, numb almost, leaning against the side of the boat, drenched like the rest of them, shivering with cold. The release of the first flare had also helped temporarily, but the increasingly ominous silence which followed did not. Firing the second flare had again eased the tension, but there was still no sign of the helicopter.

"Show me again where you think we are," Michael said, looking at the wet map over Driver's shoulder, peeling it off the boat's instrument panel and managing to tear it in the process.

"Careful! Anyway, what's the point?" he said, rolling with the swell and holding onto the side of the boat for support. "It won't make any difference."

"Please."

Driver reluctantly showed him. He drew a line with his finger between Chadwick and Cormansey. "That's the bearing I've been following, but like I've already told you, I don't have any way of accurately measuring how far we've traveled. We could be a couple of miles from the island, we might not even be halfway."

"I know, I know . . ." he mumbled, staring hopefully at the map as if he hoped to somehow find a missing clue, something he hadn't noticed before. Any kind of marker would do. *Anything*.

"Rocks," Lorna yelled from the stern of the boat. The entire group forced themselves around in the enclosed space, feet splashing through several inches of water. *Christ*, Michael thought, *she's right*. Out on the horizon was a small rocky outcrop. He turned to face Driver, who was already poring over what was left of the map, trying to match up what he could see. He circled an area south of Cormansey.

"Look at this. Lots of little islands. It's got to be one of them, hasn't it?"

In the complete absence of anything else on the map, Michael thought he had to be right.

"Head for them?"

"Safest option. We can use them to navigate. Even moor up for a while if it looks like we're going to run dry."

There was no more discussion. Suddenly revitalized, the others held onto anything they could as Driver turned the boat and began to sail for the rocks, praying that more of them would come into view as they got closer. Michael said nothing, but he glanced around at the other faces here with him, and then at the ocean which seemed to stretch away forever. The vastness of the water brought home his individual insignificance. It didn't matter a damn how smart or how lucky he'd been to get this far, how brave or how strong, his fate and everyone else's now rested on this increasingly unsteady boat and the rolling waves through which they sailed. Even Driver was of little use now. He remained at the controls, valiantly doing all he could to keep the boat on course, but his actions seemed to be having little effect.

Jagged spears of rock began to spring up on either side of

them. The water swirled and splashed the boat around with renewed vigour, dragging the hull down then forcing it back up again, at one point sending it spinning through almost a complete turn before seeming to change direction, then sweeping them back the other way. The bottom of the boat scraped along a rock.

"Is this the part where the boat gets smashed to pieces and we all drift off in different directions, hanging onto bits of wood?" Caron said unhelpfully.

"Shut up!" Lorna snapped at her, beginning to think she might be right. The hull scraped again, a loud, sickening noise, then the boat lurched as a tall wave crashed against the nearest rock and broke over them.

"There!" Michael yelled before ducking down as another wall of ice-cold spray crashed down over them. He'd been pointing at something, but the violent rolling motion made it impossible to see what he'd seen. More as a result of the movement of the water than anything Driver had or hadn't done, the little boat was pushed away slightly, then sucked in toward the rocks again. But that brief moment was enough, and Driver saw it: a small outcrop with a narrow strip of shingle beach.

"Just aim for that," Michael said, holding onto Driver's shoulder and trying desperately to keep them both standing upright as the boat rolled. "Just get us ashore."

The water level inside the boat was increasing, and not just as a result of the waves now. Harte saw that they'd sprung a slight leak, but he kept his mouth shut and covered it with his foot, knowing there was no point adding to the panic now. Kieran leaned over the side and looked down into the swirling waters, trying to gauge how deep it was and how strong the currents were. He was so desperate to stand on dry land again that, for just a second, he seriously considered jumping.

"Don't do it," Howard yelled, grabbing his arm and pulling him back. "If the waves don't smash you against the rocks, the cold will kill you."

"Recognize anything?" Driver asked Michael as he fought with the controls. The boat's small, stuttering engine was having next to no effect now. It was going wherever the sea wanted it to.

"Not a damn thing," he shouted back over the wind. "Just get us onto land and we'll take it from there. Keep the last flare with you whatever you do. We should try and set it off when we've landed."

Now, finally, they appeared to have circumnavigated the rocks and were getting closer to the shingle beach. And with unimaginable relief, they felt the direction of the boat change too. The waves and the engine combined to send them closer to the shore, forcing them into what looked like a small cove.

"What was that?" Kieran asked, and he leaned down over the side of the boat again until he was sure. And then they all heard and felt it: the bottom of the boat scraping along the seabed. Michael didn't stop to think about what he was going to do next. He jumped over the side of the boat and fell into the surf, losing his footing and going under. The ice-cold temperature stunned him and stole the air from his lungs. He managed to get his head out of the water but cracked the back of his skull against the hull of the boat. Barely able to coordinate his movements now, he forced himself to try and swim, then managed to dig his feet into the shingle and start walking. Harte followed his lead, landing with a little more success, and between them they managed to catch the mooring rope and pull the boat to shore, the waves at last helping, not hindering, their progress.

And then, finally, they stopped. The boat listed over and became still. No more rolling or lurching. The waves continued to crash around them but the boat had at last come to rest. The others disembarked and immediately went to Michael and Harte's aid, wrapping them in layers of their own slightly less wet clothes.

"We need to find some shelter, fast," Howard said, scouting around the small beach, looking for somewhere they might be protected from the biting wind.

"Use the boat," Driver suggested. "We can drag it further up the shore."

"Do we have any food?" Caron asked. "Anything we can give to these two?"

"Nothing," Kieran replied.

"Anything we can start a fire with, then?"

Harte dug a trembling hand into his pocket and threw Caron his lighter. He was shaking violently, blue with cold. Caron tried to flick it into life but it was dead, as wet and useless as everything else.

"There's nothing we can burn, anyway," she grumbled.

"Well, we need to do something," Lorna said. "If we're out here much longer we'll all end up with hypothermia, never mind these two."

"I'll go and look around," Kieran said. "I'll try and get up onto the rocks and get a better view."

He was gone before anyone could say anything. Lorna and Caron helped Michael and Harte to get as far as they could from the water, then nestled up with them beneath a slight overhang. Howard and Driver were close behind, Driver having fetched the last flare from the boat. *Might as well take it*, he thought, *though Christ knows what good it's going to be.*

Kieran returned a few minutes later, clambering down the rocks, then running back down the beach toward them.

"Anything?" Howard asked. Kieran nodded as he struggled to catch his breath.

"It's not much, but it's something," he explained, still panting hard. "There's a wreck. Looks like a fishing boat or something. It'll get us out of the wind for a while, at least."

The seven of them began the unsteady climb up the rocks to find the wreck Kieran had discovered. Lorna had images of huge trawlers in her mind, and was disappointed when she saw that it was just a small vessel, and that it appeared to have been there for some time. It had crashed at the bottom of another rock face, and she hadn't even seen it until she'd been almost on top of it. At first glance it appeared to be little more than a few scraps of corroded metal and wood.

"Is this it?" Caron asked.

"It's better than nothing," Kieran said. "It'll have to do."

She gingerly moved closer to the wreck, recoiling when she saw that what was left of a crewmember was still onboard. His skeleton—stripped of all flesh and bleached white by months of beating from the saltwater waves—had been trapped among what looked like a block of rusting winch machinery.

"Wait . . ." Michael said, but his throat was dry and his body was shaking, and he couldn't finish his sentence. They looked at him and he looked back, but still he couldn't speak.

"What is it?" Lorna asked. He looked from her face, to the wreck, then back again. Barely able to function, he had to summon his very last reserves of energy to talk again.

"I know this . . . seen this before . . ."

Kieran immediately seized on the importance of what he was saying. The others took a little longer, but he didn't waste time explaining. He raced up the rocks in front of them, then stopped when he reached the top. He gestured for the others to follow and they did, climbing up the slippery rock face painfully slowly, pushing and pulling each other toward the top.

Finally they were level with Kieran. They found him sitting on a low stone wall.

"Well, we're either back on the mainland," he began to say, "or . . ."

Michael stared up ahead, almost unable to believe it. He looked around in all directions, trying to get his bearings, and then he broke free of the others and started to walk. His legs were numb and he struggled to keep moving, but he knew this was it.

No more running. No more fighting. One last push.

It seemed to take forever, but it was less than ten minutes later when he reached the door of the small cottage. It was locked. He hammered on it to be let inside. After a delay of a few seconds, it opened inward.

"You took your time," Emma said.

"Sorry," he replied.

"Are you going to stay here now?"

"Forever."

Two Years, Seventeen Days Since Infection

63

THE LAST FLIGHT
DONNA YORKE

Have we done the right thing? Our first night on the mainland in an age, and it feels strange . . . almost like we're trespassing. The first night of the rest of our lives, Cooper said.

Two years. Five deaths. Three births.

Life on the island has been hard but successful. We've done well—better than any of us ever thought possible—but things have steadily changed there and I don't feel the same about the place as I used to. Neither of us do. The birth of Maggie, Michael and Emma's first child, was a turning point for all of us. When that little girl was born last year, we all knew we had a better chance of surviving long term than we'd originally thought. We sat in the pub and held our collective breath on the night she was born, waiting for the germ to kill her, not expecting her to survive. When she lasted a minute I began to believe the impossible might have happened. Days later and we were still expecting the infection to get her, but it didn't. And now she's over a year old and Emma's pregnant again, and I couldn't be happier for them. Lorna is pregnant too, but that's not for me. Not yet, anyway.

The babies have taken the edge off the air of finality we've all felt since the day the world died. For a while things started feeling less hopeless than they had been. But while most people on Cormansey seem to think that everything's changed and we're back in control now, I don't. As it happens, I still think our days are numbered. It's just that we might have a few more days left than we expected, that's all.

So we're going to make the most of them.

I came back to the mainland once before with Jack and Clare, but it was too soon. We weren't ready. We thought we could live here again but we were wrong. We lasted a while, then got ourselves picked up again when Richard and Harry came back for more supplies.

Things feel different this time. Coop and I hitched a lift and I don't think we're ever going back. I don't know if we can. The flight that brought us over here had been planned for some time. Richard said he thought it might be the very last flight, depending on how hard the winter proves to be on Cormansey.

Jack used to love to read. When we were over here before, he was always telling me how he used to like a good end-of-the-world story more than anything else. He talked a lot about them, and on his recommendation I read a few last year, but the endings used to piss me off. Often they'd finish with some smug little community of do-gooders rising up from the ashes against all the odds: a merry little band of farmers and cooks and teachers and . . . Call me selfish if you like, but I've never really gone for all of that. It's taken me all this time to realize I didn't want to just jump straight back on the wheel again and build up a carbon-copy, small-scale imitation of what we used to have. I want to do something with what's left of the rest of my time. I don't want to spend my life tending sheep, boiling water over log fires and wearing homemade clothes. Why should I? Why should any of us? I tried it, but it didn't work out.

There are too few of us left to make a difference anymore, too much damage has been done. They tried to stop us, said we'd be back like last time, but Coop and I had made up our minds.

We left just after ten this morning and we were back on the mainland by eleven. Everything has changed beyond all recognition here. Buildings have started to disappear—swallowed up by moss and weeds, a crawling layer of green slowly overtaking everything. There are huge cracks in some of the roads, craterlike potholes in others, and some buildings have already collapsed. And when you look closer, hidden among all the greenery and rubble, there are bones everywhere. Those bones are all that's left of everyone else. Jack said it was going to be like this, but until you see it for yourself, you can't begin to appreciate the scale of it all. It makes you realize how insignificant you actually are.

Before we left the island I went to see Jack one last time. He had his face buried in a book, as usual. He said he'd come across a word in the dictionary that summed everything up, and he told me to look it up once I got here.

Coop and I walked through a town this afternoon. We took tins of food from a supermarket and strolled down the overgrown high street like we owned the place, drinking wine, shouting out, and doing whatever the hell we wanted. It felt good, like a lot of ghosts had been laid to rest. Later we found this house. We checked it was empty and structurally sound, then set up camp for the night. Coop was asleep in minutes, but I can't switch off like he does. Maybe I will in the future, but not yet.

In a small office on the ground floor of the house, I found a dictionary and I looked up Jack's word like I promised him I would. *Aftermath*. I didn't know it had two meanings. The first was obvious, the one that everybody knows: something that follows after a disastrous or unfortunate event, like the aftermath of a war. But it was the second definition that struck me: a new growth of grass following mowing or ploughing. Jack was a deeper man than he'd ever admit. I thought our little community was the aftermath, but he saw the greenery which is slowly covering everything as the aftermath of the human race.

Michael used to say that all any of us can do now is make the most of the time we have left. That's exactly what we're going to do.

We are the last of the living.

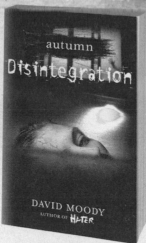

WARNING:
YOU WILL KILL TODAY

BOOK 1

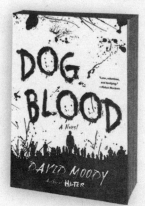

BOOK 2

BOOK 3

OWN THE ENTIRE CRITICALLY ACCLAIMED HATER SERIES

AVAILABLE WHEREVER BOOKS ARE SOLD

St. Martin's Griffin   THOMAS DUNNE BOOKS